iFLOAT

D0099659

WITHDRAWN

IFLOAT

The Jewish Messiah

The Jewish Messiah

a novel

Arnon Grunberg

Translated from the Dutch by Sam Garrett

CONTRA COSTA COUNTY LIBRARY

THE PENGUIN PRESS *New York* *2008*

3 1901 04446 1350

THE PENGUIN PRESS
Published by the Penguin Group
Penguin Group (USA) Inc., 375 Hudson Street, New York, New York 10014, U.S.A. • Penguin
Group (Canada), 90 Eglinton Avenue East, Suite 700, Toronto, Ontario, Canada M4P 2Y3
(a division of Pearson Penguin Canada Inc.) • Penguin Books Ltd, 80 Strand, London WC2R
0RL, England • Penguin Ireland, 25 St. Stephen's Green, Dublin 2, Ireland (a division of
Penguin Books Ltd) • Penguin Books Australia Ltd, 250 Camberwell Road, Camberwell,
Victoria 3124, Australia (a division of Pearson Australia Group Pty Ltd) • Penguin Books India
Pvt Ltd, 11 Community Centre, Panchsheel Park, New Delhi – 110 017, India • Penguin
Group (NZ), 67 Apollo Drive, Rosedale, North Shore 0632, New Zealand (a division of
Pearson New Zealand Ltd) • Penguin Books (South Africa) (Pty) Ltd, 24 Sturdee Avenue,
Rosebank, Johannesburg 2196, South Africa

Penguin Books Ltd, Registered Offices:
80 Strand, London WC2R 0RL, England

First published in 2008 by The Penguin Press,
a member of Penguin Group (USA) Inc.

Copyright © Arnon Grunberg, 2004
Translation copyright © Sam Garrett, 2008
All rights reserved

Originally published in Dutch under the title *De joodse messias* by
Uitgeverij Vassallucci, Amsterdam

Publisher's Note
This is a work of fiction. Names, characters, places, and incidents either are the product of the
author's imagination or are used fictitiously, and any resemblance to actual persons, living or
dead, business establishments, events, or locales is entirely coincidental.

LIBRARY OF CONGRESS CATALOGING IN PUBLICATION DATA
Grunberg, Arnon.
[Joodse messias. English]
The Jewish Messiah : a novel / Arnon Grunberg ; Translated from the Dutch by Sam Garrett.
p.   cm.
ISBN 978-1-59420-149-3
1. Jews—Fiction.   I. Garrett, Sam.   II. Title.
PT5881.17.R96J6613   2008
839.31'364—dc22
2007030302

Printed in the United States of America
1   3   5   7   9   10   8   6   4   2

Designed by Chris Welch

Without limiting the rights under copyright reserved above, no part of this publication may be
reproduced, stored in or introduced into a retrieval system, or transmitted, in any form or by any
means (electronic, mechanical, photocopying, recording or otherwise), without the prior written
permission of both the copyright owner and the above publisher of this book.

The scanning, uploading, and distribution of this book via the Internet or via any other means
without the permission of the publisher is illegal and punishable by law. Please purchase only
authorized electronic editions and do not participate in or encourage electronic piracy or
copyrightable materials. Your support of the author's rights is appreciated.

The Jewish Messiah

He Loved People

BECAUSE HIS GRANDFATHER had served, with sincere enthusiasm and a great faith in what the future would bring, in the SS—the kind of man who wasn't afraid to roll up his sleeves, not the kind of wishy-washy grandpa who never got up from his desk, who stamped an official document now and then before hurrying home to his wife and children at five, no, a gentleman, one who understood death's handiwork without bothering his own family about it, a man for whom words like "honor" and "loyalty" still meant something, a man of morals who clung faithfully to a vision even under brutal conditions when many of his buddies stripped off their uniforms and ran for it, but not him, a man who said, "A man of fiber knows his duty, a man of fiber doesn't just live from day to day," and, having said that, went on to fire every last round in his clip—the grandson wished to serve a movement with enthusiasm and faith in the future.

It was only by accident that the boy found out about his grandfather's achievements, one Sunday afternoon while borrowing money from his mother without asking, when he discovered documents, photos, and a book she had hoped would never be found.

Even in the darkness of puberty he was a good-natured fellow, with a fine eye for life's pleasures. Clouds, pasta, babies in their cradles, the aroma of wine, shop windows full of nice clothes, magazines full of titillating photos, art that had withstood the ravages of time, fast cars, and people, not to forget people, people's legs, arms, heads, hair, noses, hands, wrists, those thin, pale little wrists that first turn pink in the sun, then slowly redden. The boy loved people, and they loved him.

Europe had been at peace for so long by the time he was born. The war was far, far away, at least *that* war was, and other wars were, too; around the time he first became interested in the enemies of happiness, experts had already declared that the Second World War was now over and done with, that chapter was finished. A melancholy chapter, perhaps, but a finished one. And, after all, weren't all wars melancholy by definition? All those victims, all that senseless violence, all those homeless people?

Suffering was something the boy did only when in the company of friends and acquaintances with a less refined eye for the joys of living. He regarded suffering as a skill, as much a part of acquired etiquette as the proper way to eat lobster. As long as you knew how to pick the meat from the shell, you were good company at any table. There were moments—while brushing his teeth, for example—when he wondered why others seemed to suffer so sincerely, whereas he did not. Nature is marked by diversity, he decided then. In the same way some plants thrive in the rain forest and others do well only in desert soil, one also had people who were made for pleasure, and others created for suffering. He was of the former ilk.

Between the ages of fourteen and sixteen, he had frequented a synagogue in Basel, the city where he was born after twenty-four hours of uninterrupted labor, and where he continued to live with his well-bred and rather uncommunicative parents. But between the ages of fourteen and sixteen he had also done any number of things one might have termed wayward. More because he felt they went with his age than from any desire to rebel against his parents, the school, the state.

The boy's visits to the synagogue were prompted by curiosity. At school he was known as intelligent, socially minded, and conscientious. He devoured books with titles like *The Young Investigator*. He owned a miniature steam engine and played regularly with a chemistry set. Until he realized that the chemistry set was not the world, merely a model of it. And a rather ramshackle model at that.

It was around that time that he started to become interested in suffering. People's suffering. That animals could suffer, and perhaps even trees and violets, was bad enough, but their suffering did not say nearly as much to him. He saw in it no mystery, no possibility of a deeper truth, in the same way that he saw his father's vegetarianism as a riddle not worth solving. The good man ate no meat and no fish; he seemed bent on eating nothing substantial whatsoever.

People suffered, that much was certain. So why not the boy? What was wrong with him?

One day, after school, he went to the emergency entrance of the local hospital to watch what was brought in there. It was a relatively quiet afternoon, but it was enough for him. "Aha," he said, "aha." This was better than his chemistry set. The day after, the chemistry set went out with the trash. But he was not yet able to bid farewell to the miniature steam engine.

For days he thought about the wounded, the mutilated, the dying he had seen at the hospital entrance. Evil was indeed a problem, just as his teachers had said. Soon he announced at school that the pursuit of beauty was his highest aim. For he had seen that human suffering was nothing but an emergency exit out of beauty. The boy's drawings were competent enough, his art teacher couldn't deny that. The perspective was a little messed up now and then, but that might have been due to his age, or to his lazy eye.

He resembled his grandfather, a handsome man with a kindly face who had been killed by an advancing Russian army because his outlook on life would not permit him to run from the enemy. He had remained loyal to his leader, even when they started shooting at him from all sides. His grandfather had fought against the enemies of happiness wherever he could fight them, he had killed them with his own hands, a couple dozen of them, perhaps a few more, he hadn't kept track too carefully. His grandpa had killed the enemies of happiness the way other people ate oysters. "Make it three dozen. After all, on a night like this, who's count-ing?" His grandfather considered himself the final line of defense against the Judeo-Bolshevik conspiracy. And when the enemies of happiness and their cohorts seemed on the point of winning, his grandfather did not run away. He would not neglect his mission, not even in the final hours of his life. Heroism ran in his family, at least on his mother's side.

On occasion, when his parents were away at a cocktail party, the grand-son would rummage through forbidden drawers. He read in the forbid-den book, always the same passage, the one that said that everywhere in the world there were three kinds of people: the warriors, the indifferent, and the traitors. And he held up his face to that of the grandpa about whom they never talked. Talking about family was something they never did, not even about aunts and uncles who were in Africa combating illit-eracy. They spoke little of other subjects, either. That there was really very little that needed to be said was a conviction that fortified his parents as they plowed through life. But they lived quite nicely, even by Swiss stan-dards. On Sunday afternoons, when he would stand at the mirror exam-ining his face, in one hand the photo of his grandfather in uniform—a lovely uniform, they'd had a highly developed aesthetic sense, you had to give them that—he couldn't help feeling a bit melancholy. Like two peas in a pod. The eyes, the mouth, the eyebrows, the shape of the face. The nose. He was no traitor, and he was not one of the indifferent; he was a warrior. His grandfather could have been his twin brother. There were Sunday afternoons when he gave in to the temptation to talk to his grandpa. Standing in front of the bathroom mirror, he would whisper a few words to the yellowed photograph. In the book, he had read that the writer had been "nauseated by the thought of living at a desk as a man in servitude."

"Did the thought of working in an office nauseate you, too?" the boy asked the photo. "Is that why you suffered? Why do people suffer? What good is suffering? Shall I start a movement to free people from suffering?"

That is how the grandson generally spoke to the late SS officer, though on some afternoons he tried to keep the conversation a little lighter.

"Stop acting so crazy," his mother would have said. But she was never there when her son talked to her father's photos. It was one of the things he did in seclusion. He loved his parents, and he didn't want to upset them.

Former teachers and friends have characterized him as an unassuming boy. But in front of the mirror, with his grandpa's photo in his hand, he did not feel unassuming. He felt his genetic material trying to tell him something. His appearance was a part of Nature's, or the Creator's, plan: in his appearance a message lay hidden, and all he had to do was decipher it.

BECAUSE HE WAS a sensitive boy, he realized that it must have been hard for his mother to grow up without a father, and indeed without a mother, either, for Grandma had survived only two years longer than the Third Reich. On occasion he would put an affectionate arm around her shoulder. Or, on his way to bed, he would sometimes keep his mouth pressed to her cheek a little longer than necessary. When he had time left, he would go with her to the supermarket and help her carry bottles of mineral water. She was a slight woman, and when the weather turned humid her knees began hurting.

He kept his dark hair combed neatly (there was always a little comb tucked away in his pants pocket), even after he had dyed it blue. He had gone to this latter extreme only because the young people he associated with had switched en masse that month, it was in May, to a brighter hair color, and he felt it was his duty to support them not only with words but with deeds. By nature, he felt the need to make others comfortable; he had a knack for politics and diplomacy. But the thing that drew him most was beauty. The beauty of the uniform, of the human being, of art. The beauty of blood.

He joined a Jewish youth association, after having a dream in which the phrase "international Judaism" appeared. There were definitely not many young people who dreamed about international Judaism, and the fact that *he* did backed up his idea that he was different from others. Called. Chosen. Branded.

The student members of the association were being prepared for their forthcoming emigration to the Jewish state, and he was welcomed with open arms. The Jewish state could use all comers.

That summer, when the weather allowed, he would often jump into the Rhine in late afternoon and allow himself to be carried along a ways before swimming to shore, running back to where he had started, and repeating the whole ritual. He convinced the leader of the youth association that it would be good for them to all jump into the Rhine together on a warm evening, and to let themselves be carried off downstream. Physical exercise was absolutely essential preparation for life in a young country still under constant threat.

That was music to the ears of Mr. Salomons, the leader of the youth association. At last, a potential emigrant who showed a little initiative. That summer, one could often see him swimming in the Rhine with a group of Zionists. It was a fine sight: he out in front, behind him about twenty youthful bodies, some of them a bit nervous, others fast and bold. There were pretty girls among them who could summon up little interest for ideology but knew all there was to know about the latest bathing fashion.

His first encounter with Zionism was very much to his liking. He didn't have much real contact with the other young people, but that would change; for the time being, swimming in the river together was more than enough. Beauty is a fine thing, but a person needs ideals that go further than aesthetics alone. Zionism was an ideal that fit him, a suit made to measure.

The Irony of History

MR. RADEK, the grandson's father, was a hardworking architect. The grandson's mother, Mrs. Radek, was a housewife, but hardworking as well. For generations his father's side of the family had lived in Basel; his mother's came from Saxony. After the war, his mother had fled, arrived in Basel after a great many detours, and ended up in a foster home. She fell in love and became pregnant, or vice versa. A child came wriggling out of her belly. They called him Xavier. And that was it: no other children came out of her belly.

Xavier Radek. The name said it all. Sometimes he wrote out his name twenty times on a scrap of paper, as though he couldn't believe it went with his body.

Xavier's parents did not demand a great deal from him. As long as he went to school and kept a low profile in public, they were at peace. His visits to the synagogue, which could not remain a secret in a city like Basel, were tolerated. His parents would rather have seen him visit prostitutes, if he absolutely had to go in search of the exotic, but one had to make do: at least their son was healthy and not some heroin addict.

On a lovely summer evening, after he had been swimming in the Rhine with his young Zionists again, his mother said during dinner: "The Germans are the modern Jews. Look what a burden they have to bear."

Xavier's father, who never said much, but who could always be counted on for a clever remark at the right moment, said: "That's the irony of history."

Swimming with Zionists was a phase, his parents figured. Just like the blue hair, which had already grown out almost completely. Other children his age struggled with homosexuality, or suffered sudden attacks of kleptomania. It would blow over, would vanish as though it had never been. Just like Xavier's grandfather.

AT THE SYNAGOGUE, he sat on a bench all the way in the back, where he occasionally entered into a conversation with a misfit. Houses of prayer tend to attract misfits. They were places where one could smell that death had once walked abroad. And perhaps that was the Almighty's intention, because only death points unequivocally to Him.

Because Xavier was well mannered and, of all the misfit men, the most interested in Jewish rites and customs, and because he did not stink or walk around dressed improperly, one Saturday morning the rabbi struck up a conversation with him.

The rabbi asked him to come to his house for lunch. God expects His people to be hospitable, especially on Saturdays and other holy days.

"I'd like that," said Xavier Radek.

"What's your name?" asked the rabbi, who had thirteen children and the fatigued air of a man whose patience was often tested by his offspring, but more often by God, to say nothing of his wife.

"Xavier," he said. He would rather have given a different name, David, for example, or Aaron—good biblical names. But he did not possess the art of lying.

"Xavier what?" the rabbi asked.

"Radek." He slicked his neatly combed hair down even flatter. On his head was the crumpled skullcap he had been handed by the doorman of the synagogue. The man was from Armenia, and he watched over the synagogue to earn a little money on the side. He had bad teeth. Because he himself wasn't Jewish, he was able to do what the Orthodox Jews did not allow themselves on the Sabbath. In actual practice, his duties as guardian were marginal; he peered through the peephole (which was senseless, because he let everyone in anyway), he turned up the heating when it was cold, and he passed out crumpled skullcaps to misfits who didn't have their own. Misfit men who probably all had real problems, all except for Xavier, who felt glad to be alive.

Later, when Xavier became a radical but successful politician in Israel, he would think back on the synagogue in Basel, the smell of death and the doorman's teeth, and he thought of the future as a set of Armenian teeth that would make even a dental hygienist throw up his hands in despair.

"Xavier," the rabbi repeated, while a group of children fought to take his hand. The rabbi let them fight. "Xavier Radek, have you had a religious upbringing?"

"No," Xavier said, "not really. Not to speak of."

The rabbi held his tongue tactfully. Or perhaps he was merely bored. His beard was long, there were spots on his black jacket, and when Xavier came close to him he smelled the smell of food that had been on the stove all day. But Xavier didn't let odors put him off.

Along with a few of the gentlemen from the synagogue, they were now strolling towards the rabbi's house. "What is it you would like to learn?" the rabbi asked. Two children had won the struggle for his hand, a girl and a boy. The girl had white skin with the occasional freckle, and hair that was more red than blond, particularly in sunlight. She wore white tights, black patent-leather shoes, and a plaid skirt.

Xavier couldn't imagine how he had put up with the steam engine and the chemistry set for so long. What did a steam engine really signify, anyway?

"What do you mean, rabbi?"

"Don't call me rabbi. I'm Mr. Michalowitz."

"Mr. Michalowitz." Xavier ran over that name a few times in his mind, so he would not forget it.

"Would you like to learn something about Judaism, about the customs of your ancestors? Where do they come from?"

"Who?"

"Your parents. Where are they from? Are they Ashkenazim?"

How it had happened he was never able to figure out. Perhaps it was the color of his hair, his eyes, his physique, his white shirt, his gestures, his lips that seemed always on the verge of a smile, but in the synagogue at Basel no one doubted that Xavier Radek was a Jew. That was how he gained a culture, and a tradition; it was all that simple. This, too, could be no coincidence. He thought of his grandfather's photo, the resemblance, the words he had whispered to the photo on quiet Sunday afternoons, the questions he had asked him, the most important of which had to do with the sense of suffering.

"Poland." It was the first thing that came to mind. While they were swimming in the Rhine one evening, Mr. Salomons had told him that his parents came from Poland. It was in the Rhine that the fraternization had begun.

"From Poland, yes," the rabbi said. "Of course, but *where* in Poland?"

Xavier thought for a moment. "Central Poland," he said.

Apparently this was enough to place his parents, for the rabbi asked no further questions—at least not about that.

"And what is it you would like to learn?"

"I want to learn about suffering," Xavier Radek said.

The rabbi stopped in his tracks. The children were pulling on his arms. The lonely men who, just like Xavier, had been invited to have lunch at the rabbi's walked on. They didn't notice a thing, immersed as they were in a discussion of the political situation in the Middle East.

"Which suffering?"

"Your suffering," Xavier said. "Suffering in general." He realized that his throat was dry, as though he were alone in a room with a woman for the first time and, halfway through some bland conversation—about the Rubik's Cube, for example, she had suddenly removed a crucial item of apparel.

"Can you read Hebrew?" the rabbi asked.

"No."

"Well, start with that."

Then the rabbi walked on, and said nothing more to Xavier the rest of the way to the house.

The wind had come up. Occasionally Xavier had to put his hand on his head to keep the skullcap from blowing away. And because he was a social animal—there was no helping that—he joined in the single men's discussion. He felt like a trained pig that had just found itself in the vicinity of truffles. He said: "The Jews need *Lebensraum,* too."

AT THE TABLE, he sat between two of the rabbi's sons. The oldest boy went by the name of Awromele; the other one's name he only half understood, and half-names were impossible for him to remember. Across the table from him was a girl with braces on her teeth, who stared at him throughout the meal. He ate with relish, this food of the Jews. You couldn't call it refined—they would have to wander at least another forty years in the wilderness before getting to nouvelle cuisine—but they did have a healthy appetite. Heroism didn't need to be anything huge; this was good enough for starters. Xavier decided he should do this more often. Visit their homes.

He had washed his hands in ritual fashion, just like the others. He had heard the wine being blessed, he had drunk of the sweet wine itself, and he reveled in his new role. There was singing. At first Xavier Radek was prudent enough to keep quiet, but he had a good feeling for music, and the second time the refrain came around he could restrain himself no longer. He hummed along. He felt at ease amid the enemies of happiness, and so he hummed more and more loudly all the time, until his humming drowned out all the others, except for the rabbi. The girl with the braces tossed him glances of annoyance, but Xavier didn't notice. He enjoyed the music; he lost himself in it.

The chosen people liked to sing at the table, just like the Boy Scouts.

All details that he had never stopped to think about before, and that you never read about in the paper. The enjoyment bothered him, though. Enjoyment is shallow. You can enjoy yourself all morning, but around noon the *tristesse* of superficiality always strikes.

When the singing was over, Awromele, who had curly blond hair down over his ears, asked him: "Do you speak Yiddish?"

"No," Xavier said, "I'm afraid not."

Fortunately, the rabbi was not paying attention to them, he was busy explaining that a man does better to leave the choice of a wife to others who can be more objective. "That's too bad," Awromele said. "When you speak Yiddish, you can tell the filthiest jokes in the tram and no one understands you." He shook his head ruefully when his father said: "I've helped more than twenty men to find a bride; they were happy then, and they are happy today. I can help you men find a bride as well, but you will have to be open to my counsel. You can't turn down every bride I come up with—you mustn't start finding fault in advance."

"You know what?" Awromele said. "Tell me a dirty joke, and I'll translate it into Yiddish. What's the dirtiest joke you know?" He beamed, his face glowing red. It was not a blush, it was the excitement of life itself rushing through him, as though Awromele had no other reason to exist than to translate jokes sneakily into a slowly dying language.

Xavier felt a shiver run through him, without knowing why. He thought: That's surrendering to life, what this fellow's doing, surrendering to life head over heels. That's what a warrior must do. But he said: "I don't know. It's not really the kind of thing I'm very familiar with."

"A joke so dirty people would go nuts if they heard it."

"I'll think about it," Xavier said. He didn't know any jokes like that. He barely knew any jokes at all.

When the misfits got up to say goodbye—no agreement had yet been reached concerning their brides-to-be—Xavier got up as well. He thanked the rabbi profusely, and murmured something along the lines of "we must do this again sometime soon." He tried to shake hands with the rabbi's wife, but she didn't respond. All she said was *"Gut Shabbes."* He went down the steps in a daze.

When he was outside he realized that he was still wearing the black skullcap. He put it in his pocket.

AT DINNER THAT EVENING, the skullcap was lying like a huge insect in Xavier's white soup-bowl. By the time he arrived at the table, his father and mother had already dished up asparagus soup for themselves. His own bowl was standing there, half filled with something that, in this setting, was clearly obscene.

He looked at it and realized that his parents had gone through his pockets. Undoubtedly with the best of intentions. Parents do everything with the best of intentions.

"Enough is enough," his mother said.

He saw tears in her eyes. It made him sad.

"Enough is enough," his mother said again, but a little louder now, putting a little more stress on the final word. Then she picked up the ladle and filled Xavier's bowl.

He looked at the light-green liquid. The black skullcap came slowly floating to the surface like a huge squished beetle. More tears could now be seen in his mother's eyes. This wasn't such a disaster, was it? No one had died. They hadn't lost any money. The house hadn't burned down.

"Is this from a package?" Xavier asked.

"What?" his father asked.

"Is this soup from a package?"

"No, of course not," his mother said. "Since when do we eat soup from a package?"

Asparagus heads were floating in the soup as well. Green asparagus. Xavier looked at them.

He picked up his spoon, wiped it on his napkin, wished his parents a *bon appétit,* and began to eat.

For a moment he thought: I'm eating the Jews' lice. That thought occupied him, and even excited him a little, the way forbidden thoughts will sometimes excite young people. Life was even more mysterious than Schopenhauer and Nietzsche had predicted. He thought about Awromele, and was afraid for a moment that his parents might be able to read his thoughts.

"Xavier," his mother said after he had taken a few bites, "take that thing out of your soup."

"I didn't put it there."

"Xavier, take that thing out of your soup. I'm not going to ask you again." She made it sound as though a catastrophe were looming over them. It wasn't anger he heard in her voice, it was fear.

"Mama, I didn't put it in there. Besides, it tastes wonderful, there's nothing wrong with this soup. So, please, *bon appétit.*"

Patient but unflinching. That's how Xavier was. That is how he would always be.

The twentieth century had not yet come to an end, there was still room for a little last-minute heroism. The vague events that had composed the story of his life until now had to be more than just coincidence, a little pile of happenstance—life wasn't supposed to be like that.

At first his grandfather had guarded the enemies of happiness, then he had killed them with his own hands, without much in the way of technical resources, sometimes with nothing more than just a club. Grandpa had performed his duties conscientiously and, unlike many employees, had shown true initiative. And now he, Xavier Radek, created in his grandfather's image, was eating the lice of the enemies of happiness. The irony of history, that was he himself.

"Xavier," his mother said, and for the first time in his life he heard her raise her voice—one could even have called it screaming—"this is unhygienic. What you're doing there is filthy."

"I didn't put it in my soup. And like I said, it tastes wonderful. You've outdone yourself again. Thank you." His sense of fair play was keen. And hard as crystal.

His father, who was unable to come up with a clever remark at that particular moment, said: "I understand your being curious, we're all curious sometimes, but in the long run it's not the kind of thing for you. That's all we're trying to say."

Xavier didn't think about the long run. Heroism was not about the long run.

The irony currently attached to heroism had rendered itself obsolete, now that everything had become ironic: the wars, the newspapers, the news itself. It was time to get serious.

"As from today," said Xavier, who had forgotten that he meant to spare his parents grief, "count me among the chosen people. I love both of you, but I belong to the chosen people."

From that evening on, Xavier considered himself a foe of irony and moral relativism, which often went hand in hand. The relativism that claimed there was no black and white, only gray, was always ironic. His mother was fond of saying, with a certain regularity, "Xavier, the victims are always culprits, and the culprits are always victims."

For a few seconds nothing happened, the way almost nothing ever happened in the villa where Xavier lived, especially nothing uncouth. Then his mother took his bowl away from him and threw it, soup and all, into the wastebasket. Carefully, because she didn't want spots on the parquet. Standing beside the wastebasket, the mother then glared at her family with hostility.

Xavier looked and tried to find something of her father in her, but he couldn't; nothing about her face reminded him of his grandpa. His mother's father now lived on in him, and in him alone.

Favorable Light

HE COULDN'T REMEMBER exactly how he'd come up with the idea; the thought had simply struck him while he was sitting outside a wine bar with a few girls from school, pricking toothpicks into little blocks of cheese. Pleasure was shallow by nature, but that was no reason to swear off it completely. He had continued to frequent the wine bar.

Xavier Radek was a mild-mannered, handsome young man. When the two top buttons of his shirt were open, you could see little tufts of hair on his chest. He said little, and above all nothing untoward; that made some people think he was shy, while some found him mysterious.

Sitting in front of the wine bar, he had a sudden flash of inspiration. He would photograph Jews. It seemed like a brilliant idea. He would place them in a favorable light. They could use that. Xavier would succeed where others had failed. After all, he was possessed of a great sense of beauty, and an optimistic nature.

Most photographers-to-be focused on plants, teenagers at the beach, mass tourism. One of his father's friends had stirred up quite a fuss in and around Basel with a book of photographs about scooter accidents. It had sold well: modern man loves the sight of a catastrophe.

Just as the fashion photographer tries to capture the model at her best at the sublime moment, so he would go after the look in the eye, the wisdom, and the incomparable humor of this ancient people.

"I'm going to photograph Jews," he told the girls at his table.

They stared at him blankly for a few seconds, until a girl with big earrings said, "Well, have fun."

Being misunderstood went with the *status aparte* of the man with a mission. He decided not to tell anyone else about it.

He waited a few days, then called the only Jew whose house he had ever visited. Starting with the rabbi himself might be a bit presumptuous. Could I take your picture? You couldn't just blurt that out to a man like that. No, better to start with his son.

At the end of the afternoon—he was so nervous that he'd taken a cold shower, just to be on the safe side—Xavier dialed the number. It was a lovely phone number, with three sixes in it, the sign of the Beast.

A woman answered. In a shaky voice, he asked to speak to Awromele.

"Just a moment," the woman's voice said.

It took him two minutes to explain to Awromele who he was, but then the boy said: "Oh yeah, now I remember, it's you. Have you got a joke for me?"

"A joke?"

"You were going to come up with a joke for me, right? A dirty one— then I'll translate it for you, and you can go around telling it without anyone knowing what you're saying. Have you got one? It's got to be really filthy. One with a clit in it, for instance."

Xavier didn't know any jokes with clits in them.

"I haven't quite gotten around to that yet," he said. "But there's something else, and, well, sorry to intrude like this, but I'd like to take your picture."

"Who?"

"You."

"Me? Take my picture? Why?"

Xavier had to speak quietly. He was afraid his mother would hear, and that would only increase her suffering. He had begun skirting the truth for his parents' sake. Things that made your parents suffer had to be tucked away like Easter eggs; otherwise their lives would be ruined. Later, you had to alleviate the suffering of your husband or wife, and then that of your children, and so you spent your entire life alleviating the suffering of others.

For the time being, though, Xavier limited himself to the suffering of his parents, and that of the Jews.

"Because you're good-looking," he told Awromele.

"Me, good-looking?"

Good-looking is always good, Xavier thought. Who doesn't want to be good-looking? Besides, Xavier thought, Awromele really was good-looking, young and fresh, like an angel with those curls, which wasn't something you could say about Awromele's father. Angels don't smell of food that's been on the stove for twenty-four hours.

"Yes, extremely good-looking."

"Says who?"

"What?"

"That I'm good-looking."

"Nobody. I figured it out for myself."

"Oh. How?"

"By . . ." Xavier had to swallow a little excess saliva. "By looking at you. But I need to ask you something. That is, if I'm not intruding, if you've got the time."

Xavier felt he was starting to sweat, and began speaking louder in spite of himself. His mother was downstairs, soaking raisins for the apple pie. She was good at pies. Just like her mother before her, who had baked pies in Saxony. Even when the news from the Eastern Front had become grimmer, she had gone on kneading the dough and stirring the batter.

"I've got some time," Awromele said. "What was it you wanted to ask?"

"What I just said, whether I could take your picture."

"You already said that, yeah."

Xavier grew even more nervous. Nothing ruffles an enthusiastic optimist more than a closemouthed Jew.

"Are you still there?" Xavier asked.

"Hello," Awromele said. "Yes, I'm still here, I'm just thinking it over." The line seemed to fall dead again.

"What are you going to do with it?" Awromele asked at last.

"With the photo?"

"Yes."

"Keep it. Exhibit it, later on."

"Exhibit it. Here in Basel?"

"For instance. Or else in Zürich. You're good-looking. These are going to be art pictures. Architecture is the king of the arts, second only to music. I read that somewhere. But photography is the queen. I want to get the emotion across."

"Emotion? What emotion?"

"Art tries to get emotion across. When I see you I feel an emotion, and I want to get that across. So other people will feel that emotion, too. Suffering is the emergency exit of beauty."

"Do I have to take my clothes off?"

"No, why would you do that?"

"Oh, just wondering." Awromele sounded disappointed. "But you're saying you don't have a joke for me, one I can translate, a joke with a clit in it? Or something like that?"

Xavier promised he would bring a joke like that along with him when they met for the picture, maybe even more than one joke. Xavier would have promised anything just to hear Awromele say yes: the heavens, the stars, a nation, a kingdom.

They agreed to meet the next day on the Mittlere Rheinbrücke.

Downstairs, in the kitchen, Xavier's mother was still soaking raisins. She was wearing an apron with pictures of all kinds of vegetables on it.

She looked at her son as he came in and picked a raisin from the bowl, but said nothing. He laid a hand on her shoulder, as he often did to comfort the orphan who was his mother.

"Xavier," she said after he had eaten three raisins, "back then everything was different. What is done is done. It wasn't pleasant for anyone, not for my parents, either. That's all in the past now; we have to keep our eyes on the future."

They Had Nuclear Weapons, Too

BEING A METICULOUS young man, Xavier had not only bought a camera, an Olympus, but also a joke book. He read it twice, from cover to cover, but the word "clit" was nowhere to be found. The jokes didn't make him laugh, either. Maybe it was just him—he couldn't rule out the possibility that he had no sense of humor. Humor, he'd learned at school, was born of deficiency. Once he finally started to suffer, the humor would take care of itself.

When the appointed time came, he walked to the Mittlere Rheinbrücke. By heart he had learned four jokes that could pass for smutty.

As he was walking through Basel with his camera, the second flash of inspiration came to him. It mustn't stop at photography; people would say that was only a pose. They wouldn't take his attempts seriously, would say that others had done it before, that these days a project like his was simply a way to play it safe, that if he was going to do it he should have done it fifty years ago—which was easy enough for them to say, because he hadn't even been alive then. He may have been born under a lucky star, but at least he knew what made people tick. Their main goal was to not have to feel their own pain. A goal that often didn't pan out.

What they forgot—his father, for example—or overlooked—his

mother, for example—was that once you were dead you didn't feel anything anymore, not even pain. Xavier wanted to combine the advantages
of life with those of death. Therein lay comfort. Great minds before him
had lived in and strolled through Basel. They inspired him, seized him by
the hand, and drew him in the right direction.

He had to comfort the Jews. No halfway measures, not an adhesive
bandage here, a bit of mercurochrome there. To comfort and to comfort
well—that for starters—then the rest would come of its own accord.
Xavier felt a deep and formidable sympathy for them. For personal reasons, but also in general, for reasons of science.

The Christians had Jesus, the capitalists had profit maximization, the
Buddhists could gradually melt into Nothingness, the socialists could up-
lift the wage slaves—three evenings a week, in the open air when the
weather allowed—but the Jews had nothing. No messiah, a God who
never showed, and everyone hated them, perhaps not as openly as before,
a bit more sniggeringly, in the men's room at the coffeehouse, behind
drawn curtains, at meetings where the press was not invited, but they
hated them nonetheless. There had to be a reason for that.

What's more, you also had Jews who hated themselves, Xavier had
read in an encyclopedia, the self-hating Jews. When it came to comforting, those were the ones who should be first in line.

He wasn't exactly sure how to go about it. He hadn't comforted all that
many people in his life. He'd tried to soothe his mother's pain, but her pain
was chronic, so soothing it didn't help much. It even seemed to irritate
her. She would push him away and say, "Stop slobbering all over me,
Xavier, you're too old for that now." And his father would say, "Keep your
hands off your mother—that's unhealthy."

But he wasn't about to be discouraged. The desire to comfort was a part
of him, the way tragic humor is a part of the clown.

When he stopped to think about it, though—he was almost to the
bridge now—the Jews might have nothing, but at the same time they had
everything. They had a country of their own; they had nuclear weapons,

too; they had Einstein and Billy Wilder. He had read somewhere in a book: "Has there actually been anything filthy, any brazenness in any form whatsoever, especially in the area of culture, in which at least one Jew has not taken part?" Even Muhammad Ali had Jewish blood in him, it seemed. And they had suffered as well. What, in fact, *didn't* they have?

Then, as he stood on the Mittlere Rheinbrücke, waiting for Awromele, who was late, Xavier was struck by a flash of inspiration that would change his life.

They had filthy Yiddish jokes, translated by Awromele; they had Yiddish music, melancholy songs once sung by partisans but today performed by people who, though not Jewish themselves, had a great deal of affinity with the Jews, and who therefore sang in Yiddish while accompanying themselves on violin and guitar. In that way, the leftovers of a decimated culture could be warmed over and dished up to the public in plastic containers. Only when a culture had been decimated did people become interested in it, and Xavier couldn't blame people for that. Staring at mishaps, that was people's favorite pastime.

But did they have a Great Yiddish Novel? Xavier Radek had never heard about it. No. There were Jewish Nobel Prize laureates, some of whom had even written in Yiddish, but that was it. Whenever anything filthy or brazen took place in the area of culture, at least one Jew was involved, but the Great Yiddish Novel remained unwritten. And if something didn't happen fast, it would remain unwritten for all time.

He would write the Great Yiddish Novel.

To provide structural comfort for the Jews.

What better comfort than a novel in a language everyone said was dying out? A novel like that would combine the advantages of death with those of life. The book would be full of death and the dead—across the Lethe one no longer needed to feel pain—but it would also be an ode to the *joie de vivre* of the young pioneer.

Xavier would utter the final, heartrending gasp of an almost dead language. The way all of life should be, a final, heartrending gasp before dying.

In the distance he saw Awromele approaching, a black dot against the sun.

That morning Awromele had risen early and trimmed his pin curls with a pair of nail scissors. He wanted to look good for the camera, and for Xavier.

Xavier was sweating; he unbuttoned another button on his shirt, so the hair on his chest was easier to see.

They shook hands, a bit stiffly and uncomfortably.

Now that Xavier had Awromele before him, he realized what an awkward situation this was. Far more awkward than swimming in the Rhine with Zionists.

He was a comforter now, but he had no idea where to begin. Where did it hurt most? In which part of the Jew's body was most of the pain concentrated?

"What do you want me to do?" Awromele asked. Under his shirt he wore a prayer shawl; its tassels hung down the front of his pants. Lovely, thought Xavier, who had decided to find everything lovely when it came to Awromele's person.

"Lean against the railing," Xavier said. He hoped no one would see him, at least no one his parents knew, no one who would tell them right away whom he had been seen with.

Xavier photographed Awromele. When he had shot three rolls of film and didn't dare go on any longer, he said: "Well, that was it. You want me to tell you those jokes now?"

"Do they have clits in them?"

"No, actually, they don't."

"Well, then, forget it."

"Could I buy you a drink, then?"

"Not really," Awromele said. "I have to get home, *lernen*. I go to Talmud school." He took Xavier's hand, then dropped it right away. "Not a word about this, right? If you see my father, not a word. He's such a hothead."

"The rabbi?"

Awromele made a smacking sound with his lips. "He's not really a rabbi, he just acts like one because it's the only way he can earn money. He used to have a matrimonial agency, along with Mother and my aunt, my mother's sister, God rest her soul, but he ruined the matrimonial agency by being such a hothead. He'll just light into you all of a sudden, for no good reason. And if he gets the chance, he'll box your ears, too, or tweak your nose. People looking for a partner don't want verbal abuse—maybe from their partner, but not from the matrimonial agency. Besides, he molested my aunt, my mother's sister, God rest her soul. Can you imagine that?"

Xavier couldn't imagine that. The only thing he could imagine was taking Awromele's hand and holding it, holding it for a long time. He didn't care which body part contained the pain. Any old body part was all right by him. Still, he said, "Yes, I can imagine that very well."

"And then that business with the grant."

"What grant?"

"The municipal grant."

"What about it?"

"You never heard about it?"

"No," Xavier said. They were still standing on the Mittlere Rhein-brücke, but he had forgotten all about the Rhine, his parents, and the fatherland.

"Every Jew in Basel is talking about it."

"We don't do a lot of talking at home," Xavier said. "We're quiet Jews."

"We got a subsidy from the city to build a new community center. My father and his brother split half the grant between them. The rest of it they invested, but it was an unsound investment. An extremely unsound one."

"You're kidding!" Xavier cried. He forgot his good manners for a moment and shouted, "That's horrible!" He wasn't naïve, he knew how things went in the real world, but there were some things you were never really prepared for, things that always came as a shock when you were confronted with them. These people embezzled public funds like there was no tomorrow. Of course, that was no reason to club them to death, but they needed to exercise a little more discretion. It's never wise to give people a reason to club you to death. If there's no way to avoid it anyway, well, then, better simply to have it happen. To be clubbed for clubbing's sake.

Xavier had been raised to believe that stealing was inherent to capitalism, but that one should never steal grant money. Subsidies, after all, were a socialist invention for the fairer distribution of capital. His father was an architect, but he had his heart in the right place. He designed buildings for banks and for pharmaceutical companies that had written off Africa as an export market because they subscribed to the—not entirely illogical— view that people who had no money to get better would sooner or later fall ill again, and could therefore better be left ill right from the start. His father made up for those clients by working on all kinds of social housing projects. He had also built prisons, and had tried in his own modest fashion to see to it that drug dealers were given bigger cells. In this way, he did his best to relieve his conscience, burdened as it was by all the office buildings he'd built for the pharmaceutical industry.

Xavier noticed anger welling up inside him. So there you had it. He had come to them with the best of intentions, with no other intention than to comfort them, and within ten minutes they had lived up to all the clichés. You couldn't photograph fast enough, or write fast enough, to make up for that, not even if you wrote *ten* Great Yiddish Novels. No, if they couldn't keep their fingers out of the cookie jar, there wasn't much use in trying. And Basel was having a hard enough time of it as it was. The municipality was feeling the crunch from all sides—less money for welfare, less for theater, less for the roadworkers.

His parents had warned him. His mother had said: "Give them a finger and they'll take the whole hand, and then your whole arm. I'm not saying that because I'm a racist, it's just the way they are. They can't do anything about it, either—that's the tragic thing. Their history has made them that way."

Xavier couldn't hold back. What he wanted to do most was to take Awromele's hand and say that it was no problem, that nothing was a problem anymore, because he was here. But stealing grant money was down-right indecent, especially when it was stolen by people like the rabbi, who served as an example to others.

Just as some women were apparently asking to be raped, so, too, some Jews were apparently asking for a pogrom. Before he knew what he was doing, he had reached out and boxed Awromele's ear.

Autism

AWROMELE LOOKED AT Xavier confusedly for a moment. Then he said quietly, "Just like my father."

"What?" Xavier asked.

"Just like my father. He does that all the time, too. Suddenly loses control, then he smashes something against the wall or starts hitting people. My mother says it's because he's autistic and can't see the big picture."

"I'm sorry."

"You don't have to be—I'm used to it."

"But I'm sorry anyway. I lost control."

"He only sees little pieces of reality, and he can't put those little pieces together."

"The rabbi?"

"My father. He's not a rabbi. He's autistic."

"But autistic people can be rabbis, too, can't they?"

Awromele had to think about that one. "In principle, yes," he said.

"I'm sorry."

"Are you still talking about my ear?"

"No, yes, well, that, too, but I meant about your father being autistic. That above all. I'm sorry. That must be difficult."

"Oh," Awromele said, "for an autistic person he's actually quite sweet;

he can't do anything about it. No one can do anything about it." For a moment, a dark cloud seemed to pass over his face, but then he smiled broadly again. "He just pretends, that's all."

"He pretends to be autistic?"

"No, he pretends to be a rabbi. He never passed the exams. When his matrimonial agency went down the tubes, he had no choice but to become a rabbi—there was nothing else he could do. Especially not after he molested my aunt, God rest her soul. She was the sweetest aunt I had."

Xavier suggested that they find a better place to talk. Awromele's excitement was making him nervous.

They started off in the direction of a wine bar that Xavier knew well. Then he realized that it would be better not to show up there with Awromele. Before you knew it, rumors would be flying. So he took him instead to the Drei König am Rhein Hotel.

"He had sired eight children," Awromele said as they crossed the lobby, "before he found out." Awromele walked through the hotel as though he'd been coming there for years. He barely seemed to notice his surroundings, taken up by his story and relishing the way Xavier listened to him. Apparently they didn't listen to him much at home.

"Before he found out what?" Xavier asked.

"That he was actually in love with my mother's sister, and that she was in love with him. They couldn't keep their hands off each other. After he'd made eight children with my mother. You'd think of that beforehand, wouldn't you? Does your mother have a sister?"

"No," Xavier said, "no sisters. She's an only child. An orphan, to be precise."

"That's better, less risky—to have no sister."

They found a table on the patio with a view of the Rhine. Xavier had often swum by here in the past, alone at first, later with his friends the Zionists.

Awromele ordered sparkling water, then nipped at it a bit, as if it might be poisonous.

"Are there people you can't keep your hands off of?" Awromele asked.

Xavier thought about it. "No," he said after a moment, "there's no one like that. I can keep my hands off of everyone."

They were a strange pair. People were looking at them.

"So your parents are assimilated," Awromele said as the ice in his sparkling water slowly melted away.

"Assimilated?"

"They act as if they aren't anything."

"I guess you could say that," Xavier said. "That's what they do." His wineglass was empty, but he didn't want to order another one—he didn't want to make an unfavorable impression on Awromele.

The worst that can happen to you is to have no goal in life, not to be anything. Xavier had read that somewhere. In the forbidden book, he had also read that Jews systematically brought girls and women to ruin. He couldn't imagine Awromele doing something like that: he wouldn't bring anyone to ruin. Xavier's wisdom came from books. His parents were silent most of the time, and his teachers doubted everything, except for the man who taught the classics. He believed that Aristotle had an answer for everything.

Something about Xavier's recently chosen goal in life caused him to blush one moment and grow desperate the next. But that desperation was nothing compared with the real suffering which he craved. The suffering of others.

"Is that why you're an only child?" Awromele asked.

"What?"

"Your family being assimilated, I mean. Assimilated people never pro-duce a lot of children. That's how they destroy their Jewishness, my father says. In the long run, they do what Hitler did, but demographically. Has your family always been assimilated? Or was it something you became?"

"No, we've always been like that."

"So you don't know any better."

Awromele looked pensive again, and Xavier felt the urge to grab hold of a body part that was causing the pain. He had the impression that Awromele's pain came from all his body parts.

"Do you mind if I ask you something?" Xavier asked.

"I have to get home pretty quickly—you know how my father is."

"It won't take long."

"Go ahead. Just ask."

"Are you a Zionist?"

Awromele started laughing. He laughed loudly, he laughed in abandon, not like Xavier's mother, who didn't laugh much anyway. And when she did, it sounded like the laughter of an actress who doesn't feel like playing her part.

More and more people on the patio of the Drei Könige am Rhein Hotel were staring at them. The more people stared, the uneasier Xavier felt. You saw people like Awromele walking down the street sometimes, but you never saw them at chic hotels. They always kept to themselves.

"Of course I'm not a Zionist," Awromele said. "First the Messiah, then the Jewish state. You know that. We have to wait for the Messiah; then the state will come of its own accord. You don't know much, do you? What have your parents been teaching you all these years? Are you even circumcised?"

Awromele talked rather loudly, and his voice was high for his age, so half the people on the patio could hear what they were saying.

"Circumcised," Xavier said as quietly as he could, without actually whispering. "Not really. We didn't have the time for it, or the money. Not in those days. And we're assimilated, I told you that already."

"All the assimilated Jews I know are circumcised. Circumcision doesn't interfere with assimilation. Were your parents really *that* assimilated? What did they think about when you came along?"

"I don't know what they were thinking. My father is an architect; he's awfully busy."

"And then that stuff about the money being a problem. What kind of excuse is that? A circumcision doesn't cost anything. Sixty francs, some people will do it for twenty—maybe with less sophisticated instruments, but that's no problem for a baby. A baby can take a lot. My mother used to have us eat off the floor, to build up our resistance. Maybe it was a kind of revenge, because my father was doing it with her sister, God rest her soul, but still. One of my father's cousins was a circumciser. He had a butcher shop. He moved to Australia, and no one knows what he's doing over there. Do you have smegma?"

"Excuse me?"

Xavier began to regret bringing Awromele to this hotel. They didn't have any manners. They were an ancient people, okay, but they'd left their manners behind in the desert. He knew it wasn't right to generalize, but if you intended to apply the principles of science, you didn't have much choice. And that's what he wanted to do, to approach the Jews scientifically. To study suffering in an objective fashion, to enter the paradise of pain as a scientist. Perhaps the only justification for pain was the beauty produced by its infliction.

"Do you have smegma? I'm so curious about what it looks like, but no one will show me. Apparently it looks a little like sheep cheese. But that doesn't say much to me, either."

Xavier reached for a bowl of nuts, put two of them in mouth, and ground them slowly between his molars.

"I wash myself carefully," he said after both nuts had been ground to a pulp. Then, just to change the subject, he asked, "Do you mean grass cheese?"

"Grass cheese?"

"Yeah."

"Isn't that a real white kind of cheese?"

"That's right," Xavier said, "that's it exactly." Cheese was the only thing his father ate on bread, so he knew a lot about it.

"No, I mean sheep cheese, real sheep cheese. Do you have to scrape it off, or does it fall off in the shower? I've never met anyone who has smegma. You're the first."

Xavier choked and started coughing.

Awromele got up and pounded him on the back. That morning, Awromele had locked himself in his room and smoked a cigarette. After that he had trimmed his hair with a pair of manicure scissors. For a few minutes he had entertained the hope that, from now on, everything would be different. The worst thing about life was the endless repetition, the same holy days each year, the same Day of Atonement, the same matzos, the same hut roofed with branches, the same God who could write people's name in the Book of Life or in the Book of Death. The repetition was the worst, but the rest wasn't too great, either. Despite his age, Awromele had the sneaky feeling that there was nothing new, that there never would be anything new, that he already knew everything, and that the things he didn't know yet he could easily guess about. Then he lay down on the bed with his clothes on and studied the lines on his hand. He'd had his palm read at a fair once and was fascinated by fortunetelling. If you knew the future, there was no longer any need to change it. All you had to do was know it, and then hide from it. That, in fact, was what Awromele saw as his task in life, and in the lives of others.

"What about blow jobs—isn't that a problem?" Awromele asked after he sat down again.

Xavier's coughing had become the hiccups. "I have to be going," he said. Despite his size and the interest shown in him by a lot of girls, he was still a virgin. "Could I ask you one final question?"

"Of course."

A waiter interrupted them to ask if they wanted anything else, but Xavier simply asked for the check. The way his father always did, sounding slightly irritated at having to think about anything as banal as a check.

"How do you deal with the Holocaust?" Xavier asked.

"Deal with the Holocaust? What do you mean?"

"Nothing special. How you deal with it. Do you talk about it a lot at home?"

"Twice a week."

"Only twice a week?"

"In the winter, three times a week."

"And then? Do you try to cope with it?"

The ice in Awromele's glass had melted completely. A piercing, almost inhuman giggling came from Awromele's mouth—inhuman in the way his beauty was almost inhuman. Too lovely. Too soft. Too glorious. Too wonderful. Not that everyone could see it. A lot of people probably didn't notice, they only recognized as beauty a picture in a fashion magazine. But Xavier was a frequent visitors of museums, both those of natural history and of medieval art. He had seen countless pictures of the saints and the Redeemer. Some beauty, but not much, was changeless. And it was one single drop of that changeless beauty that he recognized in Awromele. In this young Jew he recognized something that destroyed his appetite, that frightened him to death.

"I want to ask you one more thing," Xavier said. "Or, actually, I want to make you a proposal." He feigned distraction for a moment; the hiccups had finally stopped; he paid the check.

"Would you consider tutoring me?" he asked. "I'll pay for it, of course. I want to learn Yiddish."

Awromele looked concerned, like an older brother, almost suspicious.

"Yiddish? Why do you want to learn Yiddish? You're not even circumcised."

"I want to be circumcised as well. But first I want to learn Yiddish."

"First you're going to learn Yiddish, then you're going to get circumcised. Are you feeling all right? Why?"

"Because."

"Just because? Nobody just wants to learn Yiddish. Have you had enough of being assimilated, is it getting old?"

"I want to write a book."

"A book? What kind of book?"

"A book that will comfort people."

"What people?"

"You know, people. You, for example."

"Me?" Awromele looked disgusted. "What do you want to comfort me for?"

"For . . . well, for everything."

Awromele got up. Xavier did, too. They walked to the entrance. People were watching them go—Xavier could tell even without looking back. The talking would start now. Out on the street he said, "Thanks for a pleasant afternoon." They shook hands.

Awromele's fingers were soft. If there was anything soft and feminine about Xavier, it wasn't his hands. He had the hands of a workman; in the winter, his fingers quickly turned ruddy from the cold.

"Are you serious about this?" Awromele asked.

"About the lessons? Yes, completely serious. See me as a friend."

Awromele looked amazed, then started laughing loudly. "That's a good one, I have to remember that. You know what my father always says? He says it so often it makes you sick, but, then, he says everything so often it makes you sick. He says: Jews have no friends."

Awromele's laughter was contagious.

Xavier started laughing a little himself. But not wholeheartedly. He leaned forward. Without asking himself what he was doing, he kissed Awromele on his milky-white cheek. "Teach me, Awromele," he said quietly. "Teach me."

Xavier walked home with a bounce in his step. The Jews had a friend at last. If passersby had seen him walking along, they would have known: there he went, the friend of the Jews.

A Little Roughhousing

SOME PEOPLE ARE in search only of a home, a few molecules of happiness, a daily conversation about the weather; they're content with a little chamber music and a bit of social status, but definitely not too much, for that only produces unrest, and unrest is the enemy of the family. For them the world is the size of their home, including front and back yards, supplemented perhaps by a swivel chair. As long as the world doesn't interfere with them, they won't interfere with the world. Perhaps they will vote now and again, but that is not really interfering with the world, it's more like an innocent ritual. And then you have people in whom there dwells a burning ambition. The chamber music of happiness means little to them; they're out to make their mark in the world, rearrange that world, and are willing to pay a high price to do so.

Xavier Radek was of the latter sort, even though he had no name for that burning ambition and barely knew that it dwelt within him. His parents had always sung the praises of modesty, in fact of nothing less than anonymity. For lack of a better way to put it, Xavier referred to his ambition as comforting a lost people. Comforting Awromele. Soothing the body part where the pain was located.

Xavier ran from the Drei Könige am Rhein Hotel all the way home.

When he came close to the villa where his parents lived, he remembered that he had left his camera on the hotel patio. But that wasn't important right then. What he had asked for, Yiddish lessons, would be given unto him.

He locked himself in his room and put on a record of klezmer music. Occasionally, while listening to the melancholy sound of the violins, he uttered an almost animal cry. His parents heard the music and the animal cries, came upstairs, and stood listening at the door of their only son's room.

"This isn't normal," his father said after a while.

Another terrible cry sounded behind the door.

"No," the mother said. "This is not normal." She knocked quietly on the door, but the son didn't hear her.

Because Xavier's parents were fairly passive, they remained standing there aghast for a few seconds, then went back downstairs.

Xavier turned up the volume on his stereo system, filling the house with klezmer music.

"I am a Jew," Xavier shouted in his room. His happiness was what one might call orgiastic.

Downstairs, in the living room, his parents were sitting stiffly at the coffee table.

"Let him get it out of his system," his father said. "It's his age." He leafed through his address book, looking for the phone number of a psychologist he knew.

"Maybe we should buy medicine for him," his wife said.

The architect slammed shut his address book. "This is all because of your father," he said quietly. "Couldn't he have simply been a follower, like any other respectable person? Why did he have to go marching out in front with that big, fanatical nose of his?" Xavier's mother winced and went to the kitchen.

One floor above, Xavier fell onto his bed. He buried his face in the pillows and fell asleep. Happiness had worn him out.

.   .   .

STARTING THAT VERY afternoon, the architect did his best to talk to his son man to man—no longer just as a father, as an institute of learning, but also as a friend. For starters, whenever he ran into Xavier in the living room at night, or in the bathroom in the morning, he gave him a jovial whack.

Xavier almost always shouted, "Hey, you're hurting me!"

"Come on, buddy," the father said. "A little roughhousing never hurt. You're a man." And he would push his son against the wall and playfully rub up against him.

The architect bought a punching bag, in the conviction that an adolescent needed to vent his aggression. But he himself was the only one who used the punching bag. He played with the punching bag so much his wife couldn't take it any longer and said, "If you have too much energy, why don't you join a rowing club, like any other respectable person?"

The architect stopped pummeling the bag for a moment, looked at his wife disapprovingly, and said: "That's great, coming from you. What did your father do with his surplus energy? Okay, tell me, what did he do with it? Too bad they didn't buy him a punching bag—it would have saved us a lot of trouble."

His wife shook her head and went off to soak some raisins. There was nothing that helped her forget she was alive like baking apple pies and marble cake.

The punching bag clearly wasn't the answer, so the architect asked his son to go along with him on a business trip: in Singapore, he was going to build the offices of a big pharmaceutical company. But Xavier said he'd rather stay at home.

One evening, over dinner, the architect realized just how fruitless his attempts to make friends with his son had been. Looking up from his plate, Xavier said, "They're hushing it up for political reasons, but research in Africa has shown that circumcised men have eighty percent less chance of getting AIDS."

"In Africa," was all his mother said.

Nine days after their talk on the patio at the Drei Könige am Rhein Hotel, when Xavier had still heard nothing from Awromele, he called him up.

"It's me," he said, after he finally got Awromele on the phone.

The line sounded dead.

"It's me," he said again. "Xavier Radek, I took your picture."

There was still no reply.

"Hello!" he shouted. "Awromele, is that you?"

Finally, Xavier heard something. "Am I speaking with the uncircumcised Jew?" he heard.

They're on to me, he thought, afraid he was going to faint. He had counted on their catching on to him someday, but not so soon. He cleared his throat. "How are you?"

In a strange voice, Awromele asked, "Am I speaking with the Assimilated One?"

"Is this supposed to be a joke?" Xavier asked.

"I was trying to be funny, I'm sorry. I have no sense of humor."

To his relief, Awromele's voice sounded normal now.

"It was a good joke. One of your best."

"I have no sense of humor; I'm sorry."

"No need to be sorry. What you don't have you can always acquire."

"Listen, I've found someone for you."

Xavier started relaxing, yet he still wasn't completely sure of Awromele's friendship.

"Did you hear me?" Awromele asked. "I said I've got someone for you."

"I hear you very clearly," Xavier said, "as though you were standing next to me."

"Someone who will do it for forty francs. That's as cheap as it gets. That's a gift from the Almighty."

"Someone who will do what?"

"What do you think?"

Again Xavier had the creepy feeling that they were on to him, that he was being put to the test, the way God regularly put His people to the test.

"You mean, what we were talking about at the Drei Könige am Rhein?"

"What's the name of that place again?"

"Drei Könige am Rhein."

"Yeah, that's it. Circumcision. You have any idea how much that usually costs?"

When Xavier heard the word "circumcision" he flinched, as though someone had laid a whip across his back.

"How much that usually costs? No idea."

Maybe the situation wasn't as dire as he'd thought. Xavier was glad he had called Awromele at a moment when his parents weren't home. It was important to not make his parents any unhappier than they already were. Sooner or later they would follow him. In the long run, his parents would become Jews as well, but the time wasn't ripe to confront them with that.

"An adult male, like you," Awromele said.

"So?"

"How much do you think that usually costs? Guess."

"No idea. I really have no idea."

Awromele sounded like he was talking about the price of a haircut.

"A lot, let me tell you. We're not talking about a baby here, or a housecat; we're talking about an invasive procedure, the kind the insurance doesn't cover. You can't really call it a medical necessity. But I've found someone who will do it almost for free, because your story touched his heart."

"My story?"

"That your parents are so assimilated that they didn't want to have you circumcised, that you don't know anything, but that you want to learn. I told Mr. Schwartz all about it."

"You didn't have to do that."

"Forty francs, and I'll do the aftercare."

"What do you mean, aftercare?"

"For if it gets infected."

"Oh. Is there a big chance of that? Did you get an infection?"

"Big, big? What, do I sound like an expert? You think I arrange illegal circumcisions every day?"

"What's so illegal about my circumcision?" But Xavier heard his mother at the front door and said, "I have to go now."

"Mr. Schwartz wants to meet you."

His mother came hurrying up the steps, as much as his mother ever hurried.

"I have to go, I'll call you later."

"Mr. Schwartz wants to meet you; your story touched his heart."

"Some other time," Xavier said. Then he hung up. His mother was standing before him. She was panting.

"Who was that?" she asked.

"Some girl."

"From school?"

He nodded.

Xavier withdrew to his room, where he practiced declining a few Latin words to the accompaniment of klezmer music. He had trouble concentrating, because the term "illegal circumcision" kept running through his mind.

How many people each year, in a city like Basel, underwent illegal circumcisions?

You-Know-Who

BECAUSE HIS PARENTS had decided that everything would turn out all right once Xavier had a girlfriend, Xavier went looking for one. His eye fell on Bettina. She was in his class at school, a senior. She had been born in the canton of Graubünden. Bettina had a button nose and an active social life. She looked like a real woman.

In her bed, where she had taken the virginity of two other boys, she took Xavier's virginity as well.

Along with her family, Bettina had adopted a village in India. And because that had gone so well, they were planning to adopt another one, also in India.

After his deflowering, she told Xavier: "For ten francs a month you can be part of it. That's barely two glasses of wine—less money than you'd ever miss—and it can save an entire village."

Quid pro quo, Xavier realized. So he said: "Sure, where do I sign up?" Even though all the deflowering had left him with was the feeling of having been punched in the stomach, hard.

Still naked, she began rummaging around in a desk drawer. She pulled out a few forms in triplicate that he, also still naked, had to sign and furnish with his bank-account number. That way the ten francs could be deducted automatically from his account each month. She was a real go-getter, in more ways than one.

"Okay," she said after he had signed the papers. "That's another hundred liters of clean water."

He put on his clothes. Only then did the feeling of having been punched in the stomach go away, and he asked, "So—do we have something going?"

"Of course we have something going," Bettina said, tucking away the forms he'd signed in a file. "We're a couple."

"Good," he said. "My parents will be pleased."

Fortunately, the perforator jammed right then, so she didn't have time to think about his remark.

Bettina was good at gymnastics, Xavier remembered as he left the house.

And so it happened that, at the age of sixteen, Xavier adopted a village in India.

XAVIER'S FATHER RETURNED from Singapore. Because he suffered lower-back pain, the architect had had himself massaged there by an Asian lady. That was so moreish that he'd had himself massaged again the very next day, by a young Asian boy. Barely thirteen years of age, yet already physically mature.

The architect noticed that his body felt like it was tied in knots—probably from all those hours at the drawing board. So, a few hours before leaving for Basel, he'd had himself massaged again, this time by two twelve-year-old gentlemen, old hands at their trade.

He could, of course, have had himself tucked and rolled in Basel, but somehow that seemed less fitting. He was a man with a highly developed moral sense. One did not do such things in one's hometown.

Back in Basel, he called his wife during lunch hour.

"What's wrong?" she asked. "Aren't you coming home for dinner?"

Whenever he called, it was to say he wouldn't be coming home for dinner.

"No," he said, "it's just that I think it's time for us to bring things out in the open."

She knew right away what he was talking about.

That weekend, the Radeks went to the Jura. They stayed at a good hotel with a sauna, a solarium, a tanning bed, and a fitness center.

On Saturday afternoon, when it started to rain, the architect said, "Come on, let's go to the sauna."

They undressed in their room, put on their bathrobes, and took the elevator to the basement. It was not a big sauna, just big enough for the Radeks.

They spread out their towels on the wooden benches and lay down— Mr. Radek on the top shelf, his wife and son down one lower.

"It smells like eucalyptus in here," the architect said. "Nice and tangy. Come on, Xavier, take off those swimming trunks."

"I'd prefer not to," his son said.

"You're not supposed to wear swimming trunks in the sauna; everything has to air out. We don't have to keep any secrets from each other."

"Oh, leave the boy alone," the mother said.

There was an hourglass hanging in the sauna. Xavier turned it upside down. The sand was pink.

"We need to talk to you," the architect said. "I'm sure you know what it's about, don't you?"

"No," Xavier said. That was the truth. He had no idea what his parents wanted to talk to him about. He couldn't remember their ever having talked to him about anything.

"About your grandpa," the architect said. "Your mother's father. You never knew him. He died long before you were born. But I'm sure you've wondered at times: What kind of person was my grandfather?"

"Not really," Xavier said after a moment's pause. Such thoughts had never bothered him, and he had no reason to believe this would change.

The sand trickled down slowly. Xavier's cheeks tingled from the heat. He felt as if he couldn't breathe anymore. What he had often thought was: Exactly what kind of people were the enemies of happiness? Were they all like Awromele? He had often been troubled by that, but not by his grandfather.

"Xavier, everyone wonders on occasion: What kind of man was my grandfather? Or: What did my grandmother look like? Did she bake nice pies? That's completely normal. A person needs to know more about the blood that flows through his veins. A person needs to know where he comes from."

"I come from Basel," Xavier said.

"Of course, but before that. Once you were a sperm cell. And an egg. Isn't that right? You know all of that, but it's good to stop and think about it sometimes. Look, at a certain point you become interested in your family history, the way you used to be interested in your miniature steam engine."

The architect rubbed his chest. He didn't know how to go on. He rarely talked so much or for so long, especially not with his family. He thought about the masseurs he had met in Singapore. What a service they provided, what excellent knowledge of the human body they possessed! They were privy to all the special spots. The young gentlemen knew their way around the male body, without ever being arrogant about it. And, like all respectable people, they barely said a word.

"In any case, your grandfather was a hardworking man who loved his family a great deal."

"And a patriot," his mother said.

"And a patriot," his father echoed. "In principle, your grandfather was a kind and sensitive person. But then, well, then You-Know-Who came along."

"He had friendly eyes," the mother said.

The pink sand kept trickling down. Xavier couldn't stop looking at it. He seemed mesmerized.

"And soft hands," the mother said. "Very soft hands."

"You can't judge customs, rites, and morals from the perspective of our times, from the point of view of what we know now," the architect went on. "To give you an example: In the Middle Ages they burned witches; people thought that was completely normal. No one minded. People even thought it was a good thing."

Sweat gushed from the architect's pores. A sauna purifies the body.

Someone knocked on the door. "Occupied," the architect shouted, "it's occupied. We'll be finished in a bit."

Xavier thought he was going to faint. He was glad that he was already lying down: if he fainted, at least he wouldn't hurt himself.

"Where was I?" the architect asked.

"In the Middle Ages," his wife said, "but you don't have to drag that into it. Otherwise we'll be in here all day."

"The Enlightenment. Yes, that was it. The Enlightenment is not a straight line from point A to point B, Xavier. Are you listening? Sometimes the Enlightenment takes a step back, and then, in the next decade, it takes two steps forward."

"Lovely, that eucalyptus," the mother said.

Xavier thought about school. Most of the boys in his class talked about girls all the time, which was not unusual for boys that age, but Xavier thought Jews were a lot more interesting. There, in the sauna, Xavier felt the need to someday cover a Jew in kisses, from head to toe. The thought caused him such anguish, or so much joy, he couldn't quite say which, that he almost began to weep.

"I'm hot," Xavier said. "Could we open the door?"

"It's always hot in the sauna," the architect said. "That's what saunas are for. It's the only way to get all the dirt out of your body. The heat burns the body clean."

"I feel like my eyebrows are getting scorched," Xavier said.

"Don't forget," the architect said, pulling the towel a little straighter beneath him, "that it wasn't your grandfather's first choice. He would much rather have done something else with his life."

"He would much rather have worked on the land, with cows," the mother said. "But back in those days, normal, everyday people didn't run the show."

"Normal, everyday people still don't run the show," her husband chimed in.

"Can't we talk about this some other time?" Xavier asked. "I feel like my head's on fire."

"Your grandpa had to watch over the Jews," the architect said. "That was all he had to do, watch over them, to make sure they didn't run away or do crazy things. But because he had so much energy, sometimes he hit one of them."

"He had a lot of energy," the mother said. "He was hyperactive. He didn't need much sleep, either. All he had to do was close his eyes for two or three hours and he was fit as a fiddle. These days, people take pills for that."

Xavier said nothing. He couldn't look at the pink sand anymore. He was starting to see things.

"Jogging, for example, didn't exist back then," the architect said. "What were people supposed to do with their energy?"

"Could we open the door?" Xavier asked.

"Fitness," the architect said, "things like that. You've never known anything else, Xavier. Today every town, every neighborhood, every village has its own fitness center. But that's all fairly new. Fitness didn't exist back then. Can you imagine that? No. We can't imagine that anymore, any more than we can imagine life without a telephone or television. Even this hotel has a fitness center, and later on we're going to use it. Right?"

The father thought about Singapore again. Bringing things out in the open wasn't his favorite activity, but he knew it was necessary at times.

"Sunday," the mother said, but she choked and couldn't finish her sentence.

Xavier thought that if he stayed in the sauna any longer he would end up with third-degree burns.

"On Sunday," the mother said, changing her position, "Sundays, he never beat anyone to death, because he honored the Lord's day. Even under such extreme conditions."

"Do you hear that, Xavier?" the architect asked. "Do you hear that?'

No reply came. The son was having visions he couldn't place, visions that he forgot immediately. All they left him with was a vague, unpleasant feeling, rather like the feeling he'd been left with when he lost his virginity.

The architect said: "If they'd had fitness back then, history would have been very different. People like your grandfather didn't know what to do with all their excess energy."

"And he never hit anyone without a reason," the mother added.

Xavier got up and tried to open the door. But the father slid off his shelf, gave his son a playful punch, and said: "Not yet, buddy. Our fifteen minutes aren't up yet. Let that sweat pour!"

Xavier sat back down on his towel. After standing up so quickly, he was afraid he was going to pass out. He was dizzy.

I have to spare my parents, Xavier thought, it's hard enough for them as it is. He took the hand of his father, who was still standing beside the door to make sure it wasn't opened, and said: "Papa, later on we're going to have a great workout." And then he kissed his father's hand, more times than he could count.

THE FITNESS CENTER wasn't much bigger than the sauna. Loud, monotonous music was coming from the speakers. The father settled down on a machine where you had to push weights apart. Just to please his parents, the son climbed onto a bicycle. His mother had withdrawn to the solarium. Normally she didn't like sunlamps much, but since it was included in the price of the room, she thought it would be a waste not to use it.

The father panted. He was wearing knee-length red swimming trunks, and he was pushing the weights apart with abandon. He, too, had sur-plus energy.

Xavier loved his father, even though he had never been able to find the words to say so, even though he had never found access to gestures that would make that clear. But he felt it, even now, seeing his father panting away in the fitness center—even now, although Xavier had to admit that his pity for this man seemed greater than the peculiar business they called love.

The father got up from the machine and poured himself a glass of water. His body was drenched in sweat.

"If they'd had fitness fifty years ago," he said, "the concentration camps would have been gigantic fitness centers where the Jews could have worked off their excess fat. Believe me, if fitness had been invented a lit-tle earlier, history would have looked very different."

Xavier climbed off his bicycle, walked over to his father, and embraced his wet body. You couldn't actually call it suffering, not yet, but he did feel something. Something to which could you could really only react with an-imal growling, or with a knife. Xavier discovered that it was easier to feel alive when you were in pain.

"Come on," his father said, "let's see how your mother's doing."

Her feet were sticking out from under the sunlamps.

The father lifted the lid.

His wife was lying there, naked, with a cloth covering her eyes like a corpse. She was startled. "Are you having a nice roast?" the architect asked.

"I took off my bathing suit," she said. "Otherwise you can see the lines, and I think that's so ugly."

She got up and pulled her bathing suit on quickly. It was a blue one, with fish on it.

THAT EVENING, the Radeks dined in the hotel restaurant, by candle-light.

"If people would talk to each other more," the father said, "there wouldn't be any war. The only thing to do about it is talk to your enemy. Lay your cards on the table, the way we did today. If that would take place on a large scale, peace would have a chance. If the Jews had talked to the Germans, man-to-man, without starting to shout right away, peace would have had a chance."

He took his wife's hand and patted it softly. On his lap lay a pink napkin.

Like Hotcakes

LESS THAN FOUR WEEKS after the family talk in the sauna, Xavier's parents split up. Without fighting, without screaming or making a scene.

One afternoon, when Xavier got home from school, his mother had disappeared, taking along her dearest, most valuable possessions. Lying on the table was a typewritten note in which she simply expressed the hope that now everyone would be happier.

That evening, the father shed a few tears.

Two days later, he told his son: "I've spoken to your mother. It seems best to me that the two of you stay together. You two need each other the most. And I'm out of the country so often. They need me again in Singapore—I'll be leaving in ten days."

To get over the divorce, his father began staying in Singapore for increasingly long periods of time, much longer than necessary. There he had himself massaged by Asians of all genders and ages. In a Buddhist magazine he read that massage frees the soul from the body, so he started saying to himself, before going to the massage parlor, "I'm going to church."

Xavier searched the house where he was born and had lived for sixteen years to see whether the pictures of his grandfather, and the book, were still there. But his mother had taken them with her.

·   ·   ·

WITH THE HELP of her ex, the mother and Xavier found a neat apartment in another part of Basel. The kitchen had recently been refurbished and had all the amenities. To get over the divorce, she bought new towels, a famous Italian brand.

The mother and Xavier didn't remain alone for long. After a couple of weeks, Marc, a soundman at a Swiss radio station, moved in with them.

Marc had hair down over his ears, which he tied back in a pigtail when he was working. He came from a little village in the French-speaking part of Switzerland, but had been unable to find work there. His passion was the flight simulator. His computer had a program that provided him with the illusion of piloting a Boeing 737. Every free moment he had, he spent at the computer. He never grew tired of it. Sometimes he offered Xavier a chance to fly the Boeing as well, but Xavier was not particularly interested in aircraft. Her new boyfriend's passion, the mother felt, had a calming influence. All the more because he treated her in bed with the same tenderness, amazement, and stamina that he applied to his flight simulator.

ONE FRIDAY AFTERNOON, Xavier's girlfriend, Bettina, said, "I feel sorry for you, about your parents' breaking up."

"It's no big deal," Xavier said. He was sitting on her bed, rubbing his hands together. "My mother has a new boyfriend, Marc. He's nice—a little younger than my mother, but you'd never notice. And my father was away from home too much anyway."

"I still feel sorry for you," Bettina said. Her voice grew wistful, which her voice often did, especially when talk turned to India.

She pushed her face into Xavier's lap, unbuttoned his cotton trousers (Xavier was allergic to wool), and provided him with his first experience with oral sex.

"I never do that kind of thing," she said when it was over. "This is only the second time. Just so you don't think I'm, well, you know."

Then she told him that her family had adopted another village in India, and that donations were still welcome.

From a sense of duty, Xavier signed the papers again in triplicate, complete with his bank-account number.

"You're a fantastic sponsor," Bettina said. She stretched her arms lazily. Then she squeezed some toothpaste onto a toothbrush and began brushing her teeth, looking in the mirror as she did so.

"It's nothing, really," Xavier said. "Like you said, two glasses of wine a month, no more than that."

"But you're still the sweetest sponsor I've got," Bettina repeated, her mouth full of foam. "I have other sponsors, but they're not nearly as sweet as you. With you, I have the feeling that you really care about India."

He waited until she had finished brushing, which took a long time. Bettina was a conscientious girl.

She gave him a quick goodbye peck on his freshly shaven cheek and said: "Thanks again."

"Don't mention it," Xavier said.

She didn't seem to be listening; she picked up her hole punch and filed away the papers Xavier had signed.

And so it happened that, before the age of seventeen, Xavier had adopted two villages in India.

ON A WINDY AUTUMN DAY, after Xavier had read in a local newspaper that the grant money from the city of Basel for a new Jewish community center was still missing, an article that included a brief quote from Awromele's father, he went with Awromele to meet Mr. Schwartz.

The Yiddish lessons were coming along nicely, but Awromele had hinted a few times that it might be a good idea to take care of the circumcision first, before going any further with the Yiddish.

The divorce had complicated things as well. Not that it cost Xavier much time, but he'd had to get used to the idea of seeing his father only one weekend a month, and to spending almost every evening at the table with Marc, who kept trying to talk him into trying out the flight simulator.

And then there was Bettina, whom he courted primarily in order to make his parents happy. Sometimes his mother asked, "How is Bettina doing?" But his father couldn't even remember her name. On the phone he would occasionally mumble: "Are you still seeing that girl? What's her name again?" His interest in his son seemed limited to a vague regret at ever having sired a child at all. But perhaps it was more a matter of melancholy than of regret.

While his parents were busy building up new lives, Xavier was thinking about the task he had assigned himself, the comforting of the Jews. The human urge is always to concretize the abstract, so what he usually ended up thinking about was Awromele—even when he was with Bettina, or eating olives on the patio at the wine bar.

Walking beside Awromele on the way to Mr. Schwartz's house, he was happy but nervous as well. He was afraid of saying the wrong thing, or doing something that would cause him to fall from Awromele's good graces.

It was that nervousness, that fear of failure, he realized only later, that made him feel he was experiencing life in all its terror. Comforting begins with surrender. And surrendering to life, that was what Xavier wanted to do. He, who was born for more important things than saving up for a washing machine, driving a company car, or flipping through travel-agency catalogues, decided to dedicate the rest of his life to this.

"Have you ever read *Mein Kampf*?" he asked Awromele.

"No, is it any good?"

"Well, good—'good' isn't really the word for it."

"So what's it about?"

"*Mein Kampf.* You've heard of it, haven't you? *Mein Kampf!*"

Xavier's mother always referred to the man who had written that book as "You-Know-Who." And sometimes his father did as well; when people spend a lot of time together, they often adopt each other's habits. His mother would say, "You-Know-Who once said . . ." or "You-Know-Who would never have . . ." Fortunately, Marc had no idea who You-Know-Who referred to, or perhaps he simply didn't care. His world was filled with the flight simulator.

"Come on," Awromele said, "of course. *Mein Kampf*—so what about it?"

"Well, the thing about it," Xavier said, still a little amazed, "the thing about it is that it's, how shall I put it, it's a disturbing . . ."

Xavier had read the book listening to klezmer music and lying on his bed. It had been tough going in parts, but he had read on, and his perseverance was rewarded. It had become increasingly compelling and exciting. In his mother's new apartment, he'd had no trouble finding the photographs and the book, in the bottom drawer of her wardrobe, down there with the towels.

"A disturbing what?"

"A disturbing book. One of the most disturbing books I've ever read."

"Is it a bestseller?"

"It *was* a bestseller. A huge bestseller," Xavier said. "It sold like hotcakes, and the sales are still trickling in. It's sold more than ten million copies worldwide."

"Ten million. Does it have pictures?"

"No, it doesn't have any pictures. Some editions have a picture of You-Know-Who on the flap, but that's all."

Awromele thought about it. "It's not a bad title. If it had been called *Mein Hund* or *Mein Weib* it would never have sold anywhere near that. *Mein Haus* would have been rotten marketing, too. Has it been translated into Yiddish?"

"Into Yiddish? Not that I know of," Xavier said. "It's been translated into all the major languages: English, French, Italian, Dutch, Spanish, you name it. But I don't think there's been a Yiddish translation. And it's a huge book. He plugged away at it—he didn't mess around."

"Anti-Semitism, that's what it is," Awromele said. "You have writers who want to be published everywhere except in Israel." Awromele looked a little flushed. "Maybe that's what we should do," he said. "You could learn Yiddish that way, and when we're finished we'll have something we can sell to a publisher. If the publisher plays his cards right, we'll sell a few thousand copies. Then we can go to a whorehouse together."

Xavier stopped in his tracks. "What did you say?"

"An enthusiastic publisher should have no problem selling ten thousand copies of *Mein Kampf* in Yiddish. Any collector would buy it. Even if you can't read it, even if you don't understand Yiddish, you'd still want to have it. We'll do a nice cover and put in a couple of pictures, so it will appeal to the *goyim,* too. I've got a nose for business. What about the copyrights— have they expired? Or is it one of those families that makes things complicated?"

Xavier hadn't moved. The nauseous feeling had come back.

"No, the heirs to the You-Know-Who estate are all dead."

"That's great."

"But that bit about having a nose for business, you shouldn't say that. That's anti-Semitic. Besides that, it's not idiomatic. You can say that you have a *good* nose for business, you can say that. Even better is to say that you have good business instincts."

Awromele wanted to walk on. But Xavier was still rooted to the spot. "And what you said after that."

"What did I say after that?"

"About what you wanted to do with the money."

"Yeah."

"You're not really serious?"

"You mean from the sales of our Yiddish *Mein Kampf?* Of course I'm serious."

Xavier had to stay calm now, that was the most important thing. Businesslike and calm. He had to act reasonably, in a fashion worthy of a comforter. Some people comforted a prodigal son, others comforted a whole family, maybe there were even people who comforted a street or a neighborhood, but he'd taken it upon himself to comfort an entire people. That brought certain responsibilities with it. "It wouldn't be a bad idea to translate the book into Yiddish. Like I said, the sales are still trickling in. It's a good idea in itself to acquaint the Jews, open-mindedly and without historical prejudices, with the ideas of You-Know-Who. There's a lot more to it than you might think. Fascinating bits about Vienna, about painting, about freedom of the press, the state, the social-democratic tradition. But I meant what you said after that. That you wanted to spend the royalties on . . . on something as fleeting as pleasure. Not even pleasure. Lust, the lowest kind of lust a man can have. A person can have. And then not just any person—a person like you, a special person. You don't really mean that?"

Awromele shook his head. "I don't think about things like that as much as you do, and I'm not worried about low lusts or high lusts. The only thing I think about is increasing the total quantity of enjoyment. People need to enjoy themselves. There are thirteen of us at home, and I'm talking only about my brothers and sisters. That teaches you to be practical."

"But you're one of the chosen people," Xavier said, and his voice cracked.

"Leave it up to me," Awromel said. "Keep your shirt on. If we sell five thousand copies, we'll take the girls along on a trip, not a long one, maybe just for a day at the Bodensee. Maybe go up into the mountains and rent a hut. Like the *goyim* do."

"Don't destroy me, Awromele," Xavier said quietly. "Please, Awromele, don't destroy me."

"I'm not destroying you, I'm taking you along to Mr. Schwartz, who is going to circumcise you for next to nothing, and who is also willing to trumpet it around that your parents were too lax to do that at the moment prescribed by law. So stop accusing me of things, you sound like my mother. Nobody is destroying you."

"Have you ever been . . . ?"

"What?"

"Have you ever been . . . ?" Xavier asked, and his voice crackled like the sound from an old radio. "Have you?"

"Have I ever been what? Stop driving me nuts. One day you can't wait to get circumcised, the next day you're talking about the books of You-Know-Who, like I don't have anything better to do than think about how many books You-Know-Who sold in which year, and all the stuff he has in his bookcase. I have enough problems with my father. My father is an autistic rabbi. So what does your father do?"

"Didn't I tell you? My father is an architect."

"So there you go. What about your grandfather?"

"Grandfather? What grandfather?"

"What grandfather? How many grandfathers do you have? Your mother's father, let's start with him."

"He's dead."

"But what did he do?"

Only then did Xavier notice the little freckles on Awromele's nose. He stared at those freckles, and his stomach started hurting.

"So?"

"I never met him."

"But that doesn't mean you don't know what he did."

"I can't remember."

All Xavier could see were the freckles on Awromele's nose. Such friendly, kindhearted freckles.

"You can't remember? How can you not remember that?"

"He mowed lawns. Now I remember. In Poland. For rich Jews. He mowed their lawns."

It was out before Xavier knew it. The subconscious is an ample but inflammable container.

"That's impossible."

Xavier's stomach was hurting even worse.

"In Poland all the Jews were as poor as church mice, they didn't have lawns. The rich Jews were in Germany. Don't worry, you can tell me—I told you about my father."

For a split second Xavier felt the urge to tell Awromele everything, the whole story, but he realized that that would be his undoing. He was no hero yet, he couldn't allow himself to go down in flames. "He cut off the dead leaves, he cut the grass a little, he did all kinds of things, like I said. He also watched over the animals."

"Oh, he was a shepherd," Awromele said.

"Yes, that's right. A shepherd."

"I didn't know they had those in Poland. Funny."

"He watched over the animals. So they wouldn't run away and do crazy things."

"I didn't know animals could do crazy things. Were these circus animals?"

"No, not circus animals. Cows, goats, lambs, all kinds of things. He didn't care what kind, he loved animals in general."

"Most of the Jews I know don't like animals, and most animals don't like Jews, either. My father always says a dog and a Jew, they don't go together. I used to have goldfish, but my father flushed them down the toilet. Jews and fish—I guess they don't go together, either. He must have been a special kind of guy, that grandfather of yours."

"Yes, he certainly was," Xavier said. He was feeling a bit better now, but still a little weak. It seemed wise to change the subject. He remembered what Awromele had said a few minutes earlier, and that memory produced a stabbing pain in his chest that was only bearable when he bent over. That way he still felt the pain, but it wasn't as unbearable as before.

"Awromele," he said, bending over like that, "please tell me the truth. I have to know."

"What do you have to know?"

"Have you ever been with a woman who accepted money from you, and credit cards?"

"Money, yes. Credit cards, no. I don't go to women like that. And I can barely hear you when you're bent over like that. Stand up straight. What's wrong with you?"

"It's nothing," Xavier said. "It'll go away. But what do you mean, 'yes'? What do you mean by that? Explain to me what 'yes' means."

"Yes, what does that mean?" Awromele said. "In principle, it can mean all kinds of things, but in this case it means 'yes.' Just 'yes.' Let's not go on about it or we'll be standing here all night. That would be stupid, because Mr. Schwartz is waiting for us, and I don't want to be late. He's an old man."

Xavier began moaning softly, the way he'd seen men do before the Wailing Wall, on TV.

"And your father?" Xavier asked with the last ounce of strength he had left.

"My father?"

"Does your father go, too?"

"To women who accept money and credit cards?"

"Yes."

"My father. Listen. He knows a lot about the Torah for someone who's autistic, and he's read a lot of the Gemara, considering that he's extremely excitable. But what he really knows about best are the whores of Basel. He knows them all, their first names, their surnames, their professional names, where they live, the kind of cars they drive, where they go swimming, their favorite foods—sometimes he even visits their parents. Whores' parents are often sympathetic, warmhearted people. And he brings them presents on their birthdays. As far as that goes, he's a walking encyclopedia, but you see that pretty often with autistic people, you know what I mean? That they know an awful lot about just one thing, and that they can repeat by heart. It's pretty amazing. I could never do it, but when you're autistic, it seems, there's nothing to it."

"But you're a devout Jew, an Orthodox Jew. And so is your father. The two of you are . . ."

Xavier didn't know what he wanted to say, or, rather, he knew but he was afraid he was going to start saying terrible things. When he finally realized that it was best to be silent, Xavier felt like grabbing hold of Awromele's legs. But he didn't dare to do that, either.

"Pull yourself together," said Awromele, who could see that Xavier was feeling poorly. "You haven't even been circumcised yet and we're already getting this. This is going to be great. A circumcision at your age isn't just a matter of circumcising, a little disinfectant, and then you're back out on the street. Are you all right?"

"No," Xavier said. "I'm not all right. I'm not all right at all."

There was not much left of the easy-mannered young man who had once been so interested in steam engines and who, when the moment was right, never lacked for an appropriate quote from Nietzsche, Schopenhauer, or Hegel. He had never read more of those thinkers than a few isolated quotes, but that was enough for his purposes.

"Listen," Awromele said, "I don't know where you've been all this time, and maybe there are devout Jews who don't go to the whorehouse, maybe there are people like that walking around, but I sure don't know them. Where are devout Jews supposed to go? To the beach? To the disco? You want them to join a volleyball club? Are you nuts or something?"

Xavier's moaning grew louder. "So what about God?"

"Stop asking me questions you already know the answers to. My father claims that he found a passage in the Kabbalah in which the Almighty gives His blessings to rabbis who pay for it. I admit, it's a passage you can interpret in two ways, maybe even three, but my father's sure that his interpretation is the right one. I don't know what kind of God you've got in mind, but the Almighty wants to see joy grow on this earth. Which is why the rabbi is allowed to visit whores as long as it increases his joy. Because, if the rabbi's joy increases, the world's joy does, too; the mathematics you can do for yourself. Of course he's not allowed to go every day—that's a different story. No one is allowed to do everything every day, because then there would be no difference between one day and the next, and that would be boring. Imagine if we couldn't tell the difference between young and old, sweet and tasty, Tuesday and Thursday, dirty and ugly. That would be a disaster. The Almighty gave us the ability to tell the difference, in order to increase the total quantity of joy in this world. But that's too complicated for right now. Exactly how God wants to see the joy distributed, opinions differ on that. And of course the rabbi isn't supposed to go home and tell his wife how his joy has increased, because, even if you increase your own joy as much as possible, you have to be careful not to decrease the joy of others. That's why God wants us to do some things in the dark, and other things in broad daylight."

Xavier felt like he was being drawn and quartered. "And what about the Holocaust?"

"Listen," said Awromele, who was becoming really irritated now. "I'll be the first to admit that the Almighty has faults of His own, and it's a good thing, too. Otherwise we wouldn't be able to stand Him. Do you know anybody who doesn't have any faults? But in principle He's a reasonable, right-thinking entity who wants the best for us and who wants nothing more than to see joy increase on earth, like I've explained to you now about a hundred times. And that's why He's given us all kinds of instruments to use, and we can't refuse to use them, because then He would be really pissed off."

"But we have to conquer our instincts, Awromele. We have to overcome them, we have to subduc them; otherwise we're lost." Xavier was almost unable to speak. Just as in the sauna, he was having visions, and, just as in the sauna, he was unable to make sense of those visions.

"No," Awromele said, "you're wrong there. That's what creates all the misunderstandings. God wants us to listen to our instincts, not overcome them. He wants us to hear the lovely music those instincts make, even lovelier than Mozart or Beethoven. But most people don't know that, because they never listen to that music, even though they have the radio turned on all day. Just try listening closely to your instincts; a world will open up to you. God didn't give us something just to have us subdue it. Ideas like that really make Him angry."

Xavier listened to his instincts. But he didn't hear much, and what he heard wasn't at all what he wanted to hear.

Awromele did a little jig. "Jews and dancing," he said, "they don't go together, either, but that's a different story. And Jews and figure skating, they don't go together at all. Listen, what you need to do is learn to sing along with your instincts. Because that's the only way to fill up the void a little."

At that moment, the instincts were telling Xavier the most horrible things. That he should cover Awromele with kisses from head to toe, then throttle him slowly. He couldn't keep listening to his instincts; if he did, he would go crazy.

A God who wanted the joy on this earth to increase—you'd have to be

Jewish to come up with that. A God like that really wasn't any God at all, more like an amusement-park ride.

"I'm not religious," Xavier said. "I'm assimilated, as you know, and I'm not feeling too hot. I can't even think anymore."

"That doesn't matter," said Awromele, who clearly had no intention of getting into a theological squabble. "As long as you spread a little joy on this earth, then He's satisfied. And so am I."

Xavier staggered over to the gutter and threw up his lunch.

Awromele came up behind him, patted him on the shoulder, and asked: "Are you okay? Are you feeling better now?"

"No," Xavier said, "I'm feeling worse than ever." He grabbed hold of Awromele's right leg with both hands and looked up at him. The way Isaac looked at his father raising the knife. The way the ram must have looked when it was sacrificed.

"So you're saying we need to spread joy on this earth?" Xavier asked.

"That's right," Awromele said. "That's exactly what we need to do. And we shouldn't put off doing that too long. Because the Almighty hates dawdlers."

Then Xavier's breakfast hit the gutter as well.

What Does the Jew Want?

MR. SCHWARTZ LIVED in a ground-floor apartment at the edge of Basel. He was short and rather stooped. His skull shone through the little bit of hair that was left on his head. What worried Xavier most was that, as it turned out, Mr. Schwartz was practically blind. Mr. Schwartz showed his visitors into the living room and said, "Please, sit down, I have to finish this article." Then he picked up the *Neue Zürcher Zeitung* and a huge magnifying glass, sighed deeply, and went back to reading the paper.

It was still early afternoon, but the curtains were closed. Though there were a few lights on, the apartment was quite dark.

As soon as they came in, something told Xavier that Mr. Schwartz found his way around this house largely by feel. The huge magnifying glass only deepened his misgivings. "Is this the guy who's going to circumcise me?" he whispered in Awromele's ear.

"Yes, that's Mr. Schwartz; he said he'll do it for a pittance because your story moved him so deeply."

"But he's almost blind."

"He's not blind, he's visually impaired."

"How can someone who's visually impaired circumcise me the way it has to be done?"

Xavier had been feeling a little better, but now a new wave of nausea came rolling in.

"To circumcise a Jew, you don't have to see well. To circumcise a Jew, all you need is *neshome*."

For a moment Xavier felt like admitting that he wasn't a Jew, not even one-eighth Jewish, not even one-sixteenth, so that it might be better for them to look for a circumciser who could see clearly, and forget about the *neshome*. But all he said was "What's *neshome*?"

"Soul, feeling," Awromele said. "But stop talking so loudly. Mr. Schwartz hates noise when he's reading the paper."

Xavier kept his mouth shut and took a good look around. He noticed that there were cheeses lying everywhere. His uneasy feeling kept growing, a feeling he couldn't really explain. In itself, of course, there was nothing wrong with the fact that a circumciser had cheeses all over his living room. Still, Xavier would rather have seen Mr. Schwartz's living room decorated with books, a bouquet, or a few nice paintings.

"What are all the cheeses for?" Xavier whispered.

"Mr. Schwartz imports."

"Imports what?"

"Cheese."

"Oh."

"Kosher cheese."

"I see," Xavier said.

Everything begins and ends with longing. He who lives on longing must learn patience. Xavier had no patience.

"In fact, he's closed down his business," Awromele said. "These are the remainders. He still imports cheese for friends, family, and acquaintances. Kosher Emmentaler, kosher Gouda, kosher Roquefort, kosher Gorgonzola, kosher cheese spread."

Just then Mr. Schwartz put down the paper and his magnifying glass and gave Xavier a long, hard look.

"Well," he said. His hands trembled. He hadn't shaved for a few days, maybe a week. His head was round, his nose was thin; he had piercing eyes.

"Well," Mr. Schwartz said again, and then a long silence descended, a silence so silent that Xavier could hear a faucet dripping in the kitchen, a silence so long he had time to think: If I have to listen to this much longer, I'll go mad.

Then Awromele said: "Mr. Schwartz, this is Xavier, the one I told you about."

On the table where Mr. Schwartz had been reading the paper stood an old-fashioned pair of scales, and beside them a few pencils and a stack of wax paper.

"I could offer you something," Mr. Schwartz said, "but I take it you've just had lunch, and you're too old for a gumdrop."

Then Mr. Schwartz stuck his hand in his pocket and popped something into his mouth that Xavier thought looked suspiciously like a gumdrop.

For a man who had lived through the Holocaust, Mr. Schwartz looked cheerful. Almost too cheerful. An ambitious comforter strives to care for the worst cases, the hopeless ones. Those who can care for themselves have little need of comfort, and Mr. Schwartz, by the looks of things, was one of those.

"No, thank you," Awromele said. "You don't have to offer us anything, you've already done enough for me and my parents. Mr. Schwartz, do you remember me telling you last time about Xavier? His parents are assimilated, they don't take part in anything, they haven't even had him circumcised."

At the word "circumcised," Mr. Schwartz's eyes began to sparkle.

"Ah yes, I remember now. Poor boy. But it's not too late, it's never too late for a circumcision. If you're in good health you can have yourself circumcised at eighty, no problem. I once heard about a man in Minsk, a traveling salesman, who decided at the age of ninety-two to have himself circumcised. He said: I'm a *yid,* I don't want to go into the world of the future uncircumcised. He had been circumcised for one day, the bandages were still on, when he died."

"What a wonderful story," Awromele said.

Xavier crossed his legs. Most of the blue dye had been washed from his hair; all that was left was a bluish shadow on the back of his head. He didn't think Mr. Schwartz's story was wonderful at all, more like extremely depressing.

"Yes," Mr. Schwartz said, "it's a wonderful story. In Minsk people called it a miracle, because if they'd circumcised him two days later it would have been too late. What's your name, son?"

"Xavier."

"Xavier what?"

"Xavier Radek."

Mr. Schwartz's eyes began sparkling again. "Were your parents communists?"

"No," Xavier said, "just liberal."

"Always liberal?"

"Always liberal."

"I was a communist," Mr. Schwartz said, "but I saw the light in time, and then I started importing dairy products, kosher dairy products. Would you like to taste some?"

Xavier hesitated. He had the feeling there was someone else in the house, someone who was hiding. The next thing that occurred to him was that he really did want to taste everything that was kosher, or that had gone through the hands of the people he was going to comfort like no one had ever comforted before. None of which detracted from the fact that he had no desire to eat a piece of cheese right now. Less than half an hour earlier he had been vomiting into a Basel gutter.

"What I'd really like to know . . ." Xavier said.

"Would you like to taste some?"

Mr. Schwartz stood up from the table. From a bookcase he pulled out a piece of cheese, and quickly cut off two slices with a cheese slicer. He held them out on the palm of his hand, like sacramental wafers.

"Are you going to taste some," Mr. Schwartz asked, "or did I cut off two slices for nothing?"

Xavier took a piece of cheese and stuffed it hastily in his mouth. Even though he hadn't been brought up to be religious, he felt as if he was devouring the body of Christ. He knew that this people had little to do with Christ, but what else could you compare it to? Kosher cheese, the body of Christ. The longer he thought about it, the stronger the resemblance.

"Emmentaler," Mr. Schwartz said, looking melancholy, as though there were some kind of link between Emmentaler and sadness.

The kosher Emmentaler tasted like normal Emmentaler, only a bit more like plastic.

"Take the other slice, too," Mr. Schwartz said. "Awromele has tasted my cheese before." Xavier put the second slice in his mouth. He chewed. He couldn't taste anything anymore; he chewed, swallowed, and chewed, but the lump of cheese in his mouth only seemed to become bigger.

"You like that, don't you?" Mr. Schwartz said. Then he wiped his hand on his trousers and, for a few seconds, seemed to forget that he had visitors.

The cheese slicer still in his left hand, he stood frozen in the middle of his living room, as though he had heard a strange noise, or was trying to remember the name of a friend from the 1950s.

After a few seconds, Mr. Schwartz began singing a song. Neither the words nor the melody was familiar to Xavier. Awromele hummed along, and Mr. Schwartz kept time with the cheese slicer. Not wildly—it was barely noticeable.

A tabby-and-white cat came in from another room. It sat and cleaned its paws beside Mr. Schwartz's feet.

Xavier looked at Awromele, but he had his eyes closed. The house smelled of sour cream. We all strive after the good, but how does one recognize it?

The singing didn't stop, it faded slowly, it grew softer and softer, for a moment it died out, then Mr. Schwartz started in on a new verse. But at last it was over, and Mr. Schwartz asked: "How much would you like to take home with you? One ounce, or two?" The cat was still cleaning itself. Xavier said: "No, thank you." A few months from now he would turn seventeen. He had to be quick about it.

Mr. Schwartz took a few steps forward, until he was standing right in front of Xavier. Xavier had the impression that the curtains in this room hadn't been opened for months. "What does the Jew want?" Mr. Schwartz asked.

Xavier realized that the question was addressed to him. A difficult question. Had his grandfather asked questions like that? Not all questions led to the same answers.

"What does the Jew want?" Mr. Schwartz asked again. "The Jew wants a little house without too many mice, a toilet you can sit on for hours without hurting your back, a wife who can find her own way to the baker and the butcher shop and come home on her own, a wife who knows that time and money—like her husband's life—are not endless, a landlord who understands if your rent is a month, or two months, late, and a Christmas tree. If you're a Jew like me, that is. Because when I was your age I worshiped Lenin, but I also worshiped the Christmas tree just as deeply and passionately. Then I abandoned Lenin, and a little later the Christmas tree as well. The portraits, the collected works, and the angels and glass balls left my home, and I became a *mohel*. Do you know what a *mohel* is? A circumciser. You are going to be my last circumcision, my boy. One last time I will show what I'm capable of, and then it will be over, I will have done what I had to do, then I will wait patiently for what He has planned for me. Do you know how many circumcisions I have performed in my life? Just guess."

He may be almost blind, Xavier thought, but he knows what he wants.

"An awful lot, I bet, Mr. Schwartz," Xavier replied.

"More than five hundred. I still have all my instruments stored neatly in the closet. Now I know what I've been saving them for—for you. How old are you?"

"Almost seventeen," Xavier said.

"Before you know it, you'll be thirty-four. I'm afraid I won't be around to see that," Mr. Schwartz said. "Not unless a miracle happens. And then you will have been circumcised half your life, and the other half uncircumcised, and then you'll have to ask yourself: Which half was the best? Today you don't know what you'll say then, my boy. Maybe the first half will have been better, maybe they will both have been just as bad. That's often the way things go in the life of a Jew. The first half of his life is miserable, the second half is even worse. But maybe you'll get lucky, boy. You don't know right now, but maybe you'll say: Yes, that circumcision put me back on the right path. And then you'll think of me, then you'll think of Mr. Schwartz. Circumciser. Importer of kosher cheeses. Ex-communist. Lover of Christmas trees. Tenor. A tenor, too, yes, you heard me right. I used to sing. In a mixed chorus."

Mr. Schwartz went back to his desk, sat down, and picked up a pencil. He gave Xavier a full minute to think about what he had said. But all Xavier could think was: I hope they're not all like this one.

Then Mr. Schwartz said, "I'm going to give you three ounces to take with you, so your parents can taste my Emmentaler, too."

He found a knife, cut off a piece of cheese, and laid it on the scales.

"Almost four ounces," Mr. Schwartz said, peering intensely at the scales through his magnifying glass, "but I'm going to give you my special price."

He wrapped the cheese in wax paper, folded an old newspaper around that, and then fastened the whole thing tightly with a rubber band. He wrote out the bill on a scrap of wrapping paper. These rituals, all together, took about fifteen minutes.

Mr. Schwartz showed the boys to the door. In the vestibule he said, "One week from today, I'll be ready for my last circumcision."

Before opening the front door, he peered cautiously through the peephole. Then he said, "The coast is clear."

Injustice Spares No Man

IN HER BEDROOM, which had gradually been transformed into a filing cabinet full of information about Indian villages, sponsors, hydroelectric plants, and reports from the World Bank, Bettina said, "We're no good for each other."

Xavier looked at her, speechless. He had never looked at it that way.

"I'm involved with India, and these days with women's studies, too. I don't know what you're involved with, but every time we see each other it's rush, rush, rush."

Xavier had just taken off his shoes and socks, and now he began playing with his socks. It had never occurred to him that it could go any other way. Rush, rush, rush had always seemed like the right tempo to him.

"We can still be friends," she said.

He thought about his parents and about his mother's new boyfriend. His father spent more time these days in Singapore than he did in Basel. Now that he was no longer married—or at least no longer living in the same house as his wife, for the official divorce was still a long way off— he was able to live by different standards, and he frequented massage parlors in Basel as well. He had always had a weak spot for older women, but these days he tended more towards the transsexual. Xavier had heard that it was mostly Asians who worked there, of both sexes.

Xavier's mother had once asked the architect, "Is there someone else in your life?" And he had replied, "No, no one. I just need time for myself."

And there was, indeed, no one in his life. Masseurs are no one. Invisible hands, invisible mouths that show up for a moment, then disappear again into the darkness.

"If you don't want to be friends," Bettina said, "or if you think we should leave each other alone for a while, I can understand that. It's not easy."

Xavier was still fiddling with his socks. He decided to put them on again.

"I bought a present for you," Bettina said. It was a book, lying ready on her desk. She had prepared this farewell beforehand, it seemed, as though it were an aid campaign for a little Indian community.

Xavier carefully unwrapped his present. It was a book about Jewish rites and customs throughout the ages. He smiled.

"I thought you'd like it," Bettina said. "But you can exchange it if you want."

"No, no," Xavier said, "I don't have this one yet. Thanks. But how did you know I was interested in this?"

"Everyone knows that," she said. "I'm interested in things like that too. I love peoples who have a real culture of their own. And I think men with a culture of their own are a lot more interesting too."

"More interesting than who?" Xavier asked.

There was no reply. She was the way all women that age should be, the way all women of all ages should be, in fact. And so she cried. First quietly, then louder and louder. Then Xavier began crying, too. At first because he figured you were supposed to do that when someone left you. But he was touched by Bettina as well, how she sat there on the bed, cross-legged, the stuffed animals—four in total—lined up against the neatly painted wall. A beloved's pain was easier to bear than her joy. Only when she was obviously in pain did you get that pleasant feeling: She needs me. I'm not here for nothing.

Xavier looked at the book about Jewish rites and customs. A book with illustrations, not like *Mein Kampf*. Written in yellow letters on the cover was "Richly Illustrated." This book contained everything about the culture of the people he was going to comfort, a threatened culture.

He thought of Mr. Schwartz.

Bettina went out and came back with a roll of paper towels.

"Here," she said.

They daubed at their faces, and Bettina put an arm around Xavier.

He looked at the stuffed animals: a dog, a bear, a lamb, and a mouse. Then he leafed through the book and looked at the typically Jewish faces. He wondered what it meant, that everyone at his school knew about his interest in this subject. Probably not much good. Jews were no longer in fashion.

"Xavier," Bettina said, without taking her arm away, "maybe we just don't fit together." Art tries to convey emotion, he recalled. This was how he had explained it to Awromele. You-Know-Who had wanted to be an artist. You-Know-Who had tried to convey emotion, even though the father of You-Know-Who forbade him to do so. Perhaps that was why You-Know-Who had started his thousand-year Reich. It must be horrible to make something, to work on something for years, and then to find out that it doesn't convey emotion.

"Xavier," Bettina said again.

She wasn't Jewish, but he still found her awfully sad.

Xavier closed his book and folded the wrapping paper around it. "Maybe ten years from now neither of us will have found anyone else," Bettina said. "Then we can start over again."

As Xavier was getting up to say goodbye, he was struck by how powerless he was to convey the poignancy he'd felt just a few minutes before. But the more he thought about how he could ever do that, the less certain he was that the feeling of poignancy had ever been there at all.

They hugged. Bettina said, "Maybe even a week from now, we'll think, How could we have been so stupid?"

"Yes," Xavier said, "we might think that."

Strange, actually, that only now, now that he was losing her—or being freed of her, he wasn't sure which—was he starting to love her. Maybe not a lot, maybe in all the wrong ways, but still. When you cried over someone, and with someone, there was a fair chance that you loved that someone.

"I'm going to bring you a present, too," Xavier said. He held the book about Jewish rites and customs to his chest, kissed Bettina on the lips, and left the room where he had been deflowered, where he had wept for the first time in the presence of another, and where he had adopted two Indian villages.

He never went back there again.

WHEN HE ARRIVED HOME, Xavier found his mother standing in the living room with her raincoat on. She looked bad. Xavier's first thought was: She's found out that I'm going to get circumcised.

But the mother said: "We've been waiting for you. We have to go to the hospital; there's something wrong with your father."

Marc came out of the bedroom. He was pulling on a blue V-necked sweater, They climbed into Marc's car, a twenty-year-old Alfa Romeo. Marc liked flight simulators and industrial design.

On the way to the hospital, no one said a word.

The architect was lying in a room of his own. Intensive care. A nurse was doing something with him, but when she saw the visitors she said, "The doctor is coming," and left.

The three of them stood around the architect's bed. He wouldn't open his eyes.

"Maybe you should wait outside for a bit," the mother told Marc. "If you don't mind."

"You're right," Marc said. "That would be better." Marc's parents were both still alive; they had constitutions of iron. He didn't see them very often—once every three months at most. He wasn't used to sickness and death. To him, death was nothing but a pig you could use to make excellent ham.

When he was gone, Xavier's mother said to her ex-husband, "Hello, sweetheart, it's us."

The architect still didn't open his eyes.

The neighbor lady had found him earlier that afternoon, lying beneath his punching bag. He must have been lying there a while. She had a copy of his house key, for vacations and emergencies. Because the architect's car was blocking her driveway, and because he didn't pick up the phone, she had decided this was an emergency and barged into his house in a fury. She hated it when other people blocked her driveway. Then she had found the architect lying helpless beneath his punching bag, and her rage disappeared. "Poor man," she had murmured, "poor, poor man." She called the emergency number. And forty-five minutes later, with a certain eagerness, she had let the ambulance crew into her neighbor's house. "So young," she told the attendants, "and there you are, lying in your own house like that. No one to care for you. I put a pillow under his head and threw a blanket over him."

The attendants had lifted the architect into the ambulance without a word. For a moment the neighbor lady wondered whether she shouldn't go along to the hospital. But she had a hat-making course to attend that afternoon.

"Xavier, say something to your father," said the mother, who was feeling at a loss.

"Hi, Dad," Xavier said. "It's me, Xavier. How are you doing?" He realized that the situation was critical. The equipment that had been arranged around the architect's bed spoke of the dedication with which the medical profession tried to prolong dwindling lives. Yet all he could think was: If this is death, it's awfully boring. He wasn't familiar with death, only from the secret notes his grandfather had left behind, death as a club, death as a simple man with simple beliefs who occasionally strikes out when all he needs to do is guard. Death was so normal, so simple, so ordinary.

Xavier's next thought was less edifying. If his father died, the only one left for him to convert to Judaism was his mother. Maybe he could convert Marc as well, but he had a hard time imaging Marc as a Jew. Besides, he wasn't interested enough in Marc to bother showing him the way to the chosen people.

"He looks so pale," the mother said, "and so sunken. We have to talk to him. Hello, sweetheart. Hello, dearest." She caressed her ex-husband's forehead, but he didn't respond.

The mother had her feelings under control. You-Know-Who had not had his feelings under control. He had listened attentively to those feelings, and had heard the strangest things.

Finally, the doctor came in. He shook hands with mother and son and led them to his office, where he tried to explain the situation. He didn't want to give them any false hope: "I want you to realize that the chances are very slim indeed, and . . ."

While he was inhaling deeply, in order to finish this sentence, the architect died.

The staff of the Asian massage parlor close to Basel's Central Station waited for him in vain that afternoon. They knew the architect as a man of the clock. It was a disappointment for them, because the night before he had called to say, "Tomorrow I want to try a transsexual."

And so the architect died without ever having tried a transsexual. Injustice spares no man, and regularly drags down the non-Jewish with it as well.

THE FIRST PERSON to notice that the architect was dying was Marc. He had been sitting in the corridor waiting while the physician on duty sat in his office, trying to explain everything to the architect's family. While he sat there being bored, Marc was suddenly overcome by curiosity about the man with whom his girlfriend had spent most of her life. He pushed open the door and entered the room.

There he lay, his girlfriend's ex, peaceful and pale but exhausted. Marc took a few steps towards the bed; the door fell closed behind him. He leaned over the face of the man who was officially still his girlfriend's husband. And although it wasn't like him at all, for he was a quiet man who lived in harmony with himself and his surroundings, he said: "Hello, you worthless piece of shit."

The architect did not respond to these words, either.

Marc walked to the other side of the bed and, to his own surprise, said: "You thought you were really something, didn't you? Well, look at you now."

Marc did not consider it immoral to say such things. The architect couldn't hear him. When people can't hear you, you may say whatever you like. Strangely enough, it made him feel relieved. Expressing feelings that he had never known he had. It was glorious to finally listen to your heart. They say the heart is good at loving, but the heart can swear mightily as well. Marc's heart swore to beat the band.

He was planning to go on tossing curses at the dying man, but then his eye was caught by the equipment to the left of the bed. Marc took a good look at the equipment, and while he was doing so, one of the instruments began beeping. Life was leaving the architect for good.

Beneath Marc's eyes the life disappeared, yet he saw nothing, and, to tell the truth, there wasn't much to see. He didn't hesitate for a moment, despite the enjoyment he felt in railing against the dying man; when the actual dying started, he sided with the living. He ran out into the corridor and shouted: "Help! Emergency!"

Within forty-five seconds, two nurses and a young intern had gathered around the architect's bed, and all three of them noted that there was not much left for them to do. For the sake of protocol, they performed a few maneuvers.

The life had gone out of the architect, and life that has gone does not easily return.

One of the nurses went to the office of the physician on duty, where he was still informing the family of the risks, the possibilities, the dangers, and the hopes for the future. Marc followed her. On their way down the corridor, Marc felt himself growing light with sorrow. Standing eye to eye with death had not left him cold.

The nurse looked at the doctor, then at Xavier and his mother. They had to turn around to see her. When they had, she said, "I'm sorry to have to tell you . . ."

That was all she needed to say. Marc threw his arms around his girl-friend and said, "I'm sorry, I'm so sorry." Then he turned and hugged Xavier, who less than two hours before had been weeping bitterly in Bettina's room, but who now could not shed a tear.

XAVIER THOUGHT ABOUT his grandfather's club, his beautiful eyes and prominent nose. He thought: I have a duty to perform, and I mustn't allow anything as mundane as my father's death to let me lose sight of that. Parents die, that's something every child has to go through. That is how things are supposed to be. They die. That's Nature. That is no catastrophe. My father died of natural causes, with the emphasis on "natural." A person can live with that.

"Of course you'll want to say goodbye to him," the doctor said. He led the family and Marc to the little hospital room, where the equipment had already been disconnected, in order to save electricity.

"Come with us, Marc," Xavier's mother said. "It doesn't matter anymore."

They stood around the bed of the man who had missed his first trans-sexual by a hair. Somewhere in Basel, that transsexual was walking around the massage parlor, shouting, "Where's my three o'clock?" And in the hospital corridor the physician on duty thought: If I have to go skiing with the family again this winter, I'm going to jump out the window. He was in the midst of a crisis. The combination of family, adultery, and work had produced first a rut, then disappointment, and finally bitterness.

The mother sighed. Marc squeezed her hand, he whispered: "Everything will be fine." Xavier examined his father's body. A steam engine that had exploded—that was the closest comparison that presented itself.

Marc, Xavier, and the mother left the room. They had said goodbye. The architect's life was over. It had been a rich life, by human standards.

"If he had been found a little earlier," the mother asked the physician on duty once they were out in the corridor, "could you have done anything for him?"

"I don't think so," the doctor said. "No, there was nothing we could have done." He was thinking about the shambles his own life had become.

The doctor shook hands warmly with the remains of the Radek family.

Perhaps Xavier was oversensitive, perhaps he had a lively imagination, but when the doctor's hand slipped into his he thought about killing as a profession, as work that had to be done, and which therefore resembled all the other work that could not be left undone. If death alone can put an end to suffering, then death would seem to be a solution, an answer. Perhaps even a prudent answer.

He wanted to ask the physician what happened to patients who turned into vegetables, but he held himself in check.

Less than a mile away, the transsexual was pacing peevishly around the massage parlor, shouting: "I could just as well have stayed at home, instead of getting all gussied up like this. And for what?" His colleagues weren't listening to him. They were smoking and drinking cola in order to pass the time. They had enough problems with their own customers, who often didn't show up, either.

MARC DROVE XAVIER and the mother back to the house. Death had made Marc silent. It took a while before his mind was once again occupied by the Boeing 737.

They had barely entered the living room when the phone rang. It was the architect's neighbor.

"How is your husband doing?" she asked. "I've been trying to reach you all day."

"He just passed away," Xavier's mother replied.

"That's terrible," the neighbor said. But it sounded as though she had expected nothing less. "I feel so bad. He was so young. And so handsome. This is a great blow for all of us, for the city, for the neighborhood, for Swiss architecture. And just this afternoon he was lying there so peacefully under his punching bag. I did what I could, I put a blanket over him and a pillow under his head, I asked whether he wanted something to drink. But he was unconscious. As though he'd been struck by lightning. But, now that I have you on the phone anyway, I know this isn't the right moment to talk about this, but your husband's Saab is still parked in front of my driveway, and I can't get out. I thought, well, maybe you could move the car up a little? If you tell me where the keys are, I can do it myself." The three of them drove to the villa where Xavier had grown up. They looked for the car keys.

The neighbor lady came, too; she offered to warm up a can of soup for the next of kin, and talked nonstop. When they said they didn't want any soup, she offered to open a can of pineapple slices. But her pineapple was not wanted, either. The next of kin were not hungry. A death on the street made the neighbor lady extremely talkative. Like so many people, she subscribed to the newspaper only for the obituaries, which she studied closely and read out loud to her husband, often accompanied by remarks of disapproval. After more than an hour, Xavier finally found the keys to the Saab on the floor beneath a dresser.

The punching bag, which the architect had originally bought for his son, hung unattended. The neighbor lady explained in detail how she had found the architect. "You never know what's going to kill a person. My husband and I know so many joggers who have dropped dead on the spot. That's why we take the car wherever we go."

Xavier went to his room. It had been stripped: only a bed, a desk, and a stereo system were still in it.

He sat down on his old bed and thought of Awromele.

Now he was completely alone with his mother and his mother's new boyfriend.

And with his grandfather. He had entered him. He had taken possession of him.

Accept, O Lord,
This Humble Sacrifice

MR. SCHWARTZ'S BED had not been made for a long time, and had not been cleaned for even longer. The sheets had probably once been blue.

This was how an old man lived if he no longer had a wife, or had never had one to start with. The neglect came creeping in, every week a bit more, every month a little of the illusion of cleanliness lost.

On the yellowed wall, Xavier saw a lighter rectangle where something had once hung.

"Do you know what I used to have hanging there?" Mr. Schwartz asked. "A portrait of Lenin. I've never felt the urge to paint over it. A waste of money."

This was the day for which Mr. Schwartz had been saving his instruments, ever since he'd officially stopped working.

"Besides," he said, "you need something to remind you of the past; otherwise you start questioning your own sanity."

Other old men sometimes went out to eat in a cafeteria or a soup kitchen, where they were welcome after a lifetime of hard work, or went to buy a paper at the newsstand. They could dress up a little to draw a smile from a waitress, freshen up for a friendly conversation with the owner of the newsstand. Mr. Schwartz subscribed to the daily news, and ate his meals in his kitchen. He could remain unfreshened; the world would never notice.

A cave, that's what his home felt like, even more than the first time Xavier had visited it. A cave in which a dying animal had holed up, knowing full well how gruesome it must look to those who had no clue about dying, who knew about it only by hearsay.

Awromele was sitting on a little stepladder beside the dresser. He had asked whether he could sit in, or whether Xavier would prefer to be alone at the moment itself. Xavier had said that he would greatly appreciate Awromele's presence. That he would need him, particularly during and after the procedure.

"Sure, why not," Awromele said. "When my little brothers were circumcised, I was there, too. I stood right up close and watched the whole thing. I thought it was wonderful. Disgusting, but wonderful. Until my mother pulled me away."

Lust has a bad name. Perhaps Xavier and Awromele could rehabilitate lust. The way Xavier hoped on his own to rid the Jews of their bad name.

Lust and suffering, those were the main ingredients of life. The rest was detail, subset, delusion.

Even Mr. Schwartz's bedroom smelled, of sour cream. Mr. Schwartz had set up a reading lamp beside his bed. He was pottering about nervously, as though inspecting his stock of cheese. His instruments were laid out on a handkerchief.

"Six years ago," he said, "was the last time I did this. I remember it well, six years ago. In August. It was a swelteringly hot day. There was no one else in town to do it, so they came to me. Always babies, if you know what I mean—you're my first adult—but the principle remains the same. I was a specialist, and once you become a specialist you never forget how to do it. It doesn't matter whether it's an eighty-year-old man or an eight-day-old baby, it's all a matter of technique. I'll be right back. Remain seated."

Xavier wasn't sitting down, and he didn't feel like sitting down. Never before had he been so conscious of what was between his legs.

He was, he had to admit, frightened. Frightened of pain, infections, complications. Of decisions he would later regret. The way some people regretted their whole lives, but steeled themselves and went on watering the plants.

In a little basket on the windowsill lay three rotten apples. Mr. Schwartz obviously couldn't see them anymore. But couldn't he smell them?

Xavier had no qualms about losing a piece of foreskin. That loss, after all, would grant him admission to an exclusive confederation.

His grandfather had also belonged to an exclusive confederation. It wasn't good to go through life as an outsider. It was important not to. At some point you had to go looking for your partners in adversity. During the last telephone conversation Xavier had had with his father, the architect had said, "They say that in Russia you need money or connections to get anything done, but Switzerland is no different." A striking statement, coming from the architect. Now his father could make no statements about the forthcoming circumcision, and Xavier regretted that. He had dreamed of walking up to his father, circumcised but chipper as ever, and saying: "Look! Take a good look, Dad. Notice anything different?" Then he would wave his penis around and ask his father, "You see it now?"

If his mother heard about the circumcision, she would go crazy. She had kept her feelings under control till now, but she wouldn't be able to take this. Sooner or later he would have to tell her. First he would let her get used to the idea. Bit by bit, step by step. The way you teach a child to walk.

At the library, Xavier had leafed through a medical encyclopedia to find out about the risks. Going for a ride in a car had its attendant risks as well, but in a car you could at least wear a safety belt.

You had to convince yourself. You had to tell yourself that it had to be this way and no other. People who couldn't do that had friends to do it for them, or social workers.

That weekend, Xavier had taken a good look at himself in the mirror. He didn't look bad, there was no denying that, but after a while he began seeing someone else. A man wearing a cap, boots, holding a dog on a short leash. Xavier liked uniforms. And, in theory, he was not void of a certain degree of cruelty, although it hadn't expressed itself in practice yet. At nursery school he had once pulled a little girl's hair, hard—she'd had long black hair—but you couldn't call that cruelty. At least, not unusual cruelty. Given, he watched the violence in films and on television with a businesslike, almost eager interest, but watching was largely passive.

Cruelty had to come from somewhere; perhaps it sprang up, the way rivers did. High in the mountains. At the foot of a glacier.

"Show me," Awromele said.

"What?"

"While it's still there. I want to see it."

"You mean . . . ?"

"Yeah."

"The thing he's going to take away?"

"Yeah."

"But why, why now?"

"Because afterwards it will be too late."

"I'd rather not. If you don't mind."

"I've never seen an uncircumcised one. Except for my brothers, when they were eight days old, but that doesn't count. In films you sometimes see them uncircumcised, but mostly circumcised."

"I never really noticed," Xavier said. "I don't watch films like that much."

"It's not easy to find an uncircumcised one."

"That's too bad," Xavier mumbled, and he felt himself growing sadder.

"Be a sport," Awromele said. "I promise I won't laugh."

But it wasn't laughter Xavier was worried about.

Outside, the street was being broken up. The sound of the jackhammer could be heard in Mr. Schwartz's bedroom. Every once in a while it stopped, only to go on even louder a few seconds later.

"That's impossible," Xavier said, holding his hands over his fly. "I can't."

Xavier's father had been buried only recently. It was already hard for him to remember the day his father died, except that it was a Sunday. The day on which his grandfather had always refrained from death, to honor the Lord. Did that fall under historical irony, or was it a coincidence? Was coincidence ironic?

"You have to get undressed anyway," Awromele said. "So what difference does it make? Or did you think you could wear your swimming trunks?"

Xavier shook his head.

"So do it already," Awromele said.

"I'm not in the mood right now."

At the funeral, the colleagues of Xavier's father had spoken kindly of his achievements as an architect, a great-uncle had mentioned the toy trains the dead man used to collect, and an aunt blew him kisses as he lay in his grave. Then it was over. Xavier had not said a word, and his mother had spoken only one sentence: "I will let Beethoven do the talking for me." Beethoven was always a sure bet at a funeral.

"Please," Awromele said. "Do it for my sake. I'm just curious, that's all. Without me you still wouldn't have been circumcised, not even ten years from now."

Xavier took off his shoes and socks. Emotional blackmail is the best form of blackmail. He was wearing a pair of black jeans.

Imagine, you're a reasonably normal person, in your own eyes and in the eyes of your surroundings, an unobtrusive person, but not so unobtrusive that people really start to wonder. You have everything other people have. And one day you discover that you enjoy cruelty. That's an altogether different thing from enjoying steak; there's probably a certain amount of cruelty involved there as well, but it doesn't have to show up on the outside, it can remain hidden.

Xavier pulled down his jeans. They didn't go very quickly—his jeans were tight. Out in the street, the drilling continued.

It had been five minutes since Mr. Schwartz had said that such procedures were all a matter of technique, which you didn't forget at the drop of a hat.

Imagine that you not only enjoy the products of cruelty, the steak, but also the cruelty itself. Even though you've never done anything that might be considered unacceptable. From the moment you discover that, you see yourself differently.

Xavier's underpants had the word "happiness" printed on them. A nice word.

The problem wasn't the cruelty itself, because all kinds of cruelty were considered acceptable as long as you didn't enjoy them in public. Xavier was afraid that a person like him, who enjoyed life so intensely, would also start enjoying cruelty.

The underpants were pulled down hastily, as in a locker room. The haste that comes from shame.

Awromele stared unashamedly. He even came a step closer, in order not to miss anything.

"Jesus," he said, "what a bunch of skin."

"That's how we're made; that's how you were made, too. This is the product of evolution."

"Yeah," Awromele said, "a weird thought. Evolution, I mean. Can I feel it?"

Awromele fingered the skin the way you finger the sleeve of a shirt in a clothing store, to see if the material is light enough for the summer.

"So where's the smegma?"

"I don't have smegma," Xavier said. He was still wearing his sweater, a sweater his father had given him. Dressed on top, undressed down below. He looked ridiculous.

"I wonder how much of it's going to be taken off," Awromele said, Xavier's skin still between his fingers.

Xavier stared straight ahead, at Mr. Schwartz's dressers. He had told his mother that he was going for a walk with friends. "Be careful," she had said. "They're predicting a thunderstorm."

"What did you ever do with those pictures you took of me?" Awromele asked. He had let go of the skin for a moment, but now he took hold of it anew and pushed it back to see what was hidden beneath.

"They didn't turn out. I'm sorry. I'll take new ones, if you like."

He didn't know what was so special about what was under his skin, but Awromele found it interesting; he was plucking at it as if it were the scab on a wound.

"Let go of me," Xavier said.

"Before long you won't have it anymore," Awromele said sadly. "Then it won't be yours anymore, it won't be part of your body, just a piece of skin that gets thrown in the garbage; maybe later it will be processed into cat food." He let go and went back to sit on the stepladder.

"You could save it," Awromele said, already sounding happier. "You could put it in a glass jar and keep it in the cupboard to show important visitors. You can ask your visitors; Would you like to see my foreskin? And then you pull out the jar. And if you ever become famous, you can put it up for auction. It wouldn't surprise me if you got a bunch of money for it. Who knows, by that time maybe you could even buy a second home from the proceeds."

The idea seemed to appeal to Awromele. His smile spread until he was beaming, but he stopped talking. The drilling outside had stopped. The silence was oppressive.

"Is it really true," Xavier asked, "that the Jews control the media?"

"I don't know," Awromele said. "The media? I wouldn't know."

Xavier noticed that the subject didn't interest Awromele much. Where in the world was Mr. Schwartz? Was he chickening out?

"What gives you that idea?" Awromele asked.

"My mother said something along those lines."

"Does she work for the media?"

"No, not that. Her friend is a soundman. She wants to start working again, though."

"What kind of work is she looking for?"

"Something with children."

"That's always nice, working with children. Do you want to work with children, too?"

"I don't know," Xavier said. "I like children, though." And he covered his sex organ with his sweater, which was fortunately a bit too large for him. It made him look like he was wearing a dress that had been washed at the wrong temperature. "In fact, I don't think so," he said. And, after a brief pause, "Awromele, aren't you interested in higher things?"

"Higher things?"

"I never hear you talk about classical music. For example. Or about opera. Or museums. About the fine arts. About beauty."

"No, I don't talk about those things much. Now that you mention it." Awromele got off his stepladder. "But if you'd like to me to talk about them more often, just say so."

"Have you ever been to the opera?" Xavier asked.

"Funny question," Awromele said. "No. Never." He pushed up Xavier's father's sweater, 100 percent cashmere, and began absentmindedly petting Xavier's member. The way you pet a dog while talking to its master about international affairs.

"Do *you* talk a lot about classical music?" Awromele asked.

"I'd like to talk about it more," Xavier said. "With you, too. I think it would be great to talk to a Jew about Beethoven. Or Wagner." He blushed slightly. "At my father's funeral they played Beethoven," he said quickly.

"We never play music at funerals," Awromele said. "We don't like that fancy-schmancy stuff. A funeral is a funeral. I've never met people as assimilated as you. It's a wonder you even know you're a Jew."

Awromele was stroking the uncircumcised member more forcefully now. "It is different," he said, "I can tell now. You can do more with it, you can apply more force, because there's less tension in it. A foreskin might be less hygienic, but it also has its advantages. Evolution probably knew what it was doing. They say that everything in evolution is there for a purpose, don't they?"

Xavier noticed that he was growing short of breath. Like that time he'd vomited on the street. "If the Jews don't control the media, then who does, in your opinion?" he asked. His voice peeped, as though he had asthma.

"It's probably not the Muslims," Awromele said. "They don't control much of anything."

"Now you've got to stop," Xavier said, trying to pull his father's sweater down farther. "That's enough."

"Your foreskin's got *neshome*," Awromele said, going on with his powerful caresses, as though it were his profession and he'd been doing it for years. "Do you know what *neshome* is?"

"You told me once," Xavier said, "but I forgot." He pulled harder on his father's sweater, but it didn't help much. The sweater had been bought in Milan, back when they were still a happy family, the Radeks. A happy family with a little secret.

"Soul," Awromele said. "That's what *nesjome* is, soul."

The drilling in the street started again. Awromele bent down; he took the foreskin and what was attached to it in his mouth.

Awromele's got my soul in his mouth, Xavier thought. He cleared his throat. "I know you've done a lot for me. But I don't know if I like this."

Awromele was making smacking sounds, the way wine tasters do when there are other wine tasters around.

"Funny," he said. "You taste funny."

The door flew open. Because of the drilling, they hadn't heard Mr. Schwartz coming. Mr. Schwartz was nearsighted, and so absorbed in the prospect of the task he would be performing in a few minutes that he didn't notice the situation in which the boys found themselves. He had two stirrups with him, stirrups he said had been given to him by a gynecologist friend who had closed shop. "A former communist, just like me," he said. "We former communists have to stick together."

With Awromele's help, he attached the stirrups to the sides of his bed. Then he looked around, as though wanting to make sure he was still in his own bedroom. He patted his hands together softly and said, "I'm ready; just let me wash my hands."

Awromele casually stroked Xavier's member a few more times. "It will work out," he said. "Mr. Schwartz used to be the most famous *mohel* in all of Basel. They said he could perform miracles."

"Will I get an anesthetic?" Xavier asked.

"A little, I guess, but you won't need much. Babies are circumcised without an anesthetic. Yours is a bit bigger, of course, but it's the same principle."

Xavier blew his nose. "So now I'll be part of the covenant," he said. "The holy covenant." It wasn't a question, it was a statement.

"Holy," Awromele said, "you're right about that. I hope Mr. Schwartz hurries up a little."

"Do you do that often?"

"What?"

"What you just did?"

"What do you mean?"

"What you did. With your mouth."

"Oh no, never. Only watched. How other people did it."

"You seemed so proficient at it."

"It's not all that difficult."

Xavier stared at the rotten apples on the windowsill, and then at the old-fashioned stirrups that had been mounted with such difficulty on Mr. Schwartz's bed. He couldn't help thinking about Mr. Schwartz's love of Christmas trees, and how that had caused him a crisis of conscience when he was young.

"Are you sure," Xavier asked, "that we shouldn't have this done in a hospital?"

"That would be more expensive. And less authentic. Jews are always circumcised at home."

"And what if something goes wrong?"

"Then we can always go to the emergency room."

"But then maybe it will be too late."

"A young body can survive a great deal. Don't worry."

Xavier wasn't so sure about that. What, after all, had his father's body really undergone in the way of trauma? He had lain beneath the punching bag, and a few hours later it was all over. Okay, he hadn't been that young anymore, but he wasn't that old, either.

Mr. Schwartz's instruments looked old-fashioned, but fortunately they were clean.

"I have to pee," Xavier said. "Excuse me for a moment."

He wasn't sure how long he'd still be able to do that. While he was peeing he imagined what it was like to have the clap, or other sexually transmitted diseases. It doesn't help to worry about things over which you have no control, but the imagination is more powerful than reason. Though Xavier's imagination was exceptionally powerful, he didn't want to turn back, he couldn't turn back, he didn't want to be a coward.

When Xavier came out of the bathroom, Mr. Schwartz was waiting in the bedroom with a tub of water and some towels.

"Do your parents know about this?" he asked.

"My father is no longer alive."

"Oh, I'm sorry."

"And it's going to be a surprise for my mother."

"She'll be very pleased," Mr. Schwartz said. "Just like your father, wherever he is now. I'm sure that he can see us, and that he's nodding in approval. So let's get started. Lie down and make yourself comfortable."

Xavier crawled onto Mr. Schwartz's bed. The smell of sour cream became overpowering. He wondered whether Mr. Schwartz had ever lain in this bed and longed for someone else, or whether you stopped doing that at a certain point.

Mr. Schwartz moved the reading lamp and leaned over him.

"Put your feet on the stirrups," he said.

But Xavier's feet kept sliding off the stirrups, and Awromele had to help. He held Xavier's feet tightly in place.

Xavier lay there, spread-eagled on the not-so-clean bed, feeling as if he were at the dentist's.

"Do you want to pay now, or later?" Mr. Schwartz asked, handing his patient a glass of water.

"Later," Xavier said. He had a hard time holding the glass upright.

"I'm going to give you some Valium," Mr. Schwartz said, "that should be enough." There were three little tablets in the palm of his hand, and Xavier gulped them down greedily. The faster the narcosis started working, the better.

Awromele watched with interest as Mr. Schwartz lifted the Italian sweater and leaned down close to Xavier's lower body. The patient felt the old man's breath against his navel.

"Everything looks fine," Mr. Schwartz said, "everything looks just dandy. Exactly the way it should. I'm not going to put on gloves, because I just washed my hands."

Xavier didn't feel the narcosis much, so he closed his eyes and prepared himself for the operation by concentrating on his grandfather in uniform. He felt Mr. Schwartz's hand lifting his sex organ a few centimeters, he heard someone make a clacking noise with his tongue, then he felt something cold against his sex organ, and after that there was only pain.

Pain that took his breath away. He didn't even notice that he was screaming. For a split second the pain seemed to subside, and he thought about the phrase he had come across in a comic book as a child: "Accept, O Lord, this humble sacrifice."

Then the pain came back, redoubled.

Xavier tried to pull his feet out of the stirrups, he tried to get up, but someone was holding his feet. Someone was squeezing his ankles.

He hoped he would lose consciousness, so terrible was the pain. But Xavier's consciousness remained alert, as though it didn't want to miss a single one of these precious moments. He screamed, he couldn't stop screaming, he lost control of his voice. Fortunately, Mr. Schwartz's neighbor was deaf; otherwise he would have certainly called the police, or come to take a look for himself.

Later, Awromele would swear he had never known that a human being could shriek so pitifully.

As regards the sacrifice, no one had asked for it, and there was no one to receive it. Nevertheless, Xavier kept repeating it in his mind, like a mantra: "Accept, O Lord, this humble sacrifice."

But Mr. Schwartz was there, and he did what Xavier had asked of him, to the best of his ability, peering nearsightedly through his reading glasses; and Awromele was there, keeping a tight hold on Xavier's feet.

Xavier still had his eyes closed. He dreamed of his father, working off his excess fat in a gigantic fitness center.

By the time the dream was over, Mr. Schwartz had removed the foreskin, once and for all.

A Dying Rat

IN XAVIER'S DREAM he could smell sour cream, and it took a while for him to realize that the smell was not a dream. He heard voices he didn't recognize, coming from the kitchen. What are they talking about? he wondered.

It was not so strange that he didn't understand them, for the voices were speaking Yiddish. Thanks to Awromele's lessons, Xavier was able to form simple Yiddish sentences. But he was nowhere near being able to follow the excited conversation between Awromele and Mr. Schwartz.

Right after the shameful realization that he was unable to understand Yiddish, the pain returned, inescapable and overpowering. He was still lying on Mr. Schwartz's bed, but his feet were no longer on the stirrups. He could see a few dark-red spots on the sheets.

Mr. Schwartz had slipped.

The screaming had unnerved him. "That kid screeched like a stuck pig," he told Awromele later. "You can't expect anyone to work like that."

The sex organ was wrapped in a white bandage; the testicles were bandaged, too. It looked as though that afternoon a mummy had grown between Xavier's legs. A cute little mummy.

Xavier had no time to think about that. The pain was searing, so sharp that he couldn't relax enough to think. He wondered what time it was; he had promised his mother he would be back in time for dinner.

And he was thirsty. "Awromele?" he cried out, but he didn't have the strength to shout loudly.

Before long he would be dead, without having had a chance to comfort the Jewish people. There he lay, without a foreskin but with good intentions, a couple of Yiddish lessons, the deep desire to become part of the holy covenant, and despite all this his chief concern was that he might be too late for dinner with his mother.

"Awromele," he shouted again, a little louder this time.

He tried to move. He couldn't.

Voices came from the kitchen again; he thought one of them was Awromele's, but he wasn't sure. He heard someone laughing, too.

The workers out in the street had put aside their jackhammer. What time could it be? Xavier closed his eyes. He had no idea how long he had been lying there. When he opened his eyes again, he saw Mr. Schwartz and Awromele leaning over him.

"You're awake," Awromele said. "Finally."

Mr. Schwartz ran his hand through Xavier's hair. "There you are, boy," he said. "There you are." As though Xavier had just come crawling out of the womb.

"You're circumcised—*mazel tov,*" Awromele said.

"It took longer than I expected," Mr. Schwartz said. "I had to get the hang of it again. But then it all came back to me."

"Could I have some water?" Xavier asked.

"Of course," Mr. Schwartz said. He stumbled out of the room.

Awromele squeezed Xavier's hand. "You're looking a little pale, but that will go away," he said.

Xavier was afraid it would never go away; he felt as if all the blood had run out of his body.

What a strange phenomenon, pain. It makes the world so small, tiny, no bigger than the point of pain itself.

Mr. Schwartz stumbled back into the room with water in a plastic cup.

"I found a straw, too," he said. He held the straw up triumphantly.

Xavier gulped down the water. Then he said weakly, "I have to go home."

With Awromele's help, he sat up. But when he sat up straight, it felt as though he was paralyzed from the waist down, and all he wanted to do was fall back onto Mr. Schwartz's dirty bed and sleep for the next twenty hours. At that point, what he wanted most was never to wake again.

The only way he could remain upright was with Awromele's help.

"There's something wrong," Xavier said. "Does it always hurt like this?"

"It will go away," Awromele said. "This is part of it." And he squeezed Xavier's hand again.

Mr. Schwartz said, "For special occasions, I keep a special bottle." He bent down and pulled something from under the bed. A bottle indeed. "Pure as nature itself," he said. "Plums and alcohol, that's all it is. This will have you back on your feet in no time." He poured the liquor into little glasses that he kept under the bed in cardboard boxes.

"I have to go home," Xavier said, after Awromele and Mr. Schwartz had helped him to knock back two glasses of slivovitz and he felt himself growing nauseous. "What time is it?" Xavier tried to get out of bed, but couldn't. "I'm dizzy," he said. "Everything's spinning."

"Of course," Mr. Schwartz said. "I just circumcised you. People who have just been circumcised often feel a little dizzy."

There were dark-red spots on the bandages now as well.

The hard liquor had relieved the pain for a moment, or, rather, had deflected it to other parts of the body, to stomach and throat. Xavier hadn't eaten much that day. He had read that it was better to go into the operating room with an empty stomach.

Outside it was already dark. He had to hurry; he didn't want to cause his mother unnecessary sorrow. Whenever he showed up late for dinner, she would look at him so sadly and ask, "Did you forget about me?"

His black jeans were lying on the floor. He tried to pick them up, but Awromele was too fast for him. He was still sitting on the bed. He felt he might faint any moment.

Mr. Schwartz stood there helplessly, as though he didn't know what to do now that his work was finished.

Xavier tried to push his foot into the trouser leg, but couldn't.

"If you like, you can sleep here tonight," Mr. Schwartz said. "If that would make things easier for you."

"No," Xavier said, "I have to go." And he eased himself slowly off the bed. Then he fell onto the floor.

His legs couldn't support him; they were like those of an old man half consumed by death. Maybe his legs would never support him again. There was a carpet on the floor. He didn't quite dare to look at the little mummy between his legs, but whenever he gave it a quick glance it seemed to him that the red spots were getting bigger.

He tried to crawl.

"Give him some more slivovitz," Mr. Schwartz said. "Quick."

Awromele poured the remains of the bottle into one of the little glasses and tossed the stuff down Xavier's throat. Then he wiped Xavier's mouth with his hand.

From the dresser Mr. Schwartz pulled a pair of gray trousers that probably fit him well but were a few sizes too big for Xavier. "You'll be able to get into these," Mr. Schwartz said. "Put them on, if you really need to go home so badly. But if you want to sleep here, that's no problem. There's enough food in the house." He rummaged through his nightstand, looking for safety pins with which to fasten Xavier's new trousers.

Awromele strained to pull Xavier off the floor. "Come on," he said. With Mr. Schwartz's help, he was able to roll the newly circumcised boy onto the bed, and together they wormed Xavier's feet into the trouser legs.

"I bought these trousers in Paris," Mr. Schwartz said, "in 1972, but you can keep them. I have trousers enough. How often can one person change his trousers? And what difference does it make if no one sees him anyway?"

For a moment, Xavier was able to forget everything—the operation, the smell of sour cream, the taste of slivovitz, the pain, Mr. Schwartz's accent. He was back with his father in a gigantic fitness center.

But that didn't last long: the pain came back with twice the intensity, as though avenging itself for Xavier's attempt to forget it. Pain is like a lover who grows surly when you stop paying attention to him.

Even after Awromele and Mr. Schwartz had fastened the trousers with two safety pins, they still sagged so badly that Xavier would have to hold them up with one hand if he didn't want to parade down the street naked. He wasn't wearing underpants. The two men had tried to put a pair of underpants on him, but the pain had made him scream.

Xavier in Mr. Schwartz's trousers looked something like a cross between a bum and someone trying to imitate an old vaudeville comedian. He lay on the bed while Awromele did his best to put on his socks and shoes.

"Help!" Xavier shouted.

"Am I hurting you?" Awromele asked.

In the living room, Mr. Schwartz was busy cutting off a piece of Gorgonzola and wrapping it in wax paper.

It wasn't the pain that made him shout. Xavier was having visions again. His grandfather often played a prominent part in his visions, but in this last vision a supporting role had also been reserved for Mr. Schwartz. Xavier had shouted "Help!" because he remembered that he wanted to comfort Awromele, and he wasn't convinced that he would be able to.

MR. SCHWARTZ CAME into the bedroom, feeling more triumphant than he had in years. He was no longer tormented by a sense of uselessness. In the last few hours, he had proved himself quite useful.

"What does the Jew want?" he asked. "The Jew wants to be healed, the Jew wants to go skipping down the street, the Jew wants to take a nice nap, and when he wakes up he wants to nibble on a piece of Mr. Schwartz's Gorgonzola."

He tried to hand the cheese to Xavier. Xavier was having more and more trouble seeing where the visions stopped and reality began.

Awromele took the Gorgonzola in its wax-paper wrapping. He said to Xavier, "We really must allow Mr. Schwartz to get some rest now."

Xavier was able to get up from the bed, with Awromele's help, and limped out of the room on his friend's arm. The limping hurt, and so did talking, swallowing, looking, breathing. Xavier felt like a dying rat.

The old Parisian trousers kept falling down around Xavier's knees, but Awromele deftly pulled them back up each time.

"Well, boys," Mr. Schwartz said, "we'll be seeing you. Get well quick." He planted a quick kiss on Xavier's forehead, and Xavier caught a vague whiff of alcohol before staggering and falling to the floor.

He was lying in Mr. Schwartz's vestibule, moaning quietly.

"I can't do this," Xavier said.

"Don't give up," Awromele said. "You're almost there. You'll be home before you know it; then you can lie down in your own bed."

Melancholy took hold of Mr. Schwartz once more. A few minutes of cheerfulness never go unpunished. He had done his very best. Okay, the knife had slipped, but it had slipped in the past as well, and that had never been a problem. Skin heals so quickly. The skin cells replenish themselves faster than you could imagine. Before you knew it, there was no sign of where the wound had been.

Awromele said: "Listen, you're the one who wanted to be circumcised. And that's what you got."

Xavier's moans grew louder. "But I didn't know it was going to hurt like this."

"It hurts for a little while," Mr. Schwartz said. "Everything hurts the first time around."

Mr. Schwartz and Awromele pulled Xavier to his feet. They ignored his grievous cries; neither of them knew how to stop his suffering.

Awromele rushed Xavier out the door in a hurry. Other people's moaning could get on your nerves.

Mr. Schwartz stood in the doorway for a long time, looking after them in the hope that they would turn and wave, but it didn't happen. Then he closed the door, slid closed the four deadbolts, and lay down on his bed without changing the sheets. He was finished. The dark-red, almost purple spots on the sheets escaped his notice.

I'm On Fire

XAVIER WALKED straddle-legged through the streets of Basel, like an animal that has been hit by a car and is dragging itself to its lair. Every once in a while, his trousers fell to his knees. Awromele hitched them up quickly, so passersby wouldn't see the little mummy. A woman crossed to the other side hurriedly, fear in her eyes, when she saw the boys coming.

From one moment to the next, nothing is left of you but the pain. At a *Biergarten,* Awromele called a taxi. Under the circumstances, public transport did not seem like an option. The first cabdriver who showed up refused to take them. The second one was more tolerant. In the backseat, Awromele sang Yiddish songs to keep Xavier from losing courage. But Xavier had already lost it.

The cabdriver, a foreigner, stopped in front of Xavier's house.

It was important that his mother not see Awromele—the time wasn't ripe for that yet. "You go on," Xavier whispered, "I'll be okay." He wormed his way out of the cab. His shame was stronger than his pain, but not much.

Only when he reached the door did he realize that his keys were in the pocket of his jeans, still hanging over a chair at Mr. Schwartz's house.

He rang the bell. Then he was finished. He tried to sit down, but he fell, flat on his face at his own front door.

Xavier's mother heard the bell, but she made a point of not opening the

door for strangers. Just like her late husband—he had always been op-
posed to that, too. Right after he had started practicing as an architect, he
had seen *A Clockwork Orange,* and had decided then and there never to
open the door for strangers again. Not even in wartime. Particularly not
in wartime.

Xavier tried to get to his feet a few times, but couldn't. It felt as though
a novice acupuncturist were jamming a thousand needles into Xavier's sex
organ. The paralyzed feeling grew stronger. Maybe Mr. Schwartz had accidentally severed something important.

Because Xavier had not come home for dinner as he usually did, the
mother decided after a few minutes to go and see who was ringing the
bell. She opened the door, but saw nothing. She was about to close it again
when she noticed her son lying on the doorstep at her feet. On his back.
Like an animal. The boy reminded her of an overgrown alley cat. She
didn't like alley cats.

"Xavier," she said, "what on earth do you think you're doing?"

Only then did she see that her son was wearing a pair of unfamiliar
trousers. She couldn't see the mummy under the trousers, which was
probably just as well.

"What are you wearing?"

"I lost my pants," Xavier whispered.

She started to bend over, to take a better look at the trousers, but
caught a whiff of alcohol. She was no fool. She knew exactly what alcohol smelled like, even though she didn't drink much herself.

"Lost your pants," she said. "Don't make me laugh! You didn't go hik-
ing in the mountains at all, you went out carousing with those so-called
friends of yours. You're a drunkard. I'm so disappointed."

Then she closed the door and went back to the table. She had waited for
Xavier before starting with dinner, but she had no intention of waiting any
longer. She dished out the food and shouted, "Marc, dinner's ready!"

"I'll be there in a minute," Marc called from upstairs. "I'm right in the
middle of a forced landing."

Outside, on the doorstep, Xavier howled as loudly as he could: "I haven't been drinking, Mama, help me, open the door. Please, open the door, Mama."

A window flew open, and a woman shrieked, "Shut up, or I'll call the police."

Xavier stopped his howling. Now there was only the pain, the pain that kept getting worse. It felt as though the circumcision were still going on, as though Mr. Schwartz were beginning over and over again on the same operation. Like a mantra, Xavier repeated quietly, "Accept, O Lord, this humble sacrifice."

Marc came downstairs at last. He had made it. He liked forced landings—they kept things a little exciting. Sometimes, when he was bored, Marc would throw his plane into a nosedive.

He poked his fork absentmindedly into the homemade mashed potatoes. Xavier's mother made almost everything from scratch.

"He's been out carousing with his friends," Xavier's mother said. "Now he's lying in front of the door. But I think I'll just let him lie there. That will teach him."

"Who?" Marc asked.

"Xavier."

"Oh," Marc said, cutting off a piece of chicken. "Where did you say he was lying?"

"In front of the door. Spare the rod and spoil the child," Xavier's mother declared, without knowing exactly why. Ever since her husband's death, she had grown more voluble. Sometimes, to her own surprise, she discovered that life actually appealed to her.

A man with a dog of indeterminate breed stopped to stare at Xavier.

"I live here," Xavier said quietly, "but I lost my keys." Then he couldn't help it anymore, he moaned. Not the way actors moan in a pornographic film, but the moaning you hear when you walk into a hospital ward in which twelve patients are just coming out from under anesthetic.

The man with the dog looked at Xavier—without fear, but also without much interest. He looked at him the way you might look at a new work of art in a local park and think: I've seen worse.

In the living room, the mother dished herself a second helping. Marc didn't eat enough, she felt, and she hadn't gone to all the trouble of making mashed potatoes just to have them wasted. "He needs to learn a lesson," she said. "Let him lie there for a couple of hours. Let him come to his senses. Later on, he'll thank me for it."

"He's a good-looking boy," Marc said, pouring a little more mineral water for himself and his girlfriend.

"Who?"

"Xavier."

"Oh."

"He looks like President Kennedy in his younger years, but with different hair."

"Well," Xavier's mother said, "I've never noticed that." Only a few minutes ago, her son had reminded her of an abandoned alley cat, and President Kennedy definitely had never reminded anyone of an abandoned alley cat, not even in his younger years.

Marc started reading the label on the bottle of mineral water. "Did you know that tap water is actually a lot better for you?" he asked.

"No," the mother said, "I didn't know that. And it's not true, either."

Outside, the man with the dog continued to stare at Xavier. The dog did its duty, and took a long time doing so. Old dogs resemble old people in that respect.

Xavier should have been able to smell it—it took place less than ten feet from his head—but the stink couldn't reach him anymore. He mumbled, "Help me, please, help me." Not too loudly—he was afraid the neighbors would call the police.

"So you live here?" the man asked, once the dog was finished. "I live here, too. I've never seen you around."

Xavier thought his balls and his sex organ were going to explode, that little pieces of flesh would go flying past his ears, and that the rest of him would then explode as well. All that would be left was a hundred thousand pieces of flesh, flying into the air higher and higher.

"I walk past here every night," the man said, "with Lou." He scratched the dog's head.

Xavier moaned, almost inaudibly, but the street was quiet, and Lou's master could hear Xavier's moan quite clearly. "You wouldn't say so from the looks of him," the man said, "but when this dog was young he took part in more than forty dog shows. Lots of honorable mentions. A couple of times he even won third prize." The man petted the dog, which had grown too old to be eligible for honorary mentions.

"Please, help me," Xavier was finally able to utter. "Please, won't you please help me?"

The man looked at him in surprise—as though he only realized now what Xavier had been saying all this time.

He pulled a one-franc piece out of his pocket and set it carefully beside Xavier's head. Then he walked on. He was pleased with himself. It was important never to lose the capacity to pick a fellow human in need out of the crowd. Helping people out a little, striking up a conversation where other people only maintained a moody silence, that was charity.

After the man turned the corner, he suddenly regretted not having given the young transient two francs, but he was too embarrassed to walk all the way back for the sake of that second franc.

"It's not just carousing with his friends over the weekend," the mother was saying in the living room. "I could overlook that. It's much more. Did you know that he's joined a Zionist youth people's club? They sent him a letter asking him to pay his annual contribution. I intercepted it."

They were having dessert. Yogurt with fresh fruit.

"What kind of youth club?"

"A Zionist one."

"Jesus," Marc said. "But, still, he's a special boy. You shouldn't forget that. Well groomed. Always friendly. Never grumpy. And it can't be easy for him, suddenly having a stepfather who's not that much older than he is."

The mother was a bit startled by the word "stepfather." It was a word she had always avoided.

"Yeah, yeah," the mother said. She ate her yogurt quickly. Marc wasn't much help, she had started noticing. He was there, but not really. Yet she had no intention of letting it go at that—she'd let too many things go for too long. The books she'd bought were full of practical tips, and she had decided to involve Marc more in her life, not to bottle things up, but to talk to him more. To struggle against what made her suffer. Suffering existed, you had to acknowledge that. That was the first step.

Prompted by one book in particular, which she was actually a bit embarrassed to own, she had decided to take the initiative in bed for a change. The book said it was important from time to time to change the location where the initiative was taken. In principle, any location was suitable for taking the initiative. You simply had to use your imagination. Xavier's mother felt that she had left her imagination unused for too long. She had to let her fantasy come barging in, like a family member showing up unexpectedly from Australia.

"Before we go to bed, I'll let him into the house," she said. "Staying out all night is too much, especially at this time of year. But a couple of hours on the doorstep, for a boy his age, that only builds character."

"He's a sensitive boy," Marc said. He put on a pair of headphones to listen to some jazz. He often listened to jazz while operating the flight simulator.

The dishwasher was filled. Out on the doorstep, Xavier's moaning subsided, until it stopped altogether.

A few times, Xavier thought that Awromele was standing beside him, speaking excitedly in Yiddish, but it was only a car driving by. A couple of times, he also thought that his grandfather was standing beside him, screaming that his grandson was a real man. Xavier's pain was no longer limited to his sex organ: it had spread to his legs, his shoulders, his stomach, even to his feet. He wanted to shout, "Mama, open the door," but he had no strength left. Besides, he knew it was no use. Once his mother set her mind to something, she never relented. After that, he couldn't think about anything anymore, not even about his grandfather or the Jews he was going to comfort, only about the pain.

.   .   .

THE KITCHEN WAS TIDY. The mother wondered whether she should
open the door for her son, or take the initiative first. She decided on the
latter. The night was still young. She took off her dress and her panties and
tied on her apron, the one she'd bought one lovely spring day in Milan,
back when her ex-husband was still alive. Then she went looking for the
right shoes; it took her five minutes, but she finally found a nice pair. She
let her hair down. It wasn't like when she was younger—it had grown
thinner in places, a bit straggly in others; these days she had it dyed regularly at one of the best hairdressers' in Basel—but it was still worth
looking at, that hair of hers.

She went into the living room. Marc was sitting in a leather easy chair
with his headphones on, his eyes closed.

She really had left her imagination unused for too long. A pity, that, but
no use crying over spilled milk.

Marc opened his eyes for a moment, then closed them again.

Out on the street, a man and wife walked by, arm in arm. Xavier
didn't try to catch their attention. It wouldn't help anyway, he just had
to wait.

The mother walked over and stood in front of Marc, took his hand, and
laid it on her stomach. Marc pulled his hand back and tapped on his headphones.

Music stands at the pinnacle of the hierarchy of the arts, they say.

Slowly, the mother began lifting her apron. Her thighs became visible,
then the rest. She took the headphones off of Marc's head as elegantly as
she could while holding the apron up with one hand.

"Look," she said.

Marc looked.

It wasn't good to think about life too long; otherwise it stopped making any sense at all.

"I'm hot," the mother said. "I'm awfully hot."

She pulled the apron up even farther.

Her legs weren't what they'd been. When she was a teenager, her legs had been pillars, but for a woman her age, her legs still got a lot of looks.

She was wearing a pink bra. Nothing obtrusive, rather modest.

"I'm so damned hot," the mother said. "I don't think I've ever been this hot."

Marc nodded, as though he understood completely, as though he was feeling awfully hot himself, then asked, "Shall I pour you a little apple juice, then, love?"

"I'm on fire," the mother went on, ignoring his question. "Can't you see it? I'm on fire inside. I've been on fire for years, but no one ever noticed, because I'm so good at soaking raisins."

"Is there something you'd like to talk about?" Marc asked, after running the back of his hand thoughtfully over his cheek a few times.

She had tried to mourn for her late husband, but it hadn't worked. Where other people had sadness, she had nothing. A hole.

She took Marc's hand again and pressed it against her stomach, still holding up her Italian apron with one hand.

She loved ironing; she even ironed handkerchiefs and underpants. It made her feel calm and contented. But that was behind her now, all that ironing. Time left its mark without mercy, but if you used your fantasy you could forget about it; if you used your fantasy you could forget about everything. She had read that somewhere; she wouldn't forget that anymore; she would think about that as she lay on her stomach and the man-beast reared over her.

"I was the woman who soaked raisins," she said, "but look who I am now." And she moved Marc's hand down slowly.

He tried to yank it away, but she held on. She felt a strange kind of strength, unlike anything she'd felt for a long time. A little struggle was going on between her and her boyfriend. He was trying to get away, but she wouldn't let him.

"Don't you know how I'm burning up inside?" the mother asked. "Don't you know that? No one knows that."

"I ate something that didn't agree with me," Marc said.

She turned around and bent over, still holding up her apron. "I'm open all the way for you," she said, bending over like that. "Can't you see? I'm open for you." Her voice sounded like it was coming from a tomb.

Marc thought about what to do. He felt compassion for this woman, who had, through circumstances he could no longer clearly recall, become his girlfriend. He put his hand on her back and caressed her absentmindedly, while she went on spreading herself wide open for him. After she had given birth to Xavier, they'd had to sew her wound shut—the baby had torn her open. Now Xavier was lying out on the street. At last the mother was able to forget him for a time—the childbirth, the sewing shut, the worries, the pressure, the shrieking. A child was like an intruder. The third person who makes a crowd.

How had she lived all those years without using her fantasy? Whole decades suddenly seemed fruitless to her, as though she had gone through a long hibernation. Her marriage had been nothing but hibernation. Her pregnancy, more hibernation. Her sex life, hibernation again. Holidays, hibernation on the beach. Christmas Eve, hibernation under the tree.

"Let's go to the bedroom," Marc said.

"No, here," she said. "Here. I'm on fire." She was still bent over in front of him, her voice still sounding like it was coming from the tomb.

The book had given her an idea, and more than just an idea. A longing had been awakened in her, so huge that it was almost frightening. But when you used your imagination, there was nothing to be afraid of. That's what the book said: "The imagination establishes its own limits; don't be afraid to surrender to them."

She stood up, turned around, shook her head so that her hair, or so she thought, flew out in all directions. She took Marc's face in both hands and bit him passionately on the lip. Marc submitted to the kiss as docilely as he could.

She took off her apron and threw it on the floor. There she stood, in only shoes and a bra. High heels and a white buckle. No panties. No more panties, never again. She was breathing heavily.

Somewhere, Marc felt affection for this woman. He couldn't deny that.

An affection that disturbed him. But it was no more than the echo of affection, and a distorted echo at that. Not much more than a buzzing.

She licked her lips demonstratively, for her fantasy said she should. "Here," she said, "you can do whatever you want with me. I'm good for more than soaking raisins, I'm good at other things, too. Extinguish me, because I'm on fire. Tear me apart."

He took a good look at her face. Her legs, with the veins running down them; her stomach, not too wrinkled yet, but already a little wrinkled. It didn't matter. He felt affection for this woman. That was what mattered. They had found each other, even though the consequences of that finding left him disappointed. He didn't want a woman on fire. Putting out fires was too much work for him. He wanted to be left alone.

"Do it," she said.

"Let's go to the bedroom," he replied calmly. "My stomach hurts a little, but we can lie in each other's arms. Wouldn't you like that? Just cuddle a little bit?" He was no monster.

She took off her bra. After a few weeks of breastfeeding, she hadn't been able to stand it and had switched to the bottle. She ran her hands over her breasts.

Marc was feeling increasingly uncomfortable. He was willing to do things for others, certainly for the woman he lived with, but there were limits. You couldn't force a person.

"Use your fantasy," she said, taking a step forward. She brought her face down close to his, ready to kiss him again, ready to bite his lip. "Use your fantasy for once." That's what the book had said: "Use not only your own fantasy, but let him use his as well."

Without thinking about it, without actually even realizing it, Marc hit her on the nose as hard as he could.

The mother staggered, took a few steps back. She was bleeding.

The apron, the one from the department store in Milan, was lying on the floor.

"Oh, I'm so sorry," Marc said when he saw the blood flowing from her nose. "I didn't mean to do that."

She pressed her arm against her nose and looked at him. She wasn't sure whether or not to be angry; spontaneity wasn't her strong suit. Only then did she feel the pain. She ran upstairs. Halfway up the stairs, she kicked off her shoes. She threw herself onto the bed. A peeping sound was coming from her mouth, and the blood kept dripping from her nose.

She felt more than the pain in her nose, she felt something else, something you could express only by screaming. And that is exactly what she did.

She screamed so loudly that her son, lying on the doorstep, heard her. Lying there, racked with pain, he found it only logical that the rest of world should be racked with pain as well, and so he didn't think about it much.

Marc found a rag in the kitchen and tried to wipe the blood off the carpet. It didn't work. Nothing to do about it. Then he picked up the bra and the apron and hung them over a chair. Remembering that his stepson was still lying outside on the doorstep, he opened the door and said to Xavier: "Come on in. Your mother's in a bit of a state today."

It took Xavier a few seconds to realize that he was now allowed to enter his own house. He crawled across the threshold, and cried out briefly in pain. But his cry was drowned out by his mother's screams.

"Shall I get you an aspirin?" asked Marc, whose mind was on something else. He wasn't just sorry about having given Xavier's mother a bloody nose; there were more things he regretted now.

Xavier was lying half naked in the doorway.

His mother's hibernation had ended, that much was certain. She had awakened with a scream.

In the kitchen, Marc filled a glass with water.

Between two stabs of pain, Xavier realized that he needed to look at the little mummy between his legs. He had to unwrap the bandages. In order to stop the pain, he needed to know what it looked like down there between his legs.

Now there was one thing Xavier knew for sure. He knew which part of the body it was that caused a Jew the most pain.

A Clean Break

WHILE MARC, against his better judgment, was trying to scrub the spots off the carpet, and his mother was lying on her bed and cursing her life, Xavier dragged himself into the living room. He couldn't remember ever having walked like a normal person. A world without wounds had become unimaginable.

Xavier remained sprawled on the floor, beside the easy chair in which Marc had been seated a few minutes before, watching the mother's act. From the bedroom came the sound of her sobbing, punctuated by the occasional shriek.

Xavier was hurting too badly to pay any attention. He needed to get the sloppily wrapped bandage, which had now turned a dark red, off of his sex organ. He had to examine and heal himself. But he didn't dare to do that in the middle of the living room.

When Marc was finished scrubbing the carpet, he leaned over and patted Xavier's warm head.

"Are you really feeling that bad?" he asked, his hand resting on Xavier's head. "What have you been drinking?"

Xavier fidgeted at Mr. Schwartz's trousers. An old man's trousers, that's what life looked like once you'd brushed all the myths off it.

"Take me to my room," Xavier whispered. He closed his eyes tightly. "Please, take me to my room."

"Oh, little fellow," Marc said, "cute little guy." And he kissed Xavier's forehead. Then he picked up his stepson and carried him upstairs.

Marc was not strong, so it wasn't easy for him, but he didn't let that show. He laid Xavier on the single bed that the mother had bought when they moved in here. His old bed was still at the architect's house.

After Marc had put Xavier on the bed, he took a good look at him, how he lay there, so helpless and alone. A feeling of regret came over him again. He wished he could help the boy, but he didn't know how.

In the next room, Xavier's mother's sobs grew quieter. They changed to deep sighs and heavy breathing. She thought about the orphan she had been, about how she'd given birth, about the way she had imagined being happy, long ago. The love she had felt once she knew she was pregnant, a feeling she now doubted. Before the conception, there had been almost no love at all. Tension, there was that, the hope of a better life, a longing for something more than poverty and shame. She didn't know whether she had ever felt love in her life. Yes, as a child she had loved You-Know-Who, but that was different, that had been a love without lust, because back then she didn't know about lust yet. That was a love born of patriotism and self-sacrifice.

She thought about the book she had read recently, about the magazine in which that book had been praised by female experts who knew how she could keep her sex life exciting. She doubted whether she had ever felt lust. Maybe she had only wanted to see desire in the eyes of the man she needed. Desire as a dire need, that was the life-insurance policy for a woman like her, a woman who only wanted to erase Saxony, the humiliation, and the poverty from her mind, to become what every woman in Basel was: a wife, a lady with a family life. But the dire need of men never lasts long, it continually changes shape, unreliable as the weather. A few weeks, six months at most, was the longest it ever lasted, she'd once heard someone say in the ladies' room. In her case: four months. Then the de-

sire that had made the architect—still a graduate student at the time—
tear the clothes off her body had turned into a long winter's sleep, interrupted only by a ritual that was always performed in great haste. After the
birth, the architect had focused on her rear end, as though disgusted by
the hole from which his son had crawled. And now she was disgusted by
it herself. She moved her hand across her stomach, across the shallow
wrinkles that, when she lay like this, were nothing more than shadows,
nothing more than the hint of wrinkles, but which would grow deeper,
deeper, and deeper, which would hollow her out as water hollows out
the stone.

She thought about her father, a modest man, who had valued nothing
so much as simplicity. She remembered her boyfriend's blow, and carefully
felt her nose. When she had noticed Marc at that cocktail party, it had been
because she had seen in his eyes something she had missed for so long: the
dire need of desire. And now look what that dire need had done: dire need
had given her a bloody nose.

Downstairs, Marc put on the headphones again. He became one with
the jazz music, the way he could become one with the flight simulator. It
wasn't that easy with people, but fusing with machines and with Benny
Goodman, he was good at that.

In his room, lying on his bed, Xavier carefully pulled down his trousers.
It didn't go very quickly. Every millimeter they descended made Xavier
feel as though his sex organ were slowly being torn from his body.

As he unfastened the clips that held the bandage in place, the pain made
him writhe. It took him a few minutes to dare to go on unwrapping the
bandage. His whispered his friend's name: "Awromele."

He remembered the pictures of his grandfather, the task he had assigned himself, the ambitions of most of the people he had known in his
life, people who were satisfied with very little, with the corruptive presence of enduring happiness, with the prison that happiness constituted.
For Xavier, who had always been happy, that prison had become increasingly meaningless.

In the bathroom, the mother was washing her face. Her eyes were still moist; her throat was raw from screaming. She put a little Nivea on a cotton swab and rubbed it slowly across her cheeks and forehead. Tears were still running down her face. Her nose was bent, she thought—she took another look at it—really bent, and it hurt, too.

In the doctor's waiting room, she had seen posters warning against domestic violence. Inquisitively, she had studied the pictures on those posters: a woman with a black eye, a woman missing four front teeth, a woman with burns on her arm.

There was plenty you could say about the architect, but domestic violence would never have occurred to him. Even when he took her up the anus, which had happened less and less in the last few years, he had done so hastily, that above all. She had had to do all the work, she had had to keep everything open and greased up; he had limited himself to what was strictly necessary.

The son slowly unwrapped the bandages from his organ. There were tears in his eyes as well, but they were not the product of self-pity, not the moist vestige of the eternal lament over a past gone by, a past that would never return but which had been so imperfect, so close, so fresh, and yet so dead. The nerves branching out from his crotch were stronger than his self-control. They were what made him weep.

Once the bandage had been removed, he looked at what he had looked at so often without undue interest—not like other boys his age, who could look at it for hours, ruler in hand. What he saw he did not recognize. What was lying or hanging there looked like part of an English breakfast. A black sausage, a little greasy, more dark-blue than black. The testicles were blue as well, and quite swollen. Bigger than ever, like little balloons that might burst loudly any moment.

During his admission into the covenant of the chosen, something had gone wrong. There was no denying that anymore. He had to tell Awromele, and probably Mr. Schwartz as well, in case he ever risked doing a circumcision again. A person can always learn from his mistakes.

The mother slammed the bathroom door; there was still a little Nivea on her face. She hurried down the stairs. "Look," she shouted when she saw Marc sitting on the sofa.

He didn't react.

"Look," she shouted, louder now.

He took off the headphones.

"What is it, sweetheart?" Marc attached great importance to harmony, even in times of war.

"Can't you see it?" she asked.

"What?"

"My nose."

"What about your nose?"

"Can't you see it? What you've done?"

Marc shook his head. "I'm sorry," he said. "I'm really sorry."

He wanted to kiss her, to press her against him, to forget everything that had happened.

"You broke it."

"I'm sorry," her boyfriend said again. He was generous when it came to apologies; at work he often apologized for other people's mistakes. "I didn't mean to do that." He took her hand, but she yanked it away. "I don't know what got into me," he said. "My stomach was hurting. I really apologize."

"It's crooked."

"It doesn't look any different. I don't see anything wrong with your nose. It's a cute little nose you've got there, and it looks just like it always has."

The mother felt the urge to punch him, to dig her nails into his face and scratch it open, but she restrained herself: single men were rare in Basel. "Take me to the hospital," she said. "Take me there right now. My nose is broken." She spoke excitedly, as though complaining at the cleaner's about a spot that was still in her favorite dress.

"Maybe it's just bruised," Marc said. "Your nose looks fine."

But he got up and put on his coat. It wasn't worth making a fuss about.

Five minutes later, they were in his Alfa, on the way to the hospital. The mother looked at Marc and thought: I'm going to break you, I'm going to break you like you've never been broken.

She had never had thoughts like that before. It cheered her up. She had always seen herself as a victim. First as a victim of You-Know-Who, who had betrayed things so shamefully by committing suicide in his bunker, then as a victim of her husband, who was indifferent to the glorious hole the good Lord had drilled into her body. There was plenty you could say about the Russian soldiers back in '45, but not that they were indifferent to holes like hers. And then she had become a victim of her son, who had come creeping out of that hole after twenty-four hours of pushing and suffering, and who thanked her now by going swimming with Zionists.

But that was done with; she was going to strike back. She wasn't going to let anyone walk all over her again. She had read about it in that book, she'd heard about it from friends. Stick up for yourself, don't let yourself be pushed in a corner, tell it like it is, say what's on your mind. That was living.

By the time she found herself sitting in the waiting room at the emergency unit, there wasn't much left of her need for revenge, and she felt just as passive as ever.

IN HIS BEDROOM, her child was still lying on his bed. Every now and then he took a look at his testicles. The color alone made him nauseous. Dark-blue, with a vein bulging out here and there, but the blue background made the veins look sick, porous, no longer fit to transport blood. They were going to burst. Bled to death, as the brief reports in the paper always said.

Xavier didn't know how he was going to survive this without help from his mother or Marc. He jabbered a few words in Yiddish, the few words he could remember from Awromele's lessons. Sometimes he stopped and whispered: "God of the Jews, do You see what they're doing to me?"

Then he shouted for his mother again; he didn't know that she had left the house.

He thought that the blue of his testicles would spread slowly, first to his legs, then to his stomach, and finally to his head. By that time he would be dead.

"Thirst," he shouted, "thirst."

AFTER AN HOUR and a half in the waiting room, Xavier's mother was examined by a young doctor who tried to put her at ease by telling jokes. They needed to take X-rays. The X-rays confirmed her fears: "Your nose is broken," the doctor said. He didn't ask how it had happened; he had his suspicions, but his job was healing people; the rest he left up to the social workers.

The mother began weeping quietly. The thought that the man she had hoped to marry had already broken her nose made her despair. The architect had ignored her, had treated her like a wall unit that you couldn't bring yourself to throw away, despite its serious defects. But ignoring was better than breaking. And what had she done to deserve this, anyway? She had spread herself open for her boyfriend, she had finally had the courage to use her fantasy. She would never open up again, at least not voluntarily; she would remain shut till the bitter end.

"Do you have to put it in a cast?" she asked. The doctor smiled. "We don't do that with noses," he said. "It's a matter of taking it easy, that's the most important thing. We can give you a nose brace, though, if you'd like. Or shall I prescribe some painkillers?"

"Yes, please," she said.

She looked at Marc, who was playing dumb. No regrets, no pleas for forgiveness, no shock at his own wrongdoing. Only restlessness, because it was taking so long. He sat beside her motionlessly.

"Painkillers, or the nose brace?"

"Both," she said, "please."

"We don't have to reset it," the doctor said. "It's a clean break." Then he felt it was his duty to ask whether she had been the victim of a crime.

"Not that I know of," she said.

"If you say so, I believe you."

"You know," she said, "victims are always culprits, too, and culprits are always victims. No one gets what he doesn't deserve."

"That's one way of looking at it," the doctor said. And, after staring briefly at Mrs. Radek's nose, he wrote out a prescription for painkillers.

WHEN NO RESPONSE CAME to Xavier's repeated cries for water, it slowly dawned on him that Marc and his mother had left the house, or perhaps retired to their bedroom with wads of cotton in their ears.

Xavier rolled out of bed. It wasn't really a roll, though—it was a fall. He lay on the floor of his bedroom, unable to move, without enough strength even to crawl like a baby. The blue of his sex organ had, as he'd feared, spread to his groin. Blisters had also risen on his sex organ; it looked like they were producing a sticky, yellowish-white substance. Because of the pain and the fear, he couldn't accurately judge whether that yellowish-white substance was coming from the blisters, or from other orifices. It reminded him of the stuff that comes out of pimples when you squeeze them.

Mr. Schwartz had ruined everything.

After that, he didn't think about Mr. Schwartz anymore, not even about Awromele. He was going to die soon.

But this was not his greatest worry; his greatest worry was whether or not he'd be buried in a Jewish cemetery.

Kosher Gorgonzola

THE MOTHER TOOK the prescription for painkillers to an all-night pharmacy. Marc waited in the car, watching as she stood shivering in front of the pharmacy until the little hatch opened.

When she sat down beside him again, Marc felt like telling her that he loved her. He wasn't pleased with what he'd done; he had never broken a part of anyone's body before. He had always thought he was incapable of that.

"I love you," he said. "And your son. About what happened tonight, I can't do anything about that anymore. But I know we will make each other happy very often in the future." He put his hand on her leg.

The mother looked up from the bottle of painkillers. "You don't know your own strength," she said. "You have to be careful if you hit someone."

He squeezed her leg.

"It runs in the family," he said. "We used to slaughter our own cows and pigs."

At the house, they brushed their teeth together in the bathroom. The mother swallowed two painkillers.

Marc slept in his T-shirt; the mother wore polyester pajamas. She had three identical pairs of pajamas in the colors pink, blue, and yellow, and a few nighties as well. Tonight she was wearing the pink pajamas. The architect had given them to her, for Christmas.

Marc was already lying in bed. He was concentrating on a computer magazine, and feeling pleased. It wasn't nice to break your girlfriend's nose, but he hadn't done it on purpose, and when you thought about how things went in other parts of the world, a broken nose was nothing to get upset about. He was immersed in an article about a new operating system when the mother walked past the nursery and saw that the door was ajar. Even though Xavier was no longer a child, she still called his room "the nursery." She had forgotten all about her son. She was planning to close the door, but for some reason she herself did not completely understand, she opened it and looked in. The light was still on.

The bed was empty. She became angry. She thought that her son had left the house again. How her father had met his end was something she had only heard from others. He had been a terrible sight, she knew that much. He had refused to surrender. Then she saw her son lying on the floor. He was a terrible sight as well.

Xavier seemed unconscious. But in fact the boy was only concentrating on certain thoughts, in order to suppress the pain. Every once in a while, he drifted off into gruesome dreams. He wasn't exactly what you'd call unconscious, but he wasn't really conscious, either.

"Xavier," the mother said. The light was rather dim, but she could see her only child's sex organ. She thought she was losing her mind. She had never seen a blue sex organ before. She hadn't seen very many sex organs in the course of her life anyway. The architect had never wanted her to look at him during the deed— —he had always preferred to blindfold her with a dishtowel first.

But this was not normal, that much she knew for sure.

"Xavier," she said again.

The boy looked at her. He saw that it was his mother, but that was all; not much was getting through to him at that point.

The mother went to her bedroom and shook her boyfriend. He had fallen asleep with the magazine on his chest. She had to yank hard.

"The boy," she said. "There's something wrong with him. Come and look, quick."

Marc was wearing a gray T-shirt with the word *Spaßvogel* written on it in pink lettering. A colleague at the radio station had given it to him. He got up stiffly and followed the mother to the nursery. She was doing her best to remain calm; that was something she had done all her life, and she was good at it. Her mother had been raped by the Russians, and she had stayed calm then as well, even though she was only a child. Someone had put a hand over her eyes, but she had seen it all anyway.

Marc and the mother were standing in the doorway to the nursery; the boy was lying on the floor.

"Look at that," the mother said, as though she were talking about a vacuum cleaner the cleaning lady had broken.

Marc bent over to get a better look. Then he straightened up again. "I can't stand it," he said. "I think I'm going to have to . . ." He leaned against the wall; he was dizzy; the bandage that Xavier had unraveled with such difficulty was still lying on the bed. The nursery smelled faintly of cheese, and also of the slaughterhouse.

"I can't stand it, either," the mother said. "But I suppose I'll have to."

"I've never seen anything like it." Marc always did his best to remain unruffled, fatherly, trying not to come down on the boy too hard.

The mother pulled up a chair. Her pajamas made her look almost youthful. Marc gazed at her lovingly.

"What happened to you?" she asked. The boy had closed his eyes again. "Xavier, sweetheart, what happened to you? What have they done to you?"

Xavier couldn't reply. He was dreaming that his mother was speaking the same words to him, and in his dream he murmured his friend's name.

The mother loved her only child—she was a mother, after all—but she hated him as well. After he was born, the architect had barely felt any desire for her, or at least hadn't shown it. He'd never shown much of any feeling at all. Ambition was not what you'd call a feeling, especially not refined ambition. He didn't want to be in her anymore, not really in her, and she blamed the child for that. But only in her thoughts; she never said it out loud. It was useless to talk about your feelings—it could even be dangerous. Look at You-Know-Who; he had listened to his feelings, and see what had become of him.

Marc went to the bathroom and drank thirstily from the tap. He held his mouth up to the faucet, even though the mother didn't allow that. His stepson's sex organ had him worried. He had seen plenty of pigs being slaughtered, so he wasn't particularly queasy, but this didn't look good.

"Xavier," the mother said, "please wake up."

The boy opened his eyes for a moment. "Water," he whispered, "water."

The mother didn't want her boyfriend to see her son in the nude when he came back, so she took a pillowcase from the cupboard and draped it over him.

The pillowcase brushed against his member, and Xavier screamed out loud.

"Help," the mother cried. She couldn't stand seeing other people in pain. Especially not when it was accompanied by stench and noise.

Marc came back from the bathroom, feeling refreshed. He had slapped on a bit of aftershave. He did his best to combat the odors of others by always smelling good himself.

"He doesn't recognize me," the mother said to her boyfriend.

Marc saw that the pillowcase was draped over the infected sex organ, and felt relieved. "I think we should call the doctor," he said.

"But it's the middle of the night."

"We could take him to the hospital." He noted with satisfaction that he was willing to drive there for the second time in one night.

"What will they say when they see him? Don't we have anything in the house to fix him up?"

"Water," Xavier whispered.

The mother dreaded taking her son to the hospital. She didn't know what she would tell the doctors. She knew many of them personally, from the Rotary Club. A broken nose was one thing, that could happen to anyone, but a dark-blue sex organ?

"It looks infected," Marc said. He didn't want the mother to get upset. Truth was, it didn't look infected, it looked worse than that. He had seen pictures of wounded soldiers from the First World War, in close-up. That's what Xavier's sex organ reminded him of most.

"I know," the mother said. "We'll put iodine on it. We still have some." Once again, there was hope. There was hope again, that monster.

Before Marc could say a word, she hurried to the bathroom. He heard her rummaging around, heard something fall to the ground, and a few moments later she came back with a vial of iodine. She pulled the pillowcase off her son's body, which resulted in another bout of screaming. She was getting used to that. Her mother had screamed a lot, too, right before she died. She had screamed horribly when the Russians raped her. Xavier's mother had thought that was strange. Screaming didn't change anything, so why scream?

"Why are you doing this to us?" the mother asked. "What have you been up to, Xavier? What on earth have you been up to?" She opened the bottle and dribbled iodine onto her son's inflamed member.

Xavier's body shook. He made movements that reminded his mother of a spastic. At least she had been spared that, a spastic baby. Horror-film noises came from the boy's throat.

"It stings a little, I know," the mother said to the boy. "But we have to disinfect the wound." And she dribbled a little more iodine onto the blue sex organ.

Her motherly love was every bit as great as her fear of what people might say. And people always said a lot. More and more, in fact. They had opinions about everything. Even if you lived the way they did, ate the same food, went on vacation to the same mountain villages, they still found something to complain about.

"It looks like he's having an epileptic fit," Marc said.

"He hurt himself," the mother said. "He was probably playing games with the other boys."

She bent over and held the boy's head in her hands. "You bad boy," she said. "Aren't you a little too old for games like that?"

"Water," the boy whispered. "Please, water. It hurts."

"He wants some water," Marc said.

"He's probably dehydrated after all that carousing."

Xavier's mother knew about feeling dehydrated. After Xavier's grand-mother had been raped and had screamed so horribly that it gave her daughter a headache, she had turned to the bottle.

Marc fetched a glass of water, moistened his stepson's lips, and poured a little water down the boy's throat. He avoided looking at the scene of the disaster. "Maybe," he said, "maybe we should call somebody."

But the mother said, "Let's wait and see if the iodine helps."

Together they lifted the boy and put him on his bed.

Xavier screamed again.

"Now close your eyes and go to sleep," the mother said. "And if you need anything, just call."

"Water," the boy whispered, "please, more water."

"What's that smell?" the mother asked.

She and Marc both inhaled deeply.

"Smells like blood," Marc said.

The blood-soaked bandage was still lying on the blanket. Marc acted as though he hadn't seen it. The mother thought the boy should learn to clean up after himself. Coddling him would be a mistake; if he was coddled, nothing would ever become of him.

"It's something else," Mrs. Radek said. "It smells awful."

The mother began nosing around. She shoved aside a few books about the history of the Jews, even came across a Jewish prayer book, but found nothing that could explain that awful smell. Then, beside the bed, she found the piece of kosher Gorgonzola that Mr. Schwartz had wrapped so carefully in wax paper.

"Look," she said, "look at this."

She sniffed at the Gorgonzola, then made her boyfriend smell it as well.

"Whew, that stinks something awful," Marc said. He didn't like cheese much; he preferred luncheon meat.

"Where did you get this?" the mother asked, waving the Gorgonzola in front of the boy's eyes.

There was no reply.

"Where did you get this?" she asked a little more loudly.

Still no answer.

"All right," she said. "If you're not going to tell me, I'll just have to throw it away."

She went downstairs and tossed the Gorgonzola in the garbage. She didn't want nasty things in her house.

When she returned to the nursery she saw that Marc was squatting down beside the bed, caressing the boy's cheeks.

"Leave him alone," she said. "He'll feel better tomorrow, and then he'll be off doing whatever he pleases."

The mother and Marc went back to their room. "Sleep is the best medicine," she had said before they left the nursery. "Xavier, sleep is the best medicine." She hated to see her only child suffer like this. A child didn't always have to get its way, but this was a bit much.

In the bedroom, Marc nuzzled up against the mother's left breast. He wanted to make up for it, the broken nose and his being so unkind when she had stood in front of him and shown him everything she'd never really dared to show him before.

But the mother wasn't about to let herself be placated so easily. She pushed him away; she was thinking about her child.

The boy lay in the room beside theirs and had to go to the toilet. He felt paralyzed, he couldn't move. There was nothing but the pain; it had spread to his head now, too. "I have to go to the toilet," the boy shouted as loud as he could, but the grown-ups didn't hear him.

"I can't, not right now," the mother said. "You have to understand that, Marc. I have other things on my mind. Less than two hours ago you broke my nose, and now you want to do it again." She took a deep breath. "Now you want to come right inside me. But that's not the way it works."

"I don't want to come right inside you," her boyfriend said. "We can also do it very gently."

"Forget it," the mother said. "You want to come right inside me, and I'm not going to let anyone come right inside me—enough is enough. After dinner you had your chance, you could have done anything you wanted with me, but you blew it. You had to go and listen to your Benny Goodman, and now there's not going to be any more coming inside me."

It was good to talk that way, she thought. She should do it more often. It would make her fantasy flare up, like bellows to a hearth.

She pulled the blanket up to her chin.

In the next room, the boy shouted, "Mama!"

And Marc said, "I'm sorry."

"So am I," the mother said. "I'm sorry, too."

Her boyfriend thought for a minute. "Would it be okay," he asked, "if I satisfied myself while I looked at you? I won't bother you. You can even go to sleep if you want."

"Don't let me get in your way," the mother said.

After a few moments, she pressed her hands to her ears—she couldn't stand the noises her boyfriend was making.

Before Marc had even spilled his seed on the ground, the mother had fallen into a deep sleep.

Xavier was sleeping now as well. He was having visions and dreams in which Awromele, Mr. Schwartz, and his grandfather appeared. This was all the hell he had ever known, so he thought he had ended up in hell. He was burning. He was burning for the sins of others as well, and in his dream he whispered, "Accept, O Lord, this humble sacrifice."

The Most Wonderful Day

XAVIER HAD DEVELOPED a high fever, and he had soiled himself.

When his mother came in at seven-thirty to look at her child, he was lying in his own feces. She smelled it right away. "What have you done now?" she asked.

The only reply was a little peeping sound, as though the infection had not only nestled in the sex organ but had reached the vocal cords as well.

"What have you done now?" she asked a little louder. "Are you going to start acting like a baby? Haven't we given you enough attention yet?"

Xavier opened his mouth but was unable to say anything, not even to cry for help. The mother yanked the blankets away. Now he screamed. But not loudly, and not for long, either.

The feather bed, which was real eiderdown, had made the wound start to fester. There were no longer a few isolated blisters on the sex organ. The sex organ had become one huge blister with yellow moisture running out of it. The same went for the boy's balls. Everything had swollen to unnatural proportions. What Xavier had between his legs was the funhouse mirror of sex organs.

The mother might have noticed, but she had no eye for her son's wounds just then. All she saw was the fecal material he was lying in. Not solid turds, but a squishy mess. She thought about the laundry. And cooking pans with caked-on fat, she thought about them, too. All her life she'd had an aversion to dirty diapers. One time she had even fainted while changing her child.

The mother loved Xavier—she was a mother, after all—but with her the love came in waves. "Do you think I don't have enough to do?" she asked. Tears welled up in her eyes. The falling in love, the Jews, the Nazis, the babies, the United Nations, everything existed and was brought to be in order to make her life difficult. She had never said it in so many words, but that was how she viewed the world, that was how she would always view the world—as an affront, a macabre conspiracy against her and every other decent person.

"Say something," she said to her son.

Silence.

"Say something," she shouted more loudly now. "Say something. I won't have you ignoring me like this."

The mother's shouts had awakened Marc. He came to her shouts like a hungry cat to a herring bone. As soon as he reached the door, he saw the condition his stepson's sex organ was in, and he knew there was no way to avoid a trip to the doctor.

When he laid his hand on the mother's shoulder, she shrank from his unexpected touch. She thought about her broken nose. Thanks to the painkillers, it didn't hurt much anymore, only when she grimaced or tried to blow her nose, but the humiliation, she couldn't forget that. She would never forget that. How her boyfriend had beaten her up when she had finally started using her fantasy.

"It might be better to call the doctor," Marc suggested.

She sighed, and said quietly, "Yes, it might."

The mother was afraid of gossip over which she had no control, deathly afraid of suggestive looks at the butcher's. So she said: "Let's wait a while and see. It will probably go away by itself. Nature is the best medicine. Waiting rooms and hospitals are breeding grounds for bacteria."

At the thought of bacterial infections in hospitals, motherly love overpowered her the way the heart attack had overpowered her husband. She knelt down beside the bed and said: "Poor Xavier, I know it's not easy for you, I know that. It's never been easy for you. I'm going to make you a nice hot cup of tea." She ran her hand over her son's forehead and did her best to love him, but all she could think of was: My child stinks to high heaven. How do I get out of here? Cow shit smells like roses compared with this.

She thought about her father, about how much he had loved cows.

After twenty-four hours of labor, when Xavier had finally come into the world and she had slowly recovered from the unbearable pain, her first thought had been: Now I'll never have a weekend to myself again.

For punishment, Xavier had sucked her left nipple until it bled. The mother thought it was his revenge for the heartless thoughts she'd had during and after his birth. She had been raised to believe that she was guilty in the eyes of God. Guilty in the eyes of everyone, but most of all guilty before God.

Her baby was aware of none of that. Not the guilt, not God, not his mother's thoughts. He didn't even know that he had sucked her nipple till it bled, but from that day on things had never been completely right between her and the child. After the bleeding nipple, she had seen Xavier through different eyes, from a distance, in amazement, sometimes even in disgust, the way you look at a child you regret having adopted.

An older woman friend of hers had adopted and raised a Chinese baby, and she had told Xavier's mother, "It's a terrible thing to say, but the happiest day of my life was the day that Chinaman left my house."

The mother often caught herself thinking: If only my child was an adopted Chinaman who would leave my home at eighteen and never come back. Later, she hated herself for having such thoughts.

Back then, her gynecologist had said: "He's hungry, that's all. Some babies suck hard. There's nothing unusual about it. Your nipple will heal, don't worry. You just have to squeeze it a little before you breastfeed him." The nipple got better, but the rest didn't.

"He's shit his bed," Marc said.

"That's right," the mother said.

"Poor kid," Marc said.

"He did it on purpose," the mother said. "Just to spite me. He hates me."

"Come on," Marc said, "don't say that, that's an exaggeration. He doesn't hate you at all."

"He hates me. From the moment he was born, he's always hated me."

"He's lying in his own shit," said Marc, who found hatred a ponderous subject for so early in the morning.

"He hates me, so he's lying in his own feces. What other boy his age would lie in his own poop on a day like this?"

She threw open the curtains. Romantic sunlight entered the room.

"He's sick," Marc said. "He hurt himself. That's why he's lying in his own . . ."

"He craves attention," the mother interrupted. "That's why he did this. He was late with potty-training. He was early with reading and talking, but late with the rest. With the rest he was always a little backward."

Her boyfriend felt the boy's cheek. "He has a fever," he said. "He's sick as a dog."

The boy was making incoherent noises.

"What's he saying?" the mother asked. Her child had lost his ability to express himself well, and she was repulsed by that. She despised weakness, and she despised weak family members even more. Deep in her heart, she had considered her husband a weakling as well, but she had disguised that thought by acting servile, by never contradicting him, and by opening her behind to him once every three months. He had lived like a weakling— died like a weakling, too. Her father may have lived by ideas that were considered objectionable these days, but at least he hadn't lived like a weakling, and he hadn't died that way, either. No, there was nothing more repulsive than weakness.

"I can't figure it out," Marc said. "But I can tell that he's running a high fever. Maybe we should have someone look at him, sweetheart. An expert."

"Oh, please," the mother said, "most of the time those experts just talk through their hats, they don't really know much more than the interested layman."

"But we should at least clean him up. Poop isn't good for the skin. I know. One of my uncles became senile, and he lay in his own poop all the time. He played with it, too, and then he came down with a skin disease."

"Senility is a terrible thing," the mother said. "A horrible thing." The two of them looked at the boy, whose breathing was labored.

In the kitchen, the mother put some water on the stove; her hands were shaking. If this ever got out, she'd never be able to show her face again. She'd be a goner, they would have to move. Before you knew it, her life in Basel would be ruined. Her life in Switzerland.

She took a bag of chamomile tea out of the cupboard, and tried to come up with a plan to save her life, and that of her family.

ALL THAT DAY, for almost nine whole hours, the mother tried to heal her son by regularly dribbling iodine on the wound and feeding him chamomile tea, and the whole time she murmured, "What have you done to us, child, what have you done to us?"

The boy couldn't hear these rhetorical questions; he was far, far away, in the world of pain.

When Marc came home from work around five, the first thing he did was to take the boy's temperature. He didn't reproach Xavier the way the mother did, he only made tender little noises.

Altruism is wonderful, he realized. It's wonderful to help people, especially defenseless people who are in great pain and can hardly move. Of course, it's also wonderful to curse people roundly once in a while—he remembered the curses he had heaped upon the dying architect in the hospital—but, all things considered, it was more satisfying to help them and be gentle with them. You really felt like a human being when you did that.

The thermometer showed that Xavier's temperature was up to almost 103. Marc carefully pulled back the blanket.

The wound was a battlefield of pus.

The bed had not been cleaned. The sick boy was still lying in his own feces, which had become hard and dry by now and stuck to his skin here and there.

It looked even more distasteful than it had that morning. But because Marc was feeling altruistic, he went on producing sounds that people usually make to babies lying in the cradle.

Then he went down to the kitchen, where the mother was making tea, and said: "We really have to take Xavier to the hospital now; his temperature is up to a hundred and three." He held his hands under the tap and asked, "Why didn't you clean him?"

"I didn't want to wake him up," the mother said. "Besides, I can't do everything on my own around here."

She had started to fear the worst as well, though, so they carried the boy downstairs and laid him, blanket and all, on the backseat of Marc's Alfa. A maneuver that hurt Xavier so badly that he shrieked a few times.

The mother went back to the bathroom and quickly applied a touch of red lipstick; she knew that in all situations one was judged by one's appearance. Then they drove like mad to the hospital. Marc liked to drive like a speed demon. It made the mother feel nauseous. The boy was already nauseous.

IN THE WAITING ROOM, where she had been sitting with her broken nose not so long before, the mother now sat with her child. He couldn't sit upright, so they had laid him across three chairs. The waiting room was crowded that day, full of casualties from a soccer game that had gotten out of hand even before it started. The mother prayed that she wouldn't see anyone she knew.

Every once in a while, Marc got up to see how the boy was doing, and to speak a few words of comfort to him, along the lines of: "You'll be okay. Nothing to worry about. It will be over soon."

The mother had put on her sunglasses and gone to the ladies' room to look at herself in the mirror. She had grown prettier since the divorce. And after her husband's death, her appearance had actually improved notably. It wasn't nice to think so, but it was the truth. Although it was possible, of course, that his death had nothing to do with it.

When she came out of the restroom, the nurse called Xavier Radek's name.

Along with her boyfriend and the friendly nurse, Xavier's mother carried the child to the doctor's office. The nurse apologized for the inconvenience, but all the stretchers were occupied because of the rioting.

"Stretchers can give you a hernia anyway," said the mother, who had read an article about that in a women's magazine.

They had to wait for the doctor to come in. "There's still some shit sticking to his skin," Marc said.

"They'll wash that off," the mother said. "Just put the sheet over it." Marc didn't want to argue, so he pulled up the sheet, making quiet little cooing noises the whole time.

Then the doctor arrived. The doctor was a woman. What's more, she was almost seven feet tall.

The mother decided right away that this was an unpleasant woman. She was relieved, however, to find that they didn't know each other from any of the social engagements she was obliged to attend each year. The architect had given generously to good causes, and generosity and social engagements went together. Now she was the one who gave to good causes—less generously, things had changed, but she always gave something. People in need could count on her.

The doctor had barely sat down at her desk before getting up again to look at the patient. One look was enough.

"Why did they make you wait so long?" she asked. Then she picked up a phone and snarled a few words into the receiver.

"What's this?" the doctor asked, pointing to something black sticking to the unconscious boy's leg.

"He soiled himself," the mother said.

Within thirty seconds, four orderlies had come into the room. They picked up the boy and ran with him through the corridors of the hospital, towards Intensive Care. The mother ran after them, still wearing her sunglasses, and Marc ran behind her.

At Intensive Care the adults had to wait outside, in front of a large window.

"What are they doing?" the mother asked.

"I can't see," Marc said. "They've pulled a curtain around him."

Two doctors, along with two other nurses, worked on Xavier for the next hour and a half.

"Why are they taking so long?" the mother wanted to know.

When the seven-foot doctor finally came out, she walked straight up to the mother and said, "So now I want you to tell me what happened to that boy."

The mother got up from the couch where she had been waiting calmly all this time, resigning herself to the hand of fate. She was still wearing her sunglasses. "He played with himself," the mother said, smiling amiably at the doctor. She had everything under control. "Boys his age do that all the time."

Pedophile Lenin

THE HEALING PROCESS took a long time. The first three days had looked bad for Xavier, and a doctor, not the seven-foot woman but a young man with brown skin, had spoken ominously to the mother about castration—about the pros and cons of the procedure at this stage of the illness.

"The colored man wants to castrate him," the mother told her boyfriend.

Upon further investigation, though, the doctors saw that that operation would not be needed. Only Xavier's left testicle could not be saved. During an operation that lasted less than forty-five minutes, a surgeon skillfully cut off Xavier's left testicle and the pouch of skin around it. To help the boy adjust mentally to this minor mutilation, two nurses put the testicle in a jar of formaldehyde, so that Xavier could see what he lacked for the rest of his life. Seeing what you lack assists in the process of mourning.

The surgeon assured the mother that her son still had his right testicle, and that the chances for reproduction had therefore not been drastically reduced. "Of course, we'll have to wait and see whether he ever has a normal erection again," the surgeon said. "But if not, we can always tap off some sperm. As far as that goes, medicine is making great leaps forward each year." When he left the room, the mother said to her son, "Don't worry, it's only your epididymis."

Within a few days after the removal of the infected testicle—which was a dark-blue color, in some places even black, when the surgeon put the knife to it—Xavier was able to talk again. The seven-foot female doctor came and sat beside his bed.

"Well," she said.

Xavier, who was still in a great deal of pain, struggled to open his eyes. He was still sleeping almost twenty hours a day. To combat the dehydration, a drip was attached to his arm.

"So—what happened to you?" she asked.

She was not particularly attractive; men tended not to fall for her, also because of her deep voice. Though she was intelligent and quite social, and therefore had a large circle of friends, almost no one dared to touch her.

"What happened?" she asked. "What did they do to you?" It had been clear to her from the start that this was a matter for the police, but after talking with a colleague she had decided to let the boy recover before exposing him to questioning.

"What do you mean?" Xavier asked.

"Your mother says you were playing with yourself, but that doesn't seem very likely to me."

Xavier looked the tall woman in the eyes. "I got circumcised," he said. Telling the truth seemed like a good idea.

"Yes, you certainly did," she said. "No doubt about that. You're lucky there's anything left." Her laugh was curt and unpleasant. She picked up the jar of formaldehyde, which the nurses had put on the side table, beside a bouquet from Marc, and jiggled the testicle back and forth before the boy's eyes. That would loosen his tongue. "Look," she said. "This is what you lost. You don't have this anymore."

The boy peered at his left testicle, but couldn't really see what was in the jar. He saw the little hairs that had grown on the scrotum. The flesh in the jar reminded him of the remains of a poorly plucked chicken that had turned blue with mold. He suddenly thought of Awromele; he missed him.

"Who did this?" the doctor demanded. "Who are you protecting?"

"I'm not protecting anyone," Xavier said. With effort, he rolled over onto his side.

The doctor picked up her chair and moved it to the other side of the bed, so she could continue to look the boy in the eye. "Who did it?" she asked again, more forcefully this time. "Who was messing around with you? We have to know. He may try to do this to other boys as well."

It had to be a man—women didn't do things like this, she knew that. As a young girl, she had been so unattractive that it had roused the hatred of her classmates. Ugliness rouses hatred. The idea that the body is the mirror of the soul is ineradicable. They had kicked her bicycle to pieces all the time. And when the children were done with the bicycle, they started in on its owner. Teachers who cared about her welfare and who knew that the body was not the mirror of the soul were nevertheless powerless to alter the opinions and behavior of their pupils. And so it was decided that she was to be allowed to leave the classroom fifteen minutes before the final bell rang, that she might bicycle home quickly and avoid the worst of it. But when the wind was blowing from the wrong direction, the older boys often caught up with her, hit her, and ruined her bicycle. One might think that when a person has been molested as often as she was in her younger years, everything after that would be easy. But it wasn't like that in her case. Little things could still reduce her to a shambles. She cried a lot, which is why she never put on mascara.

"Who did this to you?" she asked Xavier for the third time.

"No one," he said a bit dreamily. "Mr. Schwartz circumcised me."

"Mr. Schwartz," she said. "Aha, Mr. Schwartz. And where does this Mr. Schwartz live?"

Xavier told her the name of the street. He didn't know where he was anymore. He thought about Awromele and how much he'd like to see him again.

The doctor wrote it all down and held her patient's hand for a moment. Then she went to her office, where she wept bitterly for ten minutes before calling the police to give them the name and address of the child molester.

The police wasted no time. Within the hour, twelve of them were standing at Mr. Schwartz's door. He was busy weighing a piece of Emmentaler. Because he didn't answer right away, the policeman kicked down his door.

The old man was led outside with gentle coercion, but only after they had thrown him twice against a cupboard. Policemen, too, have a healthy aversion to child molesters. All this confused Mr. Schwartz so badly that he raised his left fist and shouted, "Long live Lenin!" before they threw him into the paddy wagon.

THE NEXT EVENING, a candlelight march was held around the block where Mr. Schwartz lived. More than two thousand concerned citizens had signed up, and many of them carried signs bearing the names of children who had been molested by their fathers, uncles, brothers-in-law, and other pedophiles. Some of them even carried signs with the names of molested children from Italy, Spain, and Portugal. The citizens of Basel preferred to be on the safe side.

A woman carrying a sign with the name "Lea" on it was so moved by the candlelight procession that she used her sign to shatter Mr. Schwartz's front window. Her deed met with modest applause. Concerned citizens wormed their way through the broken window into the apartment. Within minutes, they were back outside with Mr. Schwartz's cheeses, which they rolled enthusiastically down the street.

The concerned citizens, whipped to a frenzy by the sight, kicked the pedophile's cheeses. At first some of them kicked reticently, but soon they got the hang of it, and it was as though they'd been doing this all their lives. After a while, a scuffle arose, because not all the concerned citizens got an equal chance to kick the cheeses, and that, of course, was not fair.

When the kicking of the cheeses was over, the concerned citizens began dragging Mr. Schwartz's furniture out into the street. They enthusiastically kicked that to pieces as well. They were alight with indignation.

When Mr. Schwartz's window was shattered, the three policemen who had been accompanying the candlelight procession quickly went for a little walk. They couldn't stand the sight of violence.

Thanks to the coverage given the case by the local media, and later by the national media as well, twenty of Mr. Schwartz's other victims filed charges as well, including a sixty-five-year-old woman from Bellinzona. Months later, it became clear that their numbers were greatly exaggerated. Xavier Radek proved to be Mr. Schwartz's only victim. But by then it was already too late.

Young people painted runes on the boarded-up windows of Mr. Schwartz's house, and tried to set fire to it. The concerned citizens distanced themselves from these attacks. There was no sense in comparing apples with pears.

The Committee of Vigilant Parents was set up on the night of the candlelight procession. Xavier's mother was made an honorary member. She raced to the hospital to tell her son about it, but he was sleeping, and she couldn't wake him.

A few days later, wearing her sunglasses, she spoke the following words during a meeting of the committee in a local park: "What has been done to me must not be done to any other mother in Basel. We have been living for ourselves, and we have stopped living for each other. That is how this horrible, this unspeakable thing could happen."

Awromele's father, who realized that the Jewish community had to act as well, set up the Committee of Vigilant Jews. "We tolerate no pedophiles in our midst," he told a reporter from the local paper. "And certainly no pedophiles who attack their victims with scissors and knives. Mr. S.'s membership in the Jewish community is hereby rescinded, with retroactive effect."

When she read about it, Bettina immediately signed up for the Committee of Vigilant Jews. Because it was so far away, solidarity with India had become a bit too theoretical for her. She felt a growing need to put her solidarity into practice.

After his first, rather meagerly attended press conference, the rabbi visited a massage parlor; God had told him to seek pleasure wherever it was to be found. In the arms of the prostitute, a lady from the town of Thun, he wept for five minutes and said at last: "I didn't have any choice. I can't protect Mr. Schwartz. If I did that, I would only be encouraging anti-Semitism. Then there would be no stopping it."

The masseuse ran her hand soothingly over the rabbi's stomach. It occurred to her that, in this room, she had seen as many men cry as come.

A PHOTOGRAPHER from a local tabloid had no trouble sneaking into the hospital where Xavier lay. Once in the boy's room, he immediately noticed the jar with the blue testicle. "Here," he said. "Hold this—it will make a great picture."

Xavier held the jar containing his left testicle. He was still awfully sleepy.

That evening, the tabloid opened with a big photograph of the victim holding his own testicle.

In Basel, tempers really flared.

The photograph was sent around the world, and was later voted Photo of the Year, with the caption "Victim with Testicle."

The deputy mayor of Basel felt the need to make the following announcement: "The citizens of this city must never forget that there are also Jews who have nothing to do with pederasty, who even condemn such practices and see them as a danger to their little community."

At the police station, Mr. Schwartz was interrogated for hours, but all the hubbub had confused him so badly that he could only talk about Lenin and kosher cheese. A journalist from the *Baseler Zeitung* received a transcript of the interrogations from a friend on the force. That is how the popular press came to give Mr. Schwartz the nickname "Pedophile Lenin."

Xavier wasn't a Jew yet, but he was already a victim. It was a start.

King David

ONE WEEK AFTER being separated from his inflamed testicle, Xavier was still the talk of the town in Basel. But Awromele didn't talk about him, he only thought about him and wondered whether he should try to call him. It was a dilemma. Xavier had asked him never to phone, because of the situation at home.

Awromele longed to see Xavier. In Xavier he had come across something he had never found anywhere else: willpower, vision, energy, endurance.

"I miss you," he whispered to the little scrap of paper with Xavier's phone number on it. After he had whispered that a few times, he decided that this was an emergency: his longing had become too great. His father had told him that Xavier was in the hospital, and he had seen his picture in the paper.

The Committee of Vigilant Parents organized information meetings each evening, and was busy by day as well with the recruitment of new members.

Awromele decided that the time had come to evaluate with Xavier the events of the last few days, to hear his voice, to hold his rather large hand, to see how his circumcised penis was coming along. That circumcision, after all, had in a way been Awromele's circumcision as well; he had arranged the whole thing, he had been there, he had held Xavier's feet. Awromele picked up a *siddur* and recited the prayer for the dead. Of all the prayers he knew, that was his favorite.

When the phone rang, Xavier's mother was examining her broken nose in a hand mirror. Not another journalist, she thought. In the last few days, she had been inundated by calls from the press, and one time she had even appeared on TV, for twenty seconds. But all the attention and sympathy had done nothing to allay her fears. On the contrary, her honorary membership in the Committee of Vigilant Parents was hard for her to bear. She couldn't sleep at night. She was afraid that the rank and file would find out that she didn't love her son enough. Although she believed that all parents had the right to hate their children if they liked, she realized that such feelings did not jibe with her honorary membership in the committee. She was less than wildly enthusiastic about her semi-celebrity status. She often thought: Give me anonymity, I'm just a normal woman, and that's what I plan to stay. Fame, even local fame, did nothing but keep the pain at arm's length.

Since the punch in the nose, she had stopped opening herself to her boyfriend. On one occasion he had caressed her between the legs. Another time he had lain atop her tenderly. But she had pushed him off. She had told herself: I'm not going to let him come right inside me, not for the time being; that will teach him.

All these things she was pondering in her heart when she heard Awromele's voice.

"I'm a friend of Xavier's, I'd like to visit him. Can you tell me where he is?"

The mother gave him the name of the hospital and the room number. She was pleased to hear that it wasn't another journalist on the line.

"Thank you," Awromele said. "I'm going to visit your son soon."

"How nice," the mother said. She would be going there the day after tomorrow herself.

Marc had urged her to visit Xavier more frequently. But the mother said: "It's not good to lavish attention on him, or he'll never become independent. He has to learn to stand on his own two feet."

WHEN AWROMELE SAW Xavier lying in the hospital bed, he felt calm for the first time in days. He kissed him on both cheeks, and once on the lips by accident. "I'm so glad to see you," Awromele said. "You're looking pretty good." Just to be safe, he had taken off his yarmulke before entering the hospital. His father always took off his yarmulke when he visited a massage parlor. Sometimes it was better to remain incognito.

Xavier tried to smile. It didn't work; they had stopped giving him painkillers, and his member still hurt quite badly. "I missed you," he said.

Awromele lifted the jar from the side table and took a good look at it. "So that's the one." He examined the amputated body part. "It's actually only a little thing, isn't it? When you look at it like this, I mean. It doesn't add up to much. Is this what they call an epididymis?"

The head nurse had told Xavier what was in the jar. Whenever she came into his room, she would say: "Your testicle is famous, did you know that? You should be proud of it." She had urged him to look at it often, in order to speed up the process of closure. Repression could be fatal, and closure had to take place quickly, or your life would be over while the closure was still going on.

"Do you know what you're going to do with it?" Awromele asked.
"With what?"

Awromele held up the jar with the testicle and shook it back and forth.
"Bury it, maybe," Xavier said. "Or keep it."

"I'd keep it if I were you," Awromele said. "Even if it's only for your grandchildren."

Then he pulled a chocolate bar out of his coat pocket and said: "Oh, I almost forgot. This is for you." Awromele laughed shyly.

"Thank you," Xavier said. Despite the pain, he pulled Awromele down close and kissed him three times on the cheek and then, quickly, once on

the lips and on the nose. Awromele was the sweetest Jew Xavier had ever
met. If his grandfather had been able to meet Awromele, history would
have looked very different indeed.

"How long do you have to stay here?" Awromele asked. He took a good
look around. The hospital had put Xavier in a room of his own because of
all the journalists, city officials, and representatives of the Committee of
Vigilant Parents.

"For a little while, I think," Xavier said. "The pain is going away, but
slowly."

"I've got good news for you," Awromele said. "I've found a publisher.
He's enthusiastic."

"About what?" Xavier asked.

"What do you think? About our Yiddish translation of *Mein Kampf*. He
thinks the time is ripe for it, but he says we'll have to aim for the high end
of the market. He thinks it's a book for the highly educated, which means
it can be a fairly expensive edition."

"Highly educated?"

"Don't ask me how high," Awromele said, sounding a bit rankled. "The
man I talked to, he's never read the original, but he said he could tell that
it was a book for a literate audience. The high end of the market is still a
growth market, he said. The time is ripe for a Yiddish translation of *Mein
Kampf.*"

"We're in luck," Xavier said. But he didn't succeed in looking happy.

"I wrote it all down for you," Awromele said. "I knew it would
cheer you up." He pulled a notepad out of his pocket and began leafing
through it. "Here we go. He says the time is ripe. Or did I already say that?
That we shouldn't wait too long. Before long no one will remember who
Hitler was."

Xavier moaned loudly. It gave Awromele the feeling that his friend was
being circumcised all over again.

"Don't mention that name," Xavier said. "You have to say You-Know-
Who. Just like we're not supposed to say God's name, let alone write it
down, it's the same thing with You-Know-Who."

Awromele was immersed in his notepad. He wasn't really listening to what Xavier said. "The publisher says we're entering an era void of taboos, and that it would be good to grab one of the final taboos by the scruff of the neck. He wants to lighten up the book a little, with artwork from the period itself. But nothing abstract. Just so you can see what it's supposed to be saying. He's thinking about a first run of ten thousand. Great as a handout for doctors, judges, historians, linguists, journalists. Maybe the book clubs will pick it up, too—that's what he says." Awromele peered closely at his notepad; he was having trouble reading his own handwriting. "What's this?" he mumbled. "Christmas hampers. Oh yeah, that was another idea. To include the book in Christmas hampers. What do you think?"

But at that point Xavier wasn't thinking anything. He was having a pain attack. When it was over, he said, "I'm very pleased, Awromele, but what kind of a man is he?"

"Who?"

"The publisher."

"The publisher? He has a background in TV. He used to make clips for music programs, things like that, but he wants to do something different. He's very successful. But I have to go home now—they're waiting for me for dinner."

"What about Mr. Schwartz?" Xavier asked.

"He's in prison," Awromele said. "What, don't you read the paper?"

"Couldn't we do something nice for him?" Xavier asked. When he was a little boy, his mother had always told him: "Forget the nasty things and remember all the nice things. That's the secret of being cheerful." The thought of Mr. Schwartz in prison made Xavier nauseous. He grabbed Awromele's hand. "Don't go away," he said. "Stay for just a little while."

"As soon as you're back on your feet again, we'll go visit Mr. Schwartz," Awromele said. He leaned over and kissed the patient at various spots on his person. Then he hurried home, where he locked himself in his room and sat on his bed for forty-five minutes. Longing cuts you off from others. The more you long for someone else, the more cut off you become. Awromele realized that. If you wanted to free yourself from your isolation, you had to stop longing. But no matter how hard he tried, it didn't work.

When evening came, Xavier took the jar off the side table and clutched it in his arms. He started talking to the testicle. He said: "You are my rod and my staff, you have to help me."

When people answer a cry for help, it's almost always a disappointment. Compared with that, the testicle's silence was a miracle of hope and optimism.

Xavier decided that his severed body part should have a name. That would really speed up the closure. It's easier to say goodbye to things with a name than it is to say goodbye to the nameless.

"I'm going to call you King David," Xavier said to the blue testicle. "King David was the King of the Jews, and someday you will be, too."

He clutched the jar tightly to his chest, fearing that King David would be taken away from him, and closed his eyes.

A Source of Inspiration

THE DAY XAVIER was released from the hospital, he found two newspaper reporters and eight photographers waiting for him at the exit. All eight photographers asked him to hold up the jar with the testicle in it. Despite his handicap, Xavier had remained a cheerful fellow, and didn't like to disappoint people. So he did what they asked. "Just one more close-up," shouted a bearded photographer. He came closer and said, "Hold the jar up to your cheek."

Xavier did that as well, and the photographer said, "All right, that's great, fantastic."

Then Marc came up and piloted the boy through the crowd to his Alfa Romeo. The mother had stayed at home, to welcome the boy with her homemade apple pie. "We're back!" Marc shouted from the vestibule. The whole way home, he had made tender little noises at his stepson. He trundled him into the living room, where the mother was waiting.

She hugged her son. "Would you like some coffee?" she asked.

She cut him a big piece of apple pie—the last few weeks had been difficult for him—and said, "You still smell like a hospital ward."

Marc stuck his nose down the back of the boy's collar. "No," he said, "he doesn't smell like a hospital. He smells good."

"It's still warm," the mother said. She pointed at the pie.

Xavier had put King David on the table. King David stood there valiantly, beside the thermos full of coffee.

The mother had whipped the cream herself. She didn't like whipped cream from a can.

The three of them ate with gusto. The mother was an excellent baker.

"You've lost something," Marc said after he had finished his pie. "But you've gained something as well. You've made friends." And he picked up the jar to take a better look at the testicle.

"Marc, put that down," the mother said. "It's dirty."

"It looks like it's still alive," Marc said, putting down the jar. "It looks like it's taken on a life of its own, like it's started a new life."

"Could be," Xavier said. He was thinking about Mr. Schwartz. He was disturbed that the popular press kept referring to the cheese dealer as the Pedophile Lenin. Xavier had hoped to save and comfort the Jews, but so far he'd mostly seen to it that they ended up in prison. The thought chastened him.

"If you can't . . ." the mother said, and sighed deeply. "If you don't function normally down there anymore, I want you to tell me. Then we can go to the doctor. The surgeon said we shouldn't wait. That's the best chance we have that it will all turn out all right."

"Okay, Mom," Xavier said.

"It shouldn't be any problem," said Marc. "Should it, Xavier? I mean, you feel great, don't you? The rest will come by itself."

"The most important thing," the mother said, "is that you go back to school as soon as possible and make up for lost time. The Committee of Vigilant Parents has asked if you could come to their meeting tomorrow, to talk about your experiences. I told them you would, but after that it's going to be homework, homework, and more homework."

"I think I'll go to bed early," Xavier said. He kissed his mother and thanked her for the apple pie.

"I'll tuck him in," Marc said.

The mother sat downstairs and listened to the sounds that accompanied the tucking in. She thought about the committee. Every once in a while, she stuck her little finger dreamily into the bowl of whipped cream and licked it clean. After she had done that four times, she made a decision. All is lost, she said to herself. I'm depressed. I should start taking pills to make me feel happy. I don't have all that much to complain about. After all, I still have all my teeth.

THE COMMITTEE of Vigilant Parents met in an art gallery. More than forty parents had shown up to hear Xavier Radek talk about his experiences. There were also a few singles who didn't have children yet but wanted to do a little preventive listening.

Xavier felt uncomfortable. He was going to have to talk about how Mr. Schwartz had molested him, and he didn't want to do that. First of all, because it wasn't true, and he was fond of the truth. Second, because he wanted to comfort Mr. Schwartz. Not that Mr. Schwartz was particularly close to his heart—Awromele was the one who was particularly close to his heart—but Mr. Schwartz happened to belong to the people he'd decided to comfort.

Besides, it would hurt his mother badly to hear that her child had let himself be circumcised by a myopic Jew. She might not live through that. The Committee of Vigilant Parents played an important role in her life. And after a confession like that, she could no longer be a part of the committee, especially not an honorary member. Xavier didn't have much choice.

In the end, he decided to strike a happy medium. He would have to say something about being molested, but he would also say a few good and friendly things about Mr. Schwartz.

The owner of the gallery introduced him and called him a "beacon of courage" and a "symbol of optimism." Then it was his turn to speak. He climbed onto the podium, ran his hand through his hair, and told the concerned parents: "My name, as you probably know, is Xavier Radek. It was a little over a month ago that Mr. S. took me into his care, but . . ."

He held his breath for an instant and looked around at the concerned parents, to let his words sink in. ". . . but he did it lovingly."

He took a sip of water and looked at the tense faces all around. The concerned parents did not look particularly pretty in this light. Decrepit, actually, even though most of them were barely middle-aged.

"Bah," a woman in the front row shouted, "bah! How can you molest someone lovingly? I don't call what he did taking you into his care, I call that abuse." This encouraged other members of the audience to murmur in disapproval as well. A woman at the back shouted: "How can someone do such a thing? That's what I want to know!" And she added, "I'm here tonight as a mother and a grandmother, and I want you to tell me how someone can do that."

A man said: "And we're all here tonight as children, too. Let's not forget that. Some of us may even have been molested as children."

The woman with the loud voice interrupted him: "No! I'm not a molested child, and I never have been. I'm here tonight as a mother and a grandmother. I have six grandchildren, and none of them have been molested, either. At least not yet."

The owner of the gallery intervened. "It's not time for questions from the public. I hope we can talk calmly and with dignity about these matters, but for the moment let's listen to our guest tonight, Xavier Radek."

Xavier pinched himself in the arm and ran his hand through his hair again. He felt flushed. "What he did cannot be dismissed lightly," he said. "But he acted in good faith. His love has no future, but, then, what love does? Who among us today can truly say, 'My love has a future'?"

Xavier was warming to his subject; he lost himself in his words, the same way he had lost himself in an idea not so long ago.

Someone shouted, "So what about it, what about that love?"

But Xavier didn't respond. He could no longer tell whether he was talking about his grandfather or about Mr. Schwartz, or about Awromele; all he knew was that he had hit his stride at last.

Loud shouts of "Boo!" came from the crowd. At the back of the gallery, where the people were standing shoulder to shoulder, Xavier saw Awromele and the rabbi.

Xavier remained silent for a few seconds. The man who had shouted that they were all children, perhaps even molested children, now shouted: "Let the boy talk. We can all learn from what he's been through." The booing stopped. There were young people in the audience, too, probably students. They were taking notes.

"Christianity speaks of forgiveness and love," Xavier said. "We must not only forgive our molesters, we must also offer them our love."

Someone threw something at him. The murmuring grew louder and more disapproving than ever.

Xavier pinched himself in the arm again, but it didn't help. He shouldn't have come here. He couldn't talk about his experiences, at least not yet—maybe later, when he was older and Mr. Schwartz was no longer alive.

"I can't go on," Xavier said. "I'm sorry, I can't."

The concerned parents were stunned. They had been expecting alarming details, confessions that hadn't made the media. They had hoped for words of advice, tips on how to prevent such things.

A few seconds later, the stunned silence made way for hesitant applause. The applause grew louder, and the man who had just shouted, "Let the boy talk," now shouted: "We're caught like rats in a trap. We've all been conditioned to consume, that's why they molest our children. Once they've tried everything else, they think: Let's try a child. We're caught like rats in a trap."

A few concerned parents cheered in agreement, but most of them seemed to feel that the comparison with rats was tasteless.

The loud booing began again. It appeared that the Committee of Vigilant Parents was about to dissolve in internal conflicts.

Xavier took advantage of the confusion to make his way to the exit, straight through the crowd of concerned parents. He slipped past his mother and a few of her lady friends, women whom he had once been required to call "auntie." Waiting at the door was a photographer who shouted: "Where's your testicle? Don't you have it with you?"

"It's at home," he whispered.

Then Awromele grabbed Xavier's arm and pulled him outside. He wasn't wearing his yarmulke—he was incognito again.

Out in the street, Xavier saw that the man Awromele had with him wasn't the rabbi. "This is the publisher I told you about," Awromele said.

Xavier shook the publisher's hand, and the publisher said, "Congratulations, that was very nice." Xavier was exhausted from all the commotion, the attention, the interest in an event about which he could remember very little. What he remembered most was the smell of sour cream.

"Xavier," someone shouted. "Xavier." It was his mother; she seemed relieved to have found him. As an honorary member of the committee, she had duties to fulfill. "There's someone here who wants your autograph."

Standing beside her was a pregnant woman—a mere girl, really. She was holding a photocopy of the folder with which the Committee of Vigilant Parents had announced its formation. She held it up in front of Xavier's eyes.

"Would you write, 'For Nina, please be careful'?" the pregnant woman asked. She looked at him expectantly. She said, "You're a source of inspiration for all future victims."

Xavier smiled amiably. "I'm pleased to hear that," he said.

He played the part of the shy young man, because that role fit him well. He borrowed a pen and wrote in block letters: FOR NINA, PLEASE BE CAREFUL.

"She's still in my stomach," the woman said. "But she already needs all the help she can get."

Dying and Loving
You Do on Your Own

THE COMMITTEE of Vigilant Parents continued to organize information meetings, but they decided not to invite too many victims anymore; they decided to put more emphasis on prevention and education.

Xavier returned to his schoolwork, to make up for lost time, and his gait gradually became less splayed. The wound was healing. Whenever he sat on the toilet, Xavier looked at it and was glad to be alive. Despite his rather unpleasant experience on Mr. Schwartz's bed, he couldn't help being glad.

The mother made attempts not to feel her pain, but the more frequent and concentrated her attempts were, the more pain she felt.

Awromele crawled into bed with his clothes on and smoked a cigarette, half under the blankets to keep the smoke from spreading, and thought about love. He never used to think about love. He had been happier then.

Mr. Schwartz was in prison, and in the process of losing his mind. During his moments of clarity, he felt so miserable that all he could do was pound his head rhythmically against the wall. As he did so, he cried quietly for help in the six languages he spoke. It was better for him, perhaps, that no one heard his quiet cries, and help never arrived.

. . .

ONE EVENING, two weeks after being released from the hospital, Xavier was sitting at the dining-room table, learning his Latin vocabulary. The mother was out playing bridge with her friends; Marc was lying on the couch, listening to jazz. When the CD was over, he took off the headphones and asked, "Shall I make some tea for you?"

Xavier shook his head.

"Something else?"

"No," Xavier said. "Thank you."

Marc came and sat at the table. "I'm not bothering you, am I?"

"No," Xavier said.

Marc rolled up the sleeves of his sweater, the way he always did in the broadcasting studio, and laid his hand on the boy's hand.

"You know that I love your mother very much?"

Xavier nodded.

"Of course, there have been some problems, but I love her."

Xavier nodded again. He had closed the book of Latin words. On one of the pages, in pencil, he had absentmindedly scribbled "Awromele."

"Your mother is a fantastic woman—sweet, gentle, calm—and she always thinks about others before thinking about herself. As far as that goes, she's a real example to me."

King David was on a shelf in the bookcase, beside the collected works of Schiller. The mother had thought that was a good place for the testicle, central but not too prominent. The girls from her bridge club had all held the jar admiringly, and one of them had even asked, "Would you take my picture with it?"

Xavier looked at King David. He had become used to having only one testicle. When he got up in the morning, the first thing he did was go to the living room to say hello to King David. It had become a ritual, he couldn't do without it.

"But do you know who I really love?"

"No," Xavier said.

"Come on, think. You mean you really don't know?"

Xavier thought about Awromele, about his kisses, his lips, which had closed around Xavier's member not long before Mr. Schwartz had taken the knife to it. Stupid of him not to have enjoyed it, stupid of him to have let it go by so casually, like a snow flurry in winter. In fact, he could barely remember it. He was a happy person, but real happiness, persistent happiness, was something you overlooked; it seemed to leave nothing behind, except for the feeling that you had forgotten something important.

"I love you," Marc said. "The one I really love is you. Haven't you ever noticed?"

Xavier looked at his stepfather. Love was something he didn't know how to cope with. Fortunately, his parents had never smothered him in it. Gradually, he had started realizing why he'd been able to go through life so free of worries: it was because he had lived without love.

"Not really," Xavier was tempted to say, but he thought that wasn't nice—he was afraid to disappoint Marc—so he said, "Yeah, a little. I suspected something like that."

"You know," Marc said, "I didn't really want to tell you. But now that we're sitting here anyway, now that we understand each other so well, I might as well be honest, so you don't have to find out later. You're the real reason why I stay with your mother. I mean, of course, she's a fantastic person and I wish all my friends could have a wife like her, but you're the reason I'm still here."

There had been an article in the paper that evening about the Committee of Vigilant Jews. The committee was warning against certain tendencies in society that were becoming more pronounced all the time. The article had not come as a disappointment to Xavier. The more such tendencies there were, the more there was for him to comfort.

"Are you listening?" Marc asked.

"Yeah."

"I don't want to force myself on you. If I'm forcing myself on you, I want you to tell me."

"You're not forcing yourself on me," Xavier said.

"I've been hesitating for a long time about whether or not to tell your mother. Finally, I've decided that it's better to tell her. I mean, we're all grown-ups, right?"

Xavier nodded thoughtfully.

"The truth doesn't hurt that much once you're grown up, once you're emotionally grown up. The secrets are what hurt, the misunderstandings, all the lies. If you do your best to understand each other, to take each other's wishes into account, then you can live together without a problem. I read once in a science magazine that the truth only hurts when you have a narcissistic disorder. I don't think your mother has a narcissistic disorder."

"No," Xavier said, "there's nothing wrong with my mother."

"I don't have a narcissistic disorder, either," Marc went on. "That's why the truth has never hurt me. I can deal with the truth just fine. So, when she comes home later on, I'm going to talk to her. Then I'll tell her the truth. But I wanted you to know first."

"That's nice of you," Xavier said. He opened his book of Latin words. What might Awromele be doing right now?

Marc laid his hand on Xavier's arm and kept it there. "I want you to know," he said, "that you never have to respond to my feelings—never— if you don't feel anything for me. But if you do, and, I don't know, if you should feel something for me, something animal, as it were, then there's no need for you to be ashamed."

"Well, sure," Xavier said. He looked thoughtful; he sensed that this was a grave moment. Even though it didn't feel particularly grave to him— to him it was at most a little awkward.

"Xavier," Marc said. "I don't expect you to share my feelings. What I discovered as a young man was: Dying and loving you do on your own. All the other things you do together—eating, taking a walk, a little fucking, going on vacation, putting up a tent—but dying and loving you do on your own."

They both stopped talking. Xavier looked at King David. He had lost something that it turned out he could easily do without. Maybe that's what it was about, finding out what you couldn't do without. But what if you could do without everything?

"I love you, too," Xavier said, folding back a dog-eared corner of a page, "but as a stepson loves his stepfather. That's how I love you." He realized that he had never told Awromele that he loved him.

"I don't care how you love me," Marc said, letting go of the boy's arm. "You can love me however you like. Any way you love me is okay. It's not about the form, it's the content."

At that moment, they heard the key turn in the lock.

Marc moved to the other side of the table, where he prepared himself in silence for an important talk with the mother. He saw his whole life in front of him, from his boyhood in the Jura to the moment when he had decided to move in with Mrs. Radek and her son. He was nothing, he was like sand, but the sand knew whom it loved.

Relief

THE FIRST THING the mother did was go into the kitchen and wash her hands. She always did that when she came in. Then she hung up her coat, came into the living room, and said hello to her family.

"They're still talking about Xavier at the bridge club," she said to no one in particular. "But I told them that we're all back to normal in this house."

The mother went into the kitchen to make some chamomile tea, which she brought back into the living room a few minutes later in a thermos jug of Italian design that she and the architect had bought one time in Bologna.

They drank their chamomile tea in silence. Xavier had a vision in which Awromele was taking the weenies of strange boys in his mouth. He had never imagined Awromele doing such things, but it worried him.

When Marc realized that he couldn't put it off any longer, that he had to say it now, that otherwise it would never happen, he rubbed his hands together and said, "Sweetheart." Marc coughed. His hands were moist, but that could just as easily have been from the hot tea. "Sweetheart," he said again, and he looked at the mother. She was ignoring him. "Darling." Marc couldn't come up with any pet names; he couldn't even remember whether he had ever thought up pet names for her. "As far as I can see, you don't have a narcissistic disorder," he said at last.

The mother poured herself another cup of tea. She had never thought about herself in connection with disorders, but now that her boyfriend was stating so emphatically that she had no narcissistic disorder, she began to have her doubts. Did she seem less than normal to the outside world?

"Right," Marc said. "Not that. And, well, I'm glad. Because a lot of people really do suffer from that."

The mother said nothing. She didn't know what there was to be glad about; disorders she didn't have didn't do much to cheer her up.

"I love you very much," Marc said. He tried to look at her lovingly, with the fire that he had really only felt for her on one evening, a fire that had gone out as inconspicuously as it had been lit.

The mother took a little sip, the tea was still a bit too hot. She thought about the stories she had heard from her girlfriends at the bridge club, stories she couldn't join in with, stories about feelings she knew about only from magazines.

Xavier bent deeper over his book. He tried not to think about Awromele, and at the same time not to listen to this conversation. He was afraid of knocking over his cup. He noticed he was trembling, as though he were hypoglycemic.

"What I mean is, I love you," Marc said, because the mother had still not said a thing. "And in the last couple of weeks I have really come to appreciate you, as a person, as a woman. Well, as everything."

The mother looked at her boyfriend, who had broken her nose one evening when she had spread herself open for him. She had tried to forgive him, but she still couldn't. Forgiveness was a tricky business. In fact, she had never been able to forgive anyone, and she had the feeling that no one had been able to forgive her, either. Even though she had no idea what she'd done wrong.

"That's nice," she said.

"People without a narcissistic disorder can cope well with the truth, because they live in harmony with themselves and with their surroundings," Marc continued. He had good hope that she would understand everything, that it would all turn out fine, that she would be able to live with it as long as he didn't beat around the bush, as long as he was honest. "I want you to know that I love you very much, but there is one other person I love just a little more."

The mother looked at him. She had heard the words without understanding them. She'd had that problem before, not being able to understand what men were saying to her. Her late husband had often said things to her that she hadn't understood. Men—well, not that there had been so many of them. Two. Others had intruded into her life briefly, but they had stuck to being silent, and the rest.

"Don't you want to know who I love so much?" Marc asked, and he picked up his spoon and pretended to play with it absentmindedly. "Don't you want to know who I love so terribly much that it drives me crazy?"

Xavier became increasingly absorbed in his homework. He seemed to be in a trance. He saw the letters dancing on the page, and he was reminded of the Jewish mystics Awromele had told him about one afternoon in the tram. Jewish mystics had seen letters dancing as well.

"Yes," the mother said, after she'd thought about it a bit. "Yes, actually, I'd like to know."

Marc smiled; he tried to look as sweet as he had the evening he'd met her. That evening, he had looked sweet and innocent, too, so terribly sweet, and at the same time lovesick and brutish. Hungry. Why, he didn't know anymore himself—loneliness perhaps, the need to forget a whole series of women who had left him. You could grow tired of having people stick to you, but people who ran away were tiresome as well.

"Well," the mother said, "I'm all ears." Now it was Marc's turn to be silent.

The mother remembered exactly why she had let him seduce her: it was because she hadn't felt a man for decades. She had been penetrated, mostly from behind, but she hadn't felt a man, not that; as far as that went, she had only feeble memories that had grown so vague that she could no longer tell the difference between what was real and what was fantasy. She had also forgotten what it was like to drive a man wild. She did remember what it felt like when a man didn't want you anymore, when the father of your child was disgusted by what had crawled out of you, by the belly in which the embryo had grown so slowly. She had wanted to experience it one last time, before it was too late; she had wanted to know what it felt like to drive a man wild. That's why she had laughed that evening even when there was nothing to laugh about, giggled without good reason, rolled her eyes like a bad actress, tilted her head to one side, and encouraged Marc to go on, above all to go on, not to give up, never to give up. She wanted to know what it was like to have a man long for her. "Read my palm," she had said to Marc, who would someday break her nose. "Read my palm," and he had taken her hand and never let go.

"Your son," Marc said. "Your sweet son. That glorious creature."

The mother looked at her child, whom she had hated since the day he had entered the world with a shriek. Whom she had to hate, because he had made her what she didn't want to be, but what she had to become in order to be respectable in this city: a mother. She had thought it was a part of being happy, a child.

She looked at Marc and then at her tea. She took a sip. She was amazed to discover that she felt nothing, not even surprise, as though she had been expecting this for years, even back when she was taken to the hospital with contractions and all she'd been able to think was: Something terrible is going to happen, there's no way out. Something terrible is going to happen.

"I know I can tell you this," Marc said, "because you don't have a narcissistic disorder. Otherwise I would never have told you. But people like us, who love each other very much, don't have to keep secrets from each other."

"No," the mother said.

Xavier looked at the dancing letters in his book. He thought about Awromele; he thought: Save me, Awromele, save me. Get me out of here. Get me out of here forever. Life is wonderful, but not here. Not here, never again.

"I'm going to bed," his mother said. "I'm tired."

"Wait a minute," Marc said, rolling up his sleeves for the umpteenth time. "I want you to know that I'm not going to leave you. I want to stay here. I will never leave you. Nothing has to change. Between us. I'm staying with you because of the boy, but that doesn't matter, I'm staying with you, that's the important thing. I love him, so I also love you. You understand? I love everything that comes crawling out of you, and I would be so happy if more things came out of you, something that was mine as well."

"I need to go to bed," the mother said again. "It's late." She looked at her watch. A present from her late husband, she'd replaced the strap only recently.

She got up and took the thermos and the cups to the kitchen.

Before going to bed, she came back into the living room, where her son was still sitting across from Marc. "By the way, did you know about this, Xavier?" she asked.

Xavier saw the mother, whom he had wished to spare all grief, whom he had wished to spare the suffering of the world. But he couldn't give up Awromele for her sake. That would be too much. That would be too great a sacrifice. Between him and Awromele stood the mother. "About what?"

"About this. About what Marc just said. Did you know about it?"

"A little," Xavier said. "I don't know any more than you do. I don't know—"

"You don't know what?"

Xavier shrugged, and looked at his book. His freshly healed sex organ usually began hurting around this time of night.

"What don't you know, Xavier?"

"Nothing, nothing really."

The mother crossed her arms. She looked at the two men in her house.

One of them she had made—the word made her laugh—the other she had met in a museum, at a cocktail party, he had started talking to her, she had looked at him willingly. That was what she had told herself to be that evening, willing.

"Why my son?" she asked. "I mean, there are so many men in Basel, so many young men. Why my son?"

The mother's boyfriend looked at her son. All hope was longing, but why did longing have to be so complicated? He didn't understand that. Why couldn't he long for her? That would be simpler, and he had tried, he had tried so hard, even when he broke her nose he had been trying, he had been working on longing for her.

"That's love," Marc said at last. "Love is inexplicable, but beautiful. Don't you think? So huge, so all-embracing. So vast, so mysterious—that, too, my sweet, so terribly mysterious."

So filthy, he had felt like adding, so godforsaken filthy, filthy as a corruption scandal that will never completely be unraveled, filthy as a gas chamber from which the corpses have just been raked out with a hook. Yes, his love was filthy, he had always known that, and now he had reconciled himself to it. True love was filthy.

The mother nodded distractedly.

In the bathroom, she cleaned her face with a cotton ball.

Xavier came into the bathroom and put a hand on her shoulder. But she took his hand and laid it on the sink.

"Mama," he said, "I really don't know anything about this. I don't know what's gotten into him. You didn't know about it, either, when you brought him home, did you?"

Xavier waited for a reply, and when it didn't come he squeezed some toothpaste onto his toothbrush.

The mother crawled into bed. She couldn't sleep, so she took a sleeping pill. It didn't help. Marc had come in and lain beside her. He had tried to kiss her, but she had pushed his head away gently. "Not now," she had said. "Not now."

"I don't mean anything bad by it," he had answered. "I still think you're pretty and attractive. I don't want you to think that I suddenly have no more sexual feelings for you. If it had been possible, I would have liked to have a child with you. I would love to make a child with you. My dream is to have a child."

Then he had stroked her arm, but she pushed away his hand as well. All she said was: "It's still possible, just barely."

In the middle of the night, she got up and went to the kitchen. She stood there silently, for minutes. Her own breathing was all she could hear. In the semidarkness, she looked at the dishes lined up in the dish rack. She leaned on the counter.

It surprised her that she still didn't feel a thing. She tried to cry, but couldn't. All she felt was a coldness, a repressed rage, not even that, the residue of rage and eternal bitterness. She took a cup and filled it with water from the tap. She took a couple of sips. Then she pulled her pajama pants down to her knees and, still in the semidarkness, looked at her thighs.

The flesh was white.

She took a fork out of the dish rack. Why didn't she feel anything? She didn't understand—she had every reason to feel something, everyone felt something. The only thing she could catch herself feeling was a vague sense of being cold, like when you've taken a walk outside in the winter too lightly dressed.

She put the fork back in the rack.

That she had borne a child, she hated that. The rest not, the rest was over, a closed book that had left nothing unpleasant in its wake.

She moved her hand over her left leg. Her hands were cold and dry.

"Cold hands and a warm heart," someone had said to her once. She couldn't remember who, maybe Marc, that evening at the museum, that evening when she had wanted to be willing, nothing but willing.

She picked up the bread knife, Italian design, purchased in Verona with her late husband. A little pubic hair was sticking out from beneath her panties. It had once been a different color, lighter—curlier, too—she thought. She wasn't sure. She tried to picture her pubic hair as it had been twenty years ago, but couldn't.

Using her right hand, she drove the bread knife into her left thigh, close to her cunt.

She pulled the knife out of the white flesh. The blood flowed slowly, almost too slowly in her eyes, but gradually it began flowing more quickly. The edge of her panties and a wisp of pubic hair turned red.

She thought about the Committee of Vigilant Parents, about her marriage, the bridge club, the trips to Italy.

The pain was a relief.

Pain is always a relief.

She washed the bread knife and put it back in the rack.

The blood dripped down her leg and onto the pajama pants that were drooping around her ankles. She took off the pants; blood spots are hard to get out of polyester.

Now the blood was on the kitchen floor. That was a matter of a little mopping.

Never again will anyone come right inside me again, she thought, no one will ever come right inside me again. I am Yours, and Yours alone.

She wasn't sure who You was, God or You-Know-Who. Or maybe a combination of the two.

Our Genes

THE WEEKS FOLLOWING Marc's confession went by in relative harmony. There was no more talk of his love for Xavier; there was no more talk of love at all. Marc occasionally urged the mother to make a baby with him, proposals the mother refused politely. "Not yet," she said. "It's all still so new." She had never told Marc the truth about her age, and she wasn't planning to now. In the course of time, she had chipped off a few years here and there. First two, then three, now it was more than five. And after her divorce she had undergone a rejuvenation cure. She looked good for her age. Almost no wrinkles, firm buttocks, no drooping flesh. She felt young. On the street she easily overtook women twenty years her junior.

Only very sporadically did she get up in the middle of the night in order to drive the bread knife into her thigh, an act that summoned up in her a brief feeling of satisfaction. She had the motion that a gust of life blew through her as she stood there with the knife in her hand. A gust, that was all, but it was enough. After that, she returned to the kingdom of the dead, where she had resided for years.

AWROMELE SPENT a great part of each day under the blankets in his room. At first he had waited for a phone call from Xavier, but when it became clear that Xavier was not going to call again, Awromele tried to forget him. The more he tried to forget him, the more he thought about him.

Xavier did not call because he thought Awromele was angry at him. He didn't want to force himself on anyone, not even on Jews. He had his pride, and he planned to keep it. He too suffered under the silence, but even more under the way he pictured Awromele taking the weenies of strange men into his mouth.

Xavier decided to take up drawing. The world needed prettying up. Besides, the activity freed him from his unpleasant visions.

At first he used colored pencils. Later, he switched to oil paint and watercolors. Because he was often home alone with his mother—Marc did not return from work with the end of the afternoon—he asked her to pose for him.

Anything was better than a Zionist youth club, the mother thought, so she said, "Use me for your drawings."

Within a short period, he produced six paintings of the mother, which he himself thought were not bad, although Klimt's influence was perhaps a bit pronounced. While he painted, he thought about the task he had assigned himself, which he could not accomplish without Awromele.

Marc was enthusiastic about the boy's paintings. "Keep at it," he said. "You have talent. I have talent, too, but I can't do anything with it, and the great thing is that you can. There are two kinds of people, the ones who can do something with their talent and the ones who can't."

"Let the boy finish school first," the mother said. "After that we'll see."

The day Xavier began on the seventh big portrait of his mother—he had decided now to paint more in the style of Chagall—Awromele finally left the bed in which he had been drowsing, longing, and whining for the last few days. He had never been able to stand his parents' whining, but now he was on the verge of becoming a crybaby himself. "Enough," he had shouted at himself, "enough is enough." Sitting there under the blankets with his clothes on, he had felt like an Indian in a wigwam; sometimes he dreamed that Xavier came and sat in the wigwam with him, and that they played a game, or simply ate a piece of chocolate together in silence and looked at each other contentedly.

Awromele got dressed, trimmed his curls, borrowed some of his father's aftershave, and walked to Xavier's house.

The closer he got to the house, the faster he walked. What nonsense, to wait for a phone call! You could spend your whole life waiting. Maybe there was something wrong with the phone. He started running. As he ran, his yarmulke kept blowing off, so he stuck it in his pocket.

When, at last, he reached the street where Xavier lived, he remembered what Xavier had told him: he was never to call, and certainly never just to pop in, because Xavier's mother was a sensitive person who didn't like unexpected visitors; she suffered from intense migraines.

All Awromele's courage and good resolutions faded at the thought of Xavier's mother with a migraine. He couldn't just ring the bell and ask, "Is Xavier at home?" As long as he didn't ring the bell, there was still hope; but if he rang the bell, everything was lost.

He sat down beneath a tree across from the house and waited. He waited until he was chilled to the bone. Then he got up and walked back to his own house, where he climbed into bed, clothes and all, and cried as if his heart was broken. His sister Rochele heard it, but didn't want to disturb him.

Xavier was in the living room, painting with a sure hand. He had purchased a secondhand easel. Every two minutes he thought about Awromele. Which is probably why he painted his mother in pin curls. With every pin curl that took shape on the canvas, his anger grew. Why hadn't Awromele bothered to call and ask how he was doing? That was the normal thing to do, wasn't it, especially when someone had been in the hospital for a few weeks because of complications following a circumcision? You got in touch. At the very least you sent a card, without a return address if need be. He looked at the bookshelf with the volumes of Schiller on it and saw King David.

"Could you just hold the jar like this?" he asked the mother. He lifted it down off the shelf and handed it to her; she took it without protest. She didn't look at her son's testicle.

Her remedy for suffering had stood the test of time. She had nibbled at it all her life, a certain passivity, a certain compliance, living as though it had nothing to do with you. And that was how Xavier, thinking of Awromele doing dastardly things with other men, came to paint the mother with testicle.

When Marc came home that evening, he was thrilled with the canvas, which was standing in the hall to dry. He said: "You should go to the art academy. This latest painting of yours is something else. I'm no expert, but there is something very special going on here."

The mother glanced at the painting and said, "It doesn't look like me."

That evening, in his cell, Mr. Schwartz had a moment of clarity. He tore a sheet into strips and decided to hang himself. The shame of being thrown out of the Jewish community was more than he could bear. He said the prayer for the dead, although to his annoyance there were a few stanzas he couldn't remember. He started in on the prayer a few times, but finally gave up. Then he thought about his kosher cheese, and about the receipts he had written on wrapping paper. After that, there was nothing left to bind him to life—a vague feeling of abhorrence perhaps, the memory of something gruesome that you've seen and would like to forget as quickly as possible.

The hanging did not go smoothly. Life was stubborn. But Mr. Schwartz finally got the better of it.

WHILE MR. SCHWARTZ was dangling from his sheets, Xavier decided that from then on he would make only paintings of his mother with the testicle, in order to present them later as a series to an art academy. You needed a portfolio, he knew that, a portfolio with drawings, paintings, videotapes, perhaps even some clay figures. Marc's enthusiasm had strengthened Xavier in the idea that it would be wise to focus now on painting, on art. The comforting of the Jews would flow forth from the art of its own accord. Visions got him through the day, visions about great deeds in a distant future, and the smell of roast lamb in the near future. Hope is a stunning creature, rather like a horse that has hopped a fence and is galloping towards you.

He woke up in the middle of the night, having dreamed of Awromele. It had been a grim dream. "Where are you, Awromele?" he had felt like shouting. When he went to the bathroom for a drink of water, he heard sounds coming from downstairs. It might be a burglar, he thought, or a window his mother had forgotten to close. But the mother never forgot to close windows and doors.

Xavier went downstairs. He wasn't afraid. Losing Awromele was the only thing he was afraid of. There were moments when he thought he had already lost him. Perhaps on the very first day they'd met, when he had been unable to come up with a dirty joke for Awromele to translate into Yiddish.

In the kitchen, Xavier did not find a burglar or an open window. Only the mother, standing in front of the dish rack, her pink pajama pants around her ankles, a bread knife in her right hand.

A little lamp was burning above the fridge; the mother didn't need much light, she could find the wound by touch.

Blood was dripping from the mother's thigh. Xavier looked at her without a word. She put the knife in the sink, pressed a dishtowel to the wound. "Sorry," she said, "sorry." She didn't really know whom she was speaking to—maybe to herself, maybe to You-Know-Who, she wasn't sure. She stood there as though this was where she belonged, as though this was her spot, as though she was predestined to this, to this forbidden love—for love it was—between her and the knife, which could no longer be denied.

Xavier was wearing only a T-shirt and underpants. He rubbed the back of his neck. What he felt like doing the most was running right back upstairs, going back to his dreams of Awromele, horrible as those dreams were. The most horrible dream about Awromele was better than this. But the mother had already seen him; he couldn't run away. Now he had to stay in the kitchen, now he had to talk.

"Mama," he said quietly. He didn't want to wake Marc, especially not tonight. Marc had to remain asleep, deep and peaceful, dreaming about his great and naughty love. "What are you doing?" There was tenderness in his voice. Tenderness was something Xavier had a lot of.

The question was unnecessary. What she was doing was quite clear.

She looked at the boy. For the first time in years, she felt some compassion for her son. Not a lot, but enough, enough for a lifetime, as far as she was concerned. She would rather have had a daughter. Even more, she would rather have had nothing at all. But when she saw her son standing there in her kitchen, so shocked, so little and afraid—yes, she saw that, his fear, that he was afraid of her—then deep down inside she enjoyed it, for no one had ever been afraid of her. Then she loved him for a moment. Against her judgment, for she knew it wasn't good for her. The way you might put food in your mouth even though you know you're allergic to it.

"I'm living," she said. "Can't you see that? I'm living."

She smiled magnanimously, the way a loser smiles when he receives halfhearted applause, and started washing off the knife. The dishtowel fell onto her pajama pants, which were still around her ankles. Xavier said, "But, Mama, it's the middle of the night." She had to lean against the counter to keep from fainting. Perhaps she had lost too much blood, perhaps she had done it too often, stabbed too often into that same wound. Or maybe it was seeing her son, that terrible and at the same time delicious feeling of being caught red-handed. Caught at last. When she was little, she had always wanted to catch her parents at it, but she had never been able. Now she wanted to be caught herself. "You need to get some sleep, Mama," Xavier said. "It's the middle of the night. You don't have to apologize. But you do have to get some sleep."

Xavier had seen something he was not supposed to see, something that would make him look at the mother differently from now on. He would see her with a knife in the kitchen, while the rest of the family was asleep, her pajamas down around her ankles. So that was living. You did it in the kitchen, you did it at night with a bread knife in your hand, and you had to apologize for it.

The mother sighed. She bent down to pick up the dishtowel and pressed it against the wound again.

"Has he been fiddling with you?" the mother asked as she put the knife in the dish rack, beside the teacups she had washed carefully that evening.

"Who?"

"My boyfriend. Has he been fiddling with you, the way he used to fiddle with me?"

"No, never," Xavier said. "Really, never."

The mother smiled magnanimously again, as though hearing lies that she, to keep the peace, had decided not to unmask any further. She seemed to be in a trance, yet in a completely different, impenetrable world.

"If he does," she said, "I want you to let me know."

"All right," Xavier said, "I'll let you know. But it's not going to happen, Mama, really, it's not going to happen."

"He never fiddled with me much, either," the mother said, adjusting the dishtowel slightly, because the blood had started to trickle through.

"Who?"

Xavier barely dared to look at his mother; he especially didn't dare to look at the dishtowel. That bloody dishtowel at his mother's thigh seemed to exercise on him an attraction almost as great as Awromele's.

"My boyfriend, who else?" The mother stared at the sink, then wiped at it absentmindedly with a sponge. "That first night, and then two or three times after that, but no more. What about you? How often does he fiddle with you?" She squeezed the water out of the sponge.

"Never, Mama, really," Xavier said. "Really, never. I swear." He took a step towards her, but didn't dare touch her. What he saw when he looked at her was mostly the dishtowel, which had turned a dark red in places. A neatly ironed dishtowel: she ironed everything, even the dishtowels.

"Do you want me to get you a bandage?"

"No," the mother said, "no, absolutely not—a bandage. But maybe he can't do it anymore." She laughed as though this were a joke. The band-age, or his not being able to do it anymore, or maybe both.

"Can I do anything for you, Mama? Do you want me to take you up-stairs? Shall we both go up and go to sleep?" Xavier asked. His vocal cords had started to hurt from talking so quietly. But he really wanted to do something for her.

"Your father didn't, either," the mother said quietly, still holding on to the counter. "Once every four or five months, and then in a very special way. Well, he was afraid of having children—that's why he could only do it in that special way."

"Oh, Mama," Xavier said, "he's dead anyway. It doesn't matter any-more. He's dead."

"Yes," she said, "he's dead. He is, anyway."

She pushed aside a bottle of liquid detergent. Her mouth was dry. Cut-ting into your own flesh dried you out, like walking in the desert. She had friends in her bridge club who were going to go walking in the desert two weeks from now, and then spend two weeks at the beach to recover from the desert. Lazy vacations were better when you had something to recover from. If you came out of a concentration camp, all life would probably be one long, lazy vacation.

"What can I do for you?" Xavier asked. "Please, tell me, aren't you cold? Shall we have a cup of tea?"

He came another step closer; there was still half a yard between him and his mother. On the kitchen floor he saw a few drops of blood. Some-where in the distance a dog barked.

"I want you to look at me," the mother said. "I want you to take a good look at me, so you can paint me. Later on. Then I want you to paint me the way I am right now, in the kitchen. You mustn't tell anyone—no one must know—I just want you to paint me."

"Okay," Xavier said. "I'll do that, Mama. Don't worry. I'll paint you as you are in the kitchen. Exactly the way you are now. That's how I'll paint you. As often as you like." He felt that he needed to keep talking, as though to keep from having to hear his mother's next request, as though he didn't want to hear anything else at all.

"Sorry," she said when he was finally finished talking, "sorry for the inconvenience."

The mother moved the dishtowel a little to one side again.

Xavier wanted to hug her, to hold her, to hold her tightly and not let her go for the time being, but he didn't dare: he was afraid that she would start playing with knives again. That she might take something out of the dish rack and stab it into her flesh again, maybe a fork this time.

"You look like your grandfather, do you know that?" she said.

She eased up carefully on the dishtowel; the blood was starting to clot.

"Do you want something else instead of tea?" Xavier asked.

"Sometimes genes will skip a generation," the mother said. "Our genes have skipped a generation. You're exactly like your grandpa, the same look, the same nose; a handsome man your grandpa was, a hardworking man, and extremely conscientious."

"Yes," Xavier said. "I've been blessed with good looks. That's nice." He looked at the mother gratefully, as though the blessing had been her doing, as though his looks had been built to her specifications, as though she were the architect of his body and his face.

"Go on upstairs," the mother said. "I need a little time to freshen up."

She stepped carefully out of her pajama pants. The kitchen floor was cold. The stained dishtowel she put on the counter.

There were several wounds on her left thigh, but one of them was the biggest, one of them was her favorite wound. She loved her wounds the way other people loved their children, the way other people loved their pets.

Xavier didn't go away, he couldn't move. He wanted to hug the mother so badly, but she said again: "Go to your room now. I need to be alone for a little while."

They heard footsteps upstairs. Marc was awake. They remained quiet until they heard the toilet flush, then footsteps again, and a door being pulled shut.

The mother's new boyfriend was a sound sleeper. No wakeful nights for him.

"I thought about poisoning you once," the mother whispered, still holding on to the counter with both hands. "When you were still a baby. I had already bought the rat poison, the strongest I could get. I thought: I'll mix it in with the milk. I had stopped breastfeeding pretty quickly, because you sucked my nipple raw. Did you know that? You sucked it raw, my nipple. Of course, you couldn't help it. Still, that's what you did. Because you were so greedy, so wild. I thought: It will be better for both of us. I decided against it. I'm sorry."

"You don't have to be sorry, Mama," Xavier said, as quietly as he could. "You don't have to be sorry about anything. It all turned out fine."

"Yes," said the mother, "it turned out fine. Lots of mothers think about things like that, Xavier. I'm really not the only one. In nature you also see mother animals biting their sick babies to death. A sick child is a burden to everyone; a sick child is a burden to itself. If your father hadn't been so grumpy and withdrawn, I could have talked to him about it calmly, but you couldn't talk to him at all. That's why I decided and went ahead and bought the poison. At the shop, they didn't suspect a thing. I said: The strongest rat poison you have, please; they're awfully hard to get rid of. It dissolved quite quickly—all I had to do was stir. I mixed it with lots of sugar. I figured it probably tastes bitter, the poison. That's what they always say, isn't it? That it tastes bitter? And I sat there like that, the bottle in one hand and you on my lap. You were wearing green pajamas with a little bear on the front, a present from the neighbor lady. A horrible thing to look at, but I dressed you in them anyway—it would have been a waste to throw them away. Besides, she came over to the house sometimes, and I didn't want to offend her. You should never offend people, Xavier. So you were lying there in my arms, crying, because you were hungry. And I knew for sure that it was all for the best, I didn't doubt that for a moment. But then I was suddenly reminded of your grandfather, how he valued life so highly; he would never have wanted that. Life was sacred to him. He said: It doesn't matter—even if all I can do is swallow, I want to live. So

I poured the milk with the rat poison in it down the toilet. I kept the rest of the poison just in case, but it never came up again. In any case, there was never another moment when I was sure it was the best for all concerned. I had my doubts often enough, but then I thought: Forget it, today isn't the right day for it. And then, at a certain point, you were too old for it. Rat poison works best with babies. The bigger the child is, the more resistance it has. That's why you're still alive."

"I understand," Xavier said, still not daring to come any closer. "I understand completely. I'm glad you told me this. It's not a problem, Mama, it's no problem at all."

The mother nodded. She seemed to be thinking about something else.

"But, Mama, you're glad, too, aren't you?" Xavier asked. "Or are you sorry? That you poured the milk down the toilet, I mean? The bad milk."

"Things go the way they go," the mother said. "I had to flush twice, and then I had to scrub the toilet. The milk had splattered on the bottom of the toilet seat. Your father was very adamant about clean toilets. He always looked at the bottom of the toilet seat, because he didn't like splatters. Go on upstairs now. I have to freshen up."

"Okay, Mama," Xavier said. "I love you so much. You're the best mother I could wish for. Really the best. Don't ever forget that."

He meant it, too. It just so happens that you love the people who have spared your life. Besides, it's easier to love those who hate you, or who don't feel much for you except indifference, than to love those who love you. Nothing is more unbearable than love.

"I'll never forget this," she said. "It's very sweet of you to say so. You're probably right, but people don't understand that. They don't know how nature works. Sick little animals get bitten to death." She started cleaning the wound on her thigh. She became absorbed in it, as she did in the washing of teacups and the making of chamomile tea. She seemed to have forgotten that her child was there, just as she forgot the poison, the milk, the baby on her lap, the bottle in her hand, memories that she couldn't place, that she had never wanted to place.

.   .   .

XAVIER DID NOT crawl into bed; he sat down at his desk. Picking up a pencil, he drew a picture of the mother standing in the kitchen with her pajama pants down around her ankles, feeling life flowing through her. But because the drawing didn't please him, he crumpled it up and threw it away.

Then he started in on a letter to Awromele. He wrote that his mother had planned to poison him when he was a baby, but that she had changed her mind at the last minute. There was no use denying it, he was proud of it. Other parents had never even thought about poisoning their babies. It was a badge of honor.

Xavier was the baby she hadn't poisoned. That baby he had been, that baby he would remain. After a while, Xavier went to the bathroom to look at his face, his hair, his chest. So this was what people looked like who had sidestepped their fate. Fascinating. There was fate, there was the baby, and there he stood now, the product of those two. The fate that had been sidestepped. Someone had outsmarted it.

Remarkably enough, it also felt like a loss to him, because now he would never know what it was like to lie dead in his mother's arms. He had a sneaking suspicion that his mother would have loved him more as a dead baby than she would have loved anyone else. That she would have felt so much love for the dead baby in her arms, who now, at last, was no longer bothered by stomach cramps, that that love would have been enough for the whole world. That was the love Xavier had missed out on because he had gone on living.

Saddened by these thoughts, Xavier went back to his room. There was no sense in bemoaning that life anymore—it was over. The milk had been poured down the toilet, the rat poison had been flushed away and disappeared into the sewer, there was nothing to do about it.

He wrote to Awromele and asked him to meet him next Thursday at two o'clock, on the Mittlere Rheinbrücke.

When you had almost drunk rat poison as a baby, you could toss your pride to the wind. Pride no longer mattered anymore. Xavier had to talk to Awromele, he needed to see him.

Downstairs, in the kitchen, the mother was scrubbing the spots out of her pajama pants. She wondered whether maybe she should poison her boyfriend, but smiled at the thought. It had been such a long time since she'd tried to poison anyone. It seemed like so long ago that she had mixed the poison into the warm milk. She had been a rather good-looking woman, even after the baby was born. The day she had decided to kill her baby, she had spent an hour and a half at the hairdresser's.

She laughed out loud, and the sound of her laughter did not startle her. For just a moment, she experienced real pleasure.

Upstairs, Xavier closed his letter to Awromele with the words: "I need you."

"I need you." he wrote one more time, just to be sure. And then again: "I need you!" With an exclamation point. But when he looked at his letter again, that final exclamation point seemed only to stress the impotence of his need.

IN THE PRISON, the guards found Mr. Schwartz's body. They cursed under their breath. Suicides were such an inconvenience.

Customers' Memory

IT WAS FRONT-PAGE NEWS in the country's biggest tabloid: "Pedophile Lenin Hangs Himself in Cell."

The executive board of the Committee of Vigilant Parents bought ten bottles of champagne in order to throw a little party. The executive board felt that death was never a reason to celebrate, but that, in this gruesome exception, Schwartz had brought it upon himself. Xavier's mother, the honorary member, did not show up. A member of the board called her and urged her to come—he said the mother was "indispensable" on an evening like this—but she wasn't feeling well. "I'm sorry," the mother said, "I'd be pleased to join you some other time."

Awromele and his father were deeply affected by the death of Mr. Schwartz. Awromele's father said, "There was no way I could have helped; no matter what I did, it would only have made things worse." He said that to his wife, then to a few of his children, and finally he said it only to himself.

Awromele sat on his bed, under the blankets, and thought. He thought about Xavier's circumcision, and knew that it had not been a particularly good idea to let Mr. Schwartz carry out that procedure. Somewhere along the line he had made a mistake. Overlooked something important.

He waited for the sorrow to come, but it didn't, so he addressed himself instead to Mr. Schwartz, even though he could no longer hear him. Empathy that arrives too late is better than no empathy at all. "Dear Mr. Schwartz," he said. Then he said something unintelligible, the unintelligible words turned to humming, and then the sorrow came anyway. "I'm so sorry," he whispered to the wall beside his bed. The wall was yellowed and badly in need of paint. "I'm so sorry." He kept repeating those words until he felt that all the regret had flowed out of him.

We don't speak for other people, only for ourselves. We speak to ourselves without pause. The idea that anyone else hears us is an illusion, the way color is an illusion to a blind man and Mozart an illusion to the deaf. The world is filled with endless monologues, Awromele realized. Then he had a practical thought: if any more circumcising was to go on, he would wield the knife himself. He had no experience, but his hands didn't shake, or hardly at all, and that was something in itself.

Awromele had smoked hash on occasion. He'd never really liked it much, and a boy from the synagogue had warned him: "Never become friends with your dealer. Before you know it, your dealer's in prison, and then you've got a problem. Then you have to visit him, and bring him fruit and matzos at Pesach."

Never become friends with your dealer. That had been an important lesson in life for him, maybe the most important lesson of all. The rest was elaboration and frill.

MR. SCHWARTZ WAS hurriedly interred in a windy, deserted corner of the Jewish cemetery. The corner for dubious corpses. There weren't many people there, only a few pesky reporters who had decided that even Mr. Schwartz's burial was news, Awromele's father and Awromele himself, that was all. Mr. Schwartz had had no friends or family. He had had customers—many customers, in fact—but customers have a short memory. Awromele realized that, there in that windy corner of the cemetery. He felt it not only as theory but as an incontrovertible truth.

While Awromele was saying the prayer for the dead, quickly and embarrassedly, he realized that he had hastened Mr. Schwartz's demise, and that that was putting it mildly. Awromele was the kind of Jew who ran through the rituals too hastily because he did not believe in their power to heal, but who also dreaded the horrifying emptiness of a life without them. He thought about Xavier's legs, which he had held tightly while Mr. Schwartz performed the procedure with shaky hands. Mr. Schwartz had had to fetch a magnifying glass in order to see what he was doing. Missing Xavier caused him more pain than Mr. Schwartz's death. The thought of that put him to shame. As soon as the funeral was over, he combated that shame by crawling back under the covers.

WHEN XAVIER'S LETTER arrived at last, Awromele dragged it to his bed the way a predator drags a carcass to its lair. He ate four of his mother's homemade cookies before opening the letter under the blankets. Reading the letter made him happy. It was a feeling he'd never had before, at least not in this way. He had been content before, but really happy, no. Later, he would call it one of the most wonderful moments in his life. The Jews were not particularly sold on the devil, but angels existed—lots of them, in fact—and Awromele had heard that the devil was nothing but a fallen angel. He had heard that the devil wore beautiful garments that didn't smell of *cholent* or *perenkugel,* that he was more charming than the best Jewish marriage candidate you could imagine. Awromele had dreamed that the devil would bring him to life, because he wasn't really living yet—translating jokes with clits in them into Yiddish was amusing, but it wasn't living. And after that he would tame the devil, the way his mother had finally tamed the rabbi.

When Awromele read in the letter that Xavier's mother had tried to poison her son as a baby, it didn't disturb him. To have escaped death at such an early age was a sign of strength. He was used to people's being floored by adversity. It had floored them all—his father's autism, the war, his brothers and sisters, who were, in his eyes, often little more than walking adversities, his religion (safe enough to say, his origins)—it was all adversity. His whole life, Awromele had been looking for a sign of strength. He longed to have normal parents, like Xavier's.

Awromele tidied himself and his bed, drank two cups of tea without sugar at a nearby coffeehouse, and, purely out of nervousness, ate a bar of chocolate. Then he read Xavier's letter three more times. He felt like writing back right away, he felt like writing: "I'll be there, Xavier, I'll be there. From now on, on the Mittlere Rheinbrücke, any hour of the day, even on Yom Kippur."

He felt like calling Xavier to shout that same message through the phone, but he remembered his friend's admonition and realized that he should keep a low profile. It wasn't a good idea to seem too eager. It would be better for him to hide his eagerness.

He waited for Thursday the way other Jews wait for the Messiah. Never before had waiting made him so happy. To make the waiting even more pleasant, he bought himself a white shirt and a pair of gym socks. He still looked like an Orthodox Jew, but when it came to his socks he was already pretty well assimilated.

He also placed a call to the publisher who had expressed interest in the Yiddish translation of *Mein Kampf*. Awromele thought it would be a good idea to give his meeting with Xavier at least a semblance of something businesslike. And he would urge Xavier to resume his Yiddish lessons, he resolved. Xavier hadn't learned the future and past tenses yet, and it would be a waste to stop so soon.

This time, it was Awromele, not Xavier, who arrived early at the bridge. He had washed his hair; he was wearing his gym socks and his new shirt. He paced in circles on the bridge like a leopard in a zoo.

One hour before they were to meet, Xavier had launched into a new painting of the mother with testicle in hand. He now had three mothers with testicle, but it seemed wise to him to create an entire series. The creative energy that coursed through his veins knew no moderation, and he considered that to be his strength. Once he'd decided to have himself circumcised, he'd had himself circumcised; once he came up with the plan to paint a whole series of mothers with testicle, he painted a series, and having come up with the brilliant idea of comforting the Jews, there would now be a whole lot of comforting going on.

The time did not seem ripe, however, for a series of mothers mutilating themselves in the kitchen. For all his immoderacy, he was a practical being.

The mother was sitting perfectly still in her chair. "Use me for your art," she had told her son.

Xavier was looking forward to his rendezvous with Awromele, but he had other things on his mind as well. His newly discovered talent for painting; the mother, who got up in the middle of the night to do strange things in the kitchen; the rat poison she had once mixed with his milk. Strangely enough, though, that only made him love her more. Even though he couldn't help wondering, each night at dinner, whether she might have sprinkled poison on the rice, or whether the croutons floating in the soup might not actually be chunks of rat poison. That made life more exciting, more intense.

The idea that each night could be his last, even if it was only an illusion, gave his life something he had missed in his parents' house: Vitality. Tragedy. Redemption from the desperate sense that this was nothing but a pointless game.

But the mother had no intention of sprinkling poison: that period of her life was behind her now. She had found happiness in the arms of the bread knife. Her son had no way of knowing that—her son didn't want to know that, not really. In that respect he was like so many others: it was all right to see something, all right to catch a glimpse of the abhorrent, the unspeakable, but not to let it get through to you, no, that would not help.

"I'm going out in a minute," Xavier said. "We'll finish this painting another time, okay, Mama?"

He had asked her to look at the jar while she was posing, and she had done so. She had kept looking at it, too, even while he was trying to talk to her. He took King David out of her hand and put him back in his usual place. She hardly seemed to notice.

"Mama, are you listening?" he asked, just to be sure. "I'm going out in a minute; we'll finish it some other time."

He put the easel in the hall, so no one would bump into it. Then he went back to the living room, where the mother was still sitting in her chair. She was staring at King David. What a measly testicle my son had, she was thinking, what a joke, that testicle. That the Committee of Vigilant Parents could have made such a fuss about that.

She thought about saying this to the boy. It would only help to toughen him up. But she decided it was too much bother. Besides, what good would it do?

The boy put away his brushes and paint.

"What's it like to love someone?" the mother asked, still staring at King David. Her hands were folded in her lap. She liked posing; it may have been her real calling, even though her son's paintings didn't seem to her to amount to much. But perhaps Xavier, unlike King David, would grow to a kind of fullness. You could never tell. You could always hope for a miracle.

"What it's like?" Xavier asked. He looked at the dried paint under his fingernails. He had to clean them before meeting Awromele. "I don't know," he said. "You should know better than I do. You've been married, you have a boyfriend. What Bettina and I had was never really serious, dear Mama."

Ever since she had told him about the attempted poisoning, he had started addressing her as "dear Mama." A mother who was prepared to poison her son had to love her son a great deal. Murder, as far as Xavier could see, was the logical extension of love. In fact, without murder, how could you really be sure that love had ever existed?

"Yes," she said, "you're right. I should know that. Where are you going?"

"I'm meeting some people from school."

In the bathroom, he quickly cleaned his nails, washed his face, brushed his teeth, and decided: Even if Awromele isn't waiting at the bridge, that's okay, too. You can comfort people, but you can't force them to be comforted.

. . .

AWROMELE WAS WAITING. He was pacing back and forth, and when he saw Xavier approaching in the distance, he ignored his own counsel, his concealed eagerness spurted out on all sides, and he ran towards Xavier, as though the comforter of the Jews were a train that might pull out of the station any moment.

The boys kissed each other on the nose and cheeks. Then Awromele said, "Look, gym socks." He pulled up his pant legs a little to show Xavier the socks.

"Nice," Xavier said. "Nice socks."

Then Awromele unbuttoned his jacket and said, "New shirt."

"Also nice, very nice. You're looking good." But even as Xavier said that, all he could think of was: How many strange men's weenies has Awromele had in his mouth since I last saw him? How many were there? Twenty, thirty? Fifty, maybe?

Awromele remembered what he had resolved to do, and said: "I talked to the publisher. He's getting more enthusiastic all the time. The spirit of the age is changing, apparently. Have you heard about that? I haven't, but, then, I don't read the paper."

"I don't, either, not much; I only flip through it sometimes," Xavier said, casually taking Awromele's soft hand in his. The obsessive thoughts had him in their grasp.

"How's it coming along, anyway?" Awromele asked, pointing at Xavier's crotch.

"Much better, thank you. I can barely feel it anymore. I'm so happy we had that done. I'm a new man. And better than before. I feel like a complete Jew now, with all the trimmings. But I was wondering. Maybe it's kind of a weird question, but in the last few weeks have you by any chance had the weenies of strange men in your mouth?"

"Strange men? What do you mean?" Awromele stole a quick glance at his socks. He thought they were sexy.

They stood there on the bridge. Sometimes they took a few steps to the left, then a few seconds later a few steps to the right. They circled each other like dogs that don't know where to begin.

"Men in general. Boys. That's what I mean."

"In my mouth? No, of course not! What makes you think that?"

"Well, you put mine in your mouth, so I thought maybe you did that more often."

"No. I only did it to you out of curiosity. You weren't circumcised yet, and I'd never seen smegma; I'd never tasted it, either. I'm the kind of person who doesn't want just to see things, I want to taste them, too. My brothers are more abstract, but I'm the practical one. I want to touch things, and once I've touched them I often want to taste them, too. Do you really like my socks?" Awromele pulled up his pant legs again, so Xavier could see his socks.

"Yeah, they're great. But do you, for instance, want to touch me?"

Awromele let his pant legs fall back into place. "Yeah, in principle, yeah. I'm very inquisitive." He pressed his lips to Xavier's for a moment, but caught himself and said: "We need to talk about those Yiddish lessons. You don't learn a language by taking a couple of lessons and then stopping for a few weeks. Continuity, that's extremely important. If we're going to translate *Mein Kampf* together, we're going to have to meet a few times a week—in the park, for example—and then we'll have to buckle down and teach you some Yiddish."

"You're right," Xavier said. "That's exactly what we're going to do. But first we're going to go for a walk." He took Awromele's hand. "You have thin wrists."

"It runs in the family. My mother's wrists are also very thin."

"What kind of woman is your mother, anyway? I don't have a very good picture of her."

"What kind of woman is she? What do you think? She gave birth to thirteen children—she's tired. That's the kind of woman she is."

They crossed the bridge in the direction of town. There they caught a tram. In one of the outlying districts, they hopped off and walked through a park that was unusually quiet, because the weather was so drizzly.

"I missed you," Xavier said. "I really missed you."

"I missed you, too," Awromele said. He took Xavier's head in his hands, and as he did so, he broke. That was how it felt: he tore loose the way wallpaper tears loose, he peeled off like paint. As though he had been broken in two by Xavier's words, by the head he was holding, the indescribable scent of a person that he would recognize in any case because he had held Xavier's legs for so long while Mr. Schwartz performed his operation. As though his weakness refused to be concealed any longer, as though he could no longer hide the pain he'd hidden from the eyes of the world so successfully all this time, as though he'd sprung a leak, as though now, finally, for the first time, he coincided with the pain he didn't feel, the way a deaf person sees lips moving but doesn't hear the sound, as though he had forgotten that it even existed, that anything like pain even existed at all. Behind his endless joking, his lightheartedness, his energy (at least to the outside world; when the outside world wasn't looking, he climbed into bed with his clothes on and ate chocolate), behind all his stories and plans, there turned out to be something, something horrible, a sickness, a hole better left unopened. In a flash he caught a glimpse of who he was, a glimpse of himself from head to toe, naked, no more stories, no plans, no jokes, and what he had seen was a missing person. Missing in action, that was him, he saw someone who was no longer there, who had actually never been there at all, and who never would be there. It was this that made him feel nauseous, that made him deathly ill, in fact; he screamed like an animal at the slaughter. In the quiet park he screamed, holding Xavier's head in his hands for just a moment, then pushing it away. His screaming was high and loud; it cut through everything, then it died out. "Go away," Awromele shouted. "Go away, don't come to me with your feelings. We have a business agreement: I give you Yiddish lessons, then we're going to translate *Mein Kampf*, and in return I was allowed to taste your smegma. And that's it, do you hear me, that's it!"

Then Awromele took off running.

Cold and Wet

XAVIER STOOD THERE on the gravel path for a few seconds. He thought that Awromele would stop and turn around, that it was a joke, a game, that he would come back again as soon as he noticed Xavier wasn't chasing him. But Awromele wasn't running in order to come back, Awromele was running to disappear. And when Xavier realized that at last, he started running, too. He ran across the wet grass, straight through newly trimmed rosebushes, down paths, between trees, across mushy patches of lawn, shouting: "Awromele, stop! You misunderstood me. You misunderstood me completely."

But his voice was heard only by the bare trees, and a few passersby who had braved the biting wind and the drizzle: a nurse out walking a lady in a wheelchair, a mother with her child.

Awromele ran faster than he ever had during the occasional gym class he hadn't skipped at school, faster than he had run as a child after ringing someone's doorbell for a prank, even faster than he had the time he'd stolen a chocolate Easter egg from a shop. His mother had made him bring back the egg, but he had been unable to find the shop. Now he had no idea what calamity he was running from; all he knew was that he had seen something he never wanted to see again.

Xavier was catching up with him. He was in better shape than

Awromele, and unlike Awromele he had on sturdy leather shoes fit for mountain walks, and for kicking. Besides, he was a poor loser, and today he had no desire at all to lose, he didn't want to lose Awromele, not now, maybe never. When you start looking at the world from a certain perspective, everything is about winning or losing. For a long time, Xavier had thought his relationship with Awromele wasn't about that, but now he knew that he'd been mistaken. In order to comfort Awromele, he first had to defeat him.

Xavier ran and thought about King David. He saw the jar in the bookcase, he saw his missing body part hanging above him, big as life, and that body part, blue and inflamed, amputated, sick yet still alive, seemed to call to him: "You can do it, Xavier. Run—you won't get a second chance. Run, comforter of the Jews, run!"

Xavier ran like blue blazes, not allowing himself a moment's rest, the way his grandfather had fought tirelessly against the enemies of happiness, for something that was bigger than himself, something outside himself, an ideal, a fantasy that could no longer be distinguished from reality, that had become reality itself. All ambition begins with the fantasy that you can be a different person from who you are now: defeated and beaten, without a future, and, in a certain sense, without a past as well. It's the fantasy that lifts you up, drags you along, lifts you to greater heights than you'd ever thought you would reach, then leaves you behind like an empty bag. Any careful observer will see that we are merely tools in the hands of our fantasies. And it may be not even our own fantasies that we're fulfilling, but the fantasies of others, people we've never known and never will know. We fulfill the fantasies of phantoms.

Under the spreading boughs of a pine tree, Xavier caught up with Awromele at last. He jumped on his back, pulled on his blond hair, screamed his name, shouted a few of the words in Yiddish that he could still remember. He yanked and tugged on the struggling body that was still trying to run away, until Awromele fell to the ground at last. There he lay, on top of old pinecones, rotten leaves, moss, twigs, an empty soft-drink bottle, mandarin-orange peels. The ground was cold and wet, but Xavier

had no eye for the mix of garbage and decaying nature. All he saw was
Awromele, his face, his eyes, the pin curls. His mouth, his nose, his hair.

Xavier threw himself on top of Awromele and pushed his Yiddish
teacher's head against the ground. There were streaks on Awromele's
face, even a little blood on his throat, where Xavier had sunk his nails into
his flesh without thinking about it, the way the mother went looking for
pain in the kitchen, concentrating only on the deed itself, no more outside world, no bridge club, no memories, only the bread knife and the
thigh, a glorious vacuum.

"Awromele," Xavier said. "Awromele, what are you doing?"

The most important thing is to know what can't be taken from you, and
Xavier had decided that Awromele could not be taken from him. They
could take everything else, father, mother, home, nourishment, the roof
over his head, but not Awromele.

"What are you running away for?" Xavier asked. He had his hands
around the throat of the boy they couldn't take from him, and he pressed
gently against Awromele's Adam's apple. It had to hurt. It definitely had
to hurt—he wanted a confession, and confessions do not come without
pain. He wanted the truth, no more games. As though the truth ruled
out games.

"Why did you run away?" Xavier asked again. "You don't have to be
afraid of me." He let go of Awromele's throat. Awromele still didn't say
a word. He lay there looking at Xavier's face, at the head he had held in
his hands not so long ago and then quickly let go of, the way you let go of
a hot casserole.

"You don't feel anything?" Awromele asked quietly. His throat still hurt
where Xavier's fingers had squeezed it. He had a stitch in his side, his
mouth was dry, his head was pounding. There was disbelief in his voice,
as though he feared that Xavier might feel something that shouldn't be felt.
As though it couldn't be possible. As though it were too good to be true,
a lie, meant to take you in and then, once you've been taken in, to cough
you up again, to gobble you up, to make you a prisoner and a slave, be-

cause there's nothing harder than letting go of the lies for which you've sold yourself.

"What do you mean?"

"You don't feel anything?" Awromele asked.

"No," Xavier said. "I don't feel anything. Not now, and not ever. I've never felt anything." He brought his face down closer to Awromele's; he pressed his lips against Awromele's, roughly, the way a plumber presses together two lengths of pipe before welding them together. He stuck his tongue in Awromele's mouth; his tongue ran in circles around that mouth like a mouse in a plastic bag.

That is how their lives looked, that's how they lay there. They were experiencing all kinds of things, but because there was no time to think about it, because there was no way they could possibly think about it, because he was there but at the same time not—not enough, in any case—Xavier had the idea that, if only for a second, he was experiencing nothing all over again. That he was still waiting for something more real; something inevitable, something you couldn't refuse. That's why he thrust his tongue even deeper into Awromele's mouth, as far as it could go—to experience something, to find out what that was like.

Then he realized what a richness it was, Awromele's mouth, and his tongue was a richness, too, but a strange, stupefying richness. One too good to be true, and therefore probably just another lie.

Xavier pulled his tongue out of Awromele's mouth. "I don't feel anything," he said again. "That's the truth. Never in my life have I felt anything. I don't know what it is." He pulled on Awromele's hair, but not hard enough to tear it out. He tugged on it playfully, as though Awromele were a little animal.

Awromele wriggled out from under Xavier. His clothes were wet and dirty and torn here and there. There were mud spots on his gym socks. But Xavier pushed Awromele back onto the ground, onto half-decayed pinecones that animals had gnawed on, onto the peels, the apple cores, a ballpoint someone had lost or thrown away.

"We mustn't feel anything," Awromele said after Xavier had sat down on him again. "That's the most important thing." He was still short of breath. From running, from Xavier's weight, from the glimpse he had caught of himself. He never wanted to see himself like that again. As a stranger.

"We won't feel anything," Xavier said. "I promise, in my family almost no one feels a thing; it isn't hard to do, it happens by itself. We'll never feel anything."

Again he pressed his mouth to Awromele's like a plumber; he took Awromele's head in both hands like a sink that needs to be installed. He wasn't sure where aggression ended and tenderness began, he didn't know where death began and life ended, he no longer knew whom he hated more, himself or the boy lying on the moist ground and the apple cores. All he knew, but that he knew for sure, was that Awromele could not be taken from him. He was as certain of that as he was that he would comfort the Jews.

He licked the mud and the blood from Awromele's face, like a cat cleaning its kittens. He ran his tongue across Awromele's skin as though he wanted to taste everything, and couldn't stop tasting now. Tasting— maybe that was the same thing as experiencing.

Awromele closed his eyes, because Xavier's tongue was gliding over his eyelids. When he opened them again he said: "If we start feeling anything, we have to stop. As soon as we feel anything, we should never see each other again; then it will be like we've never known each other; then we have to forget each other completely; and then we have to tear up and burn every shred of evidence that shows we ever met."

"Absolutely," Xavier said. "But it's not going to happen. We'll never feel a thing, believe me." He tugged at Awromele's black plastic belt, he unbuttoned the black trousers. Awromele's father had trousers just like these. A pair of white underpants peeked out at him. The sturdy kind, underpants that had seen the inside of a washing machine on hundreds of occasions. He slid the underpants down carefully and murmured: "Never will we feel a thing, Awromele, believe me. We can't feel a thing. Where feeling starts, we end."

Awromele's sex wasn't stiff, but it was circumcised. Circumcised differently from Xavier's—better, more carefully, not as roughly, more neatly healed, that above all. Xavier stuck it in his mouth like a meatball, greedily but not too fast.

Xavier sucked, but tasted nothing. No taste, no skin, no special texture. And he thought, just as he had while lying on Mr. Schwartz's bed: Accept, O Lord, this humble sacrifice.

That was how Xavier lay there, in the park, between Awromele's legs, and at the same time he was somewhere else. On Bettina's bed. He remembered how he had adopted the two villages in India. Why did he have to think about that now? It disgusted him; he should stop making those donations. Otherwise he'd think of India every time he put a weenie in his mouth.

Awromele's sex gradually stiffened in Xavier's mouth. That was pleasant. The satisfaction of having someone else's sex expanding in his own mouth, the sensation, the hardness, he never wanted to forget that. He sucked harder.

"Ow," Awromele shouted. "You're biting me."

Xavier stopped sucking. He climbed up from between Awromele's legs and sat on his stomach again. "Sorry," he said. "I'm sorry. It was an accident. I wanted to taste you—I'm just as inquisitive as you are—that's all. I want to taste everything, too. Everything, everything. Everything."

He leaned down to kiss Awromele, and for a second, perhaps only a fraction of a second, it seemed as though he was finally able to forget who he was. His father's death, Marc's love, his mother's knife, nothing existed anymore, only Awromele's mouth.

When the kiss was finally over, when he finally took his mouth away from Awromele's and they could both take a deep breath, the world began coming back to Xavier.

At that moment, Awromele screamed, loud and high, the way he had screamed when he'd caught a glimpse of himself. He screamed like an animal in distress, and maybe that's what he was. But Xavier wasn't about to be put off by screaming. Awromele could scream as much as he liked, as long as he remained lying there, as long as he still belonged to Xavier and Xavier alone. He pushed his face into Awromele's crotch and snuffled like a dog. The apple cores, the filth, the mandarin-orange peels, the passersby—none of this mattered to him.

Xavier took the circumcised sex in his mouth again and sucked and licked obsessively, as though it were a contest, as though tenderness and aggression were made of the same substance, as though it were a prayer, a prayer to something nameless. Not a God, no Almighty, only something absent, something nonexistent, a prayer to a jar of pickles or a roll of tape, a prayer to an empty soft-drink bottle, a psalm as desperate as the most desperate prayers in this world.

Awromele submitted to it the same way Xavier had submitted to his circumcision, first as an act of torture, later in a state of partial numbness, and still later as something pleasurable and horrible as well, that, too. Something terrifying that it might be better to abolish. As if he felt that it would compromise him. He knew that the greatest minds had been felled by pleasure, that the memory of pleasure had led them to forge bonds they had never meant to forge, to go down paths they would never have taken in a moment of clarity, because pleasure distorts, pleasure is the biggest liar in this world.

And Awromele knew that he was in danger, that he had never been in danger the way he was in danger now, here in this park, on the ground. He screamed again. Higher and louder than before.

With Awromele's sex in his mouth, Xavier moved his head back and forth as though it had become a runaway steam engine, as though pleasure now consisted only of that one high scream from Awromele's lips, a scream that hurt the ears so badly that it could only be a scream of horror. But Xavier heard in it something very different: doubt. Awromele's cry was more than the cry of an animal, or of a eunuch lying on the guillotine, hearing the knife come hissing down, seeing his life pass before his eyes and realizing that he had done it all wrong. In Awromele's cry there was more than just horror. Xavier suspected that this was closeness, nothing more than that, this scream that made him think of the slaughterhouse.

Awromele's sperm flowed slowly into Xavier's mouth. Xavier went on sucking. He didn't know when to stop, he had never known when to stop.

Then the movements of Awromele's lower body told him that the pleasure had turned to irritation, to pain. He raised his mouth to Awromele's and kissed him, clumsily, but with passion. Neither of them tasted much— nothing special, in any case—at most something thicker than spittle, spicier, too, and of a higher specific gravity.

Sperm Dies Fast

IN THAT SAME PARK, a group of four boys were taking a walk after school, to smoke a cigarette and talk about friendship. They did that quite regularly, smoking, walking, and talking. They weren't very old, fifteen or sixteen at most. A little younger than Awromele and Xavier. They were likable boys who viewed the five minutes to come with the same fear and trembling as they did the remote future, but who carried on nevertheless, the way boys their age do.

The tallest of them, a boy with a wispy mustache and a gray ski jacket, said: "Hey, do you guys hear that?" He had heard someone scream in the distance. Screams like that weren't heard often in the park. Sometimes a dog's name was called loudly. A mother running after her child and desperately calling out her pet name for him—they'd heard that often enough. But screams like the one they'd just heard were new. And exciting.

The boys were fond of the out-of-doors; they had carved their names in tree trunks and sometimes in the benches that had been donated by older, wealthier citizens of the town of Basel. Eternity to them was a wooden bench in a park.

The boys paused to light their cigarettes, and heard more screaming. It wasn't far away now. Still passing the lighter from hand to hand, they looked at each other. They heard it and they shivered, the way you shiver when you see a needle penetrating flesh.

"Let's take a look," the tallest boy said. Life was boring enough as it was; when you had a chance to take a look, you shouldn't miss it. They were fond of looking. At each other, at other boys, and at women whom they tried to imagine without clothes, or at least in a swim suit. All dreams are a prison, but the sexual dream is the smallest prison of all—a badly lit cell that always reeks of human excreta.

It didn't take them long to find the source of the screaming. It was a disgusting source, they were in agreement on that right away—no need to waste breath about that. They sneaked up closer and looked at what was lying there on the ground. Two boys. One of them was lying on top of the other. They weren't fighting, although it looked like they'd fought. But the fight was over now. The one on top had beaten the other. The boys looked at it the way you look at an animal you've hit on a deserted country road. What were you supposed to do with it? Drag it away, take it along, drive off? Skin it?

They sneaked up even closer. Horror has the drawing power of a rare butterfly.

What they saw then stirred their emotions. They had never seen anything like this, not in the park, and not outside the park, either.

Xavier thought again, Accept, O Lord, this humble sacrifice—even as Awromele's sperm was dying in his mouth. Sperm dies fast. He no longer heard a thing; he was absorbed in his thoughts, in the heat of Awromele's body, in the taste of the spittle, the scent of the earth; that was why he hadn't heard the boys approach. He was immersed in his illusion. A few seconds, then a few seconds more, just one more moment, please, just a moment.

The tallest boy leaned down and tapped Xavier gently on the shoulder. Xavier looked up. All four of them grinned; you could see their teeth, flawless teeth; they had been raised with fluoride tablets, and they all flossed at least once a week. The tallest one nodded to Xavier reassuringly, as though to say: Don't worry, we only showed up here by accident anyway.

Xavier swallowed the sperm and rose quickly to his feet. He arranged his clothing, looked at the strange boys, and wiped his mouth, an instinctive gesture.

The tall boy who had tapped Xavier on the shoulder said, "Hi." And he held up his hand, a clumsy, almost poignant gesture.

Awromele saw none of this; he was still lying on the ground, his pants still pulled down awkwardly around his knees. He was stunned. His thoughts were elsewhere—on the promise they had made, Xavier and he. If we start to feel something, we have to stop. That was how it was, that was how it had to be.

"Hi," the tallest boy said again. He looked reticent, as though he felt uncomfortable about the whole situation. As though he was sorry about having crept through the bushes, but now that he was here anyway, it wouldn't be polite to just walk away. The other boys said hi as well. They felt the overwhelming excitement of the unknown.

Xavier had swallowed, but he could still taste the sperm in his mouth. He knew what the boys had seen, even better than they did. He would never forget what they had seen. He took a step back.

They looked at him thoughtfully. They stood in front of him the way people stand in front of a painting in a museum: they'd seen the reproductions, but the real thing is so much more impressive.

"We're not interrupting you, I hope?" the tallest boy asked.

Their faces were shining with joy. They radiated vitality.

Xavier shook his head slowly, and stepped back a few more inches.

Now the boys took a step forward. The hijinks they had witnessed had given them new energy. They were feeling reborn. They wanted to get closer to Xavier.

"We don't want to interrupt anyone," the tall boy said. His friends nodded. The tallest one spat on the ground, and one of his friends, who had borrowed his father's blue raincoat that morning, pulled the belt a little tighter.

"If we're bothering you, just tell us," the tallest of them said. And he spat on the ground again.

They were smoking, all four of them. They smoked and they looked. They were well dressed for boys their age. A little too primly, perhaps, but these boys liked to dress well. They were not afraid of work; what they wanted was eternal friendship, a house, a child, and a wife, no more than that, perhaps a car or two. One for shopping, the other for longer distances. Everything they wanted could be achieved, if only one worked hard enough; that was why they dressed so neatly when they went for walks in the park.

"We said hi," the tallest boy said. "We don't say hi to just anyone."

"We don't say hi to almost anyone," said the boy in the blue raincoat, inhaling greedily. Never had a cigarette tasted so good to him.

"Hi," Xavier said. More to himself than to the boys. It dawned on him how wonderful Awromele's mouth had tasted. Bettina's mouth had always had something dry and cheesy about it, as though the drought of the subcontinent had stuck in her craw. He noticed how special the sperm of the Jew tasted when one let it melt on one's tongue. Melting was perhaps the wrong word—sperm didn't melt. It wasn't ice cream, more like a little bonbon.

"We want to talk to you guys," the tallest boy said. He tossed his cigarette on the ground and stepped on it. "At least, if you want to talk to us. Would you like that, to talk to us? Are you two guys a little lonely?"

The other boys tossed their cigarettes on the ground now as well.

On the ground, Awromele was busy pulling up his pants.

Xavier looked at Awromele, at his legs, his hands, his pretty hair, and all he could think about was that one desire: to forget everything. That was the best he could hope for. To lie between Awromele's legs and forget everything.

"It's nothing to be ashamed of," the tallest one said, "being lonely. It happens to the best of us. The important thing is how you deal with it, what you make of it. There are so many ways to be lonely." He sniffed; the cold air was making his nose run, and he didn't have a handkerchief.

The other boys chimed in. "We're all lonely sometimes," said a smaller boy, whose voice was still changing. And the boy in the blue raincoat said, "Come on, let's shoot the breeze a little, no obligations." He made little jabbing moves, like a boxer. His friends pounded him on the back till he choked.

"Would you guys mind going away?" Xavier asked. His voice sounded timid, but he knew what he was asking. His voice at this moment sounded like that of his father, the architect, who preferred to be silent and used his voice primarily for handing out orders. Always remain polite: your subordinate is a person, too.

"That's not very nice," the boy in the blue raincoat said, looking around at his friends as though trying to assay the degree of Xavier's unniceness.

"We don't appreciate that," the tallest boy said. "We come here to offer our friendship, and the only thing you can do is ask whether we'll go away? We're just as fond of these bushes as you guys are. No, that is really not nice, the way you're treating us."

At that same moment, the tallest boy lashed out. He hit Xavier in the eye. Unexpectedly, and not very expertly.

The tall boy was furious. The senseless suffering of others filled him with hatred. To him, the time seemed ripe for meting out blows.

Xavier staggered but didn't fall. He stood bent over, holding on to a branch. First there had been only amazement, then shock. The pain came only later, the pain skipped along behind.

"We came here to talk to you," the tallest boy said. "But then you guys have to let us talk. A good conversation is a two-way street." He rubbed his hand. The punch had hurt him. It was never pleasant to have to punch someone in the eye.

Xavier saw that Awromele was still lying on the ground, trying now to fasten his trousers. The boys approached slowly, like a bride and groom coming down the aisle. Then Xavier did what he should have done before, long before, maybe even at the moment Marc had moved in with him and his mother: he started running. Away from the boys, away from here. Away from everything.

He ran as fast as he had when chasing Awromele, but this time he didn't shout that it was all a misunderstanding. Xavier ran without a word.

He could still hear how Awromele had screamed, how he'd screamed when Xavier was lying between his legs, high and loud, as though he would never stop screaming. As though, for the rest of his life, this was how we would approach the world: by screaming. Xavier ran, propelled now not by a fantasy, but by the only thing stronger than fantasy: fear.

Two of the boys started after Xavier, but the tallest one said: "Let him go. We still have this one to talk to."

Awromele had buttoned his pants by now, but he still lay shivering on the ground, waiting for what was on its way. The thing that was usually on its way was sorrow. Indefinable, and for no clear reason. But now something else was on its way, something stronger than sorrow, with clear boundaries, with a precise time limit, something about which you could say: It lasted from four-oh-five to four-oh-nine.

"Why do you scream so weird?" the tallest boy asked.

The four boys were standing around Awromele, and seeing this peculiar figure lying on the ground added to their joy: His gym socks with their mud spots, his torn and spattered shirt, his excessively long hair, his too-pale skin. His youth. Talking to older people is nice as well, but talking to young people is much more pleasant; young people are less set in their ways.

So familiar but so horribly strange—that's the way Awromele lay there on the ground. But to their questions there was no reply.

Awromele tried to get up. They used their feet to push him back onto the spot where he had lain with Xavier on top of him.

"Are you sick in the head?" the tallest one asked. "Is that what it is? Are you sick in the head, is that why you scream so weird? Don't be afraid, you can tell us."

His voice sounded gentle, as though the idea of Awromele's being sick in the head made him feel melancholy. And that was true. So many people were sick in the head. And people who were sick in the head were pathetic.

A strange excitement took hold of the boys, the excitement of life itself, the excitement that accompanies the crossing into borderlands. What stopped here, and what began? Where would it go wrong, how far could you go before breaking something, which branches would hold your weight, which others would snap and break?

"Spit it out," the boy with the wobbly voice said. "Are you sick in the head? Do you want us to help you?"

Awromele had no answer to their questions.

"Loneliness is nothing to be ashamed of," the tallest one said, and spat in Awromele's face.

Then the other boys began spitting on Awromele as well, in his face but also on the rest of him. They gathered spittle in their mouths and spat without pause, like people with a task to perform.

Then they started laughing. Quietly and shyly, later loudly and with abandon. They felt free; their unbearable lives seemed bearable for the moment, although they couldn't have told anyone what was so unbearable. Probably that one thought in particular, the one they couldn't shake: That life could be different. That they were missing the best of it. That they had already missed the best of it.

Between gobs of spit, they asked Awromele questions and whispered to him encouragingly. "We're your friends. Now that you've met us, you'll never have to be lonely again."

The tallest boy was particularly adept in his attempts to soothe Awromele. "We will always be one of your warmest memories." He had soothed so many people, he knew how it went. He was standing close to Awromele's head.

When they were finished spitting, when spitting had lost its charm the way a new love ultimately loses her charm and becomes as horrifying as the one before, the tallest boy took a few steps back. Then he ran up and kicked Awromele in the ear as hard as he could, as though Awromele's head were a football.

Awromele was too late to raise his arm and protect the side of his head. Blood came dripping out of his right ear.

"Our friendship is everlasting," the tallest one said solemnly. "Nothing can detract from that friendship. From now on, we belong together. You enjoy our protection." It was important to reassure people. They needed that, in whatsoever state they found themselves, come rain or shine. Reassurance.

The tallest boy swung his foot back again and kicked as though taking the definitive penalty shot in an important match. But this time Awromele protected his ear with his hand, so the tall boy's shoe hit the hand instead of the ear.

A bone in his hand broke. Unnoticed. In passing.

"A good conversation is a two-way street," the tallest one said. "We communicate with our feet. Do you understand? Can you hear us?" He saw the blood dripping from Awromele's ear and wondered whether the boy could still hear him. Maybe the ear was clogged with blood. He wasn't a specialist when it came to ears, so he began speaking slowly and clearly: "Kierkegaard said that the surest way to say nothing was not to be silent but to speak. That's why we talk with our feet. We're afraid of saying nothing. What do our mouths have to offer you? Empty promises, the devil's whispers. Our feet offer you true friendship. Don't say no to the friendship of our feet."

The boy whose voice was still changing whispered, "Yeah, Kierkegaard." As if it were goat cheese from the Bern highlands, available only a few months a year.

The other boys, too, said quietly, "Kierkegaard." They giggled.

A boy's bone isn't hard to break, especially when one is being a bit playful. It starts off as a game and, whoops, there goes the bone. The language of feet is a wonderful, albeit rudimentary, thing.

The other boys could not stand by idly; they kicked Awromele in the ribs, the legs, the stomach, the head, but with less conviction than the tall boy. They did it hurriedly, as though they actually wanted it to be over soon.

Awromele's body rocked like a ship on the high seas whose captain has lost control of the rudder. But he had stopped screaming. His left hand had swollen like a balloon.

Then the boys stopped. They spat one last time, but the magic was over. Finally, they threw dirt on Awromele's body, though they didn't go on with that for long. The ground was too wet—they didn't want to get dirt under their nails.

"We'll be going now," the tallest boy said. He looked for the last time at his new friend, lying still on the ground. "Loneliness is nothing to be ashamed of," he said quietly. "But from today on, you'll never be lonely again. Wherever you go, you'll always think of us, you'll never forget us. We will be your best friends, even if you never see us again. We will always be with you." Saying these words made him feel good. He brushed a few strands of wet hair from his forehead.

"Man is a social animal," the tallest boy said to his friends as he searched for his lighter. "Life is all about communicating. It doesn't matter what part of your body you use to communicate, as long as there's communication going on. We need each other, we can't go off sneaking through the jungle alone." He breathed deeply, in relief. He had found his lighter, a gift associated with some fond memories.

The boys walked away. When they got back to one of the paths, they all lit their cigarettes. They were filled with wistfulness. A gentle rain was falling.

AWROMELE'S BODY WAS lying beside the mandarin-orange peels. It didn't move. He had his arms crossed over his face. Blood was dripping from his ear. The ear and the hand hurt. The rest felt numb.

After a minute or two, when he was sure that the boys were gone, he took his arms away from his face.

There were scrapes all over his body. His body looked like one big scrape.

"Xavier," he shouted hoarsely. But there was no reply.

"Xavier," he shouted again. Nothing.

Darkness was falling slowly.

"Xavier," Awromele screamed, as loud as he could, but the screaming hurt his ribs.

"Come out. Where are you?"

Xavier couldn't come out, for at that moment he was running through the streets of Basel as though he were being chased, as though they were coming after him to blacken his other eye as well.

When he got to his house, he stopped, searched for his keys with shaky hands, opened the door, and ran upstairs, without saying hello to his mother.

Xavier took off all his clothes, avoiding the mirror, and took a hot shower. Only when the water was pouring over him and he stared at his own body did he think about Awromele. How had lain there in the park, under the tree, his pants down around his knees.

"Awromele," Xavier cried then, "Awromele." But the sound of the water drowned out his words.

In the kitchen, his mother was breading a schnitzel.

Without a Flashlight

ONCE AWROMELE REALIZED that Xavier was no longer there, that he hadn't hidden behind a tree, he could have struggled to his feet and dragged himself home. But the only protest he could think of against the treatment he'd been given, against the friendship the boys' feet had offered him, was not to get up, to remain lying there where he lay.

Awromele rolled onto his side and pulled his legs up. The movement caused him pain. He didn't dare look at his left hand. He didn't dare look at anything. He felt bad enough already.

Every once in a while he screamed, but his cries were no longer high and penetrating, not like when Xavier had been lying between his legs. It was a powerless hollering, to which the passersby paid no heed.

While Xavier was warming up in the shower, examining his body, and coming to the conclusion that he would not be able to use his blackened eye for a while—he didn't dare dab at his eyebrow again, it had felt like sponge cake—he thought about Awromele. His dearest, that's what he should call him: of all the Jews Xavier would comfort, Awromele was the one dearest to him.

A comforter is not supposed to run away; a comforter should protect. If he had been able to think clearly, he would definitely have stayed in the park, he would have thrown himself on Awromele like a bodyguard on his president. But he had not thought clearly, and now it was too late.

Maybe, Xavier thought, maybe the boys only wanted to talk to Awromele; maybe I was the one they were after. Maybe they just offered him a cigarette and asked him a few questions about the Day of Atonement. Jews were no longer in fashion, but you always had young people who didn't quite keep up with fashion. Yet this thought, too, failed to ease his mind.

Xavier had run away, that's what he had done, run away just as he had brought Awromele into his life: on impulse, without thinking about the consequences. But if he had let himself be kicked to death, the Jews would someday have no comforter. He had saved his own skin in order to protect them later, twice over.

Xavier dried himself quickly and, after he had put on his underpants, mustered up enough courage to look at himself in the mirror. His one eye had indeed turned blue, almost black, and his eyebrow looked torn. He dripped some iodine onto the eyebrow and took two aspirins, he hesitated for a moment, then popped a third one into his mouth.

As he dressed, he thought about Awromele. He hid his soiled clothing under his bed.

In the kitchen, the mother was breading a third schnitzel. She heard her son coming down the stairs and couldn't repress her feeling of disgust. "Dinner is almost ready," she shouted.

Xavier went into the kitchen. The mother had the schnitzel in her hand, already breaded, now to be fried. In fact, cooking disgusted her as well.

"I have to go out for a minute," Xavier said. "Marc's not back yet anyway." He wanted to protect the mother from unpleasant discoveries. Only when he had truly become a comforter would he tell her everything. He would rock her in his arms, the way he would one day rock the Jews.

The mother dropped the schnitzel into the pan; the fat hissed and spattered. She looked at her son and saw his black eye.

"What happened to you?" she asked, picking up an oven mitt. "Did you get in a fight?"

"A little accident," Xavier said. "Nothing to worry about. I'll be back in a bit."

"Don't be gone too long," she said. "We're going to eat soon."

She spoke mechanically, like a machine. She looked at the lettuce, which she had washed three times already. She was afraid of accidentally eating little insects.

THE ROUTE BACK to the park Xavier took running as well. It was dark. The aspirin hadn't helped his headache, which had been located only behind his eyes at first but had now spread to the rest of his head as well.

With every yard he ran, his melancholy grew. When he arrived at the park, he went looking for the place where they'd lain beneath the pine tree, but couldn't find it. He remembered where they had stood when Awromele suddenly took off running, but not where they had run to.

It had all happened so quickly. The way two bottles of wine will usher in forgetfulness, he could no longer remember what had happened between the moment Awromele had run from him and the punch in the eye. Maybe you could get drunk on sperm as well if you kept it in your mouth long enough.

He shouted his friend's name. There was no one walking in the park anymore; the only sound was the wind, and distant noises from the street.

In the study at his home, the tall boy who had mistaken Awromele's head for a football was reading Kierkegaard. He was holding a pencil and marking certain passages.

"Awromele," Xavier shouted, "where are you?" Just as loudly as Awromele had shouted Xavier's name only half an hour earlier.

In his mind's eye, Xavier saw a dead Awromele, a corpse, cold and stiff and cleaned by the funeral attendants, but he suppressed his fear by telling himself: Of course, he's gone home already, he's probably sitting at the dinner table with his twelve brothers and sisters, he's probably forgotten everything that happened in the park by now. I'm getting all worked up about nothing.

Xavier walked across a lawn he had crossed when he was running after Awromele, but halfway to the other side he could no longer remember whether it was the right lawn. There were so many lawns in this park. His eyes were smarting. The bruised one, and the other one, too.

He stepped in a pile of dog shit, or maybe a molehill—he didn't see it, it didn't interest him anymore, either. He slipped, fell to the ground, got up, ran on, and shouted again, as loudly as he could, "Awromele."

In the kitchen, the mother was putting three schnitzels on a platter. Marc had come home; he was upstairs, at the computer, taking off in a 737. His mouth was hanging open in concentration.

AWROMELE DREAMED. Images blurred together, he heard snatches of conversation, but wasn't sure whether they were real or whether he making them up on the spot. The blood that had come out of his ear was clotting. His left hand had stopped swelling, but he couldn't move it anymore. He had to let the hand dangle, the fingers—the whole arm, really. The slightest movement caused him pain, but he didn't have enough energy to worry about that. For the first time in a long time, he wasn't worrying about anything at all. He wanted to disappear, to dissolve, to become one with the mandarin-orange peels and the empty Coke bottle.

The cut on his ear was slowly turning into a black scab. He was dreaming, he was sure of that now, about the cleanser his mother used to scrub the sink, or, rather, about the way that cleanser smelled, and then about a field trip he had taken in the school bus, long ago. They had gone to visit a rabbi who some people said could heal people.

Xavier walked into the bushes. He was afraid that a late passerby or a policeman would mistake him for a rapist. He had the feeling that he had ruined everything. Without Awromele, all was lost. Stupid of him to have left home without a flashlight, stupid to have run away. And why? Simply because of a stupid punch in the eye. He was furious with himself; he tolerated no faults in himself, strove for perfection in everything, but above all in his relationship with Jews.

He squatted down beside a bush; he couldn't go on. All the running and searching had exhausted him. His head had become a zooming bumblebee he wished he could swat and kill.

Nausea grew inside him. Still, he shouted one last time, very loudly: "Awromele, where are you!" His eyes were watering so badly that even if it had been daylight he couldn't have seen a thing. But he didn't cry.

Awromele was not far away, fifteen or twenty yards at most. Awromele dreamed that someone was calling his name, but because he wasn't sleeping, only trying to forget the pain and humiliation, he realized after a few seconds that someone really was calling his name. It wasn't a dream, it was real, like the pain in his ear. His ear felt as though it were being sawed off. He'd never known ears could hurt like that.

Awromele knew who was calling him; he recognized the voice. That voice was one he would always recognize.

For a moment he felt the urge to cry out, for a moment he felt an intense joy, for a moment he felt like shouting: "I'm over here, Xavier! Help me!"

But he stopped himself. He was not going to move. He would remain lying there without a sound. He would punish the one who had betrayed him. His pride was stronger than his desire. This was the only meaningful protest against a world that had given him something he did not deserve, and which it was therefore right for him to spurn. His parents would be worried, but he didn't care; they needed to be punished as well.

Barely twenty yards away, Xavier vomited until his stomach was empty. He threw up all over his shoes, and got a little on his trousers as well, but he couldn't see that; it was too dark to see.

After he had thrown up everything he had in him, he walked home. For the first time in his life, he suffered. At last he was up to his bellybutton in the pool of suffering, and all the future he could see promised more of the same. It tasted the way the last bits of vomit in his mouth had tasted, so bitter that it hurt his throat.

THE MOTHER AND MARC had finished their schnitzels. The boy's schnitzel was growing cold on its plate.

Xavier came in, washed his hands, rinsed his mouth, and sat down at the table.

"What happened to you?" Marc asked. He looked at Xavier's eye. Then he got up and laid a hand on Xavier's shoulder, to give the boy some support. Xavier began eating, reluctantly. The meat was gristly.

"Isn't your schnitzel cold?" Marc asked, after glancing at the mother and returning to his seat. He looked at the mother like that more often lately, as though to make sure he wasn't going too far.

"No, it's fine," Xavier said. He choked down the meat, bite by bite. He did it for the mother, who had spent all that time over a hot stove.

"Come on," Marc said, looking at the mother again, "we'll heat up that schnitzel, it will only take a minute."

"It's fine like this," Xavier repeated. He gagged, and hoped that no one noticed.

The mother thought: I'll smack him over the head with a frying pan. I should have done that a long time ago. Long ago. When he was still a child. That would have saved me a lot of grief. One solid blow with a frying pan, that would be enough. She looked at the wooden bowl, purchased in Pisa, that still held a few leaves of lettuce. She restrained herself.

"Buddy," Marc said, "who did this to you?"

His mouth full of meat, Xavier said, "No one."

Marc wanted to know everything. When you love someone well, you want to know everything. "Who hit you? You can tell me, and your mother, too. We can keep a secret."

The mother looked at her boyfriend. Despite her self-control, she felt herself growing livid. She said: "Did you know that he broke my nose, Xavier? You didn't know that, did you? Yes, Marc broke my nose. I don't hold it against him. Do you think my nose looks any different?"

There was no reaction. Xavier chewed on his gristly schnitzel. Marc was blushing, but no one noticed. The mother took a deep breath before going on: "The doctor says it will heal slowly. Well, I'm in no hurry. But before we start fussing over your eye, I thought I should just let you know."

She had said nothing about it until now, about the incident with her nose. She had found it too embarrassing, a boyfriend who broke your nose, and a boyfriend like Marc, a namby-pamby like him. But now she poured out her feelings. It didn't make much of a difference. She felt no different from the way she had before she said it. Filthy, that was it, filthy through and through.

"I can't see anything, Mama," Xavier said. "Really, I can't. You look beautiful. Much better than you did a couple of weeks ago. Don't you think so, Marc?"

Marc smiled shyly. He played with his silverware. As a boy, he had done a lot of magic tricks. He had also been quite good at juggling. But that was all behind him now, now that he had discovered the flight simulator.

"I'm sure he didn't mean anything bad by it," Xavier said. "Did you, Marc? You didn't mean anything bad by it?"

"No," Marc said. "I really didn't mean anything bad by it."

The mother ran her fingers over her nose. Even as she did, she was ashamed of the gesture, and dished the last few leaves of lettuce onto her plate. She had made the salad dressing herself; she hated dressing from a jar or a tube, no matter how much work it was for her to make it herself.

"It has to heal slowly," the mother said. "Well, then, we'll just have to wait, won't we?" She began chewing on her lettuce.

Marc rested his head on Xavier's shoulder. He felt an overwhelming need for warmth, but not from the mother. Not all human warmth is equally welcome. "It was an accident," he said, his head still on Xavier's shoulder. "I would never do it again. I was confused about my sexual identity; that's why it happened. Now I've found my sexual identity. Now something like that could never happen."

Xavier gently pushed Marc's head away. He thought about Awromele, wondering where he was now and whether Awromele would ever want to see him again. For the second time in his life, he felt suffering. It changed the world, made everything dull, reeked of death.

"I'm a sensual woman," the mother said with a bitter little smile. "But my sensuality wasn't appreciated. You can't force sensuality on anyone, it's take-it-or-leave-it. Now I'm sensual for myself, and I'm not missing a thing." She looked triumphant. Victorious.

"You mustn't say that, Mama," Xavier said. "You really mustn't say that. I'm sure there are people who appreciate your sensuality. Papa, for example—he stayed with you all those years, didn't he? Men like sensual women. You just have to give them time."

The mother laughed in a way that frightened Xavier.

"I gave him time," the mother said. "And Marc, too, all the time in the world. And what did he do with it?" She looked at her boyfriend. "He played with the flight simulator." Again she laughed. Not long, and not cheerfully, either.

Marc bowed his head. "I hadn't found my sexual identity yet. The thing is—not just with sexual identity, with all kinds of identity—you're not born with it, you have to find it gradually."

Xavier was feeling increasingly ill, the headache had not gone away, and Marc's words were only making it worse.

"I'll paint you again real soon," Xavier said. "Mama, are you listening? I'll paint you again real soon. And this time I'll paint you as a sensual woman."

Marc went to stand behind his stepson and massaged the boy's shoulders. One hand slid into Xavier's shirt.

"You're tickling me," Xavier said, but Marc pretended not to hear. Xavier didn't dare repeat it—he was afraid of drawing his mother's attention to something to which she would be better off not paying attention.

"Your son," Marc said, "is a gifted artist. Right now we're the only ones who know it, but soon the whole world will know." He pressed his crotch against the back of Xavier's chair. "This boy," Marc said to the mother, "this boy has something rare. The fire of art is burning inside him. I have an eye for that, because when you work in radio you see fire like that passing by every once in a while. Not often, it's rare, but every once in a while you see it shuffling past, and that is also a wonderful moment. I am so grateful that you have given me the opportunity to spend my days close to this fire." Then Marc bent over and planted two little kisses on the top of Xavier's head, so the mother wouldn't see how his face was twisted with desire.

That's what happens when you find your sexual identity. You become a predator, the world becomes your hunting grounds, and when you don't have the world you can always prey on your family.

The mother didn't look at Marc. He left her cold. Everything left her cold.

Marc remained standing like that for at least two minutes; he kissed the top of Xavier's head again; he was acquiring a taste for it. Then the mother finally came up with something to say: "Didn't the two of you think the schnitzel was a little tough? Maybe I should try another butcher. This one has started looking at me so strangely, ever since he heard that I'm an honorary member of the Committee of Vigilant Parents."

Xavier tore himself away and stood up. "You're very sensual," he said. "Don't ever forget that. Of all the mothers I know, you're the most sensual."

"I know," she said as she piled up the dishes. "I'm also much more sensual than the girls at your school, a lot more sensual than that Bettina. I always have been. But the world was never interested."

In the kitchen, she put the dishes in the sink, and because she couldn't help herself she took the bread knife from the dish rack and looked at it, the way—in a different world—she might have looked at a man: With love. With desire. With passion.

In the park, the cold was settling deeper and deeper into Awromele's bones. He began shivering, and regretted having wanted to punish the traitor he loved so much, regretted not having replied when Xavier had called his name. That was why he shouted now, "Xavier!"

But Xavier was no longer in the park; he was in the living room, waiting for the mother to come back from the kitchen so he could say good night to her. There was a thin string of gristle between his front teeth, and he plucked at his with his nails. He was feeling dizzy. He hadn't been able to finish his schnitzel, but fortunately the mother hadn't said anything about it.

"Should we put a little ice on that eye of yours?" Marc asked.

Xavier shook his head. He looked at the bookcase, and prayed silently to King David. "King, dear King, please let me find Awromele, let us be together again. Dear King, please."

When the mother came back into the room, he stopped praying and said: "I'm going to bed, I'm exhausted. I had a rough day at school."

The mother stared at the hem of his trousers. "What are those spots on your pants?" she asked. "Did you soil yourself again?"

Xavier looked at his trousers. "I was walking in the park," he said. "The grass was wet."

"You're going to the dogs," the mother said. "Don't forget, Xavier, that you have only one testicle. You will always have to do your very best, because other men have two." She smiled, and for a moment she looked truly sad. Then she looked at King David, up there beside Schiller, and all her sadness disappeared. She caught herself feeling sorry that her son hadn't lost both his testicles in the hospital. That would have taught him a lesson; then he would have been another person, once and for all. Failing to experience enough loss in your life turns you into a swine.

"I'll never forget that, Mama," Xavier said. "And I'll never let myself go to the dogs, either. I know that I have only one testicle, and that's why I'll always do my very best."

"Some people," the mother said, "have only one kidney, and they have to be very careful with that kidney, because if they lose it they don't have anything left. You're down by a point, Xavier, and you'll never catch up." She said it dreamily. Xavier kissed his mother good night and went to his room.

· · ·

SITTING ON THE BED in his well-furnished room—a little TV, a bookcase, a fan, a jar of paper clips in all different colors—the tall boy took off his shoes and said to himself, "Man can no longer speak with his lips, but he has learned to talk with his feet." The thought satisfied him. He took off his sock and rubbed his right foot until it grew warm. "Speak, feet," he said. "Speak. I'm all ears."

He squatted down to hear what his feet had to say, and as he did that he was filled with the awareness of finitude, of absolute finitude, not only his own, but of everything. He could almost smell the finitude; he could, if he was very still, hear the finitude creeping up on him. The realization of that made his life grander, and important. For a single moment, he believed he could take on the world, squatting there beside his bed and listening to the language of the future, the language of feet.

Xavier crawled into bed naked, laid a hand on his sex in order to hasten sleep, and decided not to think about Awromele. Otherwise it would become an obsession.

Downstairs, in the kitchen, Marc was helping the mother with the dishes. As he dried a plate, he said to her, "It's good for our relationship to be able to sort of chitchat."

Jerusalem

AWROMELE'S PARENTS couldn't sleep. Earlier in the evening, they had gone to the police station. The officer on duty there had said: "Just take it easy and wait. If he's not back by tomorrow night, come by again."

After that, the rabbi had called the members of the Committee of Vigilant Jews. He was afraid that the anti-Semite had struck; he could think of no other explanation for his son's disappearance. He wasn't the kind of boy simply to run away—he had always been content to lie under the blankets in his room.

During a few of those leisurely hours in bed, Awromele had translated the first few pages of *Mein Kampf* into Yiddish, but the rabbi knew nothing about that. He thought the boy had been studying the Mishne Torah or the Pirke Avot. But whatever he had been doing in there, the anti-Semite had struck now, that much was clear to the rabbi.

For years, Awromele's father had lived in dread of the moment the anti-Semite would strike. Sometimes he would wake up in the middle of the night and shake his bald wife until she awoke. His wife had shaved her head so that her wig would stay put. Her husband was the only one allowed to see or touch her hair, but she had shaved her head anyway, just to be sure. She had no intention of showing her real hair to anyone; hence the wig. Not even to her husband. Especially not to her husband. And in the middle of the night, the rabbi was therefore able to ask the bald woman beside him, "When was it that the anti-Semite was going to strike again?"

On some days it was no longer clear to him whether he was waiting for the arrival of the Messiah or the anti-Semite. In some strange fashion, the fact that it had finally happened came as something of a relief. The anti-Semite had come, he had arisen from his rat hole and shown his true colors.

Just before midnight, the most active members of the committee gathered at the home of Awromele's parents. Some of them wanted only a Coke or a Fanta, but others asked for vodka. It was an animated gathering. Bettina had been recruited as well. Whether it was India or the Committee of Vigilant Jews, she applied herself 100 percent. She was one of those people with a keen sense of responsibility.

In addition to Bettina, the committee had a number of other non-Jewish members who sympathized, for any number of reasons, with the Jews. One man had joined because there was no other club that would have him for a member.

"We have to go looking for him," the members told each other. "Awromele has fallen into the hands of the anti-Semite."

"Or into the hands of the PLO," said the man who couldn't join anything else. He had already knocked back four vodkas, and with each glass his decisiveness grew.

"Why did he pick Awromele? We're not Zionists," said Awromele's mother. Her eyes and hands were red; nervousness immediately triggered her eczema. "Why is the PLO homing in on us? All we want is the Messiah. Until then, there's nothing else we want, and certainly not a Jewish state. Only the Messiah, that's all. Is that asking too much?"

One of Awromele's younger sisters, a girl with braces on her teeth, said: "It doesn't even have to be a big messiah, not the kind that performs miracles. A little one would be okay too." And an even younger sister, Rochele, said: "I want a messiah who can fly. Then I'll climb on his back, and he'll take me to America in two seconds. Then I'll say: Dear Messiah, now I want to go to the North Pole, where the Eskimos live. And then I'll climb onto his back again, and he'll fly me right to the North Pole."

The rabbi pounded his fist against the wall, so hard that flakes of paint fell to the floor. "Rochele, don't sin against God," he shouted. "The Messiah isn't a private jet. And that you should talk like that on the day your brother has disappeared!"

"Stop screaming, Asher," his wife cried. "Don't get yourself in an uproar. Think of your heart!" Then she turned to the other members of the Committee of Vigilant Jews and said, "My husband is autistic—he can't help it."

The rabbi pounded his fist against the wall again, even harder now, so that even more paint fell. The baby of the family awoke with a shriek. "How dare you say that!" the rabbi shouted. "How dare you accuse me of being autistic? And that on the day that Awromele has been kidnapped by the anti-Semite! And God only knows what the anti-Semite has been up to with our son."

The rabbi's wife took the baby from its cradle and stuck a pacifier in its mouth. The baby calmed down soon enough; it was used to shouting. "But, Asher," the rabbi's wife said, "everyone knows you're autistic. It was even in the synagogue newsletter. The whole congregation knows. There's nothing wrong with being autistic. I've been living with an autistic man for thirty years. They're people, too!"

The rabbi muttered under his breath and poured himself a glass of cola.

"I could just as easily have said," his wife went on, "that you fooled around on me for years with my own sister, until she died of a horrible illness that I don't wish to name out loud right here. My own sister, and if she'd been prettier than me, okay, but, no, she was older and uglier, God rest her soul. And her personality was worse, too. It's a mystery to me what you saw in her, but I don't go around saying things like that, because that's no one else's business. All I said was that you're autistic. And that's the truth. That's all I'm saying."

"No, no," the members of the Committee of Vigilant Jews said to each other, "we don't want to hear this, we don't want to know. We came here to help look for Awromele."

The rabbi said nothing more, only shook his head and took little sips of cola. Between sips, he muttered furious curses at his wife and his family. "Okay, so tell them," he shouted at last. "Tell them everything. Tell them I embezzled funds, for all I care—you can't keep your mouth shut anyway."

Rochele, who was standing in one corner of the room with a doll in her hand, said, "I know for sure that the Messiah is a bird."

Her brothers and sisters laughed at her. "What kind of a bird?" they wanted to know. "A parrot, I bet it's a parrot, or is he a sparrow? Or a pigeon?" They named all the kinds of birds they knew and laughed wildly. There was never much laughter in this household, so when the opportunity presented itself they took full advantage of it.

"No," Rochele said, "a tropical bird. I know for sure. I dreamed about it."

The rabbi's wife put the baby back in the cradle, picked up Rochele, and said to her guests: "Maybe the Messiah *is* a tropical bird. Who knows what kind of tricks the Almighty is willing to play on us? Maybe He'll send us a messiah in the form of a tropical bird, because of our sins." As she said that, she stared pointedly at her husband.

The committee member who had signed up only because no other association or club in Basel would have him, asked: "But what kind of tropical bird? Doesn't the Torah give us a clue about what kind of tropical bird we should be looking for?"

Then the rabbi pounded on the wall a third time and shouted: "Enough of this nonsense! Enough, or I'll throw you all out of the house. How dare you talk about the Messiah like that on the day the anti-Semite has struck? The Almighty is not going to send us a messiah in the form of a tropical bird, no matter how much we've sinned—He would never do that. The Messiah is a man of flesh and blood, not a bird, not a hippopotamus, and not an elephant, either. Don't ever talk like that again, not if you hope for a long and prosperous life."

At one-thirty in the morning, the members of the committee left the house to look for Awromele in groups of two or three. Some of the members took the search seriously. They waved big flashlights back and forth and shouted at a few automobilists, "Dirty anti-Semites in your fat BMWs!"

Three other members, including Bettina, felt that a search only made sense if you had a plan. They stopped in at a kebab place run by an Egyptian. They hung out at the bar of Jerusalem Kebabs, waiting for a plan to come to them. But it didn't come.

The Egyptian had chosen that name for his restaurant because he was planning to liberate Jerusalem, once he had earned enough money selling kebabs. The place he'd had before was called Bethlehem, the one before that Nazareth, and before that he'd even had a restaurant called Jericho. The time was ripe, he believed, for doing things in a big way: Jerusalem Kebabs. Twenty seats, standing room for thirty.

Like Bettina, the Egyptian was a virtuous person. Part of his profits he donated to Hamas charities. His conscience bothered him on occasion, and when it did he tried to soothe it by supporting Hamas, which did a lot of good work in and around the Occupied Territories.

After making a donation like that, he would feel better, and could go back to boosting his market share in Basel without being bothered by scruples. He had to work hard, because the competition was capable of almost anything. His donations to Hamas were really only symbolic, a couple of thousand Swiss francs here, a couple of thousand Swiss francs there. He had opened a Swiss bank account for them. No self-respecting charity could get by these days without one of those. In Switzerland the Egyptian's donations wouldn't have gone far, but in Gaza you could buy a couple of Uzis for that money, from Israeli soldiers who didn't mind a reprimand in return for a month's supply of hash. Any soldier serving in the Occupied Territories needed hash as badly as he needed a weapon.

Many of the Egyptian's best customers were Jews, and he got along wonderfully with them. Money doesn't discriminate. He had even made friends with some of them. He sent them cards at the Jewish New Year. He could even speak a few words of Yiddish.

Three members of the Committee of Vigilant Jews were now sitting at his bar, talking about the Middle East and the exchange rate for the dollar, as though both the Middle East and the exchange rate were some wayward woman who refused to listen to their good advice.

One of the committee members, a bald man who had dropped out of law school and now worked in an office as an archivist, said to the Egyptian, "Hey, pal, how about a few of those M&Ms?"

The Egyptian tapped on the counter the way croupiers do in the casino, to show that he'd understood the code. He went to the back room, opened the refrigerator where the M&Ms were kept hidden behind a big bottle of condensed milk, and brought back a few. The bald man handed the Egyptian a pile of banknotes and retired to the men's room.

"What are you people doing out so late?" the Egyptian asked. He poured himself a glass of tea. "Is it already time for carnival?"

Bettina said, "We're looking for a boy." She was from a staunch Catholic family, and had been raised in a village, Ilanz, not far from the town of Chur, before her family had moved to Basel when she was twelve. She said proudly: "The anti-Semite has struck. We're looking for our rabbi's son."

"Oh," the Egyptian said. "That's terrible. That breaks my heart. We're cousins, did you know that? We come from the same family. You've heard that before, I guess?"

The Egyptian's wife ironed his shirts. He liked to wear white ones, with the top buttons always open, even in winter. The hair on his chest was grayer than the hair on his head; he was pleased with the hair on his chest, felt that it lent him a certain authority, something mystical, something he couldn't quite put his finger on. In any case, women seemed impressed by it.

"Abraham was your patriarch, but he was ours, too. So we're family," he said.

He took Bettina's head in his hands, pressed it to his chest, and said in his deep voice: "I feel for you. What's your name?"

"Bettina," she whispered. In a short time, she had learned so much about Jewish history that she could relate ten-minute anecdotes about famous Jews at the drop of a hat.

The Egyptian felt the urge to stick his tongue in Bettina's ear, but restrained himself. "Bettina," he whispered, "would you like a couple of M&Ms too?"

"How much does it cost?" she asked. She had heard from other members of the committee that Jerusalem Kebab sold more than just skewered lamb. Happiness, pure happiness, with nothing to be said against it except, perhaps, that it lasted only briefly. The Egyptian named a price. She was stunned. You didn't get rich by supporting and protecting Jews, or by adopting Indian villages, but if the other members of the committee were trying M&Ms, how could she refrain?

"I don't have that much with me."

"Doesn't matter," the Egyptian said with a charming smile, scratching the hair on his chest with his left hand. "There's a cash machine just around the corner. Money doesn't discriminate. Not against me and not against you. That's why we get along so well. I love you people."

The Egyptian thought he was talking to an authentic Jewess. "Everybody hates us," he said, pouring Bettina a glass of peppermint tea. "Everyone is against the Arabs, everyone is against the Jews. The only one who isn't against us is money, and money needs the night the way a man needs a woman. That's why we like the night. The night doesn't discriminate, either; the night is there for everyone. My wife is Swiss; she's from Rapperswil. At first I thought she wanted to marry me because she loved me, because she thought I was handsome, because I *am* handsome and I used to be even more handsome. I have the stamina of six wild horses. But do you know why she married me? Would you like to know?"

Bettina nodded. She wanted to know everything.

"Because money doesn't discriminate against me."

Then he couldn't control himself any longer; he leaned over and stuck his tongue into Bettina's ear.

The moment the Egyptian's big tongue touched her earlobe, Bettina began to giggle. Giggling was always the right thing to do. Her face turned red. That encouraged the Egyptian to stick his tongue even deeper into her ear. Naïveté is a glorious thing. The blushing of a young woman was perhaps as alluring as nakedness.

But Bettina was not naïve. She just blushed quickly, there in Jerusalem Kebabs. For her life began there where the Jew began, but the Arab wasn't exactly chopped liver, either. It was no accident, both of them being Semites. She had suspected that, even back when she lived in Ilanz. And only now did she discover how right her suspicions had been. She'd always wanted to be exotic. She had dreamed about that when she was only nine years old.

After the Egyptian's tongue had licked her ear clean, Bettina felt more exotic than ever. There was indeed a huge difference between theoretical solidarity and solidarity that was put into practice with a passion.

"Hurry up, go to the cash machine," the Egyptian said. "Look, it's almost getting light. It's not a good idea to postpone happiness. Happiness can't take that. It dies."

Bettina slid from her bar stool and put on her yellow jacket. Now that she had joined the committee, she enjoyed wearing bright clothes. It was raining, but her jacket had a hood. She put up the hood and ran to the cash machine.

Five minutes later, Bettina came back into Jerusalem Kebabs and slipped the Egyptian her banknotes. That was all the money she had for the rest of the month, but the important thing was to live. What good was the future if you skipped the present?

The Egyptian shuffled back to the refrigerator, took out a packet of M&Ms, and handed them lovingly to Bettina.

"What's your name, anyway?" she asked the Egyptian.

"Ibrahim," he said, and stuck out his hand. Because he found a handshake rather meager, and because he was pleased to do a little something extra for new customers, he stuck his tongue in her ear again. "But everyone calls me Nino. I used to work at an Italian restaurant in Rapperswil, and in an Italian restaurant you have to be Italian. That's why they call me Nino.

When I go back to Egypt, to my mama, then I'm Ibrahim again, but for you I'm Nino."

BETTINA ENJOYED the feeling of his tongue in her ear more than she had the first time. Life was a table spread before her, and she felt like taking a second helping.

In her bedroom, the baby on her arm, the rabbi's wife was murmuring prayers for Awromele's well-being. The eczema on her hands had spread; her wig was on crooked. She feared the worst; she didn't know how she was going to live through this, or whether she even wanted to.

Only vaguely did she know why she had to live through this—for her children.

The Vegetable Garden

EARLY THAT MORNING, Xavier awoke from the most horrible dream he'd had in months. He got up and looked out the window. It was still raining, and the first morning light was as weak and miserable as Xavier himself. He pulled on a jogging suit and went to the bathroom, where he looked at his eye in the mirror. It was bluer than the night before. What difference did it make? He had lost a testicle—a black eye was the least of his worries. He had to go back to the park.

Xavier was almost sure that Awromele was no longer lying beneath the pine tree. But the important thing was to have looked for him: the comforter's task was to do the impossible. The important thing was to have tried everything. He would never forgive himself if he stayed in bed and waited until after school before going back to the park. The hardest thing is to forgive yourself. Other people you can forgive. After a while, you simply say, "It doesn't matter, let bygones be bygones." And usually it really doesn't matter. But in your own eyes, every mistake is a fatal one, an unforgivable one. That's why you need other people, to grant you what you can't grant yourself: forgiveness. And that was what Xavier wanted to grant the Jews most generously: forgiveness. For all the wrongs they had committed throughout the centuries. For the guilt they had imposed on others. For the almost unforgivable guilt they had imposed upon themselves, by being born.

Xavier brushed his teeth vigorously and splashed on some aftershave. However slight the chance that he would find Awromele, he wanted to smell good for him.

The mother and Marc were still asleep. The mother was sleeping soundly. She had gone down to the kitchen again that night; the game of love had been more intense and bloodier than ever. The love game was becoming lovelier and lovelier, down there in the kitchen. First it had been only lust and infatuation, but slowly it had turned into something real, something deep and abiding. Real love. There was no longer any use denying it—the mother loved her knife.

But Xavier knew nothing about that; he had slept and dreamed of Awromele. He locked the front door behind him. He was wearing his Walkman, it was playing Pergolesi's *Stabat Mater*. Although his headache had not gone away and his eye was still swollen, he knew, listening to the music, that things would turn out all right for him and for Awromele. And therefore for the Jews as well.

Before he started running he said quietly: "I'm going to find you, Awromele. I'm going to find you now; there are no two ways about it, because you're my Awromele."

Then he ran to the park to which he had run the night before, but he ran differently now—not faster, but with more love, more tenderness. And as he did so, there beneath the pine tree, beside the mandarin-orange peels, Awromele was contracting a slight case of pneumonia. His lips were blue, his hands had turned red, but he had punished the world. He had not surrendered his pride.

Because he felt that he had punished the world enough now, he whispered, "Xavier." He had rolled onto his side. His body was stiff and wet; his feet were numb, mud was clinging to his wounds. He had been lying in the rain for more than twelve hours, like a dead animal. He lost consciousness.

Xavier stopped on the lawn where he had stood the night before, but in the morning light he recognized everything and headed without hesitation for the bushes where he had lain with Awromele.

The *Stabat Mater* was blasting in his ears, driving him on. Faster than he had expected, he reached the bushes where he had sworn never to feel a thing.

He saw Awromele's body, lying rolled up, like a fetus. The clothes were torn. The ear, topped with clotted blood like a cherry on a cake, stared at him.

"Awromele," he said, kneeling down beside him. "Awromele." He took his head in his hands, held it, and kissed it carefully. He sat down beside Awromele, laid his head in his lap. Awromele's body felt so wet and cold, as though it had ceased to exist.

It couldn't end like this; nothing could end like this. If people died like this, it was better for them never to have lived at all.

"Don't die," Xavier said. "Awromele, please don't die." He took the boy's hair in his hands and kissed it.

Xavier remained sitting there like that for a few minutes, with Awromele's head in his lap. He had taken off the jacket of his jogging suit and draped it over Awromele's chest. As though he were holding a drowned man in his arms, as though he had arrived too late, hadn't run into the surf in time—that was how he sat there. Every once in a while he asked, "Can you hear me, Awromele?"

Xavier tried to hum. Humming always soothes. He felt as though his own life had come to an end. Xavier felt numbed, far removed from everything, without hope, without faith in the future. He rocked back and forth, the way devout Jews do. "Please say you can hear me, Awromele." As though this was all he needed to do, as though this was what comforting was all about, stroking a few hairs, wiping away a little blood, humming senselessly beneath a pine tree.

He didn't know what to do, where to go, whom to ask for help. Xavier, who otherwise always knew what to do, who was never at a loss for words in the classroom, who had even, he felt, responded appropriately when he caught his mother in the kitchen with the knife, didn't have a clue. All he knew was that he had run away from the boys, that he had taken a shower, and that he had arrived too late.

Xavier used the hem of his T-shirt to wipe the dirt and blood from Awromele's forehead. "Dear Awromele," he said, "don't worry, I'm here now, I won't go away again." He didn't dare to touch the wounds: experts would have to do that later on. He murmured, "You're safe now, they won't come back."

Awromele began shivering. He wasn't dead. His wounds were throbbing like an overheated steam turbine. But when Xavier asked him to stand up, or when he shook him gently by the leg, Awromele didn't react. "You can't stay here," Xavier said. "You'll get sick. This place will be the end of you."

Xavier carefully lifted Awromele's swollen left hand and laid it on his stomach. There was mud and blood sticking to it, but he didn't dare wipe it clean. The hand looked too mangled.

"It's me, Xavier," he said again. He thought that if he said it often enough Awromele would finally hear. "You helped me get circumcised; we're going to translate *Mein Kampf* together. We belong together, and I swear to you, I don't feel a thing, and you don't feel anything, either, Awromele. That's why we belong together. Do you hear me? Awromele?"

After a few minutes had passed, when Xavier noticed that he, too, had started shivering, just like Awromele, he saw that staying in this place was not a good idea. There was no use waiting for a reply any longer. He tried to pick Awromele up. First he pulled on his legs, but the body didn't budge. He heard a joint pop. Xavier put his hands under Awromele's back and tried to pick him up, as though the Jew were a sack of flour, but that didn't help, either. He tugged on his arms, to get him to sit up. Awromele didn't move; his body was unwieldy. His back rose from the ground a little bit, just a few centimers. But when Xavier heard bones cracking again, he was so afraid of breaking anything else that he let the body fall back onto the ground. It fell like a dead thing.

Xavier knelt and murmured: "I'm sorry, Awromele, sorry. I was startled—your bones were making so much noise. That's why I dropped you. Don't be angry."

He laid the swollen left hand back on Awromele's stomach. He put his mouth up close to Awromele's good ear. "I'm sorry," Xavier said. Even in this condition, Xavier could see how gorgeous Awromele was. "I'll be right back. Stay here. Wait for me."

Xavier walked away slowly, remembering when he had run from this spot while the boys were standing around Awromele. He thought he was leaving a corpse behind. When he arrived at a path, Xavier started shouting: "Help, help, there's been an accident."

It had stopped raining at last, although the wind was still blowing. But it was too early for people to be out walking in the park. Even the dog owners had decided to avoid the park for the moment. No one heard him. Xavier ran through the park again, looking for help. An inexplicable rage took hold of him. He saw Awromele's face, the swollen hand, and again, each time anew, the ear that had bled—the ear that had stared at him like a madman's eye. An eye that seemed to demand only one thing: Why did you run away, why you? Why did you have to run away?

And for as long as the ear continued to ask Xavier that unanswerable question, he ran on through the park, screaming for help.

IN THE RESTROOM at Jerusalem Kebabs, Bettina tore open the little bag and looked at the powder for which she had paid so much. She had never done this before. She had seen it in movies, in documentaries, too, and she had read about it in books. She had been planning to do it for a long time—she wanted to experience everything. But now that the time had come, she hesitated. The hesitation was suddenly more powerful than her desire.

She remembered her father's advice, her mother's worries, the prayers of her grandmother who had gone to church every day until she broke her hip, and had then turned her bedroom into a chapel. The real world was suddenly a bit too real for Bettina. Yet she knew there was no going back.

You can leave Ilanz for the real world, but once you've arrived there's no going back to Ilanz.

In the end, she won out over her hesitation. It would be a waste of all that money—she could hardly trade it back in for kebabs. Feeling a slight aversion, she sniffed deeply, as though sampling a rare wine.

It tickled. This expensive stuff, which had cost her almost as much as she earned in a month of waitressing two afternoons a week, reminded her of sneezing powder. Maybe it *was* sneezing powder. Maybe she'd been tricked; maybe the Egyptian had sold her something from the trick shop. Bettina's parents had done their best to encourage their daughter's wariness, and they had succeeded. People were waiting everywhere to cheat you; on every street corner, in every kebab shop, they waited to press counterfeit goods on trusting souls, and she was trusting, because she knew nothing about cocaine. That thought made her cry.

The torn-open sack of M&Ms was lying beside the sink; some powder still clung to the back of her left hand. "It's sneezing powder," she whispered, sitting on the toilet. "It's just sneezing powder. No one takes me seriously."

XAVIER RAN THROUGH the park and screamed: "Help, there's been an accident! Police!" He was running in circles. He didn't dare go too far away from Awromele. Only at the start of his fourth lap around the park did he notice the shed belonging to the Municipal Parks Service. It had once housed two men whose job it was to keep up the park, but as of late there was only one. The parks service was having trouble making ends meet. Beside the shed was a vegetable garden. In the garden Xavier saw a couple of shovels, a few bags of earth, five garbage cans, and a wheelbarrow. He stopped at the fence and stared at the wheelbarrow the way a child stares at creampuffs in a baker's window. The wheelbarrow was rusty, but that didn't matter. With that wheelbarrow, Xavier could roll Awromele all the way to the doctor.

Around the garden, where the park attendant grew a little parsley and chives for himself and his brother—he was still a bachelor—stood a makeshift fence. A few wooden posts and some chicken wire, that was all. An adult could step right over it.

And that is what Xavier did, without taking a running start, without climbing; he hurt himself, he scraped the inside of his thigh, but he didn't even notice.

In the wheelbarrow was a little puddle of water and a few gardening tools. Xavier put the tools on the ground and took the wheelbarrow by the handles. They were rusty as well. Now he had to find a way out of the garden. He could climb over the fence himself, but he could never lift the wheelbarrow over it.

Xavier thought about Awromele, the way he had been lying there beneath the pine tree; he thought about the testicle in its jam jar at home, beside the collected works of Schiller. "King David," he whispered, "give me strength, please, give me strength."

Then he seized the wheelbarrow, rolled it straight across the chives and the parsley, and, with everything he had in him, rammed it against one of the fence posts.

The post shook, but remained firmly in place.

The park attendant had built the fence himself, tapping at the posts with a rubber hammer for a long time to force them deeply into the ground. He was fond of a job well done and took his work seriously, often remaining in the park longer than necessary. The park attendant loved the trees and bushes. And they loved him.

Xavier rolled the wheelbarrow back to the spot where he'd found it and began his second run at the fence post. "King David," he shouted, "stand by me." He trod the chives and the parsley underfoot, but didn't notice: he saw neither chives nor parsley, he saw only the post. He saw Awromele.

The second collision with the post was so forceful that Xavier fell over, into the wheelbarrow. He didn't care; he didn't feel the scrapes and bruises. He scrambled out of the wheelbarrow and took another run at the fence. His lips murmured the name of the King as he saw his inflamed testicle before him again; he didn't notice that he had hurt his hands, didn't look to see whether anyone was watching, forgot that what he was doing was against the law, that he was destroying the vegetable garden of a loyal employee of the city of Basel. He was in a state of ecstasy.

He slammed the wheelbarrow against the post five times in total, until he was able to pull it out of the ground. There was nothing left of the vegetable garden; the vegetable garden had been plowed under; what the rain had not destroyed had been mashed beneath the wheel of the wheelbarrow and Xavier's shoes.

It was fairly easy now for Xavier to push the wheelbarrow over the broken fence. He didn't notice how heavy the thing actually was. He was not accustomed to wheelbarrows, and his only thought was to save Awromele.

Pushing the barrow, he ran to Awromele. His dearest, his very dearest, his loveliest. Running was perhaps putting it too strongly. He walked quickly: the wheelbarrow was heavy, and destroying the fence had cost him much of his strength. Occasionally the wheelbarrow slipped from his hands, the rusty handles wet with sweat.

THE EGYPTIAN KNOCKED on the restroom door. "Are you okay?" he asked. He was worried. In principle, he had nothing against overdoses. Money discriminates against no one, not even those who seek refuge in the overdose. But not in his restroom.

He didn't want any trouble with the police. When people died in restrooms, it meant trouble. Respectable people die in bed. He himself hoped to die in bed.

Nino paid the police of Basel, but not the way he paid Hamas. Hamas he paid out of idealism and a feeling of guilt; the Swiss police he paid of necessity. When he was still living in France, people had said to him: "The Swiss police are incorruptible. Don't go to Switzerland—stay here." But it wasn't as bad as all that. They weren't incorruptible, only very expensive, ridiculously expensive, the most expensive police in Europe. Nino had never known that the police could be so expensive. And even if you did pay the police, it was better not to have corpses in the restroom at your workplace.

He knocked on the door again, a little louder this time. The more expensive the police, the more prosperous the country, and the more prosperous the country, the more expensive the women. Why didn't he go to a less expensive country, where the police were honest enough to make do with a pittance? Ten, 20, these days sometimes even 30 percent—he barely kept anything for himself. He couldn't stand it anymore, but where could he go? He had no choice.

"Everything okay in there?" Nino shouted.

No answer came.

"Everything okay?" he shouted again.

"No, not really," Bettina replied, after she had blown her nose. You could tell from her voice that she had been crying. Her voice sounded weak and shaky—no longer brash and self-assured, no longer the voice of a woman who wanted to put solidarity into practice.

"Open up," the Egyptian said, "I'll help you."

Two other members of the Committee of Vigilant Jews were still sitting at the bar. They had split a bag of M&Ms, then drunk two glasses of whisky. Jerusalem Kebabs wasn't actually allowed to sell hard liquor, but to his best customers Nino sold everything under the counter. That was his way of getting back at the government, which didn't like Egyptians, not even if their name was Nino. The government was no good; the government was no good anywhere. The policemen who came by once a month for a cup of tea felt exactly the same way. They said, "If the government gave us a decent paycheck, we wouldn't have to do this." "I know," Nino would say then, "tell me about it." And then he would pour the policemen a little more peppermint tea. He felt sorry for them. The government forced them to take money from an Egyptian who, in their heart of hearts, they despised. The government forced them to go through life as less incorruptible than they really were. All over the world, respectable people hated the government.

Bettina opened the restroom door a crack.

The Egyptian slipped inside and quickly bolted the door behind him. He could see that Bettina was nowhere near an overdose. He looked in the mirror, straightened his shirt so that the hair on his chest looked authoritative, and turned to his new customer. "What's wrong? Why were you in here so long?"

"I don't feel anything," she said. Her mascara had run. "I don't feel it at all. It's sneezing powder."

When that final word crossed her lips, she couldn't help herself, she started to cry. Right there, with the Egyptian in the restroom. Her body shook.

The Egyptian stuck his tongue in her left ear: her sorrow was so huge, yet it was nothing compared with what was coming.

After he had ministered to her other ear as well, he realized that she was trouble. It was always the sorrowful women who betrayed you. Nothing was more dangerous to a man than a woman in sorrow. It seemed best to him to remind Bettina how attractive she was, how sexy he found her, even with a tear-stained face. True attractiveness cuts straight through all the tears. "Don't cry, girlie," he said. "This is excellent stuff. All the Jews buy from me, and Jews don't settle for second best. You know how they are. The best of the best still isn't good enough for them."

Then he pressed his lips to Bettina's, and hesitantly she began to kiss back. She had slept with eight men, but she still felt that she was inexperienced and made a lot of mistakes in bed. Foreplay still gave her nightmares.

Once the weenie was in her, though, nothing much could go wrong.

But this, this was still part of the foreplay, foreplay in a restroom.

She wanted so badly to be perfect. She thought about nothing else, only that, only her perfection and why it had remained undiscovered. She didn't think about what she was doing here, in this restroom, or why she had joined the Committee of Vigilant Jews, why she had adopted villages in India; she didn't even think about the sneezing powder, she only thought that she wanted to be perfect. She wanted to please men. That, in fact,

was the same thing she had wanted back when she had stood on the bridge
over the Rhine at Ilanz and thought about imperialism. It was in her last
year of primary school that she had first thought about imperialism.

Of course, she wanted something in return for that pleasing. She
wanted to be adored, and not by one man, but by all men. Was that asking too much, was that really asking too much? After all she had done for
India and the Jews?

She felt the Egyptian's hands running over her, the way her own hands
tested fruit in the produce section at the supermarket, in search of the best
of the lot. Adore me, she thought, adore me. I want to drive you crazy. I
can drive you crazy—yes, I can.

"I'M COMING!" Xavier shouted to the sky, the trees, and the clouds.
He had taken off his T-shirt and wrapped it around his right hand. He'd
had to bandage the cut on his right palm; otherwise he couldn't push the
wheelbarrow. Now he was running bare-chested through the cold park.
His jacket was still draped over Awromele. "I'm coming, Awromele," he
shouted. "I'm almost there."

Two passersby with their pets saw Xavier limping along half naked behind the wheelbarrow. They stayed out of his way. Avoid eye contact,
that's the only way to prevent incidents. That was what they had been
taught, the lesson they put into practice.

A lady out walking her two little dogs thought about calling the police,
but after looking at her watch she realized that she had no time for that
this morning. It would have to wait until tomorrow. She had an appoint-
ment at the swimming pool with a friend. But what if children were to
see this, what would they think? She didn't know what offended her most,
the wheelbarrow or the bare chest. Energy and initiative, that was what
the world lacked, in both politics and business; everywhere you went, you
came across the same spinelessness.

Xavier saw no passersby. He missed Awromele; he saw Awromele before him. He missed him now truly, the boy, the handsomest boy he knew.

That missing had felt different before today. Voluntary, that's how it had felt. Now it was mandatory, he couldn't do anything about it, the missing tormented him now.

Despite the T-shirt, the cut on his hand was bleeding more heavily and leaving spots on his clothing. Obviously, he wasn't used to hard physical labor, but what was a cut on the hand compared with the missing like a buzzing in his ears? A buzzing that wouldn't stop, a swarm of infuriated bees that followed him, that's what it was like.

NINO SHUDDERED in excitement. He pressed Bettina against the wall of the restroom, put his hand on her leg, and slowly slid it upwards. Bettina pushed his hand away; she wanted to please, but strategic refusal was a part of that pleasing. She was wearing a little yellow skirt with black stripes that went well with her jacket.

The hand she had pushed away came back to her leg and crawled up it again, like a big hairy insect.

"Nino," she said. "Nino." She pushed the hand to one side, but she felt herself growing weaker. She had always been drawn to the exotic. The naughty. And this was naughty, even naughtier than joining the Committee of Vigilant Jews.

Nino tugged on her underpants, tried to rip them apart, pulled on the elastic band, then on the cotton, but the cloth was too sturdy, too sturdy for his old hands. Then he tried to pull down the black underpants at a single tug, but wasn't able to do that, either. Bettina had to help him. And she did, she couldn't bear his fumbling any longer. She took it personally. If she had been more seductive, if she had been more in control of the foreplay, he wouldn't have to be dilly-dallying around like that, this old man with his greasy hair and his fat belly. The coitus wasn't the problem, but everything up to that point it made her flesh crawl.

The kebab king's hands trembled, he felt himself growing weak and dizzy, and at the same time, and this surprised him, he felt more manly than he had in a long time. He had forgotten about the money that didn't discriminate, he had forgotten his wife who did discriminate, the restaurant in Rapperswil, Hamas and the other designated charities that he tried to support as much as he could, even though he had enough problems of his own with the Swiss police, who detested the government as much as he did. He was with Bettina, with this little Jewess. Now just a few more fantasies—sexual arousal couldn't thrive without that. A few tender memories, cheap pictures he remembered from long ago, then he would no longer be alone, at last.

She stepped out of her underpants. She did something wrong. Whenever she undressed in the presence of a man, she thought: I'm doing something wrong. She couldn't help it—it happened automatically.

"Bettina," the Egyptian whispered. "Bettina, baby." He sounded hoarse; this was the voice of a man who had forgotten everything. He was no longer the Egyptian standing in front of his refrigerator, realizing that he had lost everything, including himself. He was no longer the boy who went back to Cairo and whose mother received him mockingly with the words "Is that all you brought with you? Is that it, is that all you're willing to give your parents, or did you bring something else? He calls himself Nino, do you hear that? Because he's supposed to be Italian. Nino, and he waits on rich Swiss people in Rapperswil. Are there really rich people in Rapperswil? I don't even know where that is, Rapperswil. Does it actually exist? Your brothers bring more with them when they come home, they bring substantial sums, and you, just look at that miserable little stack of bills. A dog would be ashamed to drag home something like that." And she threw the banknotes in the air like confetti.

None of that existed anymore. He was no longer a dog, and he didn't have to be ashamed like a dog anymore, either. He was a man, and, like a man, he pulled up Bettina's little yellow skirt.

He stared at her crotch. The skirt slipped from his hands, and he took a step backwards.

"What's wrong?" Bettina asked.

The Egyptian shook his head.

"Is there something wrong?" she asked. "Tell, me, please. You can tell me anything."

There was nothing she hadn't heard before. She was ready for anything, she was strong, a woman of the world, a man-eater. And she was bad, terribly bad. But that's the way she wanted to be, the way she had to be.

Nino shook his head in disgust.

"Tell me what's wrong," Bettina said.

He wiped his lips with the back of his hand and turned his head away.

She looked at herself, lifted up her skirt, but couldn't see anything different. "What's wrong?" she asked. "Please, tell me."

"You're bald," the Egyptian said, his head still turned away.

She looked at herself again, longer and better this time.

"I shaved myself," Bettina said at last. "Like a little girl, don't you think?" She laughed the most seductive laugh ever. She had practiced it in the mirror, as far back as Ilanz, laughing, looking, moving, running her hands through her hair, all of it in front of her bedroom mirror, for the men of the future.

"You like it, don't you?" she asked when she was done laughing.

He shook his head again. His mood had crumbled, and he felt like a dog again. The dog always came back, always at the moment when he was least wanted.

"It's horrible," he said, and he smiled because it was unpleasant to say that to a young woman. "It's unnatural."

"What?" she asked. "Nino, what's unnatural?" She lifted her skirt again, as though she wanted to show him how cute it was: all you had to do was get used to it, like a new dress, and after a while you'd start seeing how cute it was.

"Have you got some kind of a problem?" he asked.

"No. Do you?" She'd had men with sexual problems before. She was used to it. She solved them, those problems. They went away. She had known a man once who told her, "I had sexual problems all my life, until I met you."

The Egyptian no longer had his head turned; he was looking at her, straight in the eye. Problems, what was she talking about? Who did she think he was?

"Your cunt is a baby cunt," the Egyptian said.

Bettina looked at him, puzzled. She felt like kissing him, but she was afraid that might not be a good idea. Instead, she said, "It's awfully wet." She had read that in *Cosmopolitan,* that you should say that, to make an impression on the man you wanted to please.

"Like a little kid's," the Egyptian said. He didn't have children—they hadn't been able. He had two dogs, he and his wife from Rapperswil. First they'd had one dog, and when that turned out okay, they bought a second one. He turned around and started washing his hands.

"Everyone does this," Bettina said. "All the magazines say so. Bald is in fashion, and it's hygienic, too. When you have to wash up, you can get to everything. There's nothing to get in the way."

Again she laughed her most seductive laugh. She widened her eyes, as wide as she could, she tried every trick in the book, but Nino wasn't looking at her, he was washing his hands carefully with soap and thinking about the money he had brought home to his parents. The money he was supposed to be ashamed of, because there was so little of it. His father was dead now, his mother was ill; he didn't have to be ashamed of his money anymore; he earned so much he could even donate to Hamas. But the shame had remained, the shame conquered all. This Jewess's cunt reminded him of chicken cutlets in the supermarket, chicken cutlets on special.

"You make me horny, Nino."

He didn't like meat from the supermarket; he bought everything from the Islamic butcher. Not because he was religious, but from force of habit.

Bettina searched for words that would drive him crazy, this man in his white shirt, with all that hair on his chest, his thick eyebrows, this man who smelled of sweat and fried falafel balls. She wanted him, without knowing why. There was no reason for it. There was only that desperate longing of hers. "I haven't felt like this for a long time; I've never felt like this, Nino," she said, "so excited, so wet."

The Egyptian dried his hands. A dog, his mother was right. Look, look at him standing here in the restroom at his kebab place. No, less than a dog; a dog would be shamed by this; a dog had its own bowl, knew what loyalty came from. His dogs knew that, but did he? What did he know, anyway?

He looked at the young woman and shook his head. "Chicken cunt," he said quietly, hanging the towel back on its hook.

"What do you mean?" Bettina asked. "You don't think it's nice? That doesn't matter. Once you're in it, you don't see it anymore. Everyone at the gym has it like this, but it grows back. It's blond when it grows back, dark-blond. Kind of like my hair, but then a little darker."

"Ugly things discriminate against me," Nino said, leaning back against the little sink. "You understand? Ugly things discriminate against re-spectable people. Ugly things discriminate against you, too, because deep down inside you're a respectable person."

"You're right," she said. "But shall we do it now?"

"Your cunt is ugly," Nino said, and his words made him even sadder than he already was. "Your cunt discriminates against me."

The Egyptian was disappointed. Disappointment was a cumulative thing: each new one breathed life into the old. He had been robbed of his masculinity, his pride, his dignity. He had been robbed of his pride long ago, but now it was happening again. He didn't want a baby cunt, he wanted a woman's cunt, a real one. Although he had his doubts about that now as well. He had been in so many cunts, and it hadn't helped a bit.

Bettina started crying, but she didn't give up. "This is in," she said. "All my girlfriends wear it like this. And their boyfriends are happy about it. Just try it. Once you're in there, you won't notice it all." She felt like a saleslady chasing a customer around with something off the back shelf.

She took a step forward, and, as much as it frightened her, as scared as she was of doing something wrong, she did it. She put her hand on the Egyptian's crotch. She mustn't be left alone. The Egyptian couldn't ditch her now; she didn't want to stay behind alone in this restroom. Anything, but not to stay behind here. Not to be left alone like this, like a wet rag that wasn't worth the trouble to wring out. As seductively as possible, she said, "My pussy doesn't discriminate against anyone." "My pussy"—she'd read that somewhere, too. That it helped to say "my pussy" during love play. When it came to love play, what hadn't she read? She'd read everything, even though the magazines all contradicted each other.

The Egyptian raised his big hands to emphasize his words. "Ugly things discriminate," he said. "Everyone hates the Arabs, everyone hates the Jews. I hate the Jews, I hate the Arabs. But I'm Nino from Rapperswil. You understand what I'm trying to say? The only one who doesn't discriminate is money. You understand that, girlie? No, you don't know about that. You couldn't know about that yet. But money loves everyone. The one thing that Allah, Jesus, the Almighty, and whatever else their names are promised to people but never gave them, money gives them: love. You're still young, you don't know about the way people look at you when they hate you, the women who look at you and don't like you because you're an Arab. Money is the only one who always likes you. Money doesn't have an accent and doesn't hear accents, because money doesn't have ears. Your cunt . . ." The Egyptian choked back a little excess spittle; he was getting wound up. The sadness was growing inside him, turning everything gray, his business, women, the Palestinians, even his two dogs.

"Somebody has to speak the truth. I'm telling you the truth, I get sick when I look at you. With no hair." He pointed at her skirt.

This wasn't the moment for her to start crying again, and she didn't. She concentrated, she tried to remember the bits of advice she'd read, bits of advice with which she had won victories in the past.

"Shall I . . . ?" she asked. She couldn't speak the words, but she made movements with her lips that made her meaning clear.

The Egyptian pushed her hand from his crotch. He shook his head.

"Is there something else you want? Tell me what you want. I'll do anything." And as she said this, she saw herself standing on the bridge over the Rhine in Ilanz once more.

Nino shook his head again. "Leave me alone," he said. "Just forget it.

Would you like something to drink? A cola? I'll get you a cola. Get dressed, then we'll drink a cola together. Let's just forget about it. Bald cunt, no bald cunt, you're alone, I'm alone. That's all that matters, that's why I'm going to treat you to a cola, a nice cold cola, courtesy of the house."

He unlocked the door and left Bettina alone in the restroom.

In the kitchen, he poured a cola, and a glass of peppermint tea for himself. In his mind's eye, he kept seeing the bald pudenda. He stared into space and murmured curses in his mother tongue, addressed to the Westerners, the decadence that was spreading like the plague, and finally to himself. Then he went back to the bar. The two men from the committee were still sitting there. Instead of looking for Awromele, they were carrying on a conversation about apartheid.

Bettina locked the restroom door again, picked up her underpants, and sniffed at them. She didn't understand this—it was the fashion. Fashion had betrayed her, so it couldn't be trusted, either. What was so ugly about it? How could something like this make you sick, something so nice, something any healthy man would want to have?

Bettina sat down on the toilet seat. She was falling apart. So this was what was behind that desire to please, to please everyone she met. She sprinkled the rest of the powder into her hand and swallowed it. Then she rinsed her mouth with water, as though she'd just been to the dentist.

Someone knocked on the door. She didn't open it. She pressed her hands against her ears. There was no difference between everyone and no one. No one adored her, not even the man from the kebab place. No one wanted to discover her, no one wanted to gobble her up. Nothing would remain of her but the gifts that she had offered men and that they had been unable to accept.

Bettina pressed her hands against her ears even harder, so hard that it hurt. What a humiliation—an Egyptian with a beer belly thought her bare cunt wasn't worth the trouble. She washed her face. She decided that her misery had to do with the way she smelled. She was sure about that now, and that came as a relief. She no longer had to wonder where the misery came from, not like before. Once you knew where misery came from, you could do something about it.

There was no need for anyone to stink, not in this day and age. Before you knew it, she would drive that Egyptian crazy as he'd never been driven crazy before. But first she had to go to the doctor, as soon as possible.

She sat down beside the other members of the Committee of Vigilant Jews. The Egyptian put the glass of cola down in front of her and whispered in her ear: "You're still young; you'll get married, you'll have children, that's how things go. But you shouldn't shave yourself. The Creator gave us hair. And everything we have, we have for a reason." And then he said, a little louder now: "Women shave themselves too much, and what do they get for it? Rashes. I used to have a beard, I used to have bad skin. Now I don't have bad skin anymore, so I don't really need the beard. My skin is old, but it's not bad. My wife wants me to go along to the cosmetologist—she says there are little black spots on my nose and cheeks—but I'm not going to any beautician. Women are always seeing little black spots, because they have nothing better to do. I'm going to close the place. So drink up and go home."

The two members of the committee nodded groggily. There was still a little whisky in their glasses. It was too late—or, rather, too early—to go by the rabbi's house and inform him of their findings. They could do that tomorrow, once they'd caught up on some sleep. The Egyptian clutched Bettina's head to his chest; he didn't want to disappoint his customers.

When he let go, Bettina finished what was in her glass. She was falling apart—she had already fallen apart—so she needed to go to bed. First get some sleep, then go to the doctor.

The Egyptian looked at her and felt bad. She was still so young. He whispered: "I have responsibilities of my own, you understand? I have my responsibilities—I'm a married man, I run this place—but someone has to tell you. You shave yourself in places where a razor has no business going."

She stared at him, at this man, this foreigner. No one had every talked to her like this before—you didn't say things like that. What did he know about the laws of the razor? The razor could go wherever it liked.

Without a word, she got up and walked out of the kebab place. She was a wreck, a wreck from the provinces. Everything she had promised herself seemed ridiculous now. Going to the doctor, driving the Egyptian crazy, India, women's studies, an active role in the Committee of Vigilant Jews—she wasn't even Jewish.

She walked down the street amid the first commuters of the day. At a tram stop she paused for a minute; she still had a strange taste in her mouth.

The Egyptian showed his last customers to the door. He opened his refrigerator and looked at his stock, back behind the bottle of condensed milk. He thought about Bettina, and decided to make an extra contribution to Hamas. They could use it.

The guilt was more than he could take. He had already lost so much—money, women, kebab places, business partners, brothers, himself. As he stood in front of the fridge, it seemed to him as though all he had lost was himself. "Father," he said, "listen. Only money gives us love, only money." He clenched his fist, punched the refrigerator, hurt his hand, then punched the refrigerator again.

Worse than the guilt was the shame. The shame remained; it didn't run away from the money that flowed to the family members of freedom fighters. It was always there, just like his mother.

I Decide What's Anti-Semitic

THE WHEELBARROW was parked beside Awromele now, and Xavier was panting. It was brighter now, despite the low cloud cover. Morning had broken, people were going to work, taking children to school, but Awromele still wasn't in the wheelbarrow.

Xavier called to him, but nothing was getting through. "We have to get out of here," Xavier said, with no real hope of a reply. He pulled on Awromele's legs, no longer afraid to hear the popping of bones, the scraping of chafed skin against dirt. He lifted the feet first, then one leg, then the other, and so he was able to work Awromele's lower body into the wheelbarrow. But his torso and head were still lying on the ground.

I need help, Xavier thought, but no one's going to help me the way I look now. I'm half naked, I've got a black eye, I have cuts on my hands—they'll think I'm crazy. They'll laugh at me and lock me up, that's what they do to crazy people.

He tipped the wheelbarrow onto its side and tucked Awromele up into a ball as well as he could, as though the injured boy were a pile of clothes that had to be forced into an undersized suitcase. Xavier did his best not to bump against Awromele's swollen hand. He used his hands and knees to push the rolled-up body into the wheelbarrow, and when he had done that he tried to push it upright. "Help me, King David," he cried.

Xavier was able to raise the wheelbarrow with Awromele in it off the ground a little, but not to push it upright. He worked harder than he had ever worked before. Sometimes, in his frustration, he kicked at the wheelbarrow, but each time he apologized afterwards and said to the rolled-up body, "I'm sorry, that was my fault." He found a big broken branch and tried to use it as a lever. He tore his hands open even more.

After a few minutes, he stopped and planted little kisses on Awromele's forehead—the head the boys had kicked in order to express their admiration for Kierkegaard, in order to share with a stranger their esteem for that thinker. Even after a night in the park, Awromele's head still smelled nice.

Xavier cursed, leaned against the wheelbarrow, and pushed, but it didn't help. He went to the other side and pulled. For a moment, it looked as though Awromele was going to roll out onto the ground, but finally he was able to pull the wheelbarrow upright. Despite the cold, sweat was running down Xavier's back. His jogging pants and his stomach were muddy. His hands were covered with smaller and larger cuts, his face was streaked with dirt. He struggled to tear his dirty T-shirt into strips, then wrapped them carefully around both hands. "Now we're going to the doctor," he said. "We're going to get you some help." He caressed the hair of the boy who was tucked up in the wheelbarrow like the remains of cannon fodder that had to be brought to a final resting place. Xavier loved those remains, he longed for them. "Dearest," he said.

Xavier heard the sound of hoofbeats. Not far from the park was a riding school. He seized the handles of the wheelbarrow and turned in his thoughts to King David. The wheelbarrow was so heavy now that Xavier had to put it down and rest every three steps. Slowly, he succeeded in leaving behind the sacred place, the bare spot beneath the pine tree. The spot where he had taken Awromele's penis in his mouth, where he had been given a black eye, where he had listened to his friend's bloodcurdling screams, and where he had come to the conclusion that without Awromele his life would end.

·   ·   ·

AWROMELE'S MOTHER FIXED breakfast for her remaining twelve children, and said quietly to her husband, "It's our fault, Asher; we should have taken better care of him."

"What do you mean?" the rabbi said. "Take better care of him? Who should have taken better care of him? Me? I don't have time. How can we hope to protect ourselves against the anti-Semite? The anti-Semite is strong, and we are weak. The anti-Semite is big, we are little; the anti-Semite is everywhere, we are nowhere. What were we supposed to do? We can't lock up our children, we can't turn their bedrooms into prisons, can we?" He had spent a sleepless night and was even grouchier than usual, early in the morning.

"Dirty Jews," his wife said, sprinkling cornflakes in the children's bowls.

"What did you say?"

"Dirty Jews."

"Who?"

"All of you," the rabbi's wife said.

"What do you mean? What are you trying to say?"

"What have these dirty Jews from the Committee of Vigilant Jews done for us? They sat here, drank our coffee, drank our vodka, emptied the cookie jar, and now they're laughing at us behind our backs. Especially at you, because you're autistic. And have they found my Awromele? Have they found even one hair of his head? Even one little shoelace? Maybe they didn't even go looking for him. I wouldn't put it past them, those dirty Jews."

"Why do you keep saying 'dirty Jews'?" The rabbi was wearing a wrinkled white shirt; his coat was still hanging over a chair in the living room.

"Because they're dirty Jews, Asher. Dirty Jews they are, and dirty Jews they'll remain."

"Don't talk like that. That's the language of the anti-Semite."

His wife put the box of cornflakes down on the counter, picked up a pack of low-fat milk, and upended it into the bowls, so that it splashed all over. "I'll say 'dirty Jews' whenever I feel like it. I'm not going to let you tell me what to do anymore. What I'm allowed to say, what I'm not allowed to say. What kind of shopping I'm supposed to do, and when I'm supposed to do it. Cursed be the day I met you, cursed be the day the Almighty created the world, cursed be the dirty Jews, cursed be me for being a dirty Jewess, cursed and cursed again."

And then the rabbi's wife picked up a dishcloth, smacked it on the counter a few times, and cried out: "I want my Awromele back. Oh God, I want my Awromele back, give me back my Awromele!"

She put the bowls of cornflakes on a tray and took it to the living room, where most of her children were already waiting at the table. Some of them were still in their pajamas, others were already dressed. "Eat," she shouted, "eat. And don't let everything fall on the floor the way you always do." She went back to the kitchen, where the rabbi was still standing speechless. His wife had never called him a dirty Jew before. "You," she said, "you. Go do something. Go look for Awromele. Get out of the house. Cheating on your wife with her sister, you're man enough for that, and if my sister had been prettier than me I could have forgiven you, but she wasn't, she was ugly as sin. And she had a bad personality, too, no personality at all, she was as fickle as the wind, she was always like that. God rest her soul, but I don't know what you saw in her; I don't know, and I don't want to know, either. And now you're getting out of the house, now you're finally going to go do something, go look for your firstborn, because I want my Awromele back."

She pushed him out of the kitchen, grabbed his overcoat, threw it over his shoulders, and pulled him towards the door.

There he put up a little resistance, but it was more for show. He said, "Shouldn't we wait to see what the Committee of Vigilant Jews has to report?"

"Stop it!" she shouted. "Enough already with those dirty Jews. Go find your child."

Then she pushed her husband out the door and bolted it.

The rabbi stood on the pavement. His wife went back to the living room, where the children were spooning loudly at their cornflakes.

Rochele said: "Mama, mama. Now I know. The Messiah is a pelican."

The rabbi's wife couldn't take it anymore; years of grief came rushing out. She hit Rochele over the head with the box of cornflakes, so hard that the box tore and the cornflakes rained down on Rochele's head. "Stop it," she shouted. "A pelican. Knock it off. I don't want to hear any more about it. Dirty Jews. A pelican! Shut your mouth and eat."

"Don't call us dirty Jews, Mama," said Jehoedele, one of Awromele's brothers, stirring his cornflakes listlessly. "We're not dirty Jews. That's anti-Semitic."

"Mama," said the girl with the braces—Danica was her name. "Jehoedele's right. You shouldn't call us that. That's really nasty." Danica wasn't pretty, but she was intelligent. That was why she didn't go to Hebrew school: she was allowed to go to the Gymnasium.

"But you're all a bunch of dirty Jews anyway!" the mother shouted. "Just like your father. And I'm the one who decides what's anti-Semitic around here. You don't have any say in the matter, so shut up and eat. I don't want to hear another sound—it's too much for me this morning."

Then she went into the kitchen and sank down in a chair. She closed her eyes and began to pray.

The rabbi wandered the streets of Basel. He didn't feel too great; he'd been wearing the same clothes for the last twenty-four hours. And he didn't get a lot of searching done. Every once in a while he looked in a doorway, but he didn't see Awromele anywhere.

XAVIER HAD ROLLED the wheelbarrow onto a path. They were still in the park, but at least it was a path. He checked Awromele's pulse and thought he detected a little movement there. That gave him hope. "Here we go," he said.

More people were out now, not only dogs with their masters but also joggers wearing headphones. A couple of commuters were cutting through the park. They looked strangely at Xavier but didn't stop cutting through the park, not even when he waved his arms.

"They're afraid of us," Xavier said, leaning over the wheelbarrow. "But soon we'll get to the doctor, and then we'll take a shower. I know it's not very comfortable for you, dearest, but I can't carry you." He took three steps and had to put the wheelbarrow down again.

A young woman in a pink jogging suit came running up. Xavier shouted, "Can you help us for a minute?"

The young woman in the pink jogging suit started running even faster. Ever since she was a girl, she'd been hearing stories about rapists who pretended to be people in trouble.

Xavier looked into the wheelbarrow as though it were a baby carriage and said, "We're almost at the doctor's, Awromele, hang in there." The jacket of his jogging suit, which he had first draped across Awromele like a blanket, he now rolled up and tucked behind Awromele's head.

The strollers were moving past quickly. The day was becoming brighter, and the more the people saw, the faster they walked.

A woman in her fifties with a spaniel was the only one who seemed intrigued by the sight of a half-naked boy pushing a wheelbarrow. She didn't pick up the pace, she didn't turn and hurry away—she stopped to look. Then she slowly walked up to Xavier.

"She's coming towards us," Xavier said to Awromele. "She's coming towards us. She's going to help us." He had put the wheelbarrow back down; he had to stop and rest every two steps now. He pulled the strips of T-shirt around his hands a little tighter, so the cuts wouldn't show.

"Ma'am," Xavier shouted when she was only ten yards away, "I need your help." He took Awromele's hand, the one that wasn't broken, and squeezed it gently. "I'm giving you strength," he said quietly. "Do you feel it? I'm giving you strength. The worst is behind us now." He hardly believed it himself.

The woman was rummaging through her purse for change. She sang in a church choir, and she liked giving away money.

"Come a little closer," Awromele shouted. "We won't hurt you."

More and more psychiatric patients had to live out on the street these days. The spaniel's mistress took that as a personal affront: her own sister was a psychiatric patient. Fortunately, though, she didn't live out on the street.

At last she found a couple of coins, which she held clutched in her right hand.

"You can come closer, ma'am," Xavier called out.

These were psychiatric patients, she was sure of it. The face of the half-naked boy somehow seemed familiar. Maybe she had seen him in the park before. She came here often with her dog, Armin, and before that with her husband, who had spent half his life in a wheelchair. The ones people called bums were actually psychiatric patients. She talked about that often with the other members of the choir.

"Come on, Armin, don't dawdle."

She dragged the dog along behind her.

The boy's face really did look familiar. He looked awful, almost naked; he had a black eye, and his hands were bleeding. It was terrible to see what happened when the mental-health people didn't arrange for shelter. Her sister ended up in an isolation cell sometimes, but even that was better than how these boys had to walk around in the park. She had told the director of the psychiatric hospital: "I'd rather have my sister put in isolation than have you people let her go. Once she starts wandering around town, she'll go downhill fast." She never said so, but she actually felt relieved when her sister was put into isolation, because at least then she didn't have to visit her. It took forty-five minutes to get from her house to the hospital by public transport. He looked young, this boy. And that child in the wheelbarrow, maybe that was his little brother. That's what you got when you started making cuts in the welfare system: children living in wheelbarrows. She voted a socialist ticket herself.

She took a few steps towards the boys, the coins held tightly in her right hand. They could use them to buy themselves a nice hot cup of tea.

"Don't be afraid," Xavier said. "Don't be afraid, ma'am. Please. We won't hurt you."

And then she saw it, at last she saw it: she knew this boy. But not from the park; she knew him from someplace completely different. She was relieved that she'd finally remembered.

"Armin," she shouted, "stop it. Be good."

She dragged the dog along another foot or two.

"I know you," she said. "Or am I mistaking you for someone else? You were in the paper, weren't you?"

"That's possible," Xavier said. "I don't remember."

"You're the one who was molested, aren't you?"

"The Jew was beaten up," Xavier said. "By four boys. Just like that. For no reason. He needs to see a doctor."

"That's right, I know you," Armin's mistress said in a tone that allowed no contradiction. "I saw you on television, too. You were the one who was attacked by that man, weren't you, that strange man?"

Now she understood completely. This poor child had been molested, and then he had become confused. That happened so often, much more so than people realized. That's what she told the other people in her choir all the time: once molested, always molested. No wonder they were so confused—when you were abused like that, it turned you into a psychiatric patient. Her sister hadn't been molested, and she'd still become a psychiatric patient. But that was something genetic. The doctors had explained it to her. She should count her lucky stars that she hadn't turned out like her sister.

"What was his name again?" she asked. "That man who molested you? He had such a famous name."

"The papers blew it all up," Xavier said. "It wasn't that bad. I need to get him to a doctor—he's been lying in the park all night. He was beaten up."

She glanced at the wheelbarrow. "His name is right on the tip of my tongue," she said. "The name of that man who molested you. Wait a minute, don't tell me, I've almost got it. It was Lenin, wasn't it, isn't that what they called him? Pedophile Lenin, that was it, wasn't it? I've got a memory like a steel trap; that's important, it keeps you from going senile.

People who remember a lot, who have to remember a lot of things for their profession, take longer to become senile. That's why I do crossword puzzles all the time. Not because I like them so much—they bore me to death—but they help against senility. If you don't do anything and then you get it, you have only yourself to blame. You have those people who sit in front of the TV all day and never bother to remember anything— well, no wonder one day they can't even remember their own names."

She peered at the wheelbarrow. Poor little things, that's what they were, poor little things.

"Ma'am," Xavier said, "I would really appreciate it if you would . . ."

She looked at Xavier. He looked different from how he'd looked on television: he wasn't as tall as he'd seemed.

"On television you looked a lot taller," she said. "But I guess people say that all the time, don't they?"

She wasn't sure whether she should give her money to the boy. She put the coins back in her purse. Maybe it would be better to buy him a sweater, or a nice warm coat. There were special department stores where you could buy perfectly good clothing for very little.

She had nothing to do that day—her husband was already dead, Armin had a heart condition and slept almost all day—there was no reason why she couldn't buy the boy a warm sweater, or two sweaters; then his little brother would have one, too.

"Yes," she said, "I read all about you. I even saw you on TV. You were molested by Pedophile Lenin. It's so nice to meet you in real life. I think you put up a brave fight. I don't know whether I would have been as courageous as you. I've never been molested, but if it happened I don't know what I'd do. Maybe I'd scream, maybe I'd scream real loud, but maybe I wouldn't. You never know. It's so easy to lean back in your chair and say: If I were molested, I'd do this or that. When I read about you in the paper, I often wondered: What would I do if an old man like that started fiddling with me? And, to be perfectly honest, I just don't know."

"Ma'am . . ." Xavier said.

"Müller," she said, "I'm Mrs. Müller. Oh, I can tell, you're all confused. And who is that? Is that your little brother?" She bent over the wheelbarrow and saw the ear that was full of clotted blood.

"Oh," she said. "Oh, how awful."

Then she brought her face up close to Xavier's, as though to make absolutely sure that this really was the victim of Pedophile Lenin.

"We were attacked," Xavier said, "by four boys; we need help."

"Yes," she said, "I can see that. What can I do for you?"

She rummaged through her purse, but found nothing useful.

"You know what? I'll go and buy two warm sweaters for you boys. I know what you've been through. My sister is in a psychiatric hospital, and she should count her lucky stars. At least I'm happy she's there. There isn't enough room for most psychiatric patients, not with all the spending cuts. What did you say your brother's name was?"

"Awromele," Xavier said. He didn't feel like explaining what Awromele really was to him.

"Awromele—a strange name, but pretty. I'm Gesine. That's not a strange name, but it's not a pretty name, either. I've thought about changing it—to 'Sophie,' for example, or 'Marlene,' like Marlene Dietrich, but then I met someone who was actually called Marlene and I thought: No, 'Marlene' isn't right for me, so I stuck to 'Gesine.' "

Without waiting for the boys, she and Armin started walking. "There's a department store near here—I know we'll find a warm sweater there."

Xavier slowly rolled the wheelbarrow along behind her. He couldn't go any faster; his hands hurt, he had no strength left in his arms. To Awromele he said: "We've found a nice lady who's going to help us. She's going to buy us a nice warm sweater."

AS THEY WALKED along the shopping street, Xavier and his wheelbarrow received quite a few more looks than they had in the park. Fortunately, it wasn't too busy yet. People didn't start spending their hard-earned money until later in the day. In the early-morning hours they restrained themselves. Xavier was glad about that: he didn't like being stared at.

Gesine and Armin kept walking faster. She was pleased about having met the boys, the tall one had looked at her so gratefully. Like a dog— they could look so grateful, too. Every once in a while, she stopped to wait for Xavier and his wheelbarrow. She thought about how she would tell the other choir members what had happened to her. This was better than their stories about vacations. Now they would have to listen to her, they would have no excuse to shut her up.

The door of the department store was being watched by a uniformed guard. She felt flustered, and decided it would be better for the boys to wait outside. You couldn't take a wheelbarrow on the escalator.

"I'm going to pick out two nice sweaters for both of you," she told Xavier. "I know what young people these days like. Wait here, I'll be right back."

Xavier parked the wheelbarrow against a blind wall in a dead-end alley beside the department store and waited there for Mrs. Müller. After a couple of minutes, the uniformed guard came and stood at the top of the alley. He stared at Xavier. Using his walkie-talkie, he informed his superiors that a couple of suspicious individuals were hanging around the service entrance.

Meanwhile, Gesine Müller and her dog were searching the men's department for a turtleneck, but the prices were shocking. Then she went to the children's section. There she was accosted by a salesgirl. Salespeople got on her nerves, so she snarled, "Don't bother, I'll wait for the end-of-the-year sale." She poked around a table full of remainders, but there were no affordable sweaters there, only T-shirts. That would be of no use to the two boys outside. That was more of a summertime thing.

Hard Nuts to Crack

FOR THE FIRST TEN MINUTES, the uniformed guard of the department store ignored Xavier and his wheelbarrow. Then he decided that he'd been lenient enough. He walked up to the boys, holding his walkie-talkie in one hand. He hadn't been working security for very long and was afraid that, at crucial moments, he might not exude enough authority. "Hey, you there," he said. "You're not allowed to park vehicles here." It may have been a blind wall, but no vehicles were supposed to park there.

"This isn't a vehicle," Xavier said, "this is a wheelbarrow." He was slapping his arms against his chest to keep warm.

"A wheelbarrow is also a vehicle," the guard said. "I've been tolerant— I let you stay here for a while, I gave you enough time to beat it—but you're still here. So now I have to act. I gave you a finger, now you're trying to take the whole hand. Now I'm giving you two minutes."

"This is a wheelbarrow," Xavier said. "To carry my friend in. We're going to see a doctor. He was beaten up. And Mrs. Müller just went in to buy us a sweater." His lips had turned blue; he kept waving his arms to keep warm.

Xavier believed there was no reason to be ashamed of the truth. Before long, Mrs. Müller would come out of the department store with two sweaters; then he'd see the look on the guard's face.

A crackling sound came out of the guard's walkie-talkie, and he raised it to his ear. There was no voice, just more crackling.

He sighed, turned down the volume of the walkie-talkie, and took a good look at the half-naked boy. He recognized him from somewhere; the kid had probably been picked up a few times before. The hard nuts to crack always came back. No matter what you did to them, they were like junkies. The hard nuts to crack didn't scare easily, you had to lock them up.

"Maybe you think," the guard said, printing the boy's face in his memory, "that I don't know about your kind." He was young, twenty-three, but he was ambitious, and he had a child.

"I studied petty crime," the security guard told Xavier. "I know all about shoplifters. Ask me a question about shoplifters."

The guard looked expectantly at Xavier, but Xavier had no questions in mind.

"Come on," the guard said, "what do you want to know?"

"I'm waiting for Mrs. Müller," Xavier said quietly.

"Then I'll ask myself a question. How does the shoplifter operate? The shoplifter operates in groups of four or five. Lots of Southern Europeans or Bulgarians, often young Gypsies too, who learned it from their parents, who learned it in turn from *their* parents. There's nothing they can do about that—it's in their blood. And this is where it happens." The guard looked around, as though finding himself in the zoo, before a cage full of rare birds. "In this alley is where I deal with the shoplifter."

A crackling sound came from his walkie-talkie again. He turned down the volume. "Where was I?" he asked.

Xavier hopped from one foot to the other, but that didn't help against the cold, either. He laid his hand on Awromele's head and hoped Mrs. Müller would show up soon with those sweaters.

"The professional shoplifter does not operate alone. That's where I was. The seventeen-year-old girl who steals rouge, that's shoplifting, too, but the major damage is done by the professional. One group causes a fuss, the other group makes their move. It's an old trick. I think you're here to cause a fuss. That's why you've got a wheelbarrow, that's why you're half naked. That's why there's some guy dying in the wheelbarrow. I can tell from your face that I've got it right. Are you the shoplifter who's supposed to cause a fuss?"

"I'm cold," Xavier said, pounding even harder on his bare chest. There was still some mud sticking to his back. Arguing made no sense in cases like this, especially not in the state he was in. "Mrs. Müller is buying us a sweater; she'll be right back. Then we'll leave. I'm not here to cause a fuss."

"I do not," said the guard, taking another step forward, "and I'm being completely honest about this, I do not have the authority to arrest you. As long as nothing has been stolen, we're not allowed to lay a finger on you." There was melancholy in his voice.

"Yes," Xavier said. "You're right about that." He needed to stay on this man's good side, especially looking the way he did now. Friends, that was the most important thing in a squeeze. He prayed to King David for friends. More friends.

"Are you trying to run away?" the guard asked. And he took another step forward. He had chased many a shoplifter before. If necessary, he was prepared to run all the way to the next tram stop. He'd trained for it, too. Other people trained in order to lose weight. Not him, he was skinny enough already; he trained in order to keep up with the shoplifter, to jump one when the time was right.

"I'm waiting for Mrs. Müller," Xavier said. He could barely keep it up anymore, he had to pee that badly. But he didn't dare to do it here, not with the guard standing beside him.

"Let me tell you about the procedure. When I catch the shoplifter, I keep him here till the police arrive. Sometimes that takes a while—they're short-staffed. They don't show up for every single shoplifter."

Xavier nodded; he took Awromele's good hand and squeezed it gently. His bladder was about to explode.

The guard searched for his lighter, found it after a while, and, with a satisfied look on his face, lit a cigarette.

"If the shoplifter decides not to wait for the police voluntarily, we exert a moderate form of physical duress. When we speak of physical duress, what are we talking about?" The security guard inhaled. Sometimes he'd had to wait more than an hour for the police to show up. Sometimes they only showed up when you told them they could pick out something to take home. A pair of jeans, a bottle of perfume, a nice vase. *Quid pro quo.* "There are a number of possibilities. This is what they teach you in class. I sit on him. I assume a seated position on top of the shoplifter. And then I keep sitting there until the police finally show up. Simple, but effective. I've been working here for a little over four months, and so far there have been nine occasions on which I have had to sit on a shoplifter, and let me tell you, it's not a lot of fun. Not for the shoplifter, and not for me." He inhaled again. The guard preferred not to—he lost sleep over it—have to sit on the shoplifter; he had nightmares about it. Sometimes they were men; occasionally they were women, children—that happened, too. He had to sit on them. It wasn't his fault. The department store did all it could to keep this from happening. But they came back, the gangs of children, they came back, and it seemed like they had his number. As though they knew he didn't like to do it.

Xavier nodded.

The guard looked at the smoke he had exhaled.

"First you apply pressure to the throat of the shoplifter," he said solemnly, "and as you do that, you slowly lower his body to the ground. Then you sit on him with your full weight, on his chest, on his stomach, applying pressure to his throat the whole time, in order to discourage him from struggling. If the proper authorities are too long in coming, then they sometimes have to call an ambulance for the shoplifter. These are unpleasant incidents." That never happened very often with him. And when it did happen, he would skip lunch afterwards. Then he would take a walk through town and ask himself: Did I deal with the situation correctly?

"In ninety percent of all cases, everything is fine," the guard said. "No one has to call an ambulance. The percentage of shoplifters who die in custody is negligible." He ground out his cigarette with his shoe.

Xavier nodded again. He had to pee so badly now that he really couldn't hold it anymore.

"Look," the security guard said, "we're standing here, talking man to man, so I can tell you that sometimes there are customers who complain, who say: It's Friday afternoon, we come into the department store with our children to have some fun shopping, and the first thing we see is you sitting on a shoplifter. So they send a letter to the management: 'We come to your store with young children and see situations to which we do not wish our children to be exposed.' I can understand that, as a private individual. I have a child myself. For a little girl of five or six, a man of my size sitting on a shoplifter, applying his full weight, is not a pretty sight. But the management covers my back. Because I do everything by the book. Don't forget, it has a preventive effect as well. There are plenty of potential thieves walking around, and they hesitate: Are we going to buy it, or are we going to pocket it? Well, then they see me sitting on the shoplifter and they figure: Let's take this one to the cash register. Twenty, maybe thirty percent of my work is preventive. Setting a good example, showing what happens to people who set a bad example. I wouldn't want you to take it personally, because we're talking here man to man, but take someone like you, for instance, standing here like this with your wheelbarrow. You're setting a bad example."

Xavier had stopped pounding his bare chest to keep warm. All he did was hold Awromele's hand. "I'll be gone in a little while," he said, "I'm going to the doctor. We're just waiting for Mrs. Müller. She's coming right back with two sweaters."

The guard took a few steps forward. He was standing right in front of Xavier now. "So what are you guys going to steal today?"

Xavier looked around; there was no one else in the alley.

"Nothing," Xavier said. He smiled as brightly as he could, and added: "We're on our way to the doctor." But it was no use anymore, he couldn't help it, he peed in his pants. It felt pleasant for a moment, warm and soothing, like a bed for which you've been longing all day. Then it began to cool.

The guard turned off his walkie-talkie. He didn't seem to notice that Xavier had peed in his pants.

"We're not part of a gang," Xavier said. His jogging pants were completely soaked now, and the moisture was no longer warm—it was cold, ice-cold. Strange the way urine cools off so quickly. He picked up the wheelbarrow and put it down again a few yards away. He wanted to get out of this alley, he needed to find a doctor.

The guard took up a position in front of the wheelbarrow. It was not a lot of fun, but someone had to do it. And he always did his best to be reasonable. He was a human being. A human being in uniform has to put up with all kinds of prejudices. That's why he always talked to shoplifters, to explain the procedure. So they knew what was going to happen.

"We're not part of a gang," Xavier said. "You have to believe me." The more he begged, the less credible he sounded, but he didn't want this guard to sit on him, not now, not in his condition. And definitely not on Awromele. He picked up the wheelbarrow and put it down again a few yards farther away.

"It's your word against mine," said the security guard, approaching Xavier slowly. "Who do you think they'll believe? In the past, when times were different, we gave the shoplifter the benefit of the doubt. But that's not possible anymore. We have to set examples. Soon we're going to start checking bags—everyone who comes into the department store will have to open his bag. We're doing battle on two fronts. On the one front, we do battle against the thief, and especially in organized form; on the other front, we do battle against the terrorist. Starting next month, we'll look in the bags of everyone who comes in here. We guards have a serious responsibility. We have to make the customer feel safe. And in that way the strange situation can arise in which we, the adversaries of the shoplifter, are transformed into the guardian angels of the shoplifter. Because the terrorist does not distinguish between the paying customer and the customer who comes here to rip off goods."

The guard took a deep breath. He didn't usually talk this much. His colleagues were always staring at the TV in the canteen. His neighbors were never home. His child never said much. The only ones he could actually talk to were the shoplifters.

"You're wondering," the guard said, "What kind of example could he possibly be setting if he sits on me now? Who's going to see us in this alley? There's no one here. Don't kid yourself. Thousands of eyes see us. Thousands of eyes are looking at us. Ten thousand people are counting on us." The guard pointed up at the sky, and, indeed, Xavier saw two video cameras attached to the blind wall.

"The management sees us, too," the guard said. "The management is not stupid. The management says: A customer who doesn't feel safe doesn't buy anything. Customers like that mean the end of our department store, and do you know what that means? It means that a thousand people are out of work. So, if I sit on you in a minute, if I start applying pressure to your throat to discourage you from putting up a struggle, then that's not something between you and me. It's much bigger than that—it's about the good example and the bad example, it's about good and evil."

Xavier felt like running away, but he couldn't leave the wheelbarrow with Awromele in it behind. Never again would he leave Awromele behind. Never again.

The guard was standing right in front of Xavier now, and had already laid his hand on the throat of the boy in whom he saw the shoplifter. He was poised to carry out the procedure he had learned in class.

"Please," Xavier said. "I'm on my way to the doctor. That's all I want, a doctor, for him." The guard looked the boy in the eye, but instead of forcing Xavier to the ground and sitting on him, he began caressing Xavier's Adam's apple with two fingers.

He smelled the scent of urine.

The guard went on caressing Xavier's Adam's apple.

The boy trembled. The guard could see the fear in his eyes. Christ, did that boy tremble! He was afraid, afraid of him, the security guard. He put his mouth up close to Xavier's ear. He flicked his tongue in and out of the ear of the trembling boy. "We're trapped," the guard said in a whisper. "We're all stuck in the trap. They're everywhere. In every business, every organization, at every train station. You don't recognize them, but they're everywhere." Then he took a step back and straightened his uniform. "Do you promise never to come back here again?" he asked. "Do you guys promise to stop stealing?"

Xavier nodded.

The security guard caressed Xavier's Adam's apple with two fingers again, and brought his face closer to Xavier's once more; for a moment it seemed as though he was going to bite Xavier on the nose; then he let him go.

"Get out of here," the guard said. "Go, quick, before I change my mind, little Gypsy."

Xavier had thought he wouldn't be able to, but he picked up the wheelbarrow and pushed it along the blank wall in the direction of the shopping street. His wet underpants chafed against his body.

"A thousand eyes are looking at you," the guard shouted after him. He turned his walkie-talkie back on.

GESINE MÜLLER left the children's department. Maybe it hadn't been such a good idea after all to offer those boys sweaters. It only encouraged dependency. Before you knew it, they wouldn't be able to stand on their own feet. They had to stay far from the machinery of the social-welfare organization, because once you were caught in it you could never get out.

She stopped and looked at the coats, but the prices were completely out of the question. Armin was breathing heavily again. Was her dog about to have another coronary? She held his head between her shins and whispered his name lovingly. She had done the wrong thing; she shouldn't have become involved with those boys. One sick dog was enough.

The Door of Happiness

THE RABBI'S WIFE took Danica to school, and came home asking, "Did anyone call?" But Rochele, who had been told to sit beside the phone and not to move, could only shake her head. No one had called, not even the rabbi, who was out wandering the streets.

When she saw Rochele shake her head, the rabbi's wife opened her mouth and wailed, "Awromele, where are you?"

She didn't really believe in anything, except that she was the rabbi's wife, and that after death worms would be her share.

Rochele was so startled by the wailing that she slipped off her chair beside the phone and hid beneath the table, where she tried to forget her mother's desperation by concentrating on the pelican that was the Messiah. She found a pencil and a drawing pad and began making a drawing of the bird that would lift her up and take her to America and then, if she wanted, to the North Pole.

TO HIS OWN AMAZEMENT, Xavier succeeded in pushing the wheelbarrow a long way in the direction of the hospital where he'd been treated after his operation at the hands of Mr. Schwartz. He was even able to walk quickly part of the way. He was afraid that the guard would come after him and sit on him anyway, and maybe on Awromele as well. Fear gives wings to the exhausted soul.

Xavier stopped at a traffic light. The wheelbarrow slipped from his hands; everything was shaking now, his arms, his head, his legs, the whole world seemed to be shaking. He staggered and fell. He no longer had the strength to get up. First he lay still, then he began moving his lips silently, until at last you could heard him murmur, "An ambulance, please, call an ambulance."

Because he looked so frightening, many people were afraid to stop and listen. He lay there murmuring for about five minutes, until a man stopped and bent down. The man heard the word "ambulance" and asked, "What's your name?"

"Xavier, Xavier Radek."

"Are you in pain?" the man asked. A seemingly silly question, perhaps, but there were a lot of people who faked it.

Xavier nodded.

In a perfume shop, the man called the emergency number.

"I am the comforter of the Jews," Xavier had called out after him, but the man didn't hear that.

While the man was placing his call, Xavier sat up. "Forgive me," he said to Awromele, who was lying in the wheelbarrow like a crumpled piece of parcel post, "forgive me." And he seized the wheelbarrow with both hands. Awromele felt so cold and looked so pale, even his lips were white. Xavier wondered whether this was what the dead looked like. Had his grandfather's prisoners looked like this? Probably not—they had never been identified; they were ash floating in the breeze.

The shopping street was gradually becoming busier.

When Xavier's last bit of strength left him, he let go of the wheelbarrow and slid back onto the pavement.

The charitable man had no time to wait for the ambulance. When he came back from the perfume shop, he found Xavier lying beside the wheelbarrow and said, "The ambulance is on its way."

He paused for a moment, but Xavier didn't reply. The man walked on. He had total confidence in the paramedical personnel of Basel.

Within ten minutes, the ambulance arrived. A man and a woman carried Awromele into the hospital on a stretcher, but when they tried to put Xavier on a stretcher he began struggling and cried out, "I'm not a shoplifter, I'm the comforter of the Jews."

They looked at each other, raised their eyebrows, shook their heads. When Xavier shouted, "I am the comforter of the Jews," for the second time, they decided to give him a shot of sedative.

IN THE SCHOOLYARD, the tall boy was walking around with a volume of Kierkegaard under his arm, as he did almost every day. "Here," he said to his friends, who were walking around with him; they were inseparable. "Listen to this. 'The door to happiness does not open in. It opens out, so there is nothing to be done about it.' That's what Kierkegaard wrote. Remember that. There is nothing you can do about it."

The bell for classes had already sounded, but they had a free period. They hung around in the schoolyard, citing Kierkegaard, until they caught sight of a girl who was late for class.

They didn't know her: she hadn't been at their school very long and was in one of the lower classes. She was ugly, especially because of the braces she wore. But she wouldn't have been very pretty even without the braces. Her book bag was big and bright-pink. She stuffed far too much into it, she took books to school that she wouldn't be needing that day at all. Her hair was light-blond.

The boys drove her into one corner of the schoolyard, shouting at her quotes from Kierkegaard that she could only partly understand, because she was numbed with fear. She was wearing a blue skirt and suspenders.

At last the boys succeeded in driving her into a corner of the schoolyard where the teachers couldn't see them, not even if they looked out the window.

They took her book bag away from her. They examined the books quickly and wistfully. How well they remembered having bought and read these same books themselves. Time flew, the school was a sausage factory, the office was a sausage factory, the family was a sausage factory. Hospitals were sausage factories. Train stations, airports—there one encountered sausages in transit.

After they had flipped through the books and put them back neatly in the bright pink bag, they looked in her pencil case. There wasn't much in it—three pens, a pencil, an eraser, a protractor, a calculator.

"Kierkegaard is our hero," the tall boy said, holding her pencil case in his hand. The case had a picture of Snoopy on it. It had been a gift back in primary school, but she still used it. She liked Snoopy.

"We read him and reread him," the tall boy said. "We'll keep reading him till we're dead. Kierkegaard. Who's your hero?"

Because the girl was mad with fear, she couldn't answer them at first, but the boys insisted. "Tell us," they said, "you can tell us. We can keep a secret." After a little while she succeeded in whispering, "Papa and Mama."

Her father was a friendly rabbi who did a bit of matchmaking in his free time. Her mother had given birth to thirteen children.

The boys were disappointed with her answer. It made them sad.

"These are the days of superficiality," the tall boy said, after consulting with his friends in a whisper. "We live in the age of sausage. The difference between life and death has been reduced to a minimum. The dead seem alive, the living seem dead. And the people seem like sausages. This is supposed to be the best school in Basel." He pointed to the old, slightly dilapidated building. "At this school we became acquainted with Kierkegaard; others became acquainted with Kleist, and others with Plato. And with whom have you become acquainted? Your papa and mama. That hurts us to the quick. We look at you and we see that your papa and mama are of no consequence, we see that your papa and mama are ugly people. We look at you and we see a culture in decay."

His friends chimed in. The boy who wore his father's raincoat went up and stood right in front of the girl. "Those who look at you," he said solemnly, "see the end of days."

The tall boy took the calculator out of her case. It was a simple machine, Texas Instruments. It had been passed down to Danica by Awromele.

"What is this?" the tall boy asked.

A sound came from Danica's mouth, but it was unintelligible.

"What is this?" the tall boy asked again. "What am I holding in my hand?"

Danica was frightened, but still able to say "calculator."

"Precisely. Very good. A calculator." He pronounced the word emphatically, as though speaking to a deaf person. "This calculator is no good to us. It won't help us, it won't help you. Technology that falls into the hands of the incompetent leads to catastrophes, catastrophes lead to death, one death leads to another; death is everywhere, can't you smell it?" He took a deep breath, stepped forward, pressed his nose against hers, and asked: "Don't you have a nose? Are you the sausage that can only smell ketchup?"

Danica shook her head with conviction. "I can smell it," she said quietly. "I smell death."

"She can smell it!" the tall boy said mockingly. He looked around at his friends and said again, "She can smell it." Then he mumbled, to no one in particular, "This is how our culture dies." As though he were a magician who had to mumble a bit of hocus-pocus before completing his trick—because the audience expected it.

He put the calculator down carefully on the ground and looked lovingly at the girl with the braces. He was so moved by his own words that he truly believed that, when looking at this child, you could see a culture going down the tubes.

"Your heroes are your papa and your mama," he said. "My God. Jesus Christ."

He slammed his heel down on her calculator.

It was quiet in the schoolyard; you could hear the wind blowing through the trees, the sound of a few cars in the distance. You could hear how the calculator shattered.

Then the girl could no longer contain her tears. The four boys looked at her and her tears and were moved.

She saw her pencil case dangling from the tall boy's hand. She had to stop crying now. That would only make things worse. That's what her mother had always said: the weak scream and weep.

"There's so much sorrow in an individual," the tall boy said. "It's inexhaustible." He put his hand on the girl's shoulder, and the touch startled her so badly that she took a step back.

"Listen, little girl," he said. "Don't be frightened. Kierkegaard once said, The door to happiness opens out. There is nothing to be done about it. But you are trying to open the door to happiness from the outside. It doesn't work that way. That makes us sad, that causes us pain."

His friends nodded. They loved Kierkegaard; without him they would be nothing.

"We are on the other side of the door," the tall boy said. "And that door keeps hitting us in the face. Because you keep trying to get through."

The tears that were running down her cheeks gave the tall boy goose pimples. He was sentimental by nature, especially in the morning.

"We're going to put you to the test," he said. "Because we want only the best for you, we are going to test you, and if you pass that test you will enjoy our protection for the rest of your life."

STILL UNDER SEDATION, Xavier was carried into the hospital. A nurse recognized him right away. "It's that boy," she told the doctor. "You know, the one who was manhandled so terribly."

The doctor nodded and subjected Xavier to a quick examination.

In another room, a doctor and two assistants were working on Awromele. He was suffering from hypothermia and dehydration, to say nothing of his broken hand, the many wounds on his body, and the ear that had been kicked. That ear in particular worried the doctors. They had already seen the X-rays of his broken hand; they had put it in a cast.

The nurse began disinfecting Xavier's cuts. A sense of pride came over her, pride in the fact that this boy, who was rather famous in Basel, and certainly in medical circles, was now dependent on her care. That she was now tending to his wounds, yes, that made her feel good. This was why she had become a nurse.

"Look," she said to the doctor, "I think he's waking up." Xavier's eyelids trembled. He opened his eyes, only to close them again a few seconds later.

The doctor wasn't paying much attention to her; he had the stethoscope in his hand and wanted to listen to Xavier's heart.

"Maybe we should call his parents," the nurse said. "His mother—I saw her here a few times, if I remember correctly."

The doctor shook his head impatiently. Xavier's eyes were open wide now, and he was asking for Awromele. When no response came, he said again, a little louder this time: "Awromele, where's Awromele? Where's my wheelbarrow?"

He tried to sit up, but the nurse pushed him down gently and the doctor took a step back in irritation. He couldn't work like this. Patients had to lie still—lie still and don't get up—that was the crux of the matter. That was the mother of all recovery.

"Your wheelbarrow isn't here," the nurse said. "You're in the hospital, but you'll be better soon."

"My wheelbarrow," Xavier said, "Awromele," and with more strength than she'd expected from him, he grabbed the nurse's arm. "Where's Awromele?" he asked. "Where is he, what have you done with him?"

She tried to pull away diplomatically, speaking soothing words and reassuring sentences all the while. "I'm sure he's okay. Don't worry."

But nothing could reassure Xavier anymore. Only the sight of Awromele.

THE RABBI WANDERED around town; he was afraid to go home. He thought about his life. His sister-in-law, with whom he'd had an affair, appeared in his thoughts; the children he had made; the God he didn't believe in but still served, because he had no choice, because his last smidgen of social standing depended on that God, there was nowhere else for him to turn, only to God. And then his thoughts turned again to Awromele. His son's disappearance made him feel terrible, though his wife's sorrow made him feel every bit as bad. But he had no idea where to look for him; he had looked everywhere. He wasn't particularly good at it, at looking for children.

Then it occurred to him that there was one place in Basel where he could still go. Besides the synagogue and his home, where his wife had called him a dirty Jew, there was still one place where he could rest his weary head.

Because the sadness overpowered him, he rang the bell.

The massages were already in progress. The massages went on around the clock. In a twenty-four-hour society, one had little choice.

The transsexuals were busy this morning. They were women on top, men down below. The rabbi liked that. Somehow, in the arms of a transsexual, he didn't feel so guilty. As though he were being kneaded by a mermaid.

"I need a really stiff massage today," he told his Asian transsexual. "My son has fallen into the hands of the anti-Semite."

"Whose hands?" the transsexual asked as she did her slow striptease.

"The anti-Semite's," the rabbi said.

A bottle of body lotion was taken down off the shelf. The rabbi asked, "What's your name again?"

"Lucy," the transsexual said.

"Lucy," said the rabbi, and he told her his life story. It was an awfully sad story, and Lucy listened patiently. Halfway through the story, she realized exactly why the rabbi was so crazy about her.

AS THE MOTHER PACED the living room, wondering where her son could be, Marc tried to convince her that someday Xavier would be a famous painter. "Just look," he said, "can't you see that? Those colors, that control over the brush." He pointed to one of the paintings of the mother holding King David. "We have a genius in the house."

The mother looked at the painting, but couldn't see anything in it. Particularly not herself. The testicle in the jar—that had turned out well, she thought. "Let's wait and see," she said, putting on the table a bowl of yogurt for her boyfriend. "Where do you suppose he's gone? Back to those Zionists again? This is the end of the line. First he comes home with a black eye, then he runs off at the crack of dawn without saying anything."

ROCHELE WAS STILL under the table in the living room, thinking about the pelican that would lift her up and take her along. The drawing pad lay closed in her lap. The longer she stayed under the table, the more convinced she became that the Messiah was a pelican. She had seen pictures of pelicans. And a nature film, too. She talked to the pelican; she begged him to come and get her and take her to the Eskimos. "Pelican, come to me," she said in a whisper. "You know where I live, don't you? You've been watching me for a long time, right? You've been circling above my head for years, haven't you?"

While her mother was in the kitchen, sunk in a prayer in which she barely believed but which was better than nothing, and while her father was spreading the panorama of his life before the transsexual, Rochele was addressing the pelican.

In the little room at the massage parlor, the bottle of body lotion was almost empty now, but the story was long and doleful. Occasionally the rabbi stopped his narrative to say: "Massage me right. The anti-Semite has hold of my eldest son. Please me, while it's still possible."

And then Lucy would say, "Yes, yes, of course."

WHEN HIS QUESTIONS received no answers, only reassuring words, and Xavier could put up with reassurances no longer, he grabbed the nurse's arm again. She had already had to pull away from him a few times and hoped the doctor would finally come to her assistance. He could calm the rebellious patient, with a second shot of sedative if need be. At first she'd been proud to be treating the famous Xavier Radek, but now she was getting fed up with him.

At that very moment, the patient bit her on the arm.

She screamed. She looked at her arm, saw the blood, and screamed again. "Look," she said to the doctor, "look at what he did."

Xavier jumped off the table and ran out of the room and down the corridor, shouting: "Awromele, Awromele, where are you? I'll never leave you alone again. Where are you?"

People leapt out of his way, some of them doctors and nurses who had dealt with things like this before. A pair of underpants was all he had on, and although the mud had been washed from his body the cuts and scrapes were still clearly visible. A mad dog strikes fear into those who see it.

"Well," said the doctor who was treating Awromele, "I think we've dealt with the most serious things now." The hand was in a cast, the cuts had been disinfected; the only thing the doctor was worried about was the ear. But the true extent of the damage would not show up until later.

"We'll keep him under observation for a couple of nights," the doctor said. "He has a slight case of pneumonia, but he can recover from that at home. Has anyone been in touch with his parents?"

The nurse shook her head. In the corridor, Xavier screamed: "Awromele, I won't leave you alone now, I'll never leave you alone again. Can you hear me? Where are you?"

For a moment, Awromele thought he was back in the park, lying beneath the pine tree. He didn't reply to his friend's shouts; he lay still, without making a sound. His friend had to be punished, not only because he had run away and left him behind with the boys, but above all because he seemed to have committed the greatest crime a person could commit: loving Awromele, dreaming of Awromele.

Awromele opened his eyes and saw the fresh face of a student nurse. Realizing that he was no longer in the park, he shouted, "Xavier!"

The nurse looked at the doctor and smiled, pleased that the patient was at least capable of something. Beside the bed hung a bag of fluid that was dripping into his arm through a needle.

"Xavier," Awromele shouted, "here I am."

"Take it easy," the doctor said, "save your strength. Don't get so wound up."

Xavier had heard Awromele's shout, but didn't know which room it came from. Down the hall he saw four male nurses heading towards him. Obviously, they were not planning to put up with any monkey business. Behind them came the nurse whom he'd bitten on the arm. "There he is," she cried, "that's him. He's dangerous. He's out of his mind."

Xavier opened the door to the room from which he thought Awromele's voice had come. But there was a woman in there, in the pangs of childbirth.

The next door opened onto an empty room.

The four male nurses were almost upon him. They had been called in from the hospital's psychiatric ward. They were experienced in dealing with rebellious patients who needed to be protected from themselves.

"Grab him," the nurse he had bitten shouted. "He bit me on the arm. Grab him, before he bites someone else."

Xavier opened a third door.

"Save your strength," he heard the doctor say to Awromele. "Don't get so wound up, you're still very weak."

Despite the bandage around Awromele's head, Xavier recognized him immediately. "Awromele," Xavier cried. "Here I am. I don't feel anything, do you hear me? I don't feel a thing. I'll never feel a thing, I promise. I'll never feel anything again."

He tried to get to the bed where Awromele was lying, but the four male nurses got to him first. They threw themselves on him and applied pressure to his throat, to discourage him from struggling.

"THIS IS THE DOOR to happiness," the tall boy said to Danica. "Now you know how the door opens."

The girl was kneeling in front of him, in a corner of the schoolyard with trees all around and bushes on which cheerful berries hung in spring. The girl gagged. The braces got in the way, but she probably would have gagged even without the braces.

The tall boy said: "This is pleasure. Do you understand?" The gagging was an integral part of the pleasure. Where pleasure begins for one, gagging begins for the other. Danica couldn't reply. "You can tell me later," the boy said. "Remember the question and take your time thinking about the answer."

The tall boy's friends watched with interest. Soon it would be their turn.

"You have passed the test," the tall boy said, and laid his hand paternally on the girl's head. "From now on, you'll enjoy our protection. You are ugly. That's a euphemism; you are hideous. Yet we still love you. Anyone can love the lovely—there's no trick to that. But to love the monster, that is man's true challenge. That is what we understand Kierkegaard to say. Love the monster, then the monster will come to love you. We have given you love, we will give you our sex, so that you can do something in return. Real love is in the giving."

Then he took the girl by the ears and moved her head back and forth as though it were a machine. It couldn't take too long—the free period was almost over, and his friends still had to have their turns.

The Snoopy pencil case was lying on the ground beside Danica. She had put her hand on the pencil case while her head was being moved back and forth. She didn't taste anything anymore, she didn't feel much anymore, at most the pain in her ears, which felt as if they were being torn off her head, and the feeling that she was going to vomit, that she would vomit as soon as they took that thing out of her mouth.

She wouldn't let them take her pencil case. Her pencil case had to be protected. They could do anything to her as long as they stayed away from her pencil case, because Snoopy understood her, Snoopy was her friend.

. . .

IN HER ROOM, Bettina was arranging papers and other documentation in a new ring binder. She had stayed home sick from school, and wanted to use the day to straighten up her files. Along with her parents and a few close relatives, she had recently adopted a third village in India.

As she looked through the account book in which she had entered the expenditures and revenues for aid to India, she could not help feeling a certain satisfaction. She was finally able to forget the Egyptian.

She was young still, but her life had already made a difference.

Money, Respect, and Women

THE MALE NURSES didn't have to apply much pressure to discourage Xavier from struggling, but, just to please the wounded nurse, they roughed up the patient for a minute or two before giving him a shot of sedative. It was Xavier's second shot of sedative that day.

As he collapsed slowly, the nurses dragged him to a room where he would be given the opportunity to recover.

The nurse complained again about how he had bitten her, and showed the bite to her colleagues, who regarded it with more than professional interest. She was young and attractive, and that lent her complaint a certain added value.

Later that morning, the hospital called Awromele's house. Rochele awakened with a start from her daydreams about the pelican, and answered the phone.

"Mama," she yelled, "Mama, it's the hospital."

The rabbi's wife, who had spent the last hour wailing by the kitchen wall, waiting for news of Awromele, tore herself away from the comfortable monotony of her indictment against God.

"Yes," she said. "Yes, this is she."

"What's wrong with him?" she asked. "Where is he?"

"I'll be right there, I'll be there in a few minutes."

She hung up. The receiver fell beside the phone, but she didn't notice.

"Come on," she said, taking Rochele by the hand. Then: "No, you stay here. Watch the baby." She leaned down to kiss Rochele, but changed her mind again. "No," she said, "we'll drop the baby off at the neighbors' house. You're coming with me."

She lifted the baby from its cradle, stuffed some diapers and baby food in a bag, and rang the neighbors' bell.

The neighbor lady, who always slept late, opened the door in her bathrobe.

"Could you please take care of him for just a little while?" she said. "I have to go to the hospital, it's an emergency, I'll be right back."

Before the neighbor could say a thing, she found herself holding the baby.

"Where's your coat?" the rabbi's wife shouted to Rochele. "Hurry up, get your coat and scarf."

They ran down the steps, the mother pulling her daughter along behind. "He's alive," she said, "Rochele, he's alive, he's been saved."

She picked up her daughter, although Rochele was actually too big for that anymore, and pressed the girl to her breast. "Awromele is alive," she said again.

"But I knew that already," Rochele replied. "It's because of the pelican."

ON THE LITTLE BED that reeked of massage oil, the rabbi, secretly and in utmost desperation, addressed himself to the Almighty. He said: "Let it happen, God, please let it come, please. It's always come before, so why not today, of all days?"

Lucy paused. "My jaw muscles are starting to hurt," she said. "This is better than going to the gym."

"This *is* the gym," the rabbi said. "For me, too. What did you think? That there's some other gym I go to?"

. . .

AT THAT MOMENT, his wife was racing through the streets of Basel, holding Rochele by the hand. Her first thought had been to go by tram, but when the tram didn't come she thought: We'll walk, it's not that far. They ran along in silence, mother and daughter. The rabbi's wife's wig was a little crooked from all the wailing and head-shaking in despair, but she didn't care. Rochele had her coat on inside out; no one noticed that, either. They paid no attention to traffic lights at the crossings, but sometimes they had to stop for a moment anyway, and then she would say: "He's alive, Rochele, he's alive. It's a miracle."

Twenty minutes later, they arrived at the hospital.

"Awromele Michalowitz," the rabbi's wife said at the desk. "Quick. He was brought in today. He's alive."

The receptionist looked at her a little pityingly, then searched about and gave her the room number.

The rabbi's wife dragged her daughter down the hospital corridors. Rochele dropped her scarf, but her mother didn't notice.

They had to take the elevator, but the rabbi's wife couldn't wait, so they took the steps. She found room 534 and threw open the door.

A nurse was busy fixing the drip.

"Awromele," the rabbi's wife cried, "Awromele!"

She threw herself on the boy. "Careful for his ear," the nurse said, but Awromele's mother didn't even hear her. "Ow!" Awromele shouted. Then the rabbi's wife let go of him and simply said, "You're alive, you're alive."

"That's right, Mama," Awromele said quietly. "Of course I'm alive. And you?"

"Look who I brought to see you," the rabbi's wife said. "Your sister." She picked up Rochele and sat her down on the bed.

"Hi, Awromele," Rochele said. "I knew everything would be okay. It's because of the pelican." Then she whispered in her brother's ear, "Don't tell anyone else, but the pelican is coming to save us."

. . .

IN A BASEL suburb, the Egyptian awoke from a dreamless sleep, fed his dogs, and remembered that this was the day the policemen would come by for their money. Then, for just a moment, Bettina crossed his mind again, and he gently shook the half-empty box of dog food. His wife had already gone out. She hadn't left a note.

When the moon was full, the Egyptian sometimes crawled quietly out of bed, so as not to wake his wife, and went out into their little garden with his dogs to cry with them at the moon.

He started shaving, but stopped halfway through. "That's enough shaving," he said to his dogs. "Enough. No time today, don't feel like it today."

In the bedroom, he dressed and picked out a necktie. He always dressed up for the Swiss policemen—they appreciated that. They liked doing business with genteel people.

IN ANOTHER PART of the city, the rabbi yanked off his condom and soon rid himself of his sperm in Lucy's mouth, an event that made him feel such relief that he fired off a prayer of thanks. "I thought it would never come," he told Lucy, "I thought I was sick." And he hugged her tightly and asked with real interest, "Where do you live, anyway?"

"Downstairs," Lucy said, "in the basement."

"That's handy," the rabbi said, dressing quickly. "So at least you don't have to commute."

ONCE THE NURSE had fixed the drip and left the room, the rabbi's wife asked: "Awromele, what happened? I want you to tell us everything."

But Awromele didn't have the strength to tell everything. He took Rochele's hand with a smile and said, "Xavier knows the whole story—ask Xavier." And then he fell asleep. Still sitting on his bed, Rochele held her sick brother's hand and said quietly to her mother: "It's because of the pelican. The pelican is on its way."

The rabbi's wife said nothing, just looked sad.

Rochele said, "Mama, your wig's on crooked."

IN A USED MERCEDES that dated from his time at the restaurant in Rapperswil—he had remained frugal, so as not to disappoint his parents—the Egyptian drove to Jerusalem Kebabs.

He'd had too little sleep, and he mulled over what had happened last night. Make a donation to a charitable institution, that was what he needed to do, and soon. That was the only remedy he knew for depression. Giving to a good cause, supporting his brothers' struggle for freedom.

He unlocked the door of his restaurant. The Nigerian cleaner would be coming along in an hour, a friendly kid with great teeth who wasn't afraid of applying a little elbow grease.

The policemen would come by early in the afternoon. He hated them, really. It wasn't enough just to give them money; you had to talk to them as well, had to remember everything, their wives' names, their sons' hobbies, their favorite soccer team. If it got any worse, you'd be better off becoming a social worker, instead of a dealer. It wasn't about the money, the policemen said, it was about having a nice little talk. But it was precisely that nice little talk that the Egyptian was dreading today.

He had just poured a glass of tea and seated himself at the table in the back of the restaurant where he always sat if things were quiet when the door opened and two people came in, a man and a woman. Tourists, from the looks of them. The man had a little video camera around his neck.

"Closed," the Egyptian called out from the back of the restaurant.

The tourists didn't pay any attention.

They closed the door behind them and walked into the restaurant. Straight towards him.

Of course, they hadn't understood what he said. Tourists never did.

"Closed," the Egyptian said again. "Closed, *fermé, gesloten. Chiuso.*"

They didn't turn around right away, so the Egyptian shouted, louder now, "We are closed!"

"We only want to drink something," the man said once he was standing at the Egyptian's table. "We're thirsty." He was wearing a woolen watch cap and had a slight accent that the Egyptian couldn't quite place.

"All right, something to drink," the Egyptian said. "Fast. Drink something fast, and then go."

His weapon was behind the bar, a little pistol he had never used—he didn't like violence. In films it was okay, to look at, but he preferred not to do it himself. And he hadn't been to the movies for years. No time for that.

He thought: I'll get my gun, that's what it's there for. The Egyptian didn't like the looks of this. He had heard stories from his colleagues: the robbers didn't look like robbers these days, sometimes they looked like backpackers, and they would get all cozy with you, and when you were least expecting it, once they'd stolen your heart, they took off with the cash register. Or with your stash.

That was why the Egyptian no longer allowed his heart to be stolen. He couldn't afford it. A stolen heart meant a stolen cash register.

He wanted to increase his market share, but not at any price; he was careful, careful with the competition, too. He wasn't looking for trouble.

In any case, they hadn't come to liquidate him. If that was what they'd been planning to do, they would have done it already.

Before he could get up and move for his gun—"Drink something fast, and then go," he had said again—the man in the watch cap pushed him back in his chair.

The Egyptian looked at him in amazement. His amazement was sincere. You always take the possibility of violence into account, but when it finally comes along, you're surprised anyway, because it's always different from what you expected. Despite his muscles, which were clear to see, the man in the watch cap had something feminine about him, something gentle, yes, almost courteous, even when he spoke in a commanding tone.

"Sit down," the man said. "First we're going to talk. Then we'll drink something."

The woman he had with him was not unattractive: blonde, medium stature. She was wearing a blouse and a fairly nondescript windbreaker. She nodded amiably to the Egyptian.

They both sat down now, the man and the woman, across from the Egyptian. They looked around with interest, while the Egyptian did his best to remain who he was, the boss of the kebab place. The manager of a one-man business. A successful immigrant. A dealer with principles. A man who, in his happiest moments, sensed that he commanded respect.

The tourist across from him took off his woolen cap. He was bald.

Maybe they were just racists; maybe they didn't want to steal anything, just pound him. Pound until they were satisfied, pound until they couldn't pound anymore.

"So let's talk," the bald man said, after he was finished looking around.

If I jump up now, the Egyptian thought, and run to the bar, I can get my gun and shoot him. If I can remember where I put it. But he remained seated and asked: "Talk? Talk about what?"

The bald man didn't reply, so the Egyptian said: "I'm a busy man. I don't want to talk. I have a lot to do today."

"Cigarette?" the bald man asked. He pulled a pack of Marlboro Lights from his inside pocket.

The Egyptian shook his head. "I have a lot to do," he said again, "I don't have time to talk."

"So you mean you've stopped?" the bald man asked. He had long eye-lashes, the Egyptian noticed, and on the right side of his forehead a birth-mark, one of those fat ones.

"I don't know you," the Egyptian said, "and you don't know me. You come here, I'm closed. You want to talk. That's not good. That's not the way you do it." He tried to sound convincing, but he heard himself and thought his voice sounded like nothing. Like weakness, like a person who's been tossed aside, like an inedible piece of meat.

The bald man lit a cigarette, and asked again: "You mean you've stopped?"

Nino wiped a few crumbs from the wooden table. He mustn't forget to call the pest-control people. They needed to come by again; the kebabs might be only a front, but a modicum of hygiene never hurt. And he shouldn't forget who he was, either: he was Nino; here in Basel they still called him Nino. "You people heard me," he said, using his left hand again to wipe some imaginary crumbs onto the floor. "I don't want to talk. I've got a lot to do. I manage this place. The management says: No talking. The management says: You two are going to go home now. You two are going to go drink something somewhere else."

No one spoke. But the tourists didn't get up, they didn't go home— maybe they didn't have a home—and then the bald man asked again, "Have you stopped?"

The Egyptian tugged at his necktie and scratched the back of his head. He felt hot. Why was he still alive? Three of his five brothers were already dead. Why wasn't he dead? Why had death passed him by? Only because he was too cowardly to be a hero. If this was life, which he wasn't so sure about anymore, then he didn't really know what he was doing here. Trash was what it was, a filthy mess, full of bald pudenda and tourists who wouldn't fuck off.

"Stopped what?" he asked. "I don't know you people. You've made some kind of mistake. You've mistaken me for someone else. I don't know who, because I don't know very many people in this town. But I have to get on with my work. I'm the manager of this place. I'm going to call the police." The longer he listened to himself talk, the more he sounded like an old woman. She was lying tied up on the living-room floor, but she kept protesting, just for the record.

"That's not a bad question," the bald man said. "Yeah, what have you stopped doing? Maybe we should ask, What haven't you stopped doing? Maybe that's a better question." He looked at the woman beside him, but she didn't seem to be listening: she was meditating, or thinking about another man, or a vacation on Malta when it hadn't stopped raining for ten days. The Egyptian had been to Malta once. With a French woman. "So let's ask you that," the bald man went on. "What haven't you stopped doing? You haven't stopped dealing. You're still living, so you haven't stopped that, either. Let's see, what else haven't you stopped doing? What does a person like you not stop doing? What can a person like you not help doing?"

Nino looked at him, the bald man with the video camera around his neck. He rubbed his hands together; they felt dry. Then he stood up, but the bald man pushed him back in his chair rather forcefully, and the Egyptian couldn't help thinking about his dogs. How he had fed them that morning, how he went into the garden with them sometimes to cry at the moon. He liked that. That made him happy; he would lie in the grass beside his dogs, even if it was cold out, even if it had just rained, and cry.

"Let's talk," the bald man said. "Let's do it right now, because time is money, and before long it won't be necessary anymore."

The woman was toying with an elastic band she'd been wearing in her hair. Her hair was hanging loose now. It was kind of curly.

"There's nothing to tell," the Egyptian said, and he looked at them, these two people who looked like tourists. He kept looking at them, because he didn't understand what they wanted from him. "I'm a busy man. You two have mistaken me for someone else. That's why I don't know what you're talking about."

Maybe they would believe him. He could be very convincing at times—people used to tell him that.

"There's nothing to tell," he said again, "I'm the manager. This is my place. My falafels are famous."

For a moment, he was afraid that something had gone wrong with last month's payment, that they hadn't split it up correctly, and that the Swiss police had decided to take action. But he knew how the Swiss police operated—they worked in a different way. Besides, they didn't look like this. Swiss undercover agents talked differently, too. He knew them; he knew them better than his own family.

"I sell famous falafels. So what's to tell?"

He laughed and held up his hands. It was a good joke, too, he thought, if you stopped to think about it. When people asked him what he did, he could say that: I sell falafels.

"What is it that makes time so valuable?" the bald man asked imperturbably. "Death, that's what makes time valuable. The faster death approaches, the more valuable time becomes. A fifteen-year-old boy thinks he'll live forever—time isn't valuable to him. You don't see what we see. You don't know what we know. Our death is fast and accurate, our death never misses the target, our death leaves no trace. Our death has to be faster than that of the enemy. Our death *is* faster. But let me put it differently: since we've been sitting here, your time has become more valuable, and we want just a little piece of that time before it becomes worthless and no one wants it anymore."

The Egyptian shook his head and looked at the door. "I don't understand," he said, "I'm old—maybe I'll live twenty, maybe thirty years, probably not—I don't have any children. What do you people want? Money? Do you think I'm rich? Rich from what? Would I be sitting here if I was rich?" He thought about Malta again, and the French woman he'd been with there. Funny to think about that now—it had been months, maybe years since he'd last thought about it.

He laughed again, and the woman across from him looked at him in a way that gave the Egyptian an uneasy feeling. A bloated feeling, like when you've had too much to eat.

"Hamas," the bald man said. "Let's talk about Hamas. First you start talking about it, because a conversation has to start somewhere, then we'll tell you what we have to say. Come on, talk. Talk about Hamas as though it were your grandma. Your favorite grandma, who told you all her naughty secrets."

The woman was weaving little figures with her elastic band; she was pretty good at it. Outside, a fire engine went by, its sirens blaring.

The owner of the kebab place shrugged. "Who?" he asked. "I don't understand. My grandma? My favorite grandma? Hamas?" He laughed. "My grandma is dead. My grandfather is, too. And my grandma didn't have any naughty secrets—she didn't have any secrets at all. Listen, my hair smells like frying fat, my hands are tired from slicing lamb and running the deep-fryer, I never remember a name, I don't have any regular customers, and when I do I forget them right away. My falafels are famous, but customers can't find me because I've moved so often. First I had a place over there, now I'm here. I should try advertising, but I don't have enough money to advertise." He moved his face closer to that of the bald man. "My heart doesn't get stolen anymore," said the Egyptian. "Because the people who steal your heart steal your cash register, too. My heart is locked up."

He put his hand over his heart, and the bald man looked around wearily. Then the bald man said: "Okay, so let me tell you something. Let me tell you about your dogs. Heinrich and Günther—that's it, isn't it?"

The Egyptian cleared his throat, and looked at the door as if he expected the cleaner to show up, though he wouldn't be coming for half an hour. He often came late, never early.

"That's right," he said, after thinking for a bit. "Günther and Heinrich. That's what they're called. They're Swiss dogs, so I figured I'd give them Swiss names. You have to adapt. Which means your dogs have to adapt, too. Adapting starts with the dogs. The dogs have to speak the same language as the other dogs. You have to call them. You take them for a walk, and they run away, because they're pigheaded, or young and frisky. Then you have to call them. Then the neighbors hear your dogs' names. Don't give them names that would be unwise, I always say. Don't give them names that will give your neighbors an uneasy feeling. A bloated feeling. For Swiss dogs you have to come up with Swiss names."

He kept talking, because as long as he talked he felt no fear. His brothers were heroes—that's why most of them were no longer alive—but he was no hero and never had been. He had dreamed of being one. He looked at his hands again.

They didn't seem to have any more questions, so he asked: "What can I do for you? What do you people want from me? You're mixed up, you've mistaken me for someone else. In some places everybody's Hamas, in other places everybody's Swiss. I'm nothing."

"There's a lot you do for us," the bald man said. "Enough, in any case. What seems like a little to you might be a lot to me. Every little bit helps. I collect those little bits. You love your dogs, don't you? You're crazy about them. That's one way of talking to you. I can tell you about how much you love your dogs, and how unpleasant you'd find it if one day they disappeared. How you'd go to bed at night and see those two lovely dogs of yours being run through a meat grinder. About how you'd see them in your dreams, every single night; you get out of bed, again and again you hear Heinrich's and Günther's dying yelps wherever you go. I could talk to you like that, but I prefer not to talk to you like that. Because, actually, I find that unpleasant. I want to tell you something, and I have something to tell you. I collect, I'm a collector—that's what I do. Some people collect pinecones, other people collect stamps, I collect information. That's why I'm here. That's the only reason I'm here, the two of us are here."

The bald man stared at the Egyptian the whole time he was talking to him. The Egyptian looked him in the eye, and as he looked he thought: What can I offer this man to make him stop talking? I can't listen to this anymore; the sound of his voice makes me sick, even sicker than that bald cunt yesterday. Maybe I'm sick, because everything makes me sick. Maybe I'll die soon, maybe that's not so bad, even though I'm afraid of dying, because when I die I'll see my whole life pass by, what it was like, what it could have been like, what it should have been like, and I don't want to see my life pass by. I can't face it. That's why I have to keep living, because as long as I'm alive I don't have to look at it.

"Information, as I'm sure you know, always has something attached to it," the bald man said. "Informants are what is attached. Maybe you're starting to understand what I'm trying to tell you. Maybe you sensed it coming the moment we walked in here. I collect informants. I've collected a whole network of informants, and I take care of them, too, because you have to take care of them, the informants; otherwise they run away or forget the meaning of life. Just like women. And now that I've run into you, I want to add you to my collection."

The Egyptian tried to get up, but the bald man laid his hands on his shoulders and said: "You really shouldn't do that anymore. It's not nice."

The Egyptian sat down again and whispered, "I'm thirsty."

"Get him a glass of water," the bald man told the woman.

She went to the bar. Nino turned and watched her go. She was wearing a denim skirt. She rummaged around in the sink, rinsed a glass, and poured him some water.

He drank eagerly. When the glass was empty, the bald man said: "What do we have to offer informants? I'm sure you'd like to know. Before you can accept a proposal, of course, you have to know what it involves. What are you saying yes to? That's the question. You're saying yes to life, for starters; those who say yes to us are saying yes to life. One good turn deserves another. That's our motto. I'm going to tell you everything, and I'm going to be frank—being frank is better for all of us. If you'll be frank with me, I'll be frank with you. And the franker we are with each other, the more useful we are to each other. We offer our informants money, respect, and women.

"Let me start with respect. I talk to you as though we're on an equal footing—that's respect. You're a filthy Arab, a two-bit dealer, such a two-bit dealer that you pose no danger to the big dealers—they let you live the way other people let a fly live on a summer evening. But we act as though you're not a filthy Arab. We act as though you weren't some shit-fly. We forget about that—or, rather, we act as though we've forgotten about that—and that's respect. Respect is a rare commodity in this day and age."

The Egyptian looked at his hands again; in some strange way, he was glad that he'd put on a tie that morning.

"Everyone hates the Arab," the Egyptian said slowly. "Everyone hates the Jew. Money is the only thing that doesn't hate us." He knew whom he was dealing with now; he had no doubt about that anymore. He wasn't particularly quick on the uptake—he was like an elephant, slow to get rolling—but once he was rolling he moved straight ahead. He should have known. They were everywhere, even in Switzerland. He rubbed his hands together. He wanted to go home. Go to sleep. Walk his dogs. Go back to sleep.

"The second thing we offer you is money," the bald man said. "You homed right in on that. Money isn't everything, but it's a lot. Money on a monthly basis, good money. Something for a rainy day, a little safety, a little security—call it whatever you want—we call it money." For a moment, almost unnoticeably, he glanced over at the woman beside him, who was still playing with her elastic band.

"And, finally, we offer you women."

"Women," the Egyptian said, and he thought about his dogs again, and for a moment about his mother, too.

"One woman," the bald man said. "The loveliest, sweetest, softest of women."

"I'm a married man," the Egyptian said, quietly and not very convincingly. "Are you married?"

"What do you call that?" the bald man asked. "What do you call it when a man offers another man money, women, and respect?"

The Egyptian thought about it. He scratched his cheek; he should have done a better job of shaving, this looked like hell. If his mother saw him like this, she'd laugh at him, she'd never let him enter her house again, she'd gossip about him to her friends—he would never be able to go back to Cairo, but, then, maybe he never wanted to go back, all he wanted was peace and quiet. "Friendship," he said. "When a man offers another man money and women and respect, then those two men share a friendship. Then they're friends." He took a deep breath. That was it. He had spoken well. But it didn't help.

"Exactly," the bald man said. "Friendship. You give us information, we give you friendship."

The bald man stuck out his hand and the Egyptian took it, but didn't let go of it again. "Listen," he said, "I know who you people are—you don't have to tell me. I know already. I've heard about you; I've had friends who worked for you. They died, but that's not the point—anyone can make a mistake. I'd be pleased to be your friend. I'm a businessman, after all, I have no opinions, I hate opinions, they get me nowhere. What's an opinion? No idea. I don't read the papers. I work hard, no time for the newspaper, All I know is that everyone hates us, that everyone hates me. Even the flowers, even the plants hate me—when I bring them home they die—and the trees hate me, too—when I go for a walk in the park they hit me in the face with their leaves. Everything that lives and grows and blossoms hates me. That's why I can't afford to have an opinion. I'd be pleased to be your friend, but you know how they are. If they find out they'll slit my throat. They're excitable. You people know how that is." Then he turned to the woman, like a lawyer starting in on his final plea. "A throat is cut before you know it. And I'm a married man. I don't want to end up like that. Not like the others. I don't want to end up like that— believe me, I don't deserve that. My wife doesn't deserve it, either. She's a good woman. In her way."

"And your two dogs," the bald man interrupted, "Günther and Hein- rich, don't forget them. You not only have a wife, you also have two dogs. They need you, the dogs need you. No one refuses my friendship. No one says to me: I don't care about that friendship of yours."

The bald man yanked his hand out of the Egyptian's grasp.

The Egyptian had the feeling that all was lost. That he would be better off saying yes, just to have it over and done with.

Briefly, for a fraction of a second, the bald man laid his hand on that of the woman beside him. She stopped playing with the elastic band. The bald man waited for the Egyptian to say something, but he was silent. He was thinking about his dogs, his house, his wife, his life; again he had the feeling that he had lost himself somewhere, the way you lose a wallet with precious photos and think, even years afterwards, God, what a pity about that wallet. He was afraid, because he'd heard the stories. He dreaded what was coming, but he had been dreading that for a long time, for years.

"Don't you think she's lovely?" the bald man asked.

The Egyptian looked at the woman, at her dark-blond, slightly curly hair, her blue eyes, her blouse, the swell of her breasts. He nodded.

"She truly is lovely," the bald man said. "She's the loveliest."

The Egyptian shook his head slowly. "I'd like to," he said. "I don't even know your name, but I'd really like to. But it's impossible. I don't want to end up like that—I'm too old to end up like that. I have nothing valuable

to offer you; I don't know anything. I know nothing. No one takes me seriously, that's why I don't know anything."

The bald man got up, walked to the door, and locked it. Then he went
to the bar and searched around amid the pile of tapes and CDs beside the
little stereo. The Egyptian looked questioningly at the woman across from
him, and she smiled at him.

"Beethoven? Do you like that?" the bald man asked.

"I enjoy classical music," the Egyptian said. "I lived in France for many
years. Worked in France for many years. I'm familiar with French cuisine,
and that's where I first heard classical music. I speak French. A little.
French is classical, too."

The bald man put on a piano concerto by Beethoven and sat back down
at the table. "Look at her," the bald man said. "Look at her, my friend. I
brought her along for you. As a token of friendship. As the start of something beautiful. Look at her."

The Egyptian looked, but he was afraid, and tired—that, too—and he
was also worried about his dogs. Who would go with them into the garden at night to cry at the moon if he wasn't around?

The woman with the dark-blond hair began unbuttoning her white
blouse.

"You people will leave my dogs alone?" he asked.

"Of course," the bald man said. "Of course we'll leave them alone.
What have your dogs ever done to us?"

"When business is good," the Egyptian said, "I donate money to Hamas,
because I suffer from depressions, actually, and giving money helps. I
opened an account for them here in Switzerland. Every good cause needs
a Swiss account. I used to give a lot of money to my parents, but it wasn't
enough. They're doing good things in Palestine, Hamas is. That's why.
They're not corrupt, they believe in something. I don't, I can't help you
people, I don't believe in anything, that's why I'm depressive, that's why
my head hurts. It pounds, it pounds all day long. I take pills for it, but the
pounding doesn't stop. You two are representatives of the Zionist entity;
you must believe in something, but I don't. That's why my head pounds."

And while he spoke, he stared at the woman's lovely breasts.

"Put your hand on them," the bald man said. "Touch her tits, touch them, that's what tits are for, that's what they're made for, to be touched, to be sucked. Tits make you forget everything. The left one will make you forget that you're a filthy Arab, the right one will take care of the shit-fly you've become. The shit-fly that feeds on the excrement of others. You don't have to think about any of that anymore. You're with us now. Love has come home. You have come home."

The Egyptian reached out his hand and put it on the woman's right breast. She smiled, but said nothing. He felt how warm she was. He touched her nipple, he thought about other nipples, and then again only about this nipple, which was different from all the others.

"Is she a whore?" he whispered.

"She loves her country," the bald man said, glancing at the woman as though to make sure he'd expressed himself well, had not passed along information that would afterwards prove inaccurate. "Her fatherland. And you?" The bald man took his video camera out of its case. "Do you love your fatherland?"

The woman got up and stood in front of the Egyptian. She took his hand and moved it over her bare upper body.

"What about you?" the bald man asked again as he turned on the video camera, which made a zooming sound before he pointed it at the two of them. The recording had begun.

"What about me?" the Egyptian asked. She was loosening his tie. Truly lovely she was, beautiful the way people in movies were beautiful, voluptuous, overwhelming—a machine, really, but a luscious machine, cold and hot at the same time.

"Do you love your fatherland?" the bald man asked as he started filming.

"I don't know," said the Egyptian, whose shirt was now being unbuttoned and pulled off. "I can't lose my heart anymore. Not to people, not to countries. My heart is locked up. I have two dogs. That's enough." He took a deep breath. The woman's hand was taking his breath away, and making him nervous—that, too. That hand was now moving across his stomach, his chest. Her nails—they were painted, pink—he looked at them the way you look at an unfamiliar creature crawling up your bare leg. You're curious, and just a little frightened, too, because it's bigger than you thought.

"Is she a Jewess?" the Egyptian whispered.

"Ask her," the bald man said. "Go ahead, you can ask her. You can talk to her. Maybe we should turn on some more lights—it's kind of dark in here."

He went to the bar. The Egyptian looked at him and said, "The switches are down there, on the right."

The bald man leaned down. The little restaurant was flooded with light; the only time it was ever this light was when the Nigerian cleaner came to mop the floor. He wondered where the cleaner could be. What time was it, anyway?

The woman took off the Egyptian's shoes. He submitted, passive and mute. She pulled his socks off, too. Dark-blue socks. He sat there bare-chested, but didn't feel the draft. Lust is a strange animal. The animal was stronger than the fear, it made the Egyptian greedy. He was lost anyway—what difference did it make? Cold consolation is better than no consolation at all. He wanted so badly to feel like a man.

The bald man sat back down where he'd been sitting the whole time.

"Do we have to do this?" the Egyptian asked. "Do we have to film this?" He felt a hand on his crotch.

There was no reply. The bald man filmed on as though he hadn't heard a thing, and in the background the piano concerto by Beethoven sounded sadder all the time. The Egyptian tried to concentrate on the music. His days in France—that's what the music reminded him of.

"Get up," the woman said, "so I can take off your pants."

Her voice sounded pleasant. Gentle and helpful, the voice of a nurse, an experienced nurse, the voice of someone to whom you can surrender, someone you can trust, because you figure she knows what she's doing.

But the Egyptian didn't get up yet; his legs were like jelly; everything about him was like jelly. He had once wanted to be a pianist, a concert pianist.

"Are you a Jewess?" he asked.

She nodded. Like him, she was half naked, but she still had her shoes on—she was wearing tennis shoes. A thought flashed through his mind: She's stoned. And so is the bald guy. They're both stoned out of their minds.

The Egyptian smiled politely, but uncomfortably, too, because he was half naked. "I have lots of Jewish customers," he said. "Friendly people, good customers, we don't talk about politics. I never talk about politics."

Then he looked at the video camera. "I can't do it," he said. "Not with a man around. I have to be alone. Can't you go away?"

"No," the bald man said. "Later on, yes. I have to be there the first time. The first time, I have to film it. I keep the film, because sometimes the informant forgets what the purpose of his life is all about, and then we show him the film. That refreshes his memory. Soon the purpose of your life will be on videotape. Then you can never forget it. Even if you go senile, the purpose of your life will have been documented. That is happiness: being able to watch the purpose of your life on video."

The Egyptian struggled to his feet. She unbuttoned his pants, and they fell down around his ankles.

"Is this your job?" the Egyptian asked, looking straight in the lens. "Is this what you do every day, again and again, and the next day, too?"

The bald man laughed—heartily, for the first time. "This is my job. It's not pleasant. But it's part of my work. Don't worry, it's nothing personal. I am the eye that sees nothing. If everything goes well, no one sees a thing. By the way, I'm divorced."

"What?" The Egyptian suddenly thought about the strange birthmark on the bald man's head.

She had his penis in her hand.

"You asked whether I was married," the bald man said, "a few minutes ago. Remember? Well, I'm divorced."

"You're pretty excited," the woman said. "I can tell that I'm making you horny. You make me horny, too. You're cute. Different from the others. You don't smell like frying fat—that's not true. You smell a little like dogs, and a little like the desert." She giggled for a moment; maybe it wasn't a giggle, maybe she'd choked on something.

It grew quiet; everyone was listening to Beethoven. The woman was rolling the Egyptian's penis between her hands.

"Does he always film you?" the Egyptian asked.

"He has to film me," she said. "It's for our country, it's for the safety of the citizens of our country. Only in this way can there ever be peace."

"Are you stoned?" the Egyptian asked.

She stopped kneading, looked at him. "Sometimes," she said. "Not now. I like to be, though. When the time is right."

"They say," the Egyptian said, and the words seemed like dry, stale bread sticking to his molars, "they say that XTC makes everything very intense, too intense for words. I've never tried it, I don't know, but that's what they say."

She held his penis tenderly in her hand and looked at her informant. "Actually, I like women," she said. "I also like men, okay, but I like women more. And sometimes when I'm with a woman for my own pleasure— because when I'm with a woman it's always for my pleasure—I take XTC. It's intense, yes, that's right, it's intense." She nodded and went on kneading. For the moment they both seemed to have forgotten about the man with the video camera.

"This may not be as intense," the Egyptian said, "but it's intense enough for me. If it were any more intense, my heart couldn't take it. I have a weak heart—that's why it's locked up."

There he stood with his old body, his fat belly, the hair that grew like weeds in the most unexpected places: on his back, his upper arms, the backs of his hands, at his ankles, on his toes. But what the bald man had said was right, he was in the process of forgetting all the rest; it hadn't succeeded quite yet, but he was in the process. This was his forgetting, it had started, it was in her tit, in the representative of the Zionist entity, in her predilection for women, her desire for XTC, in the routine way she introduced informants to the purpose of life. She would numb him, she would redeem him, she would show him the deeper meaning of all this.

The woman bent down and began lightly kissing the Egyptian's partially stiff penis. Then the Egyptian looked at the camera again.

"So this is how you get by," he said to the bald man. He suddenly felt proud, no longer wounded; or, rather, he was so wounded that it no longer mattered. "This is your job. You go home tonight, and what do you say then? 'I filmed.' Is that what you say? 'I filmed another one'?"

But right away he thought: What am I going to say when I get home tonight, what am I going to say when I talk to my mother? Every day that she lives on, she acquires more venom. She'll laugh at me. Even if I don't tell her, she'll still laugh at me, because she hears everything in my voice. And I always hear her laughing, wherever I go, whoever I'm with, I hear her laughing. Only when I cry with my dogs at the moon, that's the only time she isn't there.

"This is how everyone gets by," the bald man said. "Just relax and enjoy it. That's what you need to do: enjoy, and forget the rest. That's why we're here."

The Egyptian leaned down and kissed the woman. On her cheeks, her nose, then on her lips, too.

"Are you a whore?" he asked. "Are you a Jewish whore?"

"I work for the state," she said, petting his penis. "I like my work, because it's essential. Whores don't like their work—they hate it, they despise it, they don't like their customers. If I didn't do this work, there would be no more state. Our state is a dream, but it can be your dream, too. That's why I love my work. But I love you, too, because you smell of dog and of desert, and that's why I'm not a whore. I can smell that—I smell that you're different from the rest. I'm a civil servant, I'm part of a collective. From now on, you're part of that collective, too. When you're part of a collective, individual wishes and desires no longer count. The collective frees you of needless feelings."

The Egyptian looked at her and couldn't help it, he said, "You're beautiful, yes, you're beautiful, but you have no future, what you do has no future." He wondered: How many years' difference is there between us? What age was I when she was born? He tried to figure it out, but it didn't work, it made him dizzy, all those calculations.

"So what does have a future?" the bald man asked from behind his video camera.

"My dogs," the Egyptian replied after he'd thought about it for a few seconds, and now he turned his body towards the camera as well. The woman had to let go of his penis. "If you people look at this later on," he said, "whoever sees this later on, remember this: your country has no future, my country has no future, the future is for the dogs. Remember that, whoever sees this later on, and don't laugh at me. As I am now, you will be, too, and then you won't want people to laugh at you, either. So don't laugh at me, there's nothing for you to laugh at."

I'm in league with the enemy, so I'm already dead, he thought. It's only a matter of time, of minutes, maybe seconds even. I'm like the chicken running around after its head has been cut off.

The last echo of life was lust. The lust that was registered in the bald man's video camera, in order to remind the informant of the purpose of life.

That was why the Egyptian threw himself on the woman, on the table. And while she stuffed his old, partially stiff member into herself, and kissed him and told him how nice he smelled, of desert and of dog, the Egyptian heard in the distance the piano concerto by Beethoven.

Venice of the North

THREE DAYS AFTER he was brought in, Awromele was taken off the drip. He had told no one exactly what had happened in the park. They had urged him to press charges of assault, but he had refused.

The Michalowitz family was relieved to find that their eldest son had emerged from the ordeal relatively unscathed. He had only 70 percent of his hearing left, true enough, but there was so much screaming in the Michalowitz household that that wouldn't be much of a problem.

The rabbi decided to do penance, and for three whole days he did not go to any massage parlor whatsoever. He also resolved, for two whole weeks, until the full moon arrived and with it a new month on the Jewish calendar, not to think about transsexuals.

The Committee of Vigilant Jews decided to patrol more often, under the rabbi's leadership. The members of the committee were advised to take a baseball bat with them when patrolling in the evening; if they did not have one of those at home, an old tennis racket would suffice.

Although Bettina was still a member of the committee, she decided not to join the patrols. She wanted to start leading a healthier life. And until her hair grew back, she didn't want to stay out so late anymore.

Xavier was sent home the same day he'd been brought into the hospital. The goodwill he had accumulated as a victim of Pedophile Lenin he had squandered by biting the attractive nurse on the arm.

The rumor of Xavier's actions had spread throughout the hospital. "You see it happening all around you," a neurologist said in the cafeteria as he wolfed down a bowl of granola. "The victims start resembling the culprits. You see it with the Jews, you see it with the pedophiles—lots of pedophiles were once abused themselves. And now look at that boy; he's barely recovered from being molested, and he attacks a nurse. If I went back to college now, I wouldn't study medicine. The more you help people, the more they hate you."

His colleagues nodded in agreement.

WHEN HE GOT HOME, Xavier was received in silence by his mother, who later served him his dinner in silence as well. Even when Marc said, "Say something to your son, none of this is very easy for him; you can tell that by looking at him," all the mother said was "So why don't *you* talk to him, if you're so fond of him?"

After dinner, Xavier said he was tired and wanted to go to bed, but while his mother was doing the dishes he secretly called Awromele at the hospital. The rabbi's wife was still at his bedside—she paid no attention to visiting hours—but Xavier and Awromele were still able to exchange a few words.

"Maybe you should try painting your mother again," Marc said after Xavier had hung up. "She doesn't show it much, but she really enjoys being painted."

Xavier was actually too tired, but he set up his easel anyway. When the mother sat down at the table, as she always did, to drink a cup of tea, he said: "Here, hold the jar with my testicle in it. Then I'll make a nice painting of you."

The mother let him force King David on her, and said, "No more than thirty minutes, I need to go to bed."

While Marc watched in admiration, Xavier painted with broad, restless strokes. Maybe it was Marc's admiration, or maybe it was the serene manner in which the mother sat there with the testicle in her hand, but Xavier felt the artist in himself even stronger than before.

"Were you off with your Zionists again?" the mother asked after twenty minutes had gone by.

"I was in the hospital, Mama. You remember, don't you?"

She nodded, as though to make clear that she was not about to be fooled. She seemed to be deep in thought.

"Are you going to paint me with the knife now?" she asked.

Xavier was startled, but didn't show it. "What knife?"

"You know very well what knife," the mother said.

He went into the kitchen, found the bread knife, and handed it to the mother. She put the jar with the testicle on the table and held the knife up proudly.

Xavier began painting.

"This is my lover," she said to Marc. "Look at my lover." But Marc pretended not to be listening. He said to Xavier: "Don't you think it would be a good idea to go to the art academy? Autodidacts always have a little catching up to do. Maybe Paris would be a good place for you. Or Amsterdam. I've heard good things about the academy in Amsterdam, from a colleague of mine. The avant-garde of the future is gathering there. There the artist is his own work of art. The Venice of the North is what they call it. I wish I could go with you. But I could take you there anyway, in the Alfa."

Xavier painted on and thought about Awromele, how he had been lying beside the mandarin-orange peels in the park.

The silence that followed lasted a few minutes, until the mother said: "The Venice of the South has been overrun by the Japanese. I was there with my late husband—not an Italian in sight. Asians everywhere."

She looked at her son. "Don't forget to paint my lover," she said. "You promised." And she held the knife up even more proudly. "He's very faithful, and brimming with love."

She uses that to cut my bread, too, Xavier thought. But he painted on. Even though he felt exhausted and feverish, it didn't matter to him. An artist has no need for sleep.

When the painting was finished, he showed it to the mother. Her only remark was "Reasonable," but Marc said he had outdone himself again.

In bed that evening, Xavier decided: I'm going to the Venice of the North, and I'm taking Awromele with me. We'll be alone there. And once we're alone, the comforting can begin.

ONE WEEK LATER, after Awromele was healing well enough to satisfy the family doctor—"The bruises will go away by themselves," he said, the ear was the only thing that still worried him a bit—and after the rabbi had forgotten his oath not to think about transsexuals until the moon was full, Xavier told Awromele of his plan to go to the Venice of the North and enter the art academy there.

"Will you go with me?" Xavier asked.

"But what about translating *Mein Kampf* into Yiddish?"

"We can translate *Mein Kampf* in the Venice of the North as well. We don't have to stay in Basel to do that."

A tram rattled past; they were sitting on the patio of the wine bar that Xavier had avoided at first, because of the gossip it might cause at school. Since he had achieved fame as the victim of Pedophile Lenin, though, he no longer lived in fear of gossip. He had become unassailable—there was already so much gossip circulating about him.

Xavier was holding the forbidden book in his lap.

"Listen to this," he said. "This is really fascinating."

"You have to sit on my right side," Awromele said. "That's my bad ear."

Xavier got up and moved to Awromele's right side. They'd never talked about what had happened in the park. Xavier had always meant to bring it up, but didn't know what to say.

"Listen," he said. "How about this: 'The part played by Jewry in prostitution, and even more in the trade in young girls, can be seen more clearly in Vienna than in any other Western European city, with the exception perhaps of the ports of southern France.' "

"It's a fascinating book," Awromele said. "It's got pace, it's got momentum, it's full of humor, and I think the writer has a story to tell. We've struck gold."

"I think so, too," Xavier said. "So why don't we go on translating in Amsterdam? It's an international city, and they say it's the place to be for the pure avant-garde."

"But what about your school?"

"Oh," Xavier said. "My school? From now on, you're my school. I've learned more from you in a few months that in five years of Gymnasium. At first I thought I'd comfort you people with a novel. But now I think I can comfort you even better with a translation and paintings."

Awromele thought about it. He'd never really understood what Xavier meant with this "comforting" stuff. He still didn't.

They kissed. Xavier laid his hand on the back of Awromele's neck and whispered: "Do you know that I still don't feel a thing? Nothing at all? I couldn't if I wanted to. I'm keeping my promise."

"Me, neither," Awromele said. "That's what binds us. That's our covenant."

A few people from Xavier's school came and sat on the patio. They stared at him, but he ignored them.

Awromele sipped at his tea. You could still see what a beating he'd taken in the park, but Xavier had grown so accustomed to the bruises and scrapes that he no longer noticed them.

"I've never been to the Venice of the North," Awromele said.

"Neither have I," Xavier said. "But that doesn't matter. Apparently, the art academy there stimulates the artist's inner development."

"I'll have to talk to my parents about it."

"And what if they say no?"

Awromele shrugged. "Then I'll go anyway," he said. "What about you, have you told your mother yet?"

"I'll do that the night before I leave," Xavier said. "Otherwise she'll worry too much."

"Okay," Awromele said. Good thing that they'd had Xavier circumcised already: that would be one less thing to do in the Venice of the North. Awromele didn't know any circumcisers there; in fact, he didn't know anyone there at all. He thought about Mr. Schwartz, and felt sad.

Xavier said, "You're my dearest, my very dearest."

Awromele smiled and looked at Xavier as though he were a gift from God. "You know," he said, laying his hand on Xavier's thigh, "did you know that the surest way to say nothing is to speak?" He began caressing Xavier's leg.

"What do you mean?" Xavier asked.

"I heard that somewhere," Awromele said. "I don't remember where it was, but when you want to say something you should do it with your feet, or with your hands."

Awromele pressed his lips to Xavier's and kissed him. This would never have happened if they hadn't circumcised him. That alone was enough to justify the circumcision, and Mr. Schwartz's suffering. Awromele kissed him with all the strength he had in him. It made a noise, but because Awromele was partially deaf he couldn't hear it. He kissed the way you can kiss only when you're not sure about the other person, when you don't have him yet, when you feel that you might lose the other person any moment.

Two girls who had come out onto the patio were looking at them. They had once been in the same class as Xavier. That their former classmate did it with men was one thing, but that he did it with a man who was also a devout Jew was more than they could fathom.

"I don't get it," one of them said, not very quietly.

"My father says that our morals are decaying," her girlfriend said.

They turned around and looked at the boys. Nothing was more wonderful than looking at filth. It made you feel so clean.

Xavier wrapped the book in a plastic bag and handed it to Awromele.

"Take it with you," he said. "Then you can work on it a bit. At your house, no one will notice a book like that."

AFTER AWROMELE TOLD them at the dinner table that night that he had lost his heart to Xavier and planned to go traveling with him, the rabbi couldn't eat another bite. His son's announcement made him feel like vomiting; his wife's eyes filled with tears, and red blotches appeared on her hands; and Awromele's brothers and sisters all began shouting at the same time and throwing food at each other. Danica was the only one who didn't shout. She didn't throw food at anyone, either. She sat quietly with Snoopy in her lap and ran her tongue across the inside of her braces.

The rabbi pounded on the table, as he often did, but this time he pounded so hard that his whole family fell silent. Even the baby in the other room stopped crying. "Listen," the rabbi said, "Hitler tried to destroy us, but if you go to Amsterdam with this boy you'll be doing the same thing, you'll destroy your family. There will be nothing left of us."

Awromele tried to say something, but the rabbi pounded on the table again. "Listen," he said, "let me finish. Everyone loses his heart sometimes; God gave us a heart so that we could lose it. And everyone loses his heart sometimes to a man—that can happen. And what *can* happen *does* happen, but when it happens, God help us, on a given day, when you can't do anything about it, then you keep it a secret. You resolve it discreetly, and you don't go trotting off to Amsterdam with that man and leave your parents to be the laughing stock of the entire Jewish community in Basel. And if the Jewish community in Basel knows about it, then within two days they'll know about it in Zürich as well, and then there's no life for us here. Then I can start all over somewhere else. Be discreet, Awromele, be discreet. Isn't that what I've always tried to teach you? Look for pleasure, but look for it discreetly. Because only discreet pleasure remains; only discreet pleasure has the right to exist."

"That's enough of that!" the rabbi's wife shouted. "I don't have to listen to this. I don't want my children listening to this. This is slander,

Asher. This is scandalous, what you're preaching here. How can you say things like that? Awromele, don't listen to your father. Your father is a cheating fraud and he always has been—listen to me. This boy is no good for you. This boy will drag you down into misery, this boy attracts misfortune, this boy lets himself be circumcised at an age when respectable men are already circumcised, this boy saw to it that Mr. Schwartz ended up in prison. What am I saying? This boy saw to it that Mr. Schwartz is no longer alive. This boy is not one of us; my feelings don't deceive me; this boy is bad. If you absolutely have to run away with a boy, then I can't stop you, but find a nice, decent boy who you can adopt children with, because I know you, Awromele, you're my son, one day you'll want to have children, and maybe later you'll change your mind, maybe later you'll suddenly want a woman. That happens sometimes. But if you change your mind, don't wait too long. Do it while you still have all your teeth. If you go to Amsterdam with that boy, you won't be able to do that anymore, you'll never be able to change your mind, because I'm telling you: you'll never be able to escape this boy. He'll never let you go. He's after your money."

"But I don't have any money," Awromele said without raising his voice, "and I'm going with him, Mama. I want to be with him. He's going to the Venice of the North, and I have to go along. Where he goes, I'll go; where he dies, I'll die."

"Awromele," the rabbi shouted, "it's because the anti-Semite got hold of you—you're all confused."

"I'm not confused," Awromele said. "There's nothing else I can do. I'm actually thinking more clearly than ever."

"That's because you don't have any experience in life," the rabbi's wife said. "Later, you'll be sorry."

"I will not allow you to go," the rabbi said. "As long as I live in this house, as long as I am a rabbi in Basel, as long as I am your father, you will not see that boy again. I'm going to lock you up."

Awromele stood up from the table. "I don't feel anything," he said, "but I'm going now, I'm leaving tonight, and I won't let you stop me. Because I don't feel anything, I'll never feel anything again. I won't let you lock me up. Lock yourselves up if you want. That's the only way you two know how to avoid trouble. Lock yourselves up, bolt all the doors, shut the windows—and look what it's brought you, look at what you've become. Despicable, that's the only word for it. You two talk all day, all you do is talk, you don't produce anything—okay, children who do the same thing you do—you don't produce anything, only words, misleading words. Words that come from your mouths are dead words. The language of the future is the language of the shoe, of the knee, of the hand, of the whip. That is communication, honest communication."

"You're not going!" the rabbi shouted. "You're not leaving this house, or you're no son of mine. We'll sit *shiva* for you. And if you stay, the two of us will go out on the town, the way we used to."

"Stop it!" the rabbi's wife shouted. "Don't say things like that; you going there is bad enough already. How can you drag your children along to a den of thieves like that?"

"But, sweetheart," the rabbi said, "sweetheart, darling, my dearest wife, I do it for you, I go there out of respect for you, respect and love. When I'm there, I'm close to you; I'm never that close to you anywhere else. I need the masseuse in order to love you more. To come closer to you, I need a mediator, the way the Christians need a mediator to come closer to God. The Christians have never understood that, but Jesus is the masseur of God."

"Stop it!" the rabbi's wife cried. "I don't want to hear this. This is blasphemy, this is an insult to God. How can you call yourself a rabbi?"

"That's what I mean," Awromele said. "Talking, raping the language, turning it inside out, turning it around, then inside out again. It's parasitism. That's why they call you parasites, because you don't speak the language of human beings. The language of human beings is the language of the shoe—that's plain speaking. That's clear talk; people can do something with that. That's why they tried to exterminate you, because you've raped the language. Every word is something to be haggled over, every word can mean something else; you people are even prepared to haggle over your own death."

Awromele ran to his room, gathered together his favorite trousers, his favorite shirt, his gym socks, the notebook with the Yiddish translation of *Mein Kampf,* and the book itself. Then he stuffed it all into a plastic bag. It's starting, he thought. He didn't know what was starting, all he knew was that it was starting, that something incredible was on its way. The rabbi's wife knocked on his door. When she didn't hear anything, she opened it and said: "Awromele, if you're going to go, don't go like this. Wait a little bit, until you've calmed down."

"I have to," he said. "Papa wants to lock me up. If I stay here, I'll become like him. Something important is going to happen, and I have to be there. I'm part of the future; you two are only part of the past. A horrific past, a stinking past."

"Awromele," the rabbi's wife said, "stop babbling; you've got me all worried. Future, past—what are you talking about? Everything repeats itself, everything has already happened and is going to happen again. If the past stinks, the future will stink even worse. Keep your head down— that's the best thing you can do. Keep your head down, and don't make too much noise. Stay here; you're my firstborn son."

"No, Mama," Awromele said, "I have to go. The surest way to say nothing is to speak. I have to go, in order to say something."

He headed for the front door. He didn't want to wait for the elevator, so he took the stairs.

In the kitchen the rabbi's wife was stuffing cookies into a plastic bag. She shouted: "Rochele, hurry up, Rochele, come here. Run after your brother and give him this. And tell him not to talk nonsense: he can always come back, we'll be waiting for him, I'll be waiting for him."

Rochele grabbed the bag and ran down the stairs. She didn't catch up with Awromele until they were out on the street. She threw her arms around his waist.

"Here," she said, "here. This is from Mama. She said I should give it to you. Please come back, Awromele, please. No one knows what to do without you. Papa doesn't mean anything bad by it, you know that. He's just autistic, that's what Mama says: he can't help it. People who are autistic can't do anything about anything."

Awromele took the bag of cookies. He lifted his little sister on his arm.

"Don't go away, Awromele," she whispered in his ear. "Don't go away. The pelican is coming. The pelican will help us."

He smiled a little and put her back down. He ran his hand over her hair.

"Language is in your feet, Rochele," Awromele said. "Language is in your shoes. Anything that comes out of your mouth is useless. The language of the future is in the knuckles of both hands." He showed her his knuckles, and for a moment Rochele laid her fingers on her brother's knuckles. "Awromele," she whispered.

Then he walked on, the bag of cookies in one hand, in the other the plastic bag with his most valued possessions.

"Awromele," Rochele cried, "Awromele, come back, we need you."

But Awromele kept walking, because the language that came from people's mouths was dead.

Rochele knelt down on the pavement. She looked at the sky, at the trees, the clouds, the windows hung with curtains, and the windows hung with nothing at all.

"Pelican," she said softly, "look at me. I know you can see me. Look at me."

Eye to Eye

IT WAS TEN O'CLOCK in the evening by the time Awromele rang Xavier's doorbell. In the hand that hadn't been broken, he held the plastic bag with his most valued possessions and the bag of cookies. He was sweating from his walk across town.

Awromele had stuffed all his savings into his pants pocket. He didn't know how he would get by in the Venice of the North, so he had decided to be frugal. No more public transport, no more candy, and he would jot down all his revenues and expenditures in a notebook.

Marc opened the door.

Awromele was standing there in his black suit and pin curls, the *tzitzit* hanging out of his pants.

"Have we met?" Marc asked the Orthodox Jew. He wasn't the kind of person to be flustered by strangers showing up at the door at ten o'clock at night. The way other people eat what's set before them, that's the way Marc accepted the world.

"I'm a friend of Xavier's," Awromele said. "Xavier Radek." Awromele hoped that Xavier would hear his voice and come running out. But Xavier didn't hear anything: he was painting, and when he painted he didn't hear a thing. As was often the case at this hour of the evening, the mother was sitting across from him with his testicle in her hand.

"Yes, that's right," Marc said. "He lives here." And he looked the devout Jew over from head to toe. It was hard for him to imagine that Xavier knew this boy, let alone that he was his friend. "Is he expecting you?" he asked. On the other hand, Xavier was an artist, and artists tended to have peculiar friends. Especially when they were young. The artist as a young man was an eccentric nonconformist. Conformity came only with success. Marc had read about that, and so he didn't worry about Xavier's strange hobbies. Everything would turn out just fine in the end. The people would love Xavier and forgive him everything, and in that way they would also love Marc a little, too. "Shall I call him?"

"Yes, please," Awromele said.

Marc turned to go into the living room, but thought better of it. "He's painting right now. He can't be disturbed. Could you come back tomorrow? Tomorrow afternoon, perhaps? Perhaps you should call first, to make sure he's in."

Awromele clutched his plastic bags a little tighter. He should have put the cookies in the bigger bag as well. "Couldn't I come in for just a moment?" Awromele asked. "Just for a second? I can wait in the hallway, but I need to talk to Xavier. It's urgent. It won't take long."

Marc hesitated. Letting this boy in while Xavier was working might not be such a good idea. But he decided to let the strange creature into the house anyway. The Orthodox Jew probably spoke the truth. Xavier had peculiar friends, and maybe he wanted to use the boy as a model. That was a good idea. An artist needed to work with a few different models. Painting the mother all the time had to get a little old. This boy wouldn't make such a bad model after all, with his blond locks, his authentic getup, his religious headgear.

Marc said: "If you can be quiet and not disturb Xavier, you can come in. He's painting; he doesn't talk to anyone then. Then he's in a kind of trance."

Marc showed Awromele into the living room.

When Xavier saw Awromele, he shouted, "Jesus, Awromele!" He dropped his brush. Fortunately, he had put old newspapers on the floor under the easel.

The mother was sitting motionless at the table with the testicle in her hand, but it had not escaped her notice that an Orthodox Jew had entered her living room.

"Who is that, Xavier?" she asked. She put down the jar with the testicle in it—she had a cramp in her hand. "And pick up that pencil."

"A friend," Xavier said, "an acquaintance—nothing to get excited about. And that isn't a pencil, Mama, it's a brush." It pained him that Awromele had ignored his admonitions, that he had come by unannounced. His friend's presence stirred up a panic in him that he could overcome only by concentrating on his painting. On the other hand, he was so happy to see Awromele that he felt like running to him and licking him from head to toe, like a playful young puppy.

"I'm not getting excited," the mother said. "I only asked who it was. I suppose I'm allowed to know who has come to visit me at such an hour."

Xavier picked up his brush.

"Don't let us ruin your concentration, Xavier," Marc said. "Go on with your painting."

Marc turned to Awromele. "He's working on a series, a wonderful series called *Mother with Testicle*. It's got everything, the whole gamut of human emotions and fears. Have a seat. But be quiet."

Marc showed Awromele to a chair, diagonally across from the mother, and nodding at Xavier he whispered in the boy's ear: "Do you see those hypnotic eyes? You can really see it when he looks straight at you. He can make you do anything with those eyes. With those eyes, he has you in his power. Mrs. Radek did not just bear a child, Mrs. Radek brought something very special into the world."

"That's my bad ear," Awromele whispered back. "I can't hear you unless you sit on the other side."

While Marc now whispered into his good ear, the mother stared at Awromele. The boy's face was fascinating, there was no denying that. He did seem to exude a rather strange odor, though. She liked his hair, too. Blond, curls, funny—she'd never imagined that. Her father had always talked about black-haired Jews. Maybe the blond ones were better. People also said that light-skinned Negroes were higher on the social scale than the dark-skinned kind. There had to be a good reason for that. Nothing was without a reason.

"Mama," Xavier said, "if it bothers you that I have a visitor, I can also take him to a café."

"No," the mother said, "it's interesting to meet one of your acquaintances. What's your name?"

"Awromele," Awromele said.

"Aha," said the mother. She picked up the jar with the testicle again. She longed for her knife.

"And you are an Israelite, if I may be so free?"

Awromele clutched his two plastic bags between his knees and said: "Yes, an Israelite, you could say that. I believe so. But so are you, aren't you? Xavier, isn't your family—"

"Aren't we what?" the mother asked.

"Ah, rats," Xavier said, seeing that he had messed up his painting. His concentration had left him—his surrender to the colors, the brushes, the canvas—it wasn't working. All he could think of was Awromele. "What Awromele means is that we're all Israelites. We all come from the same fountainhead. That's what you mean, isn't it? The same patriarchs, the same myths, the same mistakes. If you go back far enough in time, there's only one father and one mother."

"Oh," the mother said. "Oh. I never looked at it that way. That's news to me. Xavier, is this going to take long? I need to go to bed."

"Almost finished, Mama."

Marc stared breathlessly at the magic Xavier worked in paint, and the mother said to Awromele: "I see it differently. I'm not so sure that we all come from the same fountainhead. I'm not sure that there is only one father and one mother if one goes back far enough. A person who was born in Nepal and grew up in Nepal is fundamentally different from me. His culture isn't my culture, his history isn't my history, his primal father is not my father. Not that his primal father is any better or any worse than mine, but he is fundamentally different."

"Mama, stop moving your hand," Xavier said. "I can't paint you like this." He was trembling himself; he couldn't keep his hand steady anymore. He was afraid, although he wasn't exactly sure of what. And he was dripping paint. He had begged Awromele not to come by unexpectedly, he had spoken at length of his mother's migraines, but he knew that everything had changed since what had happened in the park. It was no use forbidding Awromele to do anything anymore; besides, it didn't matter much, he wouldn't be living here much longer anyway. Soon he would be living in the Venice of the North, with Awromele. Together they would do a lot of bicycling. Everyone did that there, he had read—cycling, cycling, and more cycling.

"I don't know how my son met you," the mother said, doing her best not to move her hand. "He's such a closed book, just like his father, my late husband. He's interested in other cultures, but that's all I know about him. My late husband was a closed book as well, but he wasn't interested in other cultures, although he did go to Singapore often on business. He always said, There's so much we don't know about our own culture. That's how my husband was. In the last few years, my son has sought contact with Israelites, and I have nothing against that in principle. Some people study birds, others raise rabbits, still others seek contact with Israelites. At one point I phoned the school psychologist about it, and he said: It's a part of adolescence. Fine, Xavier tried to keep it a secret from me. That must be a part of adolescence as well. But he couldn't, because a mother knows everything. He went swimming, for example, in the Rhine with Zionists. Things like that, you know. I try to think: Oh well, contact with other cultures can perk up an individual. You obviously learn something from it, about yourself as well. But that sword is definitely two-edged."

She fell silent. She reminded herself of her late husband, who would remain silent for months and then suddenly launch into a speech. She missed him sometimes, his silent contempt, his ineffectual aggression. She had never thought it could happen, but on occasion she longed for him and his all-pervasive coldness. The scornful way he'd looked at her, not so very different from the uninterested, somewhat arrogant gaze with which he had viewed the world in general. Yes, he had been disgusted by her, her late husband, she had no more doubts about that, not only after her child was born, but before that too. From the very beginning. Kissing, for example, was something he'd never done—he just took her right away. That was all. "Taking" was perhaps not the right word for it. He assaulted her. He didn't like kissing. He had no time for that. Yet that was precisely why she had fallen for him, because he was disgusted by her. The way she was disgusted by herself.

She looked at Awromele. Somewhat to her own surprise, that longish hair of his appealed to her. Those eyes drew her in, so blue, so clear, you'd almost say sweet if you didn't know better. But she knew what deception was. The face is a deception. They deceived you with their faces, people did, they took you in with their looks.

"I mean," she said, "that the interest must come from both sides. We exhibit interest in your culture, so you must show a little interest in ours. My impression is that most Israelites are not particularly interested in our culture—in fact, not at all. We subsidize museums for the Israelite, meeting halls, and monuments. And that's fine. He takes, we all take—that's part of being a citizen—but what does he give? That's what I'd like to know—what does he give? Don't take this personally, I'm not saying you don't give anything. Perhaps you give a great deal, but I'm speaking here in general. Sometimes I see them in the tram and I can't help thinking that they actually despise us. I see them looking at me, the Israelites, out on the street, even in boutiques where they have no business in coming, at least from the looks of their clothes, and then I think: They despise me. I can feel it. They despise me and my culture. They don't have to say a word, I can sense it anyway. Without words. A profound contempt. Every time an Israelite looks at me, he hurts me. I feel this horrible pain, an inhuman pain, simply because of his gaze. Because of his eyes resting on me, the way he looks right through me. Do you know what I mean? I've never talked to anyone about it, but I can tell you."

"Mama," Xavier said. "Don't talk so much and don't move so much. I can't concentrate."

"Yes, you might be right," Awromele said thoughtfully.

"What?" the mother asked. "What might I be right about?"

Awromele sniffed loudly; he hadn't brought a handkerchief. He felt like eating a cookie now; the long walk had made him hungry.

"About being despised. That's what I mean. There's a lot of despising going on. It's something people like to do. My parents, for example, despise each other. My mother's family, for good reason, despises my father's family, and they're quite vocal about it. But since you're an Israelite, as you put it, yourself, I wouldn't worry too much about it. You're Xavier's mother." Awromele glanced at Xavier, who was finishing up the shading on King David. Awromele remembered the promise they'd made in the park not to feel a thing. He didn't feel a thing, he knew that for sure, he couldn't feel a thing, and that was precisely why he wanted to be with Xavier.

The mother looked at him expectantly.

"Obviously, you're one yourself," he said. "As Xavier's mother, I mean. An Israelite. But don't worry. If you'd rather not have people know, I won't tell anyone. There are plenty of people who'll tell you, Oh no, not us, absolutely not. But often enough they are. They just keep it a secret, because they don't like it, because they're afraid of the consequences. Because they don't speak the right language. You have Orthodox Jews who look down on assimilated Jews, and vice versa. That's true. But as far as your son goes, for example, I never had any problem with the fact that he didn't know anything. That he didn't know the prayers, that until recently he was uncircumcised, that he didn't know any dirty jokes in Yiddish. That's never mattered to me. I accepted him the way he was, I love him the way he is. If that's what's worrying you, I can put your mind at ease." Awromele rubbed the hand in the cast. It itched.

The mother choked on her own spittle, which she often did when love was mentioned. The testicle trembled in her hand. She started coughing. She popped something in her mouth, a yellow lozenge, and started sucking on it. The tickle in her throat faded.

"But take me, for example. When I look at you, the way we're sitting here," said Awromele, "when you see me looking at you, do I cause you pain?" Awromele looked the mother deep in the eye and thought: This woman is the mother of my sweetheart. I must never forget that when I talk to her, I have to remember that. That forges a bond: no matter what she says, whatever else she may claim, that unites me with her.

"Would you like some tea?" Xavier asked. "Mama, shouldn't we offer Awromele a cup of tea? Isn't there a kettle on in the kitchen? A little tea, Mama, don't you think we should offer our guest a little tea?"

His voice was wobbly, as though he were going through puberty all over again.

The mother held up the testicle with both hands. She was serious about her task as a model. "In a minute," she said. Her arms hurt. Posing for a painting wasn't as easy as it looked. She hated her son, but she did want to stimulate him to paint. "Yes," she said to Awromele, "you cause me pain. What did you say your name was again? Exactly?"

"Awromele," Awromele said. "Awromele Michalowitz."

"You cause me pain, Awromele Michalowitz," the mother said. "Your presence, your eyes, your look, the odor you exude—because you smell different, I'm sure you're aware of that. You cause me pain, everything about you causes me pain, everything about you tears me in two, makes me, I'm sorry to have to put it like this, nauseous. I've never had the chance to talk to anyone about this, but I can talk to you, because you've come here of your own accord. I don't know what's gotten into me, but the moment you came in here I thought: I can tell him about it."

"But I don't despise you," Awromele said, wiping his nose with the back of his hand. "I hope you believe me. I don't despise you, not in the slightest; on the contrary, I respect you, because you're Xavier's mother."

The painter tried to lose himself in his canvas, tried with the help of his brushes to forget the conversation going on around him. And the mother said: "So you don't, well, all right, that's what you say now, while you're sitting on my couch, breathing my air, now that you've walked on my wooden floor, touched my doorknobs. It's only logical that you should say that. But the other ones do. You told me that yourself—my sixth sense didn't deceive me. They despise us. When you said that, I thought: Well, there you have it. So now I know. I'm not trying to justify what's happened in the past—I can't do that, I mustn't do that—but behavior does have its consequences. Those who despise their hosts cannot go on expecting a free meal. We've done our best to please the Israelites, we've tolerated their synagogues and their slaughterhouses, their clubs, their ritual baths, and whatever else they need. And don't get me wrong when I say that I'm not judging them. Fundamentally different is neither fundamentally better nor fundamentally worse." She took a deep breath.

Xavier's painting was becoming increasingly Expressionistic. The painting now contained the irony of history—he could hear his father say that—and his emotions, they were in it, too, his love for Awromele. So that was the name he would give the painting: *The Irony of History and My Love for Awromele.* He would show it to the ladies and gentlemen at the art academy in the Venice of the North, and they would have no choice but to admit him then. It was desolate, this painting, desolate as a mountain landscape above the timberline.

The mother took a deep breath and said: "Of course, because we hoped to ward off danger, that's why we gave the Israelite so much. You have to give your enemy a lot, and not merely because we've been raised to turn the other cheek to our enemies, an important ethical principle and one I have always lived by, no matter how difficult that was for me. I have turned my other cheek, each day anew. I haven't complained, because complaining is for the weak. But what I mean to say is: I've always known that you should wrap your enemy in a warm towel and gently rub him dry, that you should give him love and nourishment and something to drink, for that is the only thing that renders him helpless. You have to know your enemy, that's the start. My father used to say that no one is more to be pitied than the one who doesn't know his enemy, the man who thinks he has no enemies and is therefore no better than a sitting duck. I have never wanted to be anyone's sitting duck. I smelled them, the enemies; I heard their footsteps, their voices; I knew they could be in places you wouldn't expect— in your own home, for example. Your own husband can be your enemy, your own child. The biggest mistake fascism made was to turn against the Israelite. If fascism had absorbed the Israelite, if fascism had said to the Israelite: Come, let us join forces, then fascism would still be a vital movement, it would be the most important movement in Europe. Look at the Palestinians. The Israelite is a fascist by nature—it's in his blood, it flows through his veins. I'm a member of the Committee of Vigilant Parents, as you may know—an honorary member, because my son was molested and lost his testicle." She moved the jar a little closer to Awromele, as though she wanted to show him all her son had lost.

Awromele nodded. In the hospital he had already taken a good look at the testicle, but he thought the testicle that they hadn't cut off was nicer.

"I hear them say it every time I attend a committee meeting," the mother said. "The Middle East is a powder keg. Before long it will come to Europe. What am I saying? The powder keg *is* already in Europe. We've tried not to see it, but it's here. It's in our trams, the powder keg sleeps in our homes, it goes shopping in our supermarkets. You, for example, you're part of that powder keg, which will explode in our unsuspecting faces—you're an Israelite. I hope you don't blame me for speaking so openly with you, I'm sure you understand. You seem to me an intelligent young man, and I haven't spoken for so long. I'll be honest with you, without beating around the bush: you are my misfortune. The way you sit there, at my table, the way you look at me, the things you've brought with you, your hair—there's no other way I can put it. I've never seen my misfortune at such close range, and I'll be honest: it fascinates me, I'd like to touch you. My misfortune, I'd like to say to you, There you are at last, it was about time, I've been waiting for you so long. I'd like to examine you, I'd like to study you. I'd like to sniff at you, the way animals sniff at each other."

Her eyes filled with tears. The mother put down the testicle, rubbed her eyes, and picked up the jar again.

"I'm not saying that I approve of absolutely everything he did," she said. "You-Know-Who—that's who I'm referring to. He made huge mistakes, unforgivable ones, there's no denying that. But if You-Know-Who had finished what he started, however much I disagreed with it, however much I still disagree with it, but just if, imagine that, just as an experiment in thought, then the Middle East wouldn't be a powder keg today. Then that powder keg would not be on Europe's doorstep. If the civilized world had let You-Know-Who finish what he started back then, wouldn't we be better off today? I'd like to hear what you have to say about that. You're an insider, you know those people in a way I don't. You must have thought about it yourself. I'm sure you've drawn conclusions, perhaps less pleasant conclusions, but, still. I'd like to hear them."

"Mama," Xavier said, sounding as though he had a bad cold, "I'm almost finished; then you can go to bed. Please hold the jar up a little higher, like this, just a little higher."

"My arm is stiff," the mother said. She didn't often get the chance to air her opinions. It did her good to talk to someone, especially to someone as attentive as Awromele. He devoured her words like pure poetry, like the Song of Songs, but written specially for him. The Song of Songs she had composed for her enemy, her favorite enemy, the only one, the final one. She had the feeling that he was devouring her body with his eyes, just as he devoured her words.

"Give your acquaintance a chance to answer me," she said. "Xavier, take your time and finish your painting. I'm curious to hear what he thinks of it. I don't mean it personally—you know that, Awromele. This is about a purely theoretical hypothesis. Would the world have been better off if you hadn't existed?"

Now it was Xavier's turn to have a coughing fit, which lasted for two minutes. During the fit he dropped his brush again. He was so afraid that his mother would betray him, that his secrets would be brought to light, that his relationship with Awromele would be destroyed. He was like a philanderer caught in the act who thinks, My mistress is lovely, but I wouldn't want to lose my wife; not that; I need her; in fact, I love her very much.

Awromele didn't know what to make of all these claims, this argumentation. Xavier had a strange mother. All Jewish mothers were strange, but this one was particularly strange. He remembered the words of the tall boy, the word that had made a great impression on him; he remembered the boy's legs, his shoes, the spit that had dripped onto Awromele's face.

"The world would have been better off if I hadn't existed," Awromele said. "That's true. But that doesn't make me unique. And it doesn't bother me, either. That's just the way it is. That's how things go."

"Yes," the mother said, "yes, I understand that." She sighed deeply. "That's quite a relief to me. I'm glad you see it that way, too. I used to wonder: Is there something wrong with me? Have I gone mad? But apparently not. It's also reassuring to know that it doesn't bother you. Some things simply cannot be undone. You-Know-Who didn't get to finish what he started; you people are here; those are facts." She laughed once; she had been feeling rather anxious.

Awromele ran his good hand through his hair. He took off his yarmulke. The ribs the tall boy and his friends had kicked still hurt whenever he breathed deeply. The hand in the cast itched even worse.

"Loneliness is nothing to be ashamed of," Awromele said.

He looked around, as though in search of support for this statement, but no support came. Xavier painted on, hastily and wildly. He had to get through this, he had to survive this; then he could be alone with Awromele, alone with Awromele for all time.

The mother turned her gaze on Awromele; she liked him more than she had expected. He, too, thought the world would have been better off without him. She would have to revise her ideas a bit. Honesty was something she appreciated.

"When my son is done painting," the mother said, "I'll offer you a cup of tea."

To that, Awromele replied: "We communicate by the wrong means, with the help of noises we make with our tongues, our throats, and our lips. We shouldn't communicate like that, that's asking for problems, that's asking for destruction. Our language is the language of the knuckle. The language of the knuckle is the language of love."

He held out his hand, clenched it to make a fist, and showed the mother his knuckles. She was still holding the jar with the testicle in her left hand, but with her right hand she reached out and touched Awromele's knuckles, and she couldn't help it—she shuddered as though she'd received an electrical shock.

"Your skin is soft," she said.

Awromele smiled; the mother's hand was still touching his.

"I bet you haven't done much manual labor."

"Not yet," Awromele said. "But that will come."

"My husband," the mother said, "had soft hands. He was an architect. He died. My father had soft hands, too; he worked with his hands, but they stayed soft. No matter what he did, they remained soft until his death."

"Could I sleep here tonight?" Awromele asked.

The mother pulled back her hand.

"Where?" she asked.

"Here," Awromele said, "in your house? I ran away from home. I couldn't stay there anymore—they wanted to lock me up. Could I spend the night here? I have nowhere else to go."

"What about the couch downstairs?" Xavier suggested, moving his brush enthusiastically across the canvas and addressing himself in his thoughts to King David. This was going to be his masterpiece. Masterpieces often looked pretty terrible.

If Xavier survived this evening, he could survive anything.

"I'm not sure I understand you exactly," the mother said. "From whom did you run away? And I'm not sure I have enough food in the house for guests."

"Don't worry about that," Awromele said, holding up the bag of cookies. "My mother gave me something to take along. I'm used to living on cookies. When I was younger, I would crawl under the blankets and eat chocolate bars, but those days are behind me now."

Marc, who had been standing silently behind Xavier the whole time, now said: "Of course, the boy can spend the night here. We'll put some sheets on the couch, and there are enough blankets in the cupboard. Besides, it's not that cold. I don't think he'll even need blankets."

"There we go," Xavier said, "finished, the painting is finished, Mama. You can put down the jar now."

She put it down and rubbed her stiff wrist and forearm. "I wake up in the middle of the night quite often," she told Awromele. "When I have to use the toilet. I have a tendency to rummage around a lot at night. That's unpleasant. Well, I only mention it in connection with your own good night's sleep. In principle, of course, you're welcome to the couch. Why not? You're my son's acquaintance, and although he seldom or never thinks about his mother, his mother always thinks about him. Always about only him."

"I'm a sound sleeper," Awromele said. "And I won't bother anyone. And you don't have to worry about standing in line for the bathroom tomorrow morning, because I never take a shower in the morning."

"Oh," the mother said, "you never shower in the morning? Then when do you shower?"

"Late in the afternoon. Sometimes I skip a day. If you stay under the blankets all the time, you don't need a shower."

"Aha," the mother said. "Is that a ritual practice?"

"No," Awromele said, "I came up with it myself."

"I'll get us some tea," Xavier said. He took off his smock, put away the brushes he had used, and nodded to Awromele. They went into the kitchen together.

There was hot water in a thermos jug. Even before he had poured the water, Xavier started kissing Awromele, and Awromele kissed back, digging his nails into the palm of his hand and thinking about that time in the park.

For a moment, Xavier was happy.

"What's with your mother?" Awromele asked after a few seconds.

"She's a little confused," Xavier whispered, "from all the commotion. She acts like this fairly often. Don't worry about it, it doesn't mean anything."

"I think the things she says are fascinating," Awromele whispered.

"About me being her misfortune. That's so captivating, don't you think? No one has ever said that to me before. And it was as though she was looking right through me."

Then the mother came into the kitchen. She was carrying two dirty cups. Xavier let go of Awromele and began toying with the lid of the thermos.

"Let me do that," the mother said. She put down the cups and took the thermos jug from her son. As she poured the hot water into clean cups, she said to Awromele: "He made a big mistake. He should never have destroyed you people, because it only made you stronger. He should have wrapped you in a warm blanket, the way I'll wrap you in a warm blanket later on."

"You don't have to do that, Mama," Xavier said.

"Oh yes," the mother said, "I'm going to wrap your acquaintance in a warm blanket." And then she nodded amiably at Awromele.

Awromele looked at her in puzzlement. He thought she was a remarkable creature.

They drank their tea in the living room. The painting was drying in one corner of the room. They were silent, except for Marc, who kept talking about the future, even though no one responded to what he said.

At ten minutes to twelve, the mother said, "Marc, go find sheets for our guest."

Marc got up and went upstairs. The mother turned on the radio. It was playing quiet music, panpipes. "We'll just wait for the news," she said. "Find out what state our world is in. Then we can go to sleep."

The mother cleared the table, and when Marc came back with the sheets she said to Awromele: "The bathroom is upstairs. I'll fetch a duvet for you."

"You don't have to do that, Mama," Xavier said. "Let me do it."

"No," the mother said, "leave this to me. I'll take care of the duvet."

Awromele brushed his teeth with Xavier's toothbrush. The idea that the toothbrush had been in Xavier's mouth as well made him happy, it gave him the feeling he was attached to someone in this world. Truly attached. When he came back into the living room, the mother was standing beside the couch, holding the duvet.

"This belonged to my late husband," she said. "He lay under it for almost fifteen years. I kept it, but I never wanted to lie under it myself. And of course Marc didn't, either. Now it comes in handy. Undress—then I'll tuck you in."

Under the watchful eye of Xavier and his mother, Awromele undressed. First his white shirt, then his *arba' kanfot,* then his pants and his gym socks, until he was down to his underpants. It took a while, because of the cast on his hand. Marc came down for a look as well.

"So lie down," the mother said.

Awromele lay down carefully on the couch. The sheets had been neatly ironed; he didn't want to wrinkle anything. The mother spread the duvet and tucked Awromele in. "This is what You-Know-Who should have done with you people," she whispered. Her lips brushed Awromele's forehead. She shuddered again.

Then she went to her bedroom.

"What's she talking about, anyway?" Awromele asked Xavier.

"No idea," Xavier said. "She's confused." He leaned over and kissed Awromele. "I love you," Xavier whispered. "Don't forget that. I love you, but I don't feel a thing, and as soon as we're in the Venice of the North I'm going to comfort you. Comfort you so hard and so long, and not just you, but your entire emaciated people."

Awromele took off his underpants to make it easier for Xavier's hand. He wondered what Xavier meant with that emaciated-people business, but the pleasure stopped his waking mind. The pleasure answered all questions. The pleasure was one long answer.

IN THE EARLY-MORNING hours Awromele was awakened by the sound of thumping. First he tried to roll over and go back to sleep, but because the couch was rather narrow he couldn't turn, and going back to sleep didn't work, either. After staring at the ceiling for a few minutes, Awromele got up to investigate; he wanted to know where the thumping came from.

He put on his underpants. Because he didn't know his way around the house, he bumped into furniture in the dark.

At last he opened the kitchen door. He saw the mother standing there. There was a little light on above the stove, a light built into the exhaust hood.

The mother was standing at the sink. Her pajama pants were down around her ankles. She had a knife in her hand.

Awromele was about to close the door, but the mother looked up at him. She beckoned him with her finger. Awromele turned, and she said, "Come closer, Awromele Michalowitz."

He stood there without saying a word. He didn't dare go away—he couldn't refuse his hostess such a simple request. The mother coughed a few times. Seconds went by. Awromele stood in the doorway, but he didn't dare to leave the kitchen. That would be stupid, and stupidity was dangerous.

She said, "I've been waiting for you, Awromele, for at least fifteen minutes."

"I was looking for the bathroom," Awromele said, turning around again. He didn't go out the door.

The mother put the knife back in the dish rack. "Close the door, Awromele, there's a draft." Awromele closed the kitchen door quietly; he didn't want to wake the others.

The mother turned to face him now. "Come closer, would you?" she said. "I've been waiting for you, I knew you would come."

Awromele turned and took a step towards the mother. Like a sleepwalker, without wanting to.

He didn't want to go to the mother, who was standing at the sink in the middle of the night with her pajama pants around her ankles; he wanted to go with Xavier to the Venice of the North. He wanted to lie with Xavier in a big white bed, the way he had lain with him in the park.

A bed: that wasn't asking so much. A bed sounded wonderful to him. To slowly become unwashed in that bed.

"At night I make a little noise," she said. "When I visit my lover. Sometimes I make little cries of ecstasy, but never too loudly, because that would wake the others."

"Yes," Awromele said. "I understand."

"I hope you don't hold it against me," she said. "About you being my misfortune. You probably can't do anything about it. It's just the way nature arranges things."

She took the bread knife out of the dish rack.

"I . . ." Awromele said, "I'm going back to sleep."

"No," the mother said, "don't go to sleep."

"I really need to get some sleep. I'm sorry I disturbed you."

"Don't go to sleep," she repeated. "I want you to meet my lover."

She held up the knife. Black and gleaming. "He's from Italy," the mother said. "They say that Italians make the best lovers. I wouldn't know, but it doesn't surprise me. What do you think? Are Italians the best lovers?"

Awromele forced himself to smile. He couldn't help thinking about his own mother, about his little sister Rochele and everything she had whispered to him about the pelican, and then about the tall boy again, and what he had said. Awromele had never been to Italy: maybe the best lovers did come from there. But he had never thought they would look like this: a bread knife with a black handle.

"Come closer," the mother said. "I've always wanted an Israelite to see this. I knew it would happen one day. Only I didn't know when, or how."

"I need to go to sleep," Awromele said. "Mrs. Radek, I really need to get some sleep." He was whispering, but he still tried to speak as clearly as he could, so she would understand him, in order to rule out misunderstandings.

"I do it for you people as well," the mother said. "For the Israelite, so also for you. When I stroke him, my lover, my sweetest, the warmest, the loveliest of all lovers, then others are stroking him as well; then the Israelite is stroking him, too. I stroke him on behalf of others, the way my lover also takes me on behalf of others, forces himself into me on behalf of dozens, thousands of others. That's how it feels, as though thousands are forcing themselves into me when he takes me."

She held out her hand, but Awromele didn't dare take it. Besides, he was standing too far away to take her hand, and he didn't feel like getting any closer.

"I'll be going now," Awromele said. "I'm very grateful to you for letting me stay here for a few hours. I'll never forget it. It was a pleasure. Shall I fold up the sheets?"

"Stay," the mother said. "I want you to see this. I want you to get to know my lover. People are cold, Awromele, but not my lover, my lover is hot."

Now she took a step towards the boy. That was hard for her to do with her pajama pants around her ankles—she had to hold on to the counter. Inch by inch, she shuffled towards Awromele.

And he stood there, remembering that this woman was the mother of his beloved, that Xavier had come out of her, just as Awromele had come out of the rabbi's wife.

Finally, she stopped. The Italian bread knife was dangling from her right hand. "I've often wondered what my misfortune would look like," she said. "In the evening, when I couldn't get to sleep: at night, when I woke up, and I always woke up at night. What would he look like, what kind of eyes would he have? My husband wasn't my misfortune. My husband was the father of my son, my husband gathered me up when I was nothing, an orphan, a rag. My husband was disgusted by me, but that doesn't matter, Awromele, because so am I."

"Yes," Awromele said, "yes, yes. Of course." Now he remembered the name the tall boy had mentioned as he spoke the language of shoes and knuckles. Kierkegaard. A strange name. Kierkegaard. It sounded like a company that made Swedish crackers, and he thought of the matzos his people had to eat at Pesach, the whole time keeping his eye on the mother's lover.

"I had a hunch," the mother said, "but I wasn't completely sure. Now I know for sure, and it's strange, it's as though I've known my misfortune the whole time, as though you've always been there, from the very first day of my life, from the moment I met my husband. My husband liked to do it violently, so he could forget that I disgusted him. He explained that to me once, in a moment of weakness. Violence was the only thing that could make him forget how I disgusted him. Everything about me disgusted him, my hair, my mouth, my teeth, the way I smelled, my caresses, my holes—some holes less than others, but he told me, There's not a whole lot of difference. Because sometimes he really talked to me. Then he was tender, then he explained things: why he had to assault me, why he couldn't do it any other way, why that was the only way he could show his love. It doesn't surprise me that my misfortune is pretty, and young, and blond. That's how it should be, young and pretty and blond."

She gasped for breath; she was dizzy. She had to hold on to the counter. "I talk with him," she said, "with my lover, every night, here in the kitchen, before he takes me, before he tears me open like an animal. Before he does that, I talk with him. I caress him. His blade is cold at first, but that's only appearances; he's as warm as a person could never be. They try to be, people do, but they'll never be as warm as my lover. I tell him everything while I caress him. He likes that, it thrills him."

She held the knife out in front of her.

"I want you to caress him, too. Now that I've seen my misfortune, now that I never again have to wonder exactly what it looks like, that misfortune of mine, now that I know that, now I want you to caress my lover. Neither of us should have existed, Awromele. But it's too late to do anything about that now."

She swallowed the wrong way, coughed, and wiped her mouth with her free hand. Then she said: "He likes being caressed, he loves that, he loves being called little names. Caress him and say something to him."

She held the knife under Awromele's nose.

"I can't," Awromele said. "It's very sweet of you to offer. But I really have to go home now—my family is waiting for me—some other time, I'd be delighted. It sounds like fun, when I'm a little less pressed for time."

"No," the mother said. Her voice sounded furious, sharp as an ax. "Not some other time. Caress my lover. They've forgotten about you. If you hadn't existed, I would have been happier. But they've forgotten about me, too. I'm just as forgotten as you are. That's why I want you to stroke my lover. I want my lover to feel the hands of my misfortune, the soft hands of my misfortune."

Awromele moved his good hand towards the knife, placed his index finger carefully against the blade.

"Stroke it," the mother said, "stroke it. You're cold, my lover is hot."

Awromele carefully moved his finger up and down.

"That's good, the way you do it," the mother said. "He likes that, it thrills him. This is the love of my life, Awromele. When I'm not around anymore, I want you to remember what the love of my life looked like. I want you to tell other people: Mrs. Radek had one great love in her life, and I stroked him."

Awromele held his finger still, but the mother said: "Don't stop. Go on. Talk to him, talk to him in your language, that horrible language of yours, the one that causes me such pain, the language in which you people speak to your God. Say to my lover the prayer meant for your God. My lover wants to hear your prayers, he wants to hear prayers that aren't meant for him, and so do I. I want to finally hear a prayer in the language of my misfortune."

"That's impossible," Awromele said. "I have to go now. But I'll come back, and then we'll do everything you say."

"Say it," she said, "say the prayer." She put her left hand on Awromele's shoulder, squeezed his shoulder, then moved her hand up until it was resting on Awromele's hair, while his finger kept stroking the mother's lover.

"Pray," she said. "You're my misfortune; you have to pray for me. No one else will, no one else is allowed to."

Awromele thought: If I do it, maybe I can get out of here, and I mustn't forget that she's the mother of my beloved. And so, as he continued to stroke the knife, he said: "*Shema Yisrael, adonai eloheinu, adonai echad.*" He said it quickly and sloppily, the way a timid boy might order a loaf of bread in a crowded bakery. His voice trembled. His hand trembled. He had no feeling left in the finger that was stroking the knife.

"Again," the mother said.

And Awromele repeated the prayer. Just as quickly, just as quietly, and, for the first time since meeting the tall boy and his friends in the park, without embarrassment.

"Yes," she said, "that was good. Now he can take me again like an animal, in the place where he always takes me, every night, like a hot, panting animal, because that's what he is, my stainless-steel lover, a hot, panting beast, a sweet brute, untiring, always ready for love, always in the mood, never a headache."

She moved her left leg forward. "Look," she said.

Awromele saw the wounds on her left thigh, the scars, the scabs. The old wounds, the wounds from yesterday, the wounds from a week ago, the wounds that were jabbed open again and again. A battlefield, her leg was. He felt like screaming, but he was afraid it would wake someone. The mother's hand was still resting on his head.

He wanted to run away and never come back. Away from this house, away from this city, away from this country.

"Stay," she said, "stay, Awromele. You know that song, the one about Jewish blood that splatters from the knife? I've sung it often; it has a nice melody, it sticks with you. Do you know that song? I'm sure you've heard it before. Do you know it? Do you want me to sing it for you?"

She turned her lover around, aimed him at her left thigh.

"This is sweet," she said. "This is living. You're too young to understand that, and, besides, you're my misfortune. Young, with curly blond hair, that's how I want to remember my misfortune. If you people had been exterminated, I wouldn't have had any misfortune, but what else would I have had?"

She set the knife to her thigh and pushed it in slowly.

This time Awromele really did cry out, but the mother put her hand over his mouth. "What do I have to say?" she asked. "Quick, what do I have to say? How does the prayer go?"

She grabbed his arm and squeezed it hard. As though that were all she had the strength to do, as though she couldn't do anything else.

"*Shema Yisrael,*" said Awromele.

"*Shema Yisrael,*" said the mother.

"*Adonai eloheinu,*" said Awromele.

"*Adonai eloheinu,*" said the mother.

"*Adonai echad,*" said Awromele.

"*Adonai echad,*" said the mother.

Then she pulled the knife out of her leg.

She put her hand over Awromele's mouth right away. The blood flowed like a hesitant little mountain brook in early spring.

"It's love," the mother said. "Awromele, it's love, it's the only love on this earth, the purest, the loveliest, it's the only love worthy of the name: the hatred of the Jews. You know, my father had hands just like yours, hands just as soft as yours."

"I didn't know that," Awromele said. "He must have been a special man. I think I'll get my things together."

"You won't forget me?" the mother asked. "You won't forget me and my lover?"

"No," Awromele said, "never."

The mother let him go.

He took a few steps back, turned, and opened the kitchen door, then looked over his shoulder. The mother was still standing there with her lover in her hand. The battlefield of her left leg was illuminated softly by the lamp in the exhaust hood. She looked at her misfortune and knew for a fact that it was love, her father's love, too. She would never doubt it again, now that she had seen her misfortune up close.

Awromele said, "Have a pleasant night, and thank you for everything."

He closed the kitchen door carefully and ran upstairs, to Xavier's bedroom. He shook Xavier till he was awake.

"What is it?" Xavier asked. "Did we oversleep?"

"No, we didn't oversleep," Awromele said, "but I want to go. Are you going with me? Xavier, let's go now."

In the kitchen, the mother was carefully cleaning her lover with hot water and dishwashing liquid. "My little one," she said, "my sweetest. You're the loveliest of all. The warmest." She caressed the knife, the way she would never caress anyone again. *"Shema Yisrael,"* she said to the knife that was the love of her life. She had remembered those words—the rest she had forgotten. *"Shema Yisrael."*

Then she had to drop the knife in order to clutch the counter with both hands. She felt dizzy, but happier than she had ever felt before.

And down her left leg still flowed a mountain brook. A brook that wanted only one thing: to grow into a broad river.

In sh' Allah

EVEN THOUGH THE MOON wasn't full, the Egyptian sneaked out of his house in the middle of the night. He took his dogs into the garden, scratched them behind the ears, and in one corner crouched down beside them, on all fours, and cried with them at the moon that wasn't full.

He did that for at least ten minutes. All that time, he was thinking. He weighed the advantages against the disadvantages, until all advantages and disadvantages had disappeared, and then he made up his mind.

But he himself had the feeling that he had done nothing, that the decision had been made for him. Life had rolled over him like a wave; he had allowed himself to float along. Now he was in the process of washing ashore— he didn't know where. Soon he would feel dry land beneath his feet again. He went back into the house: he was wearing his gray slippers, so as not to wake his wife. He took his cell phone down to the basement, where there were a few bottles of wine, a washing machine, and some furniture they no longer used, and dialed the number the bald man had given him. It took a while for someone to answer.

"It's me," the Egyptian said, "from the kebab place."

There was no reaction.

"From Jerusalem Kebabs," the Egyptian said. "Nino. You two were there yesterday."

"Where?" asked a woman's voice he didn't recognize.

"At my place," the Egyptian said, "yesterday. I want to talk to her; she said I should call this number if I wanted to talk to her, twenty-four hours a day. The woman who was at my place—the blonde one. I want to talk to her."

He had been given this number to call if he had something to tell, if he heard anything important. That was the job of the informant, that was his job now. But he didn't have anything to tell, he just wanted to see her. He thought he was going crazy. He had been lying awake half the night beside his wife, but he didn't see her, all he saw was the Zionist with the blond hair who actually liked women. Wherever he looked he saw her, he heard her voice. He saw himself sitting on a chair at the back of his restaurant, felt her hands running over his stomach again. He mumbled into his pillow, "I am an informant." And he was being driven crazy by the thought of dying without seeing her again.

"Later today, the same time, the same place," the woman's voice said, and she hung up.

The Egyptian went back to the dogs in the garden. He lay down beside them in the cold grass and looked at the sky. There were no stars to be seen. They licked his hands and his face, nibbled gently on his fingers. I have to see her, the Egyptian thought. I smell of desert and dog, I'm different from the other informants. When I see her again, I'll explain everything.

MARC AWOKE TO the sound of loud talking in the room next to his. He went to see what was going on, and found Awromele and Xavier in a fervent embrace. "What's going on?" he asked. "What are you two doing?"

"We're leaving," Awromele said, without letting go of Xavier.

"We're going to the Venice of the North," Xavier said. "We'll take the train, we'll be there in eight hours. We're not going to wait any longer. Waiting any longer would be a waste of time. Now is the moment." He looked around triumphantly, almost ecstatically.

Marc thought about it. He sat down beside them on the bed. He was wondering; he could always take a day off, or even two, but he wasn't sure the mother would be very happy about that. He could just call in sick. He was never sick otherwise, they wouldn't make any fuss about that. And the mother would understand, too. When you were the mother of an artist, you had to think big. He had to think big, too, because he was the mother's boyfriend.

"You know what, I'll take you to Amsterdam," he said. "In the Alfa— that's a lot more fun. That way we'll be there in a few hours, and we can get a bite to eat together. I was there a long time ago with some friends. There's a great club there, it's called The Milky Way."

Then he hugged both boys, as though they had been the best of friends for years. As though they'd slept in the same bed for years. Xavier, in fact, was the one he wanted to touch. Awromele was simply part of the package. It was nice to hug them. He wouldn't mind hugging Xavier fervently more often, but the opportunity never presented itself. Sometimes he put his hand on the back of Xavier's neck, but usually Xavier didn't seem to appreciate that.

Marc went to his bedroom and quickly stuffed a few things into his weekend bag. Feeling cheerful, he hummed a song he'd heard on the radio a few days ago; he could only remember part of the lyrics. Yes, he had done well to stay with the mother. He had discovered his sexual identity, but he was taking it nice and easy, all in good time, no sense in rushing things.

In the room beside Marc's, Xavier asked, "What are you taking with you, anyway?"

"A plastic bag, the one that's downstairs," Awromele said.

"Is that all?"

"That seemed handier to me, to take as little as possible—it seemed practical."

"How long are we going to stay?" Xavier asked. As though he hadn't come up with the plan, as though he weren't the one who wanted to attend the art academy in the Venice of the North.

Awromele shrugged. "I don't know," he said. "Maybe forever. I have no idea."

Xavier decided then and there that he would take only his paintings, or at least the paintings that were dry, and a few pairs of trousers. What else was there to take when you went away forever? When you went away forever, you had to leave a lot behind—that was how it worked.

He rolled up the paintings, folded some trousers and two T-shirts, and put them carefully in a sports bag. It all went so quickly that he had no time to say farewell to anything—his knickknacks, his bed, his mother, his easel—and that was for the best. Leaving without saying goodbye was the most pleasant way to go. Leaving as though running out of a burning house, that's how you had to do it; otherwise it would never happen at all.

The mother was still in the kitchen. She had pulled up her pajama pants, But she was unable to move.

"I'm leaving," Xavier told her. "I'm going to the Venice of the North; I'm going to dedicate myself seriously to my painting. It's now or never. I can finish school some other time. Art won't wait."

"Oh," the mother said. "Art."

He laid his hand on hers. She was still holding on to the counter.

"We'll see each other soon," Xavier said. "I'll call when I get there. Marc is taking us. You're the sweetest mother I know. You know that, don't you?"

"Yes," she said. "I know." Her son patted her hand, but she barely felt it; her thoughts were elsewhere, although she had no idea where.

Xavier did not find it difficult to say goodbye to the mother, yet he still felt a lump in his throat at the sight of her standing there, so fragile. She had been his model. He had painted her. That was the one thing she could do, the one thing she really liked to do, pose for him.

Now that the one who had painted her was leaving, it seemed as if her life had become drained of purpose, as if all she could do was stand in the kitchen, her hands on the counter, her gaze fixed on a lover who had always been silent and always would be.

"Well," Xavier said, and he hugged his mother. She let him do it. She even put her arms mechanically around her son. "I'll let you know what the admissions board thinks of the paintings I made of you," Xavier said. "I'll tell you all about it."

And with those words, he left the mother behind in the kitchen.

He'd noticed that something was flowing down the inside of her pajama pants, but it was better to ignore that. You couldn't keep confronting people with their peculiarities.

In the living room, his eyes rested on King David. He was still on the table, a remnant of the past, the remains of a still life. Xavier picked him up and held him in his hand for a moment. "King David," he said to the testicle, "blessed King David. Of course, you're going with me. Where I go, you go. And vice versa."

He didn't put him in the sports bag—that would be too risky; the jar might break. He would carry him like this, in his hand, the way you carry a little pet.

"I'm going to give the boys a lift," Marc told the mother in the kitchen. "I'll be back in a day or so." He pecked her on the cheek. "That's okay, isn't it?"

She didn't reply. She was standing at the sink; she could feel that her left leg was wet, but she felt no pain. All she noticed was a slight dizziness. She wondered what day it was, whether she had any appointments, and if so, with whom.

"You don't mind, do you?" Marc persisted.

"No, of course not," she said. "Go on. Be careful."

It was early in the morning—still night, really. The mother didn't know whether to go back to bed or to stay in the kitchen like this. Maybe she could make some tea. But she didn't have the strength for it.

Marc hesitated. His girlfriend was being awfully quiet, he thought, standing there so still. "You're all right, aren't you?" he asked. "Does it upset you, having Xavier go away like this? He'll be back. Children always have to leave the nest. It's good for them. The sooner the better. I stayed at home for too long myself, but, then, it was awfully easy there. And pleasant—that, too."

She nodded, staring at the knife. It was so beautiful—of all the objects in this world, the knife was the most beautiful.

"Yes," she said, "that's fine."

Then she looked at Marc. He hadn't washed his face yet; there was still sleep in his eyes. "Did you know that I wanted to poison him?" she asked.

"Oh," Marc said, and poured himself a glass of water. His hand bumped against the knife, lying lonely in the dish rack. But he didn't notice. He was thinking about the drive with the boys. "Who?" he asked.

"My son," the mother said. "When he was still a baby. I had actually bought the poison and mixed it in with his milk. It doesn't take long for it to dissolve in warm milk, rat poison. The pellets are big, though—you have to stir well."

"I have to get going," Marc said. "While it's still quiet on the road. We'll talk about it some other time." He gave his girlfriend a soothing little kiss—she was a brave woman. Then he walked away. In the doorway, he turned and waved. And although the mother didn't really have enough strength to do so, she waved back.

Marc closed the door and walked briskly to his car. He was looking forward to this. They could stop along the way someplace, at a romantic restaurant.

HER DAY'S WORK was over. In the cellar where she lived, Lucy's owner chained her to a heating pipe, so she wouldn't run away and do crazy things.

The owner looked at her for a moment as she settled down in her sleeping bag. "You're lucky," he said tenderly. "Other people have to sit in the car for hours to get to work. But where you are is where your work is; you take your work with you everywhere, no matter where you go. You're a privileged person."

He sighed deeply a few times and left Lucy alone. It wasn't easy, always having to find new people from exotic countries to massage the working population. They worked long hours, true enough, but they were better off than in their own countries, and they never had to sit in traffic.

AWROMELE AND XAVIER were in the back of the Alfa. It was cozy in Marc's car. Marc was sorry that Xavier wasn't sitting next to him, but in Amsterdam there would be time enough for farewells. Never give up hope, he told himself. Looking on the bright side of life was half the battle.

They drove down the street. "Here we go," he said, and looked at the boys in the mirror. They were holding each other tight.

THE MOTHER WAS standing in the kitchen. The blood had started clotting; her pajama pants were sticking to the wound. Later, on she would have to pull it loose. That felt unpleasant. She put it off for a little while.

She noticed that the house was quiet, and because there was no one at home anymore, she lay down on the cold kitchen floor. That was nice, to lie down for a bit. She had to recover from the act of love. She closed her eyes.

Across town, the rabbi's wife awoke. She tiptoed immediately to her eldest son's room; the bed had not been slept in. Although she knew it was no use, she looked under the blanket and then, just to be sure, under the bed. "Awromele," she whispered. "Awromele, are you there?" As though he might be hiding in the closet.

Then she went back to her bedroom and shook the rabbi. "You ran him out of the house," she said, "you chased him away, you've ruined us." She pounded her fists on his chest, but all he did was mumble: "Leave me alone. What do want from me? Stop blaming me for everything. I'm not God."

·   ·   ·

IT WAS STILL EARLY when the Egyptian drove to his kebab restaurant, to prepare himself for the meeting with the woman who thought he smelled of desert and dogs. He could hardly wait. His own wife was still asleep; he had left a little note for her in the living room. He had fed the dogs.

He tapped his hands on the wheel of his old Mercedes, to the rhythm of Um Kalsum. Something was reminding him that he was alive. Amid everything that was dead—and almost everything was dead—there it was all of a sudden, life. Overwhelming, almost incomprehensible, but pleasant, terribly pleasant.

He opened the restaurant, sat down in his regular spot at the back with a few Egyptian papers he hadn't read yet and several ledgers that he kept up for the sake of appearances. Despite everything, they pleased him, the ledgers—the appearance of order seemed like quite a feat to him at his age. He didn't know what he was looking forward to, but he was looking forward, there was no doubt about that.

The city was slowly waking up. The Egyptian made coffee, and thought about opening early, since he was here anyway. He liked seeing the customers come in, the schoolchildren, the tourists doing Europe on a budget that left little room for a healthy diet, the office clerks in a hurry. Because he was hungry, he looked in the fridge and found a plate of falafel balls he had made the night before. He was thinking about the woman who had seduced him for her country only a short time before, and who'd had to admit that he was different from the others she'd caressed on her country's behalf.

Since he was waiting for her anyway, for the woman who had given him something he had never received before, he decided there was no reason not to fry up a few falafel balls. No better breakfast than falafel. He used to eat them for breakfast all the time, back when he had just started the kebab place.

He picked up the can of oil and poured a big puddle of it into the fryer. He had enough oil—he always kept up his stocks. He turned on the radio.

The music was something he vaguely recognized, something Spanish, and he tried to whistle along with it. He thought about the parties he'd gone to in France when he worked there, parties where the music was too loud and there was too much smoke. Yes, he had been a partygoer once. Long ago.

He watched the oil heat up slowly. It took so long for oil to heat up. He liked to watch it. He rubbed his cheek; last night, before going to bed, he had shaved carefully, and even used the nail scissors to trim the hairs in his nostrils.

The Spanish song began to irritate him. He turned off the radio and picked up a tape—the piano concerto by Beethoven, always a good choice. He turned on the tape player and sat down in a chair beside the fryer, a plate of raw falafel balls in his hand. He tried to summon up a picture of the woman who had come to visit him yesterday. He didn't have anything to tell her, nothing new, nothing she didn't already know; he was the informant without a story. At first she would be disappointed, but she would understand. She wouldn't mind. His story was his body. That's what she would say to him, too, as she held him in her arms. Your body is your story, your smell is the information you've collected for us.

IN BASEL IT was now ten o'clock in the morning. The mother lay in her kitchen and dreamed about her son as a baby, about how he had sat on her lap, how she had breastfed him, her wedding party, the knife. The dreams were brief and vivid. Occasionally she awoke with a start and realized that she was lying on the floor of her kitchen, but that didn't bother her. Nothing was worth getting bothered about. She didn't get up. It was good this way, the way it should always be.

THE OIL IN the fryer was slowly growing hot, gradually reaching the point where the frying could start. The Egyptian dropped in the falafel balls one by one. He was almost happy. It was wonderful to watch them turn brown. The piano concerto soothed him; he had nothing to worry about; it hadn't been a mirage; he knew what she had said to him, and she would know what he smelled like. She would be drawn to his smell. She could pick him out of the crowd, she could locate him blindly.

IN THE CLASSROOM, the tall boy and his friends were bent over a math exam. They were concentrating; for the moment, their thoughts were not on Kierkegaard or the girl with braces whom they'd recently taken under their wing. But halfway through the assignment, the tall boy's thoughts began wandering anyway. Next time I see her, I have to tell her that, he thought, the girl with the braces. It's not Snoopy who understands us. I have to tell her that: Girlie, it's not Snoopy who understands us.

THERE WAS A KNOCK on the door. Maybe she's early, the Egyptian thought. Yes, she was early. She couldn't wait to see him, either, the informant unlike other informants. She had raced to him, on a moped perhaps, or one of those Italian scooters, the kind you saw in commercials. He couldn't remember what the commercials were for, only that the people in them raced around on scooters and found each other.

He walked away from the deep-fryer.

As soon as he opened the door, two men in almost identical gray suits knocked him to the floor. A third man locked the door behind him. He was wearing a gray suit, too.

There were three of them, the Egyptian had time to think, feeling his ribs. The men were hurting him.

"My, doesn't it smell nice in here," said the man who had locked the door, while the other two remained seated on top of the Egyptian. The man inhaled deeply. He strolled around the restaurant, from back to front, front to back. Then he walked from back to front again, and at last he said: "Yes, that's wonderful. You don't smell anything like that very often."

He took a chair and put it down next to the Egyptian, who was lying on his back with the two men on top of him. He had a beard, the man who thought it smelled so wonderful, the man who radiated calm and confidence.

"He who betrays his brothers," the man said, "is less than a worm. A worm is sacred compared with the traitor." He spoke slowly, not without a certain flair, not without humor, either; he seemed to grasp the irony of his own words.

The Egyptian couldn't speak; he was having trouble breathing; he feared for his heart. He saw his dogs before him, the dogs that ran after him, the dogs that cried with him at the moon. The bald man had been right: his dogs and nothing else. Only his dogs remained. Nothing more to his life than two dogs.

The man with the beard got up from the chair and bent down until his face was close to the Egyptian's. The Egyptian could smell him: he smelled of soap, soap from a bottle, hotel soap probably. He had washed himself well before going to the kebab place to carry out his assignment. Those accursed assignments. The Egyptian knew about them, had heard about them. He had seen them from close up, the tasks people assigned themselves.

The man pulled out a pistol and stuffed it in the Egyptian's mouth, while the other two remained seated on his stomach.

At first the Egyptian had tried not to open his mouth, but the man with the pistol had pinched his nose shut, and then he had to. When he opened his mouth to breathe, the man had quickly stuffed the pistol into it. Then the man wiped it on his trousers, the hand that had pinched the nose.

The barrel was cold in the Egyptian's mouth, and big, bigger than he'd ever imagined. The Egyptian tried to swallow, but couldn't. His gums hurt, his tongue; he tasted the barrel in his mouth, the bitter tang of metal. So he was still able to taste—at least that was something.

He'd never had the barrel of a pistol in his mouth before. He thought: They're trying to scare me, that's it, just scare me, I have to stay cool. Just stay very calm, as though this happens every day. That's what I need to keep telling myself: all they're trying to do is scare me.

Still, he had the feeling he couldn't breathe anymore. No matter what he told himself, the choking remained. He made a noise that sounded like gargling. And again he saw his dogs. Why did he keep seeing his dogs all the time?

Then he thought about his heart. He was afraid his heart would stop beating.

"You know," said the man who had stuck the pistol in the Egyptian's mouth, "what we do to collaborators. What we have to do to them. Because they're collaborators."

The Egyptian had to pee; he couldn't hold it in anymore.

The man laid his hand on the Egyptian's head. It was a big hand, a heavy hand. The Egyptian felt the pressure on his head. "War is a terrible thing, little brother," the man said. "But for traitors there is only one punishment. A traitor, after all, is not a man. A traitor doesn't deserve a grave. And you're a traitor. As long as there is a war going on, there's no time to hear witnesses, to hear you, to explain our side of it, to wait for a decision. No time, you understand? We have to intervene before you become dangerous, little brother."

The Egyptian tried to say something, but the only thing that came out was more gargling. The hand was still resting on his head.

The man pulled the pistol out of his mouth.

The Egyptian panted for breath. There was spit everywhere, it ran down his lips; his tongue hurt, his gums, his throat, the corners of his mouth. He tried to swallow. The only thing he tasted was metal. He smelled the odor of burning falafel balls. He drooled.

The man with the beard held his weapon loosely in his hand, like a big key he wanted to stick in the lock again, because the door wouldn't open.

"Don't do it," the Egyptian whispered. "Please, don't do it. I didn't tell them anything." Then he couldn't help himself, he peed in his pants. The urine seeped through his underpants and then through his trousers. The floor became wet.

Only at that point did the two men on top of him notice the Egyptian's urine.

They dragged the Egyptian to his feet, sat him down in a chair, and hit him in the face a few times. Not hard, more by way of a warning.

"Enough," the man with the pistol said. He moved his chair over, right in front of the Egyptian's.

"Little brother," the man with the pistol said, "oh, little brother." He pulled out a handkerchief and wiped the Egyptian's lips. His movements bespoke a kind of tenderness.

"Oh, little brother of mine," the man said, "was it worth all this? How much did they give you? Was it a lot? Was it enough? Enough for you to be treated like this, enough for what we have to do to you now because you've betrayed us, because you didn't think about us when you should have been thinking about us? I'm afraid not. This place looks shabby. They gave you too little. Much too little. How long has it been going on? You know, I don't even want to hear about it; the details disgust me. I don't want to know. Don't say a thing. Because nothing is worse than betrayal. When you open your mouth, the betrayal starts."

Then the man took a deep breath and said: "My, doesn't it smell wonderful in here? Almost enough to make you hungry."

But the only smell was that of burned falafel balls in the deep fryer. That stench was more powerful than the odor of piss that layered around the Egyptian.

"Please," the Egyptian whispered, "please. I didn't say anything. I wouldn't know what to say, because I don't know anything, I don't know anything because no one takes me seriously. I didn't get anything, and I didn't say anything. I just want to live a little longer, that's all. Just live a little longer."

The man with the pistol put a piece of chewing gum in his mouth. The other two held the Egyptian in his chair, even though that wasn't necessary. No one had to restrain him. He restrained himself. He always had, and now more than ever.

The man stuffed his pistol in the Egyptian's mouth again. A tooth broke off. Nino's teeth weren't in such good shape anymore; he needed to go to the dentist, but he kept putting it off. He dreaded it, he was afraid of it.

The Egyptian screamed, insofar as he could scream with the barrel of a pistol in his mouth. He spat out his tooth onto the floor. The man with the beard glanced at it, then kicked it away. "Shut up!" he shouted. "Shut up, or I'll blow your brains out."

The Egyptian stopped screaming. He saw himself again, lying in the wet grass with his dogs. It hadn't been mowed for a long time; he had no time for it, and his wife said it was too hard for her, mowing grass. He could almost feel the dogs' tongues; their tongues were rough and hungry. He should have stayed at home—no, not at home, they would have found him there, too—he should have left Basel, gone into hiding, disappeared, the way others had disappeared. A different name, a different country, a different language.

"He who betrays his brothers once," said the man with his finger on the trigger, "betrays his brothers again and again; his life is nothing but betrayal. He has betrayed himself. The betrayal makes everything that happened before that time betrayal, too. He starts with it, and he doesn't stop. It's greater than all the other things he's done. That's why he is nothing more than that: a traitor. Little brother, I'm sorry. That's what you are, and that's what I've come here to tell you."

The Egyptian reached out and grabbed the arm of the man facing him. The gray suit of the man with the beard, 100 percent wool, that's what he grabbed. "No," the Egyptian mumbled, "no, please."

Red drool was running from his mouth, making him look pitiable.

XAVIER, AWROMELE, AND MARC were already close to Karlsruhe. Awromele was sleeping with his head on Xavier's shoulder; he was exhausted. Marc glanced at them occasionally in the mirror. They were pretty, both of them, yes, very pretty. Extraordinarily attractive.

.   .   .

THE MAN WHO was chewing gum shook his head slowly, without taking the pistol out of the Egyptian's mouth. He was struck once more by
how stupid people looked when you pushed a pistol into their mouth. Stupid and hideous. Like dolls. Life-sized dolls with batteries that were slowly
running down.

"This isn't my decision," he said; the chewing gum was gradually losing its flavor and becoming an unpleasant ball of rubber. "Other people
made this decision, but I can't contact them. And even if I could contact
them, they wouldn't change their minds. That's how things go, little
brother—you made a decision, too. And you didn't go back on it, either.
Betrayal is a decision like all the rest."

He looked around.

"I didn't tell them anything," the Egyptian mumbled. The barrel of the
pistol made it almost impossible for him to talk. "I don't know anything.
I donated money because I support you people. Your struggle is my struggle." His hand was still on the sleeve of the man with the pistol, but now
the man brushed his hand away, the way you brush off an animal, a spider
that has fallen out of a tree onto your suit. You don't want to kill the spider, just get rid of it.

The man took the chewing gum out of his mouth and stuck it under
his chair. His other hand tensed. The Egyptian felt the pistol being pushed
farther into his mouth. His throat hurt; the skin on his lips felt like it was
peeling off; his whole mouth hurt. Again he forced himself to think,
They're only trying to scare me. But it didn't work. No matter what he
thought, something was more powerful than his thoughts.

He pooped in his pants. It was diarrhea, and he thought about his dogs,
where they were now, how they jumped up to greet him when he came
home. He thought he was crying, but that was his imagination. Why could
others die with their heads held high, proud and dignified, but not him,
why couldn't he do that? Because he didn't believe in anything, that was
why. That was why he did it in his pants, why he had to die like an ani-

mal. Everyone hated him. Money was the only thing that didn't discriminate against him, but it wasn't here to help him now, now it was nowhere in sight.

The man pulled the pistol out of the Egyptian's mouth. He took a few steps back, stopped in front of the tape player for a moment, then looked into the kitchen and acted as if he was listening to the music. Maybe he actually was listening.

The Egyptian followed him with his eyes, without moving; his eyes were the only thing that dared to move. The man lifted the basket from the deep-fryer. The eight falafel balls had turned black.

The man brought the basket to the Egyptian, who was still sitting in his chair. The other two men were holding his arms behind the back of the chair. They were silent; they didn't make a sound.

"Look," said the man, "look, is this all you have to offer us?"

The Egyptian looked into the basket and saw the black balls.

"Is this how you welcome your guests? Is this what you call hospitality? Is this how your mother raised you?"

The Egyptian didn't speak; he didn't know what to say; he didn't know the right answers anymore. A punch landed on his face.

With a careless gesture, the man tossed the burned falafel balls into a corner. As though he did it all the time, as though he were the chef in a big restaurant and this was how he rejected the mistakes of his apprentices.

"We're hungry," the man said. He sat down in his chair again, rubbed the barrel of his pistol over the Egyptian's lips, his nose, his cheeks. "We're hungry, because we haven't eaten anything for a long time. And it's been a very long time since we've had anything nice to eat. Why don't you make us something nice?"

The Egyptian felt the feces in his pants; he could smell his own excrement. "Please," he whispered. "Please." And he reached out his hand again to the man with the pistol. But the man had no patience with him anymore. He batted the hand away.

"Hungry," the man said. "Do you understand? We are hungry." He paused for a second between the words, so the Egyptian would understand that now he would really have to put something on the table.

The two other men picked up the Egyptian. He couldn't stand on his feet anymore: he was shaking too badly, he was too weak, or too scared; maybe it was his heart, too. They had to hold him upright. That's how he stood before the judge, or at least before the proxy his judge had sent, because he couldn't be here himself.

Once he was upright, the excrement ran down his legs to the floor.

He seized the sleeve of the man with the pistol again. Like a drowning man, like a madman. He looked like a madman, too, with that red drool coming out of his mouth. "I didn't say anything," he whispered. "Please, I want to live. I didn't say anything."

The man took another piece of chewing gum out of his pocket, hesitated, and put it in his mouth. Then he pushed away his prisoner's hand.

"I believe you," he said. "You're too stupid to lie. Isn't that right, aren't you too stupid to lie?"

The Egyptian nodded like he'd never nodded before. He was too stupid to lie, sure, much too stupid.

"That's right," the man said, "too stupid to lie. Too stupid for anything. What did the Zionists promise you? Money, of course. You believe in money, little brother, and look how you've ended up. Look at you now. What can money do for you now? Nothing. Even if you had all the money in the world, it still wouldn't help you. You bet on the wrong horse, little brother, you and millions of others, on the wrong horse."

The man with the pistol couldn't help laughing a little at the strange situation in which they found themselves. Laughing seemed to mellow him a bit.

"You've won your life, little brother," he said, once he was finished laughing. "You've won it back." He patted the cheek of the trembling Egyptian; there was still a little blood on it.

"Yes, I'm giving you back your life, brother," he said. "I don't want it. I don't want to have it. Because you're too stupid to lie, I'm giving back your life. So now fix something for us to eat. It makes a man hungry, giving life back. And thirsty. Do you have some water?"

The Egyptian tried to grab the hand of the man with the pistol, but he pulled it away. "Don't touch me," he shouted. "Stop touching me!"

"Thank you," the Egyptian whispered, "thank you." He felt like kneeling down, to thank him, to show how grateful he was for this gift, his life. But he couldn't kneel, because the two men were holding him up between them. So he asked: "What can I do for you? Tell me what I can do for you. I'll do anything."

"We're hungry," the man said. "We just told you that. We are terribly hungry."

The two men dragged the Egyptian to the back of the restaurant, to the kitchen, where the oil was still boiling. They had to drag him; he couldn't walk by himself, because of the emotions and the shock.

The man with the pistol picked up the plate of falafel balls the Egyptian had kneaded the night before, and sniffed at them.

"This is still edible," he said. "Where's the basket? Where are your pitas?" One of the men went and fetched the basket from the front of the restaurant, from the spot where the two of them had sat on the Egyptian and where they had punched him in the face because he had peed his pants.

At that moment, there was a knock at the door.

"Don't open it," the Egyptian whispered. "Don't open it."

The man with the pistol wormed the barrel back into the Egyptian's mouth, but this time he didn't break a tooth.

Another knock sounded.

The Egyptian shivered like someone with a high fever. He missed his dogs' fur, the warmth of their fur; he thought he would never feel that fur again. Crazy to think about that now, about his dogs' fur, how they jumped up to greet him.

The men heard footsteps going away. The Egyptian heard it, too. The man with the pistol waited for a minute, then pulled his weapon out of the Egyptian's mouth.

"Okay," he said.

His assistant came back with the basket, but the man with the pistol put it down casually on the bar. He didn't even bother looking at the basket.

"He who collaborates with the Zionists becomes one himself," the man with the gun said. "Look at him, look at him shake. Only women shake like that."

The Egyptian felt filthy, and therefore unworthy as well. A befouled person is an unworthy person. Unworthy to stand before his judge, who, due to a shortage of time and personnel, was also his executioner. He was afraid that his filthiness would detract from the force of his arguments. He felt that they would have listened to him better if he hadn't been so filthy. That they would have understood him if he'd been a little cleaner, if he hadn't peed and pooped in his pants, if no blood had dripped from his mouth. His pleas would have made a much greater impression if he had looked a little more respectable. Suddenly he felt ashamed of his broken tooth. He was ashamed of how easily his teeth broke.

"I support the struggle," he mumbled. "I always have. You people know that, don't you? I've always donated money. I opened accounts for you, I acted as your intermediary in this country. I helped you. As much as I could. I support your struggle."

The more he mumbled, the more blood ran out of his mouth.

The man with the pistol said: "If you had been a man, we would have killed you. But you're not a man. You're disgusting. That's why we're letting you live, do you understand? We're letting you live because you deserve to live like a worm. Take off his shoes."

The man who had fetched the basket bent down and began taking off the Egyptian's shoes.

The Egyptian was suddenly very fond of his shoes. He had bought them on sale not so long ago, one afternoon while he was taking a walk, but not because he'd really needed them. Nice black shoes. The soles were leather, so they made a pleasant sound when you walked down the street. At least, it had sounded pleasant to him—he liked it. Click-clack, that kind of sound, like a horse.

"And his socks," said the man with the pistol.

Those were pulled off hastily as well. The socks were a dark blue.

The Egyptian's feet were white. Shockingly pale. There was hair growing on the Egyptian's toes. Dark hair. You could see the veins beneath the skin. The men looked at his feet as though his feet weren't really a part of him, as though they were two separate animals that had somehow ended up in Jerusalem Kebabs. Pale and hairy vermin. The Egyptian looked at his own feet now as well. And for the first time he realized how old he really was, and how ugly his feet were.

"Because you're not a man," the man with the pistol said, "but a traitor, you will live. But you will mourn every moment of your life; you will always regret being alive. You will feel the pain that you have caused your brothers, and then you must realize that your pain is nothing compared with theirs. We feel more pain than you will ever experience. You're getting off lightly. Pick him up."

The men pulled up two chairs. They stood on the chairs. Then they picked up the Egyptian. They had rolled up his pants legs first, then washed their hands right away. They were clean men, and they liked to stay clean.

The Egyptian was hanging in the air now. He was dangling in the hands of the two men. "Please," he murmured, "please." But his murmurs sounded less and less convincing. He himself couldn't believe in them anymore. For a moment, in a flash, he thought about the woman he had been expecting, the woman who hadn't come. Three men had come instead. He realized that he no longer smelled of desert and of dog; he was no different from the other informants, he was simply one among many. He could lay no claims to anything. In the end he was a traitor; to that led all the roads he had followed, all the cocaine he had sold, all the falafels he had fried, to that moment, to that point, to that day. The day he had become an informant.

Still, he couldn't rid himself of the impression that he had never betrayed a thing.

Then he peed in his pants again. This time the men paid no attention. "To make sure that you will crawl on your belly like a worm," said the man with the pistol, "we are going to fry your feet."

The men held the Egyptian above the deep-fryer. It was hard, but they did it, because they were in excellent shape. They went to the gym on a regular basis, to keep from growing fat, but also to be able to deal with traitors. It was part of their job.

The Egyptian had almost no strength left, but he pulled his legs up to his chest. He kicked. He kicked like a child. "Please," he whispered, "I beg you." He tried to turn his head to look at the man with the pistol, and hurt his neck.

The man with the pistol was standing behind the Egyptian; in front of him was the door of his kebab place; the music played on; and for one second, for a fraction of a second, the thought flashed through his mind: Who is this pianist, anyway? What is his name again?

He looked down and saw the oil like a black hole. The boiling oil had no color anymore—no smell, either, although there were still pieces of burned falafel ball floating in it. A reflecting hole, it was, no more than that, a reflecting, boiling hole.

The Egyptian screamed: "No, no, not like this. Please. I beg you."

But the more he begged, the more ridiculous he appeared in the men's eyes. The lower their esteem for him, the more he disgusted them.

The man with the pistol grabbed the left foot, slid his hand up to the shin, and dipped the Egyptian's foot in the fryer.

He didn't hold it in the boiling oil for very long—five or six seconds at most—just long enough to achieve the desired effect.

Then he did the same with the right foot.

The Egyptian's screams were horrific. The men actually grimaced at the sound of them, as though they could feel the victim's pain. It was the most horrific screaming they'd ever heard. They hoped they would never hear anything like it again.

When the operation was over, they let the Egyptian fall to the floor. He landed behind the bar. Beside the light switches, under the tape player. The piano concerto by Beethoven played on steadily. The whole thing hadn't taken long—a few minutes at most.

The Egyptian's feet had not turned brown, not even black, more like a slimy white, with pink spots here and there. The flesh had become stringy. The flesh stank.

The men climbed down from their chairs and put them back neatly where they had been. They washed their hands again. There was no towel, so they had to dry them on a roll of paper towels.

The men walked to the door. Behind them walked the man who had dipped the feet in the oil.

"That wasn't easy," he told his colleagues. "But it had to happen. You can be proud of yourselves."

He nodded and put away the pistol.

Then he offered them a piece of chewing gum. They put the gum in their mouths. All three of them were chewing gum now.

It was ten-thirty-five in Basel, cloudy; rain was expected, but it would take a while to come.

JUST AS THE Egyptian had thought, she showed up early. It was only around eleven. She found the door standing ajar and opened it cautiously. She went in. Wearing jeans and a sweater, carrying a backpack, she looked more like a tourist than ever—a young tourist, like so many others. It was the perfect disguise, and perhaps it was more than a disguise. She *was* a young tourist, more that than anything else. Her work—well, what did her work really involve? What did it add up to, anyway? When viewed in the cold, clear light of day?

"Hello," she called out.

There was no answer.

She had seen a few spots of blood in front of the kebab place, so she knew that perhaps no answer would ever come. That silence reigned here, and that here silence would continue to reign.

She smelled the odor of fried meat.

She walked over to the bar. And saw the Egyptian lying there.

She squatted down, wiped his lips with her bare hand.

Only then did she see the paper towels on the bar, and used them to wipe his face. She laid one hand on his hot cheek, but didn't dare to touch his feet and ankles.

She fought down the urge to gag, to vomit, to run away.

"Mmm," the Egyptian said. She couldn't understand him.

She poured him a glass of water, turned off the heat under the oil, which was still boiling. The stench in the kebab place was overpowering. It was almost more than one could take. She tried to give the Egyptian a sip; he had a hard time keeping the water in his mouth. It ran out again almost right away. The corners of his mouth were torn.

Then, at last, she heard what he was mumbling: "Kill me."

She took his hand, held it, pressed it to her breast. But the Egyptian kept murmuring: "Kill me. Please, kill me."

Again, he saw his two dogs—no, he didn't see them, he felt them. He felt their fur, their wet fur after they had rolled in the grass. You could give them a bath as often as you liked, they still loved dirt. Those dogs. But it wasn't the fur of his dogs he was feeling, it was the breast of the woman who had said that he smelled of desert and of dog. She had pushed his hand up under her sweater and laid it on her bare breast.

She squatted down there beside him, without a word.

Every once in a while, the Egyptian closed his eyes. He didn't really close them, they fell shut, the way a door suddenly slams shut in a gust of wind.

He remembered how she had sat across from him two days before. That had been a different world, another age. He couldn't look at her again, ever again. If only he weren't so filthy now, but he was horribly befouled. Despite the pain, which seemed to grow only more intense, he was ashamed of lying beside this woman in his own filth.

"Finish me off," he said, and squeezed her breast. "Can't you see the shape I'm in?"

She shook her head slowly, without really knowing why.

She kept shaking her head, and when the door of the kebab place opened and the bald man came in, she was still shaking her head, gently, to the rhythm of the music, it seemed.

She didn't stand up; she heard him coming, the bald man, she recognized his footsteps; and quietly, very quietly, he said her name, the name she used in Basel. She remained squatting down beside the Egyptian, his hand on her bare tit. He squeezed; it hurt a little, but she paid no attention to that. She dabbed at his lips.

The bald man came and stood beside her. He looked at the Egyptian.

He looked at the bar. The piano concerto by Beethoven appealed to him. It was nice. Serene. Peaceful. Slightly melancholy, but not overdone.

The Egyptian stared at the bald man. The first time he'd been carrying a video camera, but not today.

"Kill me," the Egyptian said to him.

His voice was the voice of a machine that doesn't work well anymore. His voice faltered. His voice rasped. It came from another world.

The bald man gestured to the woman. She took the Egyptian's hand, removed it from her tit, held it for a moment. It was warm, but not sweaty.

The Egyptian looked at her. She noticed that. She wanted to say something, just quickly. But she didn't. He opened his mouth, wide open, as though he wanted to scream, as though he was expecting the barrel of the gun to be shoved into his mouth again. Then he had to close his eyes, and he saw his dogs. He wondered who would take them outside now to cry when the moon was full. He wondered whether they would miss him. And, whether it was the thought of the dogs or seeing the bald man, he no longer wanted to die. He didn't want to be finished off anymore, no matter what shape he was in, with or without feet, with or without legs, crippled or not, it didn't matter. He just wanted to live, no more than that, just live.

The woman took a few steps away from him, walking slowly to the door. She had seen people die before. She tried to recall the exact number; she was precise when it came to death, when it came to her work; she was fond of facts. Still, there was something about this dying, something that made this death different from the others. Not all dying looked alike.

The bald man pulled out a gun. It had a silencer on it. He looked at the Egyptian; the Egyptian looked at him. There were the dogs again, the garden, the grass, and the videotape, too. The videotape bearing the purpose of his life. When he was no longer around, that would still be there. It would survive him, and probably still be looked at in a future of which he would no longer be a part. That was his eternity, actor in an erotic film made by amateurs.

Maybe that was what all eternity looked like: eroticism by and for amateurs.

The Egyptian didn't whimper, he didn't say, "Please, no, not like that." All he thought was, I want to live, it doesn't matter how, I just want to live, I want to see my dogs, I want to take them into the garden in the middle of the night and cry with them at the full moon. But he didn't dare say that; he didn't dare say anything anymore; anything he might say would only make things worse. He was silent, out of shame.

The bald man shot without hesitating. Hesitating caused pain. Pain was perhaps nothing but hesitation.

He fired three times: twice in the Egyptian's chest, once through the head.

Then he put away his gun carefully.

The bald man went over to the woman. "One less informant," he said quietly. He put his hand on the back of her neck, caressed the little hairs on the back of her neck. Only for a moment, not too long, never for too long. There was no intimacy between them; no intimacy must be allowed to exist.

The woman saw something on the floor. She looked at it but couldn't see what it was. Just for the hell of it, just to have something to do, or perhaps actually out of curiosity, she bent down and picked it up. It was a tooth. It had a gold filling.

She looked at it, hesitated, started to put it down on one of the tables, but stuck it in her coat pocket instead.

The bald man was ready to go.

They went outside.

The woman looked at the trees. She straightened her sweater. She turned left; the bald man went in the other direction.

Two minutes later, a woman walked into a department store and disappeared into the crowd. In the women's department she looked at a few summer dresses, and although she was hardened and had seen many people die, she still smelled the odor of desert and of dog.

Made for Each Other

MARC PARKED in the center of Amsterdam, along a canal. There stood his Alfa, amid all the normal cars; there stood Marc with his overnight bag, Awromele with his plastic bag, and Xavier with his rolled-up canvases.

"So here we are," said Marc, "the center of the avant-garde," and he locked the door. He had made good time.

Xavier and Awromele looked around. So now it was starting; here was where it began.

Talent—you either had it or you didn't, and, standing there beside Marc's Alfa, beside a canal that stank a little, an odor that seemed extremely authentic to Xavier, he knew for sure that he had it.

Marc offered to stay in town that night. "The three of us can find a hotel, my treat," he said. The boys didn't think that was necessary. They could get by on their own. Xavier told Marc that he should go back to Basel. The mother shouldn't stay alone too long. It couldn't be easy for her, having her son leave so suddenly.

"Yes," Marc said, "maybe that would be better." He pressed his stepson to his breast. He could barely let go of the boy; he kept throwing his arms around him, holding him tight, running his hands down his back, and pressing his mouth to his lips. And saying all the while: "Don't deny your own talent, Xavier. Don't let them take it away from you. Keep painting, no matter what happens, keep painting. And no matter what they say to you here, I believe in you."

Xavier finally put an end to the embraces by saying, "Now we really have to get to a youth hostel—otherwise we'll never find one."

"I'll tell your mother you said hello," Marc went on. "I'll tell her not to worry."

For the last time, he hugged Xavier with all his might. The sorrow inside him grew, and at the same time he felt a strange excitement, as though he had history itself in his hands. He climbed back in the car and drove to Basel. All the way to the German border, he could think only of Xavier's hypnotic gaze, his massive talent, the fact that he, Marc, had recognized that talent and awoken it with a kiss, that his career would be a glorious one, and international, that above all.

Only when he was past Cologne did he start preparing for his flight simulator.

AWROMELE AND XAVIER didn't find a youth hostel, but they found a cheap hotel, not far from the central train station. They shared a bathroom with three English punks who drew no distinction between alcoholism and anarchy.

The drain in the hotel bathroom didn't work well, which made the place smell of sewer. On the shelf in front of the mirror was an old razor blade with hair sticking to it.

"We won't stay here long," Xavier told Awromele when they were lying in their three-quarter bed at last. "Don't worry."

They cuddled up. Xavier put his arm over Awromele and planned to fall asleep like that. He was happy, despite the little bed and the smelly bathroom. "Together at last," he said.

Awromele, though already half asleep, murmured: "Please don't go feeling anything. Please feel nothing."

The very next morning, Xavier went to the Rietveld Academy. His paintings he carried in a tube under his arm. He had said to Awromele:

"Will you take care of King David? If you leave him alone in the room, someone might steal him."

Awromele wandered through Amsterdam with King David in a plastic bag. He had taken off his yarmulke. He bought a knitting needle so he could scratch himself under the cast.

In a café across from the stock-exchange building, he struck up a conversation with an American who, after about ten minutes, asked Awromele to come up to his hotel room. Awromele turned down the offer. He was reminded of the tall boy's words: "Loneliness is nothing to be ashamed of." He did make out with the American a little, though, for he also remembered the gist of what the tall boy had said: language as we know it is becoming obsolete. The language of the knuckle, the shoe, and therefore also that of the tongue that makes no sound, at most a little smacking noise, that is all the language that matters now, that is the language we must speak; otherwise we will never free ourselves of ourselves.

At the end of a long kiss, when he no longer knew quite what to say but realized that it would be a good idea to slow down kissing the American, he pulled out the jar and said: "Look, this is King David."

"King who?" asked the American, who was in Amsterdam on business.

"King David," Awromele said.

The American took the jar, saw something blue, and asked, "What is it?"

"My friend's testicle," Awromele said. "His name is King David."

The American laughed heartily at that. But when he took a better look at the jar, he grew a bit pale and asked for the bill.

Awromele went back to their hotel room. He lay down on the bed to wait for Xavier. After a while, he took *Mein Kampf* and a notebook out of the bag and tried to translate the next passage. "So first the struggle and then perhaps pacifism," he translated. "Otherwise mankind will have overshot the zenith of its development, which will then result, not in the ascendancy of some ethical idea, but in barbarism, and finally in chaos."

Awromele was getting better at capturing the author's style. There was an awful lot you could say about this man, but he certainly could write. He went on to translate a whole section, without waiting for Xavier.

He ate the last of the cookies his mother had given him.

When Xavier came back, around dinnertime, Awromele had translated more than two full pages. He was proud of what he'd done. Xavier sat down beside him and kissed him. Awromele asked, "How did it go?"

"It went," Xavier said. "They sort of have to get used to me, to my style of painting. And what about you, did you have a nice time?"

"I met an American who wanted to take me back to his hotel room," Awromele said. He was relieved that he had made acquaintance with someone so quickly. In Basel he was seen as a withdrawn boy; he could also be boisterous and tell a lot of jokes, but he'd had almost no real friends. "And I did some translating. Listen to this," he said. " 'He who wishes to live must therefore struggle, and he who does not wish to struggle eternally in this world will not be able to go on living.' " Awromele closed the notebook. "That's what my mother always says, too."

"What do you mean?" Xavier asked.

"Well, just what I said. My mother always says that you have to fight in this life. You have to stay quiet, but while you're being quiet you have to fight."

"No, I meant about that American?"

"Oh, him."

"Yeah, what was that all about?"

"Like I told you. He asked me, Do you want to go back to my hotel? He said: You feel like going with me? It's just around the corner."

"And you could understand what he said?"

"He spoke English."

"Since when do you speak English? I've never heard you speak English. I thought you spoke only Yiddish, Hebrew, and German."

"My English isn't perfect, but I understood what he was saying. It's easier for me than French."

Xavier picked up King David and put him carefully on the top shelf of the cupboard. It was a narrow cupboard. Fortunately, they hadn't brought along a lot of clothes.

"How did you start talking to him, anyway?" Xavier asked, looking closely at King David. He had the feeling that King David had shrunk, and changed color slightly as well. "Did you touch him or something?" Xavier asked. "Or worse than that? People don't make proposals like that otherwise."

"I didn't do anything, I just talked to him."

Xavier threw Awromele back on the bed, sat on top of him, and squeezed his throat. "What did you do with that American? I want to know. What did you do with him?" Xavier saw the hairy hand of an American plucking at Awromele's body, and the thought took his breath away. He was a reasonable person, but the hairy hand of the American turned Xavier into a cornered rat.

"Tell me," Xavier shouted, and squeezed Awromele's throat even harder. "Tell me, what went on?"

The Englishmen, who had gone to bed only a couple of hours before, pounded on the wall with their shoes. They liked noise, but not when they were sleeping.

"Nothing," Awromele said in a squeaky voice. "Nothing at all, sweetest, believe me."

"What do you mean, nothing?" Xavier asked. "Why did that American ask you to go with him if nothing happened? If all you did was talk to him? Something more than that must have happened, and I want to know what."

"I made out with him a little," Awromele said. "That's all."

Then Xavier boxed Awromele's ear. It was the second time he had done that to Awromele.

Awromele looked at Xavier in amazement, though he wasn't really shocked. When Xavier had climbed on top of him and squeezed his throat, he had known that anything could happen. He thought about the tall boy again, about his own head, which had been used as a soccer ball.

Xavier himself was horrified at what he'd done. He was afraid of losing Awromele, and he started petting and caressing him, and kissing him on the ear that he had just hit.

"That was my bad ear," Awromele said. "That wasn't very smart of you."

"I'm so sorry," Xavier said. "I feel so terrible." And he caressed the ear and the red spots on Awromele's throat.

"I only kissed the American," Awromele said, "after he asked me up to his room. I only did it to be polite. I didn't want to disappoint him. My mother says we Jews already have such a bad name, that's why we need to say yes to most things. He looked so sad. I can't say no to someone who looks so sad."

"Was it nice?"

"What do you mean?" Awromele asked. "Nice?"

"Did you feel anything?"

"No, of course not. I did it because I couldn't say no."

Xavier stopped petting him; he stopped kissing him, too. He just sat on Awromele and said, "So I'm not really that special, that's what it comes down to."

He climbed off of Awromele and slid from the bed.

Awromele lay quietly on the brown bedspread, rubbing his neck, which was still red from the force of Xavier's hands.

"What you do with me you can actually do with anyone," Xavier said.

"No," Awromele said, "you're something special. But loneliness is nothing to be ashamed of."

"What do you mean, loneliness is nothing to be ashamed of? Are you lonely? I've come all the way to this city with you. You couldn't wait any longer, it had to happen right away, at a moment's notice. I give up everything—my life, my mother, my school, my city, my language, my upbringing—I give it all up for you. I'm pleased to do that, it's not that, because I want to comfort you. Like no one has ever comforted a Jew before. But then, the very first day we arrive in this strange city, you say, Loneliness is nothing to be ashamed of."

"But it isn't anything to be ashamed of, is it?" Awromele said. "They told me that, and I thought, Yeah, they're right."

"Who told you that?"

"The boys in the park, those four boys."

When Xavier heard that, he was so angry and so sorrowful that he tore one of his paintings into little pieces. He couldn't understand why Awromele would listen to boys who had beaten up on him, and not to him, the comforter of the Jews.

"Why are you doing that?" Awromele asked. "What good is that going to do? Those are your paintings, you worked so hard on them. Don't do that, please. It makes me sad." He clung to Xavier like a little monkey, but Xavier knocked him away.

"I'm doing it," Xavier said, "because you attach more value to boys who beat you up than you do to me. I call that sick."

Awromele picked up the knitting needle and began scratching himself under the cast. "What are you so worked up about, anyway?" he asked. "What in the world are we talking about here? You leave me alone because you want to go to the art academy so badly, and instead of being happy that someone's interested in me, you start ranting and raving. Don't do that. I'm here with you. I'm here, aren't I?"

Xavier didn't know what to say to that. He looked at Awromele. Again he saw the hand of the American. His fantasy was more powerful than his love. He didn't notice anything of that love now. He felt only hatred, a dull, monotonous hatred.

He no longer felt like telling Awromele what had happened during his visit to the Rietveld Academy. The strange way the receptionist had looked at him, the long talk with the professor who had recommended the pre-liminary course, and then added: "But think about it for a while. Not everyone belongs at this school."

Xavier wanted to get out of the hotel room and go into town; he needed to be alone, to think.

"We agreed," Awromele said, getting up, "that we weren't going to feel anything. We have to stay a little independent, that was the agreement."

Xavier didn't know what to say to that, either. Little was left of his hopeful expectations from the day before, when they had sat together in the car. He wondered, could this be suffering?

At the same time, he sensed lust. He longed to touch Awromele, to throw him down on the bed again, not to squeeze his throat this time but to ride him like a horse, to go into him like no American would ever go into Awromele, no matter how sad he looked or how hairy his hands were.

"No, we're not going to feel anything," Xavier said. "I promise, I swear. Nothing, absolutely nothing." And he kissed Awromele, pushed him down on the bed.

"Be careful of my hand," was all Awromele said.

The Englishmen were pounding on the wall even harder.

When Awromele was down to only his shirt, and all Xavier had on were his trousers, an intense melancholy came over Xavier, insatiable, such sadness. That sadness told him, You don't mean anything to him.

He let go of Awromele, pulled on his sweater, and walked out of the hotel. Awromele shouted after him: "We weren't going to feel anything. That was the agreement, that's what you promised. Not feel a thing. Never feel anything. Don't stop in the middle of it."

Xavier had truly intended not to feel a thing. He had been willing to swear that he, just as Awromele had said, was incapable of feeling a thing, but apparently he was feeling something now anyway.

He wandered through the city. After twenty minutes, he thought about going back to Awromele, to tell him how much he loved him, but he shoved the idea aside. A little later he thought, Maybe I should put an end to it. But instead, he bought a bicycle from a junkie.

As he cycled along, he began seeing the beauty of the city he had known till then only from Marc's stories and from guidebooks. He started feeling better; there was nothing for him to get wound up about. Maybe Awromele was only trying to make him jealous, maybe he was testing him. Awromele was probably still a little confused from the beating he'd taken in the park. What he had taken was actually a bit worse than the beating itself. Little wonder, then, that, in his confused state, he had made out with some dirty American. Besides, he had only just started going out without his yarmulke, and that couldn't be easy for him, either.

This line of reasoning came as a reassurance to Xavier.

After he rode around for an hour on his new bike, he remembered the task he had assigned himself. Now that he was here, there could be no more excuses.

At a late-night shop, he bought a bunch of tulips, to surprise Awromele.

Xavier found his friend sitting cross-legged on the bed, busy translating *Mein Kampf* again.

He handed him the tulips and said: "I also bought a bike for us. Do you want to see it?"

"Yes," Awromele said.

When they were out on the street and Xavier saw Awromele beaming as he looked at the bike, he fell in love all over again. Xavier thought: We fit each other, we were made for each other. We belong together.

THE MOTHER HAD remained lying on the kitchen floor for a good eight hours. She had slept, daydreamed, thought without being able to say exactly what she'd thought about. At last she got up and made some tea.

She did a little shopping. At the greengrocer's, she talked to the owner's son. He, too, was a member of the Committee of Vigilant Parents, even though he was nowhere near having children yet. He had joined out of solidarity with his loyal customer. After he had read in the paper about the horrors that had taken place, he'd told himself, I have to do something. Joining the Committee of Vigilant Parents seemed to him like the first step.

While she was counting out her change, the mother said to him, "Did you know that I wanted to poison him?"

"No," the greengrocer's son said. "Who, if you don't mind my asking? Pedophile Lenin? Well, I can imagine that."

"No, my son," the mother said, "when he was just a baby." And she laughed the way she had once laughed at celebrations and cocktail parties. Charmingly, seductively, yet still with a certain distance. In fact, she couldn't laugh at all, she didn't see anything to laugh about.

The young man gave her a plastic bag for her groceries. He watched her go. That woman must be having a hard time, but she fought back bravely. Always cheerful, always time for a little chat.

The mother headed home, but—as though pulled along by invisible threads, as she would later describe it—she felt compelled to enter a supermarket.

The manager of the supermarket referred her to a shop that specialized in pest control.

In front of that shop, the mother stood wavering for a quarter of an hour.

Then she walked home. She was going to fix a vegetable quiche.

An Overdrawn Account

AT THE RIETVELD ACADEMY, they were more impressed by Xavier's drive than by his paintings. Yet they still decided to admit him. One of the professors told his colleagues: "He may not have much in the way of technique, but he has something special. He has character and willpower, and then there are those hypnotic brown eyes that stare right through you. That boy has something."

Awromele and Xavier found a room in a student hostel on Prinsengracht. The room would have been small for one person, let alone two, but they didn't mind.

When their money ran out, they went looking for work.

Xavier found a job waiting tables at a Mexican restaurant downtown, not far from the central train station. Despite Xavier's broken Dutch, the owner had fallen for his charm, his helpfulness, and his personality, and also for his eyes, which could have passed for those of a Mexican. Besides, the boy was always polite to customers, even when they weren't polite to him.

Awromele found a job at the Albert Heijn supermarket. Even though he was actually an illegal alien in the Netherlands, the manager of the chain store on Middenweg told him, after flipping through his passport a few times: "A Swiss citizen is never really illegal. I'll tell you what—I'll pay you half the minimum wage, and we'll leave it at that. We help you, and you help us; that way everybody's happy."

That was the kind of reasoning Awromele could appreciate. Besides, he wasn't working solely to make money, but also to meet people and make friends. And he made friends, he made friends one after another. Sometimes he made out with those friends; sometimes he tactfully shared their beds.

Despite his vow to feel nothing, these activities caused Xavier a great deal of sorrow. At unexpected moments, they also caused him to fly into a rage.

When Awromele was lucky, Xavier would pick up his drawing pad during such a fit of rage and begin sketching away furiously. At the academy, they said of the drawings he made then, "You can't really call it talent, but these days passion is a rare enough thing in itself."

At less fortunate moments, Xavier did not pick up his drawing pad, but smashed all the furniture in their room. Then he would say to Awromele: "I hope you realize that I'm doing this because I love you. Consider it a compliment. If I didn't love you so much, I wouldn't let myself go like this."

Awromele understood that, but he didn't enjoy it. "It's so agitating," he said. "I'd rather have you not feel anything, like me."

The mirror in the bathroom they shared with ten other students had been destroyed in this way, as had the bookcase they had just put together one Saturday afternoon after buying it at IKEA, when Awromele confessed that he had kissed a married man from North Brabant Province in the furniture store's coffee corner. "I can't help it, sweetheart," Awromele said, taking Xavier's hand and holding it tenderly. "I can't do anything about it, I can't say no. That's how we were raised. What would you do if you had grown up hearing, 'Don't say no, the Jews already have such a bad name'? You wouldn't resist, either. I do it out of courtesy."

"But you're *not* courteous," Xavier shouted, picking up the hammer and smashing the new bookcase to smithereens. Even though he was never

around when it happened, he could see the details of the kissing and making out in his mind's eye, in color, sometimes even with a soundtrack.

The imaginative power that won him praise at the Rietveld Academy
was a hindrance to him. His fantasies drove him to the brink of madness,
yet it was not something he could allow himself to repress. He had to
transform that energy into beauty. But it came back again and again, and
every time it came back it was more powerful than the time before. "Stop
saying that!" Xavier screamed amid the ruins of the bookcase. "The fact
that you're Jewish is no excuse for hopping in the sack with every man who
comes along. You're disgusting, that's all."

He ran out of the house. That was how most of his tantrums ended. He
had never been hot-tempered before, and never unhappy, either. It had to
be love, love changed you, love made a complete person out of you. But
he continued to have difficulty with Awromele's giving his body to almost
any man who asked. Anti-Semitism could not be combated in bed.
Awromele's behavior only made it worse.

After these fits of rage, if the line wasn't too long, Xavier would go to
the Anne Frank House around the corner. It was one of the only places
where he could regain his calm. The staff knew him. They thought he was
a nice boy, charming, interested, and helpful. In addition, he spoke a little Yiddish and had a slight knowledge of Hebrew. Despite Xavier's
tantrums, Awromele had continued to give him lessons, and not only in
Yiddish: Xavier now wanted to learn Hebrew as well. He took his task seriously. Every morning before breakfast, he would learn his vocabulary
list, and before they went to bed at night Awromele would drill him.
Comforting without discipline was for chumps.

Yes, Xavier thought as he walked through the Anne Frank House,
Awromele doesn't do much except stock shelves and screw, but I still
have to comfort him. I must and shall comfort him. Him and his people.
And then he would repeat these words to himself silently, in Yiddish.

His visits to the Anne Frank House, meanwhile, aroused his interest in
the problems of the Middle East. He bought a scrapbook and began cut-

ting out all the articles he could find about the Middle East. He pinned little flags to a map to trace the course of the First Intifada, and to his fellow students and professors at the Rietveld Academy he praised the courage and creativity of that ancient people. He told them, "You wouldn't think so to see them run, but they are fighting machines."

Xavier was a man with a mission. Nothing Awromele did could change that.

IN THE EARLY DAYS of their stay in the Venice of the North, which, as it turned out, was also referred to as "the Jerusalem of the North," Awromele and Xavier called home regularly. Later, the calls became less frequent. The mother didn't say much, mostly "yes" and "no," and the rabbi's wife mostly cried. That didn't help anyone much. And the phone bills got too high.

Xavier quickly grew accustomed to missing his mother. He still painted his testicle, without his mother now, but with Israeli soldiers and Jewish war heroes instead—Moshe Dayan, Menachem Begin, Golda Meir.

And Awromele was able to compensate for the emptiness family had left behind. Amsterdam pepped him up. He began dressing differently, and once or twice a week he would violate the dietary laws. He shaved more carefully than he had in Basel, and for the first time in his life, he bought himself a bottle of aftershave.

Awromele also developed the growing urge to talk to strange men, and to kiss them. It almost became an addiction. And the more he kissed, the more frantically Xavier painted, and the more fanatically he worked at his Yiddish lessons with Awromele.

On occasion, Xavier would ask Awromele for details: "Do you take off all your clothes?" And: "Do they touch your butt, too? I thought I was the only one who was allowed to do that." But Awromele never felt much like talking about it. He usually said: "I can't say no. Let's leave it at that."

"But I don't go around kissing other people, do I?" Xavier would say. "I feel no need for that. So why do you? I thought we would be enough for each other."

"You can say no," Awromele said. "You should be glad about that. Do you think it's easy for me?"

Because Awromele himself couldn't say no, Xavier would sometimes follow him, in order to intervene if need be. And sometimes, when he should actually have been at the Rietveld Academy working on a collage, he would take the tram to the store on Middenweg, to watch Awromele innocently stocking shelves. Spying on him like that, seeing him in his Albert Heijn outfit, lining up bottles of fabric softener, he was overwhelmed by infatuation. The simple fact that no one was fiddling with Awromele at that moment was enough to make him happy. Afterwards, he would catch the tram back to the Rietveld Academy and press on ecstatically with his oeuvre.

Although their interests these days were so widely divergent, they still worked together on translating *Mein Kampf.* Three times a week, sometimes a little more often. Once they were bent over that book, their notebooks and dictionaries at hand, they never argued. And at such moments Xavier did not feel even the slightest pang of the jealousy that at other moments drove him to the Anne Frank House.

Awromele said to Xavier: "Let's keep at it. The market is ripe right now for a translation like this. If we wait too long, maybe it won't be anymore." Then they would sit down on the bed together, with the book by You-Know-Who and with their notebooks and dictionaries. And they translated, with dedication and love. They weighed each word—each word had to be the right one. The text had to be given the treatment it deserved.

AFTER ABOUT FOUR MONTHS, the rabbi's wife came to Amsterdam in an attempt to convince her son to return to Basel. She brought with her a big box of cheese biscuits, shortbread, and creampuffs, all of which she had baked herself.

Awromele was happy to see his mother again, and launched greedily into the cheese biscuits. Xavier, meanwhile, did his best to comfort her.

She went home again two days later, without having accomplished her purpose.

Throughout the train ride to Basel, which lasted more than eight hours, she wept. A German railway conductor offered her a free cup of tea.

One week after her return, the rabbi died of a brain hemorrhage. Awromele flew to Basel, dressed for the last time in the clothing of his youth, and sat *shiva* for a whole week. Then he flew back to Amsterdam and kissed more men than ever, in order to make up for lost time.

XAVIER WAS MAKING good progress with his Hebrew and Yiddish; he learned those languages faster than the techniques of painting. But that's not the way he looked at it. He continued to paint with great discipline, despite the occasional dip. And during those dips he would think: maybe, as a painter, I'm actually an autodidact; maybe the academy is ruining me. The spontaneity is fading. They're forcing me into a mold. My own personality is getting lost.

Whenever he had these dry periods, he would suggest to Awromele that they immigrate to Israel together. Awromele had been raised with principled objections to the Jewish state in its present form. The Jewish state was to be established only after the arrival of the Messiah, not before.

"I kind of like it here," Awromele would say then. "And, besides, first the Messiah, then the state."

"Can't we do something to trigger the Messiah's arrival?" Xavier asked.

"No, you can't trigger that. These aren't contractions. What are you talking about?"

"Without Israel, every Jew is an overdrawn account. And who knows how long we'll have to wait for the Messiah? Maybe we should buckle down and do something about it. God protects those who protect themselves. The Almighty hates overdrawn accounts. We should get to work."

"I've never accounted for anything," Awromele said. "Besides, someone has to stock the shelves. So why shouldn't it be me?"

Xavier was not particularly convinced by Awromele's arguments. Giving comfort, the way he understood it, was not a metaphysical affair. The place where the most suffering and dying was going on, that was where the comforter should be ready to move. The Anne Frank House was a bit too limited for such ambitions.

"Let's go," Xavier would say to Awromele as they lay in bed at night. "Before long, there will be more Palestinians there than Jews. Then there will be no point to it. There's nothing left for us to do here—our lives here are empty—but there we have a task to perform, there we're needed."

But Awromele truly enjoyed his work at Albert Heijn. A person like him, who had never learned to say no, shouldn't take on too much responsibility. And besides, the Palestinians didn't worry him, not even if ten million of them showed up next week. He had traded in God for pleasure, and it was the best deal he'd ever made.

In the months that followed, Xavier made little progress at the academy. He kept painting the same subject, and his teachers slowly but surely began steering him towards photography. Though his painting was of debatable quality, his professors had no trouble imagining that their student might become an original photographer.

But Xavier stuck stubbornly to his canvases. Photography was beneath his dignity. "Anyone can push a button," he said. "But creating a new reality, that's a different story."

AWROMELE BEGAN STAYING away at night now as well. At such times, Xavier did his utmost not to feel anything. It wasn't easy. He lay in bed and couldn't sleep. Every fifteen minutes, he would look at the alarm clock and tell himself, "He'll be home by four." But when four o'clock arrived and Awromele still hadn't come home, Xavier would get dressed and go into town. Sometimes he would wander through Amsterdam till the crack of dawn and think, When I get home at seven, Awromele will be sound asleep in bed. But with increasing frequency, Awromele wasn't there at seven, either.

When that happened, Xavier would kneel beside their bed, pick up the notebooks containing their translation of *Mein Kampf,* and begin to read aloud. In the Yiddish translation, he read: "Hence the lie concerning the language of the Jews, which is not a means to express their thoughts but, on the contrary, a means to disguise them. He speaks French, he thinks in Yiddish, and when he puts together poems in German, he does nothing but indulge the character of his own folk."

That calmed him.

Although he was not religious, he addressed himself with increasing frequency to God: "Let him come home soon, God. Don't let him trade me in for someone else. Give me the strength to comfort him better."

The Terrorist in Beatrixpark

SUMMER CAME, and the Albert Heijn store where Awromele worked threw a party. The employees were allowed to bring their partners. Sales at their store in the last quarter had risen more that at any other Albert Heijn in Amsterdam. So the drinking and dancing took place at the store's expense.

That was how Xavier first met Awromele's colleagues. He discovered that Awromele was popular at the Middenweg store. People knew about his Jewish origins, but didn't make a thing of it. Checkout girls with bleach-blond hair told Xavier that Awromele was an excellent colleague, and never at a loss for a joke. They thought his accent was the loveliest they'd ever heard. They didn't mind the fact that he was more interested in men than in women. On the contrary, that made things easier.

A little before midnight, when the party had passed its high point, Xavier saw Awromele dancing with the manager. Their dancing became increasingly intimate, until Xavier could no longer tell where Awromele stopped and the manager began. Awromele kissed the manager. Again and again, as though he couldn't get enough of his manager's lips.

It all became a bit too much for Xavier. Feeling a fit of rage coming on, he thought, If Awromele tries to tell me again that he does this because the Jews already have such a bad name, I'll hit him.

Xavier walked out onto the dance floor and tapped Awromele on the shoulder. But Awromele didn't respond. He had lost himself in the manager's mouth. He had become one with his boss, even though Awromele had never learned to dance. Xavier had—the waltz, the lambada, the tango—he'd had to learn them all back at the Gymnasium in Basel. Xavier stopped trying to get his attention. He danced with one of the checkout girls for a while. Though he tried to dance as enthusiastically and sexily as Awromele, he couldn't concentrate on his dance partner. He kept seeing Awromele, his movements, his mouth, his lips.

Awromele was driving him crazy. And so was his own imagination. But this was no fantasy anymore. He didn't have to imagine it, he was seeing it. Wherever he looked, he saw Awromele pressing his body against that of his manager.

It had been a long time since Xavier had seen a man as unattractive as the manager. If only he'd been a handsome man, charming and intelligent, like Xavier's grandfather.

At last, in the men's room, he ran into Awromele. Still in the company of the manager. Hand in hand. Xavier whispered, "Shall we go home and translate a little *Mein Kampf*?" But Awromele said, "No, not now, tomorrow."

"Awromele," Xavier said, "let's go home. I'm not enjoying myself anymore. I can't take this."

Awromele only shrugged and waved his hand dismissively. "I always come back to you," he said. "What are you worried about?"

The manager left them for a moment, to get something to drink. They were standing in front of the lavatory door now, and Awromele said: "I don't want to disappoint him. He likes me so much, he's crazy about me. I can't help it, I can't say no."

Just then, the manager came back, without drinks. He gave Xavier a friendly nod and dragged Awromele back onto the dance floor.

Xavier stuck around for one more number. Then, bitterly and without saying goodbye to anyone, he left the party.

He walked home along Leliegracht, speaking words of encouragement to himself in Hebrew, then in Yiddish. "I should leave Awromele," he said.

"He's no good for me. What's the point of this? I don't have a friend, I'm alone. I'm all alone. The comforter of the Jews has no friends. Awromele is a beast, a Jewish beast, but where does that get me? He doesn't want to be tied down. All he wants to do is party, he has no feeling for ideals. He's a Godless Jew. Zionism doesn't interest him. What am I supposed to do with someone like that?"

Sunk in thought about whether or not to leave Awromele, and having arrived at Prinsengracht, he walked on, instinctively, in the direction of his school. It was a familiar route; he enjoyed walking to the Rietveld Academy. He walked like an automaton.

"No," he told himself half an hour later. "I mustn't leave Awromele; I have to comfort him. I have to start comforting him even better. Then he won't need other men's kisses. I haven't comforted him enough; that's why he acts like this. It's my fault. I've failed, I've driven him into the arms of the manager. I have to offer a sacrifice, to make up for it."

Xavier began humming quietly and walked on, pleased with his decision.

On Diepenbrockstraat, he saw a boy leaning over a moped. Something about him struck Xavier. The boy was standing under a tree with his moped; he looked as if he'd been standing there for a while. Xavier looked at him from across the street. Then he decided to cross. It was the middle of the night.

Xavier approached slowly. He was curious. He didn't want to spend the night walking the streets alone again, not like all those other nights, in the hope that Awromele wouldn't come home too late.

Maybe he had been concentrating too much on Awromele; maybe that was why he'd failed. There had to be more things in the world than Awromele alone.

The boy was wearing a jogging suit. His hair was a dark brown, almost black, and curly. Not big curls—more like Awromele's, tight curls. He probably used fashioning gel.

The boy looked up. He saw Xavier, and went on with his moped. He was squatting down now, busy tightening something.

Xavier came a few steps closer. He cleared his throat, put his hands in his pockets. He heard the manager saying to Awromele, Do you want to come to my place, or shall we go to a hotel? His imagination: gruesome and unconquerable.

"Would you like some help?" Xavier asked.

"No," the boy said. He barely looked up. Xavier couldn't see what he was doing. Something with the moped, that was obvious. But he couldn't tell exactly what—a flat tire, an empty gas tank, a greasy sparkplug.

The boy looked good. At least, what you could see of him looked good. And young.

Is this how Awromele would do it? Going up to boys in a park, or while they were fixing a tire, waiting for the bus, buying popcorn in a movie theater. The rest went automatically. The rest was not saying no, never saying no. Because the Jews had such a bad name already.

"Would you like some help?" Xavier asked again.

The boy looked up at him for a moment. Xavier saw his eyes. Lovely eyes. Big, that above all, long lashes, thick eyebrows. He saw it all, even in this light. Xavier saw everything.

"Fucking moped," the boy said without standing up. He lay down on his back and began messing with the engine. He obviously didn't know much about engines. The moped looked new.

Xavier was standing beside him now. He could reach out and touch him. He leaned down and put a hand on his shoulder, he smiled. He knew how to smile, how to put people at ease; he squeezed the boy's shoulder gently.

The boy got up right away. No, he didn't get up, he jumped up, as though he'd sat on a hornet. "Fuck off," he said. And as he said it, he took a step back.

Xavier was still squatting down. It was a Peugeot. Xavier put his hand on the front wheel. "Nice bike," he said. "Real nice. Peugeot."

He repeated the name a few times, like a prayer.

"Yeah, they sure know how to put them together, don't they?" Xavier said. "Peugeot." He felt content. His father had once owned a car of the same make.

The boy pushed the moped off its kickstand and began walking away with it.

The moped didn't work. It had broken down. That was all. A breakdown, in the middle of the night, on Diepenbrockstraat.

While Xavier was thinking about the boy, he saw Awromele in his mind's eye, undressing, doing things with the manager that he should do only with Xavier. He heard him saying to the manager: "I have to do this because no one comforts me. Because I can't say no. Because loneliness is nothing to be ashamed of."

Xavier got up, brushed the dust and sand off his hands. He didn't know where to go. He didn't want to go home, Awromele's absence would only hurt him more. If he lay in bed, he would see Awromele in the arms of the manager, he would see Awromele kissing mouths that should never have been kissed, he would see a blissful look glide across Awromele's face, a look he hadn't seen in real life for a long time. Awromele's absence, that was hell.

The boy was about twenty yards away from him now. He couldn't walk very quickly, pushing a moped like that. Maybe it was stolen; maybe that was the problem. Xavier could see how heavy the moped was, how hard it was to push along. "Hey," he shouted.

The boy turned off into Beatrixpark. There were two fences forming a stile at the entrance, to keep bicyclists from riding through.

Xavier followed the boy. It wouldn't have been hard to catch up with him, but he kept walking behind him at a proper distance. He didn't want to be pushy, he just wanted to be there, in case.

Occasionally the boy turned around to look, and Xavier waved. One time he shouted, "No need to worry."

The boy was close to one of the ponds now. Xavier knew this park; he had come here to paint a few times: King David with trees in the background, benches, a trash can. King David in the grass. King David and the roses.

The boy was no longer walking—he was running, insofar as one can run while pushing a moped.

Then the boy stopped. Xavier stopped as well. He waited to see what would happen. He wondered whether Awromele had ever followed boys with mopeds into the park at night. He was sure he hadn't; he was the only one who would do that, for Awromele. Everything he did, he did for Awromele; after all, what did he amount to on his own?

The boy was holding his moped upright with one hand now. He turned to face Xavier, waiting for him.

"What do you want?' the boy shouted. "Fuck off."

Xavier didn't know what to say to that. The boy spoke with an accent, too, but it wasn't a German accent. Xavier couldn't place it. Even though it was nighttime, even though he was standing close to a pond, he felt sure of himself. He knew what he was doing here; he knew why he had come here. He had to convince the boy and help him, in that order; he was good at that, at convincing people. Back at school, he had always won the class debates. Rhetoric had been his favorite subject.

"You need help," Xavier called out. He began walking towards the boy.

The boy said nothing. He didn't run, either; he just looked at Xavier, sizing him up.

Then Xavier stopped in his tracks. Something had occurred to him. "Are you Palestinian?"

There was no reply. The boy stood there, his head slightly bowed, holding his moped with one hand. He was wearing a pendant; something glistened there, just beneath his Adam's apple.

"Come on," Xavier said, "tell me the truth. Are you Palestinian?"

Xavier had never met one before, but sometimes he thought he recognized one, in the subway, in front of a department store, on the beach on a Sunday afternoon. The enemies of the people he must comfort.

The boy turned around, took a few steps with his moped. On the back of his jogging suit was a number: 78.

Xavier caught up with the boy. He couldn't move very fast. There was gravel here, which made it even harder to push the moped. The gravel had just been laid. The moped looked like it was sinking up to its wheels. Like in quicksand.

The boy stopped again, panting.

Xavier walked around and stopped in front of him. He held out his hand to him. This was how Awromele did it, making contact, kissing, not too much talking. There was nothing to say. Not in language the way people had known it until now. The old, accursed, impotent language that pointed only to death, every paragraph, every word, every comma, death.

"My name's Xavier." He placed his hand on the boy's shoulder. The same shoulder he had touched before.

The boy didn't move. He simply looked at Xavier. Tense, threatening, but curious as well.

This world was a world of eternal struggle, You-Know-Who had seen that quite clearly.

He wants me, Xavier thought. He wants me, the way I want him. He desires me. That's what we were made for, to long for each other, only for that, again and again, without end, till the end of time, till it doesn't matter anymore.

"You're pretty," Xavier said. "You're a pretty Palestinian."

He waited for a reaction, still with his hand on the boy's shoulder. Only now did he notice that the boy was trembling.

"Or are you something different? You can tell me what you are. Or are you just pretty? That's okay, too. Just being pretty is the best."

The boy pushed him away. With both hands. His moped fell against Xavier.

Xavier cursed. His right leg hurt—his ankle. The moped was lying on his foot like a corpse.

Xavier rubbed the painful places.

The boy started backing away, leaving his moped, leaving Xavier, backing towards the pond. Dignified, like an actor who doesn't want to turn his back on his beloved audience, who keeps waving and bowing until the final applause has died out.

"Come on," Xavier shouted, and went after him. When he started walking, he noticed how badly his leg hurt, but he kept walking faster. As though he was in a hurry, as though every minute mattered, as though he couldn't wait a moment longer.

When you were made for each other, it was wrong to walk right past each other. It was wrong to let each other go when you desired each other the way the boy and Xavier did.

Then the boy could go no farther. He was standing in the grass at the edge of the pond. In the distance, on the gravel, lay the moped.

The rain had turned the ground to mush.

Xavier suddenly thought about his grandfather, his mother. He should call her again soon; he should paint her again sometime as well. But she was in Basel, and he was in Amsterdam. He thought about Mr. Schwartz, and then about Awromele. And the whole time he was thinking about all this, he was walking towards the boy, who stood with his back to the fence beside the pond.

Mothers came here with their baby carriages. They would stop for a few minutes at the pond, to feed the ducks. With a moldy piece of cake. Wasted minutes. Xavier had watched them, had compared them with the mother in Basel. He grabbed the boy by his upper arm, the way you might grab a schoolboy, strict but with the best of intentions. The boy didn't seem to be resisting, as though he couldn't, or didn't dare to, or didn't want to.

Xavier pushed the boy onto the ground, in the mud. He lay down on top of him. As if he were an air mattress. "Do you long for me?" he asked quietly. "Do you long for me the way I long for you? You can tell me, you can tell me anything now. It doesn't matter who you are; it doesn't matter, do you hear me? To me you're just the prettiest Palestinian, and that's what you'll always be."

Once more there was only the look in the boy's eyes, a questioning, suspicious look. Xavier moved his face closer to him—he wanted to whisper something in his ear.

"Hey, fuck off!" the boy shouted. He pushed Xavier's head away, poked him in the right eye with his fingers.

The pain enraged Xavier. He seized the boy's head and started kissing him.

Xavier heard ducks while he was kissing, he heard them quack; he was surprised that the ducks weren't sleeping. Maybe they had woken the ducks?

The kissing soothed him; he could think clearly again, for the first time since he'd seen Awromele dancing with the manager.

Xavier grabbed the front of the boy's jacket, pulled open the zipper. He wasn't wearing anything under it. That's why he was trembling—he wasn't dressed warmly enough. He didn't have enough clothes. That was it. A runaway, a thief.

"Do you want to be comforted?" Xavier asked, holding the boy firmly to the ground. "Isn't there anyone to comfort you? Are you a foreigner?"

The boy tried to pull on Xavier's hair, but Xavier moved up to sit on his arms. He rocked back and forth on his knees until the boy started screaming. Xavier took hold of the pendant and turned it around. An animal—a camel, a dromedary, a hippo perhaps. He couldn't see what it was supposed to be.

"I'm Awromele Michalowitz's friend," Xavier said, still holding the pendant. "I saw you with your moped. I figured you could use some help. I figured you need me; that's why I ran after you. That's all. You don't have to be afraid."

The boy tried to free himself. But where could he go? His moped was broken.

Xavier pressed his lips against the boy's lips. He succeeded, despite the struggling and the screams—the boy screamed in a language Xavier didn't recognize—in sticking his tongue into the boy's mouth. Everything was right, everything fit together, everything was made for each other. Everything tasted so familiar, strangely enough, so safe.

Xavier caressed the boy's hair, kissed his nose, his lips, his cheeks. Not hard, closer to gently, tenderly, and with concentration. He kissed the boy's stomach; it was dark in the park, but the streetlights farther down made it light enough for Xavier to see that little hairs were growing out of the boy's navel, soft black hairs.

He paid no attention to the boy's struggle. He had to comfort now, tonight; otherwise he would lose Awromele.

At last there was no more struggling, no more pushing and pulling; the boy grew quiet. He liked it, he wanted to be comforted, the way all people wanted to be comforted. Wanted to be understood, to be discovered. Maybe there was no difference between comforting and not being able to say no; maybe, once you added it all up, it all came down to the same thing.

Xavier licked the boy's nipples, and when he'd had enough of that he leaned down over his face again. He felt content. Almost happy.

At that moment, at that happy, perfect moment, the boy raised his head and bit Xavier on the cheek. So hard that Xavier screamed. But the boy didn't let go.

Xavier pulled on the boy's hair, but that didn't help, either. The boy had sunk his teeth into Xavier's cheek and wasn't about to let go; he was like a mad dog; it seemed he wanted to rip flesh from bone. He bit in mortal fear, he bit like a woman.

Xavier yanked the pendant from around his neck. Nothing helped; the boy sank his teeth in farther, he wasn't letting go.

In the mud, Xavier's hand came across a stone—not a particularly big one, a little one. With the boy's teeth still in his cheek, he grabbed the stone and brought it down once, hard, on the boy's head.

Then the boy finally let go.

The boy's head fell back onto the ground. He lay there, exhausted, but looking pleased as well. Although the light was dim, Xavier could see blood on the boy's mouth. That's how hard he'd bitten. He had sunk his teeth all the way in. For no reason, without pity.

Xavier bent down over the boy. He had wanted to comfort him; of all the people in the Jerusalem of the North, he had been looking for this boy, this lovely boy who had been standing with a moped in the middle of the night on Diepenbrockstraat.

He touched the boy's cheek, but the boy didn't respond; the boy was very quiet now. In his hand, Xavier still held the stone. It wasn't a big one—half the size of his hand, maybe a little bigger. Children had played with it; they had left the stone lying here; they had been planning to build something with it, but then they'd had to go home to eat.

"You're a foreigner, aren't you?" Xavier said. "You're not from around here. You're from somewhere else. But I come from somewhere else, too, did you know that? I'm from Basel, Basel on the Rhine. Do you know that place? What's your name, anyway?"

The boy didn't answer. He looked at Xavier as though he was off his rocker. A retard, a runaway from an asylum, out in the middle of the night with a stolen moped. Someone who didn't even know his own name. Someone who had forgotten to take his pills, a boy who was nothing without his medicine.

But because of the intensity of his gaze, the color of his eyes, all Xavier could think was: You're so pretty. And because he thought the boy was so pretty, he petted his head carefully.

Xavier stopped for a moment. He panted, noticing how the pain in his cheek was gradually spreading across his whole face.

"You're a terrorist," Xavier said. "Isn't that it? Are you a terrorist? Or are you only friends with the terrorists?"

Then Xavier had no choice but to kiss the boy again. "Sweet boy," he said. "Pretty boy. It doesn't matter. When I was a baby, my mother mixed rat poison into my milk, because sick little animals have to be bitten to death. But she didn't do it—that's why I love her even more than before, because I didn't know about that before. About the sick little animals and what she did to the milk. Do you love me like that, too? Why don't you talk to me?"

He shook the boy. The pendant Xavier had yanked off was lying in the mud beside his head. Xavier glanced at it: yes, it was obviously a camel or a dromedary. Strange that a boy would wear an animal around his neck— it was what you'd expect from a schoolgirl, saving plates with pictures of bunny rabbits on them. Plates that would never be eaten from, because they were too pretty. Plates that would always stay in the cupboard and be looked at on rare occasions. Only looked at.

"Little terrorist," Xavier said to the boy. "Wake up, pretty little terrorist, say something. I want to hear your voice."

Xavier sat down cross-legged beside the boy. He was muddy anyway, it didn't matter where he sat.

He took the boy's head in his hands; he rocked it, wiped the moisture from the boy's forehead. It was sweating, the head was. Xavier said: "I came here to comfort you, even though you're a terrorist, even though I knew you were a terrorist when I saw you standing beside the moped. I could tell right away—I recognized you—but terrorists need comfort, too. I saw you, and I knew you were looking for me, pretty boy, the same way I'd been looking for you, all those nights when I walked through Amsterdam because I couldn't go home, because I can't sleep when my friend's not there. I go crazy when he's not there, and he's almost never there, because he can't say no. That's why I was looking for you, from the first moment I got here. Because I wanted to tell you this: suffering is the emergency exit of beauty. That's what I've been wanting to tell you, for so long, as long as you've existed. You don't have to be afraid, little terrorist of mine, because morality is what protects the strong and destroys the weak. That's why beauty is all there is. That's why every judgment is a matter of beauty, and that's why I'm looking for the emergency exit. I know what I've done, you don't have to tell me, I know everything, but I did it to comfort the Jews. What I did to you, too, I did in order to comfort them. I hit you on the head with a rock, but that's the only way to speak, sweet boy. Because the stone speaks on my behalf. Much better than I ever could. He tells you what's inside me, what needs to come out, about the things for which no words exist, and even if they did you wouldn't understand me. That's why I speak with a stone. All pain is communication, you understand? And all communication is pain. Words as we know them are superfluous. What I am doing now is superfluous. The stone speaks, the stone sings, the stone has sung a song of love; every time he hit you on the head he was declaring his love. Did you hear it, pretty boy? Did you feel it? It was a lovelier song than I could ever have sung for you. I can't sing—I'm not a stone."

Then Xavier looked at the stone he was still clenching and saw that there was hair sticking to it. Hair and scalp, an indistinct but sticky substance. He kissed the stone, petted the boy's cheek.

He let go of the boy's head, got up, walked to the fence beside the pond. He could step over it without difficulty. He was still holding the stone, as if it were a little daughter's hand, like a proud father out walking with his daughter for the first time, right after she's learned to walk.

The water was cold, but not as cold as he'd thought. The ducks quacked. On the other side, he saw two geese as well. He squatted down to wash his chest. He was dirty, from the mud, from the sweat. He remained sitting there like that, up to his chin in the pond. He looked over his shoulder. He could see the boy lying on the shore, the terrorist; he could barely see him. All pain was communication; if it didn't hurt it wasn't communicating, and then nothing had been said, nothing had been stated, nothing had stuck. The painless was frivolous, at the very best.

Xavier raised his hand to his cheek. His cheek was bleeding. He didn't need a mirror to tell. He could feel it. They came swimming over to him, the ducks; they were curious.

"Hello, ducks," Xavier said.

There was already a glimmer of light in the east. He had to go home, he had to get home fast, wash up, wash his clothes, wait for Awromele.

He dropped the stone into the water, with regret, full of sadness, the way you leave a loved one without being able to imagine what life will be like without her. He climbed onto the shore.

The ducks quacked as he went, as though they had grown accustomed to his presence, as though they couldn't get along without him.

For a moment, he stopped and looked at the boy lying in the mud, close to the fence around the pond. Xavier pulled up the zipper on the boy's jogging suit. "So you don't get cold," he said. "But cold is communication, too; the cold talks to you, the cold sings its song as well, lovelier than we humans ever could."

. . .

AT THE AIRPORT in Zürich, a young woman with blond curls checked
in for a flight to Tel Aviv. At the counter in the duty-free shop, where she
wanted to buy some chocolate for her mother, she searched the pockets
of her jacket for change and found a tooth. She took it out of her pocket
and looked at it, pensively but also a bit distraught. It had been months
since she'd seen the tooth; she had forgotten it was in her jacket pocket
all that time.

"Oh, forget it," she said.

For a single second, it was as though the entire airport at Zürich smelled
of dog and of desert. Then she put the tooth back in her pocket and
walked on, with no Swiss chocolate for her mother, to the gate.

Where Evil Grows

WHEN HE GOT HOME, Xavier took a shower. He cleaned his cheek; it didn't look good, bloody and inflamed, someone had really taken a bite out of it. In the bathroom, he filled a bucket with soapy water and put his clothes in it. He threw his shoes away. They were almost two years old anyway.

Awromele still hadn't come home, but Xavier couldn't worry about that. He climbed into bed naked and pulled the covers up around him. There was no way he could get warm. Sleep wouldn't come, either. He was delirious; he dreamed, he awoke with a start, called for his mother, then for God, then Awromele. He thought about his grandfather, about You-Know-Who; he took King David out of the cupboard, laid him beside him in bed, and looked at him as though seeing him for the first time.

When he heard the clock of the old West Church strike seven, he sat straight up in bed. He rocked his upper body rhythmically back and forth, the way devout Jews do when praying, and thought about the boy with the moped. At last he had beaten his imagination, shut it up for good, crushed it beneath his heel. He was no longer thinking about Awromele, about what he was doing, or could be doing; he thought about the boy with the moped, the terrorist in the park for whom he had sung a song of love. People still couldn't understand how beautiful that was, the song that had been sung there, in the middle of the night. Only the ducks had heard. But someday people would understand; someday the world would see that only pain is communication. Human beings wanted to communicate, again and again. Even the saint on his desert pillar wants that—that's why he sits on his pillar, to talk to it, to tell it everything, even if it remains silent, to love the pillar and be loved by it in return. Without the pillar, he would go mad.

But all painless conversation, all chitchat that doesn't even scratch the surface, is a diversion, fluff, oil that polishes the surface until it shines but finally ruins it. Talking makes us forget we're alive, makes us wonder whether life even exists, whether there is even anything like life, whether this isn't a form of death that we have collectively overestimated.

Xavier was still rocking back and forth. He weighed his thoughts, arranged and rearranged them, and saw the boy in the park.

Awromele came home at eight-thirty. He smelled of cigarettes and manager.

"What happened to you?" Awromele asked. He pointed at Xavier's cheek.

"Oh, nothing," Xavier said. "I was bitten."

"Bitten—you're right about that. How did that happen?" He ran his hand over Xavier's hair. He looked at the wound. Awromele couldn't stand the sight of blood.

"I got bitten because I was talking to someone. I had a good conversation, finally, I have to admit."

Awromele wasn't listening closely; he took off his clothes and crawled into bed with Xavier.

"Shouldn't you take a shower?" Xavier asked.

"Later," Awromele said. "Not now. I'm tired. I love you."

Xavier pulled Awromele up against him, as close as he could. "I made a sacrifice," he said. "All true communication requires a sacrifice. If you want to help someone escape his loneliness, you have to make a sacrifice, you have to break down the walls."

"What kind of sacrifice?" asked Awromele, who already had his eyes closed.

"A sacrifice for you," Xavier said. "Only for you. To comfort you."

"What kind of sacrifice?" Awromele asked again. The pressure of Xavier's body had given him an erection. He opened his eyes again.

"A sacrifice," Xavier repeated. "I made contact with the enemy."

"What enemy?"

"Your enemy."

"You didn't have to do that," Awromele said. "I don't have any enemies."

"Everyone has enemies," Xavier whispered in Awromele's good ear. "Everyone. You just have to recognize them, that's all. You have to say hello to them, know where they live; you need their phone number so you can call them. Their first and last names. Their ZIP code. Life is struggle, nothing more."

"Don't make any more sacrifices for me," Awromele said. He was awfully tired; he couldn't focus well on the conversation. He had spent half the night listening to the manager, who had poured out his heart to him in bed. Awromele was in the process of dropping off into a just and healing slumber.

"So how was your evening?" asked Xavier, who couldn't sleep anyway. He wanted to be close to Awromele, in whatever way he could.

"Oh, all right," Awromele murmured. "I couldn't say no again. I hope I learn someday." He looked at Xavier's cheek, and just before falling asleep he said, "We need to get you to a doctor with that cheek." Then he rolled over.

Xavier was still trembling, exactly like the little terrorist for whom he'd sung.

They would have to leave the Venice of the North. In Beatrixpark, beside the pond, lay a lonely moped. There was nothing left for him to do here. Marc had been right. He was made for bigger, more important things than the little they expected from him at the Rietveld Academy.

Then he fell asleep at last, shivering from the cold, dreaming that he held a stone in his hand. And in his sleep he spoke to the pretty terrorist, again and again, each time anew, despite everything.

They slept for the next four hours. Awromele didn't have to work at Albert Heijn that day. When Xavier woke up, he had made up his mind. He would never go to the Rietveld Academy again. He had started off as an autodidact, and that was what he would remain. Awromele was still asleep. Xavier kissed him gently on the back of the neck until he woke up. Awromele was in a morning mood, the way he often was after a night when he had been unable to say no.

"Would you like some tea?" Xavier asked. "It's late already."

"Water. Just water."

Xavier brought him a glass of water.

Awromele drank thirstily. He not only remembered the night he had spent with the manager and the manager's stories, he also remembered his early-morning conversation with Xavier. "What was that about the enemy?" he asked.

"What enemy?"

"What you told me about when I got home this morning."

"Forget it, it's not important. I was still a little drunk, I was just talking."

"More water," Awromele said. He loved Xavier, so he didn't doubt his word. But he found him so tiring sometimes, so principled, so moralistic, so impractical.

Xavier fetched some more water.

Then he lay down beside Awromele, under the blanket. The sheets needed changing, but if Xavier didn't do it it wouldn't happen, and Xavier hadn't done it for a long time—he'd been too busy.

Awromele put down the glass. They held each other without talking.

"I've decided," Xavier said after a while, "to drop out of the Rietveld."

"Why?"

"I'm an autodidact."

"A what?"

"An autodidact."

"Oh." Awromele wiped his lips, blew his nose in his hand, and then wiped it on the blanket. He was in every way a practical person. He knew that a little dirt wouldn't kill you. Exaggerated hygiene only lowered your resistance.

"I thought we came here because you wanted to go to the Rietveld so badly." Awromele held his own head in his hands, pressed his fingertips against his temples, rubbed his eyes hard; nothing helped. He felt worse than he had in a long time.

"The Rietveld isn't stimulating enough for me. You know what they told me? Go do something with plants and flowers. Flower-arranging, ikebana, working with living materials, Oriental aesthetics."

"Yeah, why not?"

"Why not?"

"Why don't you open a flower shop? I think I'd like that. I don't know much about flowers, but I think it would be romantic to start a business with you. And you have a good sense of color and shapes."

"Because I want to do more with my life than open a florist's, Awromele. I want to do more than arrange bouquets."

Xavier shook his friend. It amazed him that he couldn't see what Marc had seen. That his own friend didn't recognize the genius in him. But he was too proud to say that. He felt lonely. It was probably a temporary thing. Once they got to Israel, his talents would show themselves. He would plant forests, orange groves, olive trees. He would make the desert blossom, the way he'd tried to make Awromele blossom.

"We don't belong here," Xavier said. "There's that, too, dearest. Haven't you ever noticed how people look at us?"

"What people?"

"In the street. In the tram."

"They look at me because they think I'm pretty," Awromele said. "I never knew I was pretty, but it turns out I am. People like to look at pretty things. Don't you think I'm pretty?"

"No, that's not why they look," Xavier said. "They look because they're afraid of you. And because they're afraid of you, they despise you."

Awromele's headache wouldn't go away. He squeezed his temples—he had read somewhere that that helped. "We didn't fit in in Basel, either," he said quietly. "So it's not such a disaster."

"It *is* a disaster."

Awromele shook his head. "No," he said. "Get me some more water. I'm dying. My head."

Xavier got some more water; there wasn't anything he wouldn't do for Awromele. Especially after last night.

Awromele emptied the glass down his throat. Then he went to the toilet and tried to vomit. After hanging over the pot for ten minutes, to no avail, he climbed back into bed, sweaty and exhausted. "Never again," he whispered. "Never again. Fucking is one thing, but I'm never going to drink again."

"You mean you fuck them?"

"Who?"

"The people you can't say no to."

"Only if they insist. And if I'm in the mood. Otherwise it's just a little messing around."

Tears came to Xavier's eyes. Despite his headache, Awromele saw the tears. "Xavier," he said, "listen, I can't say no. Let it be. It doesn't have anything to do with you. And, besides, we weren't going to feel anything. We swore we wouldn't feel anything. I don't see that happening. If you ask me, you feel all kinds of things, and your feelings upset me. Your feelings make me sick. Your feelings aren't good for you, and I'm afraid they're not good for me, either."

"I really don't feel anything, Awromele," Xavier said. "I really don't, just like you don't feel anything. I know we'd go crazy if we felt anything. We'd spatter all over the place like a bomb. But that doesn't have anything to do with that other stuff."

"What other stuff?"

Xavier caressed Awromele's head, the same way he had caressed the head of the pretty terrorist, and for a moment, for one brief moment, he couldn't tell the two of them apart, he didn't know who he was caressing.

"There is one country," Xavier said, "that was made for people like us."

Awromele looked at Xavier questioningly. What was he talking about now?

"That's right," Xavier said. "That country is called Israel, and it was made for you and me."

"When I first met you," Awromele said, "you barely knew you were a Jew. It's okay by me, it's not that, but you can overdo it. I didn't know what it meant not to be able to say no when I met you; I didn't know that it involved taking off your clothes so often. But I don't really mind, I've learned to live with it. I just moved here, and I don't really feel like moving again."

"We're not staying here," Xavier said. "This is no city for me, and not for you, either. We're going to Israel. I can already speak Hebrew pretty well, I can learn the rest there. There we'll be at home, there we'll finally be among our own."

Xavier suddenly remembered the boy's pendant. Did a camel have one hump, or two? He needed to look it up in the encyclopedia. He saw himself again, sitting in the mud with the young terrorist's head in his lap.

"Actually, I want to stay here," Awromele said after a few minutes' silence. "I just signed up at the gym. I paid for a whole year—it would be a waste to go away now."

"No," Xavier shouted, "you're going with me."

"Why? Why should I, if I'd rather be here?"

"Because you can't say no. That's why."

Xavier lay down on top of Awromele. "I can't sleep," he said, "and when I can't sleep I always start thinking, and if I think long enough the good ideas come by themselves." Xavier didn't know who he was lying on; he was dizzy; he pressed his nails softly into Awromele's forearm.

"You really need to do something about that wound," Awromele said.

"It looks terrible. I don't know who bit you, but it wasn't a normal person."

"I've been thinking. About evil."

"About what?"

"Evil," Xavier said.

"Oh."

"It exists."

"Yeah."

"But where does it come from?"

"I don't know," Awromele said. "No idea. So many things exist, and I don't know where they come from."

"Where do you think it comes from?"

"I don't know," Awromele said. "Christ, I stock shelves at Albert Heijn, I know where the butter is, the yogurt, the peanut butter, the smoked sausage. That's enough. That's all a person needs to know. And you, early in the morning, while I'm lying here with a splitting headache, you start asking me riddles."

"It isn't early in the morning anymore, it's almost late afternoon."

"Whatever it is," Awromele cried, "I don't know. And get off me. You're too heavy. I don't feel good."

But Xavier didn't get off of him. "I think I know where evil comes from."

Awromele closed his eyes. He wanted to sleep; maybe that would help.

"You know where it comes from?" Xavier asked. "Where it starts, where it arises, like a river? From the cunt. Evil comes from the cunt."

Awromele wiped his lips. "Which cunt?" he asked, not sounding very interested.

"All cunts," Xavier said. "Without exception."

"Oh," Awromele said. "Well, no wonder. Shall we try to get a little sleep?"

Xavier was shivering even more than before, as though he weren't lying in a warm bed but still sitting in the mud beside the pond. "That's where it comes from," he said. "That's where it lives. That is the headquarters of evil. The good comes from the backside, the lovely, the beautiful, the un-selfish, the aesthetic —it all comes from the backside. But evil comes crawling out of the cunt. People always choose for the wrong side."

"That's not very smart of people," Awromele said. "Good of you to find that out. I really love you, do you know that? But I don't feel so well."

Xavier kissed Awromele on the forehead, on his eyelids, the eyes of the boy he didn't want to lose, without whom he was nothing. All comforting began with Awromele, but it couldn't end there—a people awaited him.

"If we want to help people," Xavier said, "we should close off the cunt." Xavier searched around under the pillow, then farther down in the bed. He found King David.

"Look," he said, "come on, look at him."

"I'm looking," Awromele said. "I know him, don't I? I know exactly what he looks like."

Xavier closed his eyes. He saw the moped lying in the gravel; he felt the pain in his leg when the moped fell against him. You had to find it, evil, you had to smell it in order to know where it came from, you had to go looking for it; otherwise you'd never know what life was, otherwise it would always remain a promise, a vague promise. Where it stopped and where it ended, you had to find out about that. What life really was.

I Take It You Have No Pets?

THE MOTHER WAS SITTING, as she often did in the late afternoon, in the chair where she'd always sat when Xavier painted her. She was sitting there with a cup of tea. She was staring into space. Occasionally she smiled, even though there was no reason for it and she wasn't thinking about anything funny. It was a mechanical stricture of the mouth. Now that she was home alone during the day, her passion for her Italian lover was no longer banished to the middle of the night. At the strangest moments, she was overcome by intense desire. Then she would get up, walk to the kitchen, and take him out of the dish rack. Every time she picked him up, she whispered the words she had learned from Awromele: *Shema Yisrael*.

The phone rang. She didn't answer it, she listened to the ringing until it died out, then went into the kitchen. There she took off her clothes. There was no one home anyway. She looked at the battlefield her left leg had become, and for their first time she failed to understand why she hadn't started in on her right leg, or her stomach, or maybe her left arm. There was so much flesh left untouched.

That morning she had finally found the time to go into a shop that specialized in pest control. She had taken the tram. "I hear them running around at night, when I'm trying to watch television," she'd told them at the shop. "The rats."

"Then we should actually come by for a look," the man in the shop had said.

"No, I want to try it myself first," the mother said. "I'm not at home much. I wouldn't want you to come all the way out there for nothing."

Then the man sold her the most powerful poison he had. "I take it you have no pets?" he asked.

The mother shook her head. "I'd like a receipt, please," she said.

Because the weather was so lovely, she decided to walk home, but halfway there she regretted it. The poison was so heavy.

Funny how she never missed anyone. Well, sometimes, in spite of everything, her late husband, because he'd been disgusted by her.

Now there was no one left to be disgusted by her. Marc lived with her, but he wasn't disgusted by her. At most a little indifferent. You needed to have someone around who was disgusted by you; otherwise you had to do it yourself, be disgusted by yourself. She slid her finger along the blade, and murmured the prayer she had learned from Awromele.

DANICA SAT ON the floor of her room, surrounded by Snoopy things—diaries, pens, a little Snoopy, a big one, a key chain. The more she fell under the protection of the tall boy and his friends, the more Snoopys she collected.

Not long before, a biology teacher had asked her: "Don't you think you hang around a bit too much with boys who are much older than you? I always see you with the same group out in the schoolyard."

"No," she'd said. Then she had walked away quickly.

IN BEATRIXPARK, they found a badly wounded North African boy. The papers didn't give it much coverage; there was more important news that day. The police didn't give the case high priority, either; a gas station had just been blown up.

.   .   .

XAVIER WAITED until Awromele had dropped off again. Then he got dressed, taped a bandage over his wound, and went outside.

He walked through the center of town, sweating, feverish, but in a strange way happy. He was pleased with the decision he'd made, convinced that in the end Awromele would follow him to the land where he belonged.

At a supermarket he bought a container of custard. Awromele liked custard; it had been his culinary discovery in the Venice of the North.

In the checkout lane, Xavier saw a woman with two shopping bags and a child. He offered to carry her bags to her bike. Always helpful, that was Xavier, always thinking of others. They struck up a conversation. She was a schoolteacher, but she was on sick leave. Calmly now, no longer shivering, Xavier told her about his painting, but avoided the parts about King David. There would be so much to explain otherwise.

He offered to walk her home—she lived close by—and when they were standing in front of her door she asked, "Would you like to come up for a cup of tea?"

Xavier looked at his watch and smiled. He shook his head, but she insisted, and finally he agreed.

He helped her carry the heavy shopping bags up the stairs.

"I'm going to put my daughter to bed," she said. "She's completely bushed." She carried the little girl into the nursery—a cute little girl in a blue dress, with a vacant expression on her face.

Xavier sat down on the sofa in the living room and looked around. A neat apartment, a bit small, but it had everything: books, CDs, plants, even a little painting on the wall. After five minutes she came back. "She's asleep," she said. "Let's go to the kitchen; it's cozier there."

She had a red teapot. She said, "Call me Rike."

Xavier watched her make tea. The conversation grew more animated.

"So—do you have a girlfriend?" she asked. The tea was steeping.

Xavier shook his head.

. . .

IN BASEL, the mother put on her clothes. She took a bowl from the cupboard and began making a cake. She hadn't done that for so long, it was about time she did. Even though her child had left home, there was no reason why she couldn't bake a cake, for herself and her boyfriend.

She put all the ingredients on the counter—the butter, the sugar, the flour, the eggs, the cocoa, the vanilla extract. She looked at her list to make sure she hadn't forgotten anything. Occasionally she felt dizzy; then she had to lean against the counter. She smiled, but it didn't mean anything, it was something she did automatically, something she'd learned from her husband.

"LET'S LIGHT SOME CANDLES," said the woman whom Xavier had helped with the groceries. "I always like that. It's so cold outside, it's like winter."

She found some tea-warmers and put them on the wooden table. She lit them with a disposable lighter.

"Do you smoke?" Xavier asked.

"Sometimes. My boyfriend used to."

Xavier nodded. He stirred his tea, took a few sips.

"Are you lonely?" he asked.

She laughed. Xavier looked at the little flames. "Well, I'm alone a lot, but I'm not lonely. I have a child."

They both looked at the flames now; there were nine tea-warmers on the table. Xavier could act terribly interested when he felt like it. And he *was* interested. He would surpass the expectations of his teachers at the Rietveld Academy many times over.

"Do you have the feeling that people understand you?" Xavier asked.

She looked out the window, then at the stove, laughed again, and said, "Sometimes."

"Would you prefer to have another language at your disposal besides the language you use now?"

"What do you mean? You ask awfully complicated questions."

She was wearing her hair in a ponytail; she took off the elastic band that was holding back her hair and rewound it. Tighter, better.

Xavier counted the tea-warmers again; there were nine of them, he hadn't been mistaken.

"Let me put it another way," he said. "Do you believe that all truth is pain? Do you think that the truth begins where pain begins?"

She ran her hand over the wooden table, plucked at a fingernail, and looked out the window. If you leaned out a little, you could see a neglected garden down below. "God," she said. "Jesus. Well, I'm not sure, I've never thought about it, but I like talking to you."

THE MOTHER STIRRED the batter. She had used a bit too much sugar, but the quantities didn't matter that much. And butter, never margarine, only butter. She thought margarine was disgusting.

She poured the batter into a glass baking dish and slid it into the pre-heated oven. For a moment, she clutched at the counter. "*Shema Yisrael,*" she said. Then she began whipping the cream. She did it the old-fashioned way, by hand.

"WOULD YOU LIKE to stay for dinner?" asked the woman whom Xavier was supposed to call Rike. "I don't have anything special, but if you don't mind that? Something simple, something quick. I belong to a salsa club, and we're having a meeting later."

Xavier was still sitting at her kitchen table. She thought he was nice, a little strange and a little young, but she liked strange men. Especially when they were young.

"I don't know," Xavier said. "Only if it's not too much bother."

"No," she said. "It's no bother at all, cooking for two or cooking for three, it doesn't make any difference." She got up to see what was in the fridge.

Xavier got up now as well; he went and stood behind her. "Will you help me?" he asked.

"With what?" The refrigerator was open; she was bending over to look at what was in the vegetable tray. Xavier saw carrots, a few forgotten green beans, an eggplant.

He seized her around the waist. "You have to help me," he said.

She turned around. The refrigerator door was still open. Xavier's hands were on her hips now.

"Did you cut yourself?" she asked. "Shaving?" She pointed at the bandage.

Xavier shook his head.

"I think I know," he whispered, "where it comes from."

"Where what comes from?" she asked. It alarmed her to feel that she loved this boy. Strange as he might be, she could learn to love him. In any case, she wanted to get to know him better; that was it; she was exaggerating, she always did that. Loving, where did she get that from? It had been a long time since she'd had such a nice conversation. That's all it was. Someone had finally gone out of his way to understand her. And that was something in itself.

"I know where it comes from," Xavier said. "I know it. But do you know it, too?"

"What? What are you talking about?" She wanted to step back to close the refrigerator door, but there was no room.

"I've seen it," he said. "I know about it. But do you want to know?"

She shook her head. "Move back a little," she said, "so I can close the fridge." She took a few things out of the refrigerator and closed it.

Xavier was trembling now, like a weak sapling tree in gale-force winds.

"It's love," Xavier said. "That's what evil is. Only that, nothing more than that."

"Aw, come on," she said. And then she took the boy in her arms and kissed him, because this was more foolishness than she could bear.

"I BAKED A CAKE," the mother said after dinner. Dinner had consisted of schnitzel, potatoes, and some mixed organic vegetables she had bought at the greengrocer's around the corner, which was also a health-food store.

Marc only nodded; he had taken note of her remark. Since Xavier had left, he had grown silent.

She cut him a piece of cake, then fetched the bowl of whipped cream from the kitchen. "Do you want some of this?" she asked. "Freshly whipped, so it's at its best."

Marc nodded. He ate quickly, like a worker in a company canteen, his fork in his right hand, leaning on his left elbow. That's how he always ate, now that Xavier had left home. He didn't have to do his best; there was no one left to do his best for.

He didn't notice that the mother wasn't having any cake. He didn't notice much lately.

She watched him eat, she was very calm. She smiled. One time Marc looked up—questioningly, it seemed. She nodded at him encouragingly. "Enjoy your cake," she said.

"I KNOW IT," said the woman in her kitchen. "I mean, I know what you're saying. When my friend left me, I was seven months pregnant. I thought: What have I got now, what are my prospects? Who's going to want me anymore? But I went on wearing pretty clothes, going to the hairdresser's, cooking nice things. That's what you should do, too."

She pressed Xavier against her and held him tight. She understood him, this strange boy, and he would surely come to understand her, too.

"It's not that," Xavier said. "I've seen it, and once you've seen it you keep seeing it. Once you've seen it you can never forget it. I know where it comes from."

"Listen to me," she said, moving some things from the counter to the kitchen table. "You need to cook something nice for yourself. When you think, What are my prospects, who's going to want me now?—then you have to cook something nice for yourself."

"HOW ABOUT ANOTHER PIECE?" the mother asked. "I baked it this afternoon."

"What?" Marc asked.

"The cake," she said. "I baked it this afternoon. For you."

Marc nodded.

She cut him another piece of cake, put it on his plate, and added a big dollop of whipped cream. She smiled again, but this time it was for a reason: she was thinking about her lover; later on, he would be with her again. And then for all time, then it would be between her and her lover. Every step she took, every glance she took at the world, he would be with her.

Marc ate even more quickly than before. His thoughts were on his flight simulator, on Xavier, whom he couldn't get out of his mind, on his future.

"Do you like it?" the mother asked.

Marc nodded.

"Strange," the mother said, "that spot being empty." She pointed at the bookcase where King David had always stood. Marc turned around. He looked at the shelf with Schiller on it and said, "Yeah, strange," before stuffing the last piece of cake in his mouth.

"WE HAVE TO be quiet," Rike said. "I don't want her to wake up."

Xavier followed her up to the bedroom. The bed was nothing but a mattress on the floor.

There was no night table, only a big plant.

"Wait a minute," she said.

She went into the bathroom. When she came back, her hair was hanging free.

It had been a long time since she'd lain in bed with a man. Almost a year, maybe a little longer. It was about time—she didn't want to forget how. That was the risk you took if you didn't do it for a long time. She shouldn't deny herself this, it was important, a little action now and then. It didn't have to be perfect, he didn't have to be perfect, the action was what mattered.

"There's no need to be afraid," she said. She sat down beside Xavier. "What we're going to do is very natural."

And, sitting on the bed, she pulled off her jeans. She was the older, she needed to encourage him a bit. If you waited until men got around to it, you could wait forever. Patience was her strong suit; she had plenty of it.

Xavier pushed his head into her lap. First into her pink underpants, and when those had been removed, into her bare crotch. He examined the place where evil came from. Shivering and everything, drooling, planning not to feel a thing, but still, despite everything, with the pretty terrorist from the park in his mind's eye.

"Quiet," she said.

"Take it easy," she said.

The harder he pressed down between her legs, the more clearly he saw the terrorist in the park. The way he'd been lying there in the mud, beside the pond, with the jacket of his jogging suit open. Xavier saw him as though he had seen him only seconds before.

Then he bit her—not nastily, more out of helplessness; tenderly, even.

All truth is pain, but he couldn't cause pain. He wasn't able. He let go of her and tore the bandage from his face. That produced pain. Finally— it was about time.

The wound on his face startled her. "Jesus," she said.

She pulled up her knees. Only now did it occur to her exactly what she was doing. She had met a boy at the supermarket, and now he was lying in her bed. A boy with an infected cheek, a boy with a cheek that looked as if it had been stuck in a garlic press. He grabbed her by the knees.

"It doesn't matter," he said. "Loneliness is nothing to be ashamed of."

She shook her head. What's he talking about? she thought. What's he raving about?

"I'll cook something for you," she said. "That's what we were going to do, wasn't it? My daughter will be waking up soon."

MARC HAD MOVED to the couch; he was wearing his headphones. Benny Goodman, always Benny Goodman. The mother hated Benny Goodman.

She didn't clear the table; she remained seated. She looked around as though this were the first time she'd ever been in this room, as though she were a visitor here.

After a few minutes, Marc bent over. His face had gone red; he was sweating.

The mother smiled. She looked at the bookcase, at the cake on the table, the delectable workaday world of her dining table. Everything was arranged so nicely— the cake, the whipped cream, her cup of tea. Almost like a museum, as though it would always stay like this. As though it would never change.

Marc got up. He groaned, he went to the bathroom. It had been a long time since the mother had heard a man groan. Her lover worked silently, and her late husband had never made much noise, either; he didn't like noise.

When Marc came back, he was red as a beet. The sweat was dripping from his forehead. He looked around nervously, like a cornered animal. Yes, that's what he reminded the mother of, an animal.

He remained standing like that for a few seconds. He was about to sit down, but then he suddenly doubled over, as though someone had punched him in the stomach. There was no one else in the room, though, only the mother, and she was sitting straight as a ramrod at the table, in her usual spot.

Marc was lying on the floor, like a big baby.

"Call a doctor," he shouted. "Help me."

The mother got up to take a better look at Marc. He was lying on the other side of the table. She couldn't see him very well from where she was sitting.

"Help me," he shouted. "Do something!"

She leaned down to look at him. His whole face was covered in sweat. He was gurgling; it looked like he was trying to vomit, but nothing came out. He was clutching at his stomach with both hands.

Marc looked at her. He reached his hands out to her like a child. His face was twisted in pain. Yes, he reminded her of a child, a pitiful child.

"You just ate a little too quickly," she said. "It'll be over in a minute."

DANICA HAD CAREFULLY arranged her collection of Snoopy things. She had examined and re-examined each object. In a catalogue she'd ordered that had come all the way from America, she had checked off the things she didn't have yet. And then, in a green notebook, the same kind of notebook she used for math, she had noted the order in which she would buy them.

She went and stood before the mirror above her sink and bared her teeth. She looked at her braces. She pressed her tongue against the braces and, at the same time, rested her hands on her breasts. Then she spoke the name of the man who the boys who protected her said would explain everything. The man who would clarify everything, and change her life.

"Kierkegaard," she said, squeezing her breasts a little harder. "Kierkegaard," she said again. "Kierkegaard. Do you hear me?"

"NO, YOU DON'T have to cook anything," Xavier said. "You don't have to. I'm not hungry yet." He tried to push Rike's knees apart, but couldn't. She had tensed up. "It's nothing to be ashamed of," he said. "As long as you remember that all pain is truth, and all truth pain. If you remember that, the rest comes naturally."

This boy was strange; he frightened her a little with his odd remarks, the funny way he acted. At the same time, though, she had to admit: he did have penetrating brown eyes. Eyes that wouldn't let go.

She stopped resisting; he pushed her legs apart.

"That's where it comes from," he said. "That's where it arises."

He pushed her legs up, even farther, and farther still.

"But something else arises there, too," he said. "Back there, behind the evil, the good arises, the lovely, the true, the beautiful." He stuck his finger between her buttocks. He felt around between her buttocks, at first only with his finger, later with his tongue as well.

"Don't do that," she said. "I'm not clean. Let me cook for you. I'm not clean."

From the next room came the sound of crying; it ruined Xavier's concentration.

MARC DRAGGED HIMSELF across the floor to the chair where the mother had resumed her pose. She had been counting the books in the bookcase, just to kill time, but now that Marc was lying at her feet, she couldn't ignore him any longer.

He grabbed her legs and shook them, which she found rather unpleasant.

"Do something," he groaned, "help me. Please, help me. Do something. It hurts so bad."

The rat poison hadn't improved his looks; in fact, it had made him revolting, ugly.

"You ate too fast," the mother said. "You were too greedy."

He was short of breath; it looked like he couldn't breathe anymore. He struggled to pull himself up to a sitting position. But he hadn't grabbed hold of the table, he had seized the tablecloth. He pulled everything down onto the floor—the cups, the plates, the leftover cake, and the bowl of whipped cream.

The mother looked at him disapprovingly. What a mess he'd made of things. He couldn't even bring this to a decent end.

Marc lay on the ground, the tablecloth draped halfway across his body.

For another minute or two, the room was filled with a strange panting sound, like the sound of a sick dog sneezing. Then, at last, it was still.

The mother stepped over the mess and went into the kitchen, where she picked up her lover. "*Shema Yisrael,*" she murmured.

She decided on her groin; she had never been taken there before. There was no one else at home but her. She could scream all she wanted.

RIKE TOOK HER little daughter into the living room and put her in front of the TV. Then she went back up to the bedroom, where Xavier was still lying on the bed. Although she hadn't been planning to, she took off her jeans again. It had been so long since she'd had some action, she wanted a little action now, even if it was with a strange boy. She didn't want to wait another year; she didn't want to wait until she had the courage to invite someone else from the supermarket up for a cup of tea.

"Lie there, just like that," Xavier said. He trotted down the stairs. He put the tea-warmers on a tray and brought them back to the bedroom. He'd made it all the way without having one of the little candles go out.

"Oh, how romantic," the young woman said. "That's so sweet of you."

Xavier pushed his head between her legs again, and after a few minutes, he mumbled, "We have to wall it shut."

"What are you mumbling about now?" she whispered. She was a little out of breath from moving her lower body up and down the whole time. She was the older; she wanted to make a good impression in bed. She wanted to show him how nice it could be.

Xavier picked up one of the tea-warmers, blew it out, ran his finger through the wax, which was still runny, and rubbed the wax on the spot where evil came from.

"Ow," she cried. "What are you doing?"

"I'm the comforter of the Jews," he said. "That's why I'm walling shut the cunt."

She sighed, she blushed. For a moment she thought she heard her daughter running down the hall, but she was still sitting in front of the TV. "You nut," she said. "You're so cute, you know you're so nice."

THE MOTHER WAS lying on the kitchen floor. The lover had taken her in the groin; there was a lot of blood coming from her groin.

If only they could see me now, she thought, if only they could see me.

She had her lover in her hand; she hadn't put him back in the dish rack. She needed to catch her breath, but later he would take her again, and again, and again, until she couldn't say "*Shema Yisrael*" anymore.

DANICA PUT SOME things into a shopping bag with a picture of Snoopy on it: a toothbrush, a pocket diary, a bar of soap. She didn't miss her father; she didn't miss Awromele, either; she didn't miss anyone. Then she went outside, to the park where her tormentors often hung out after dinner, to talk about important matters.

She hoped she would meet her tormentors; without them she was all alone, because even when they weren't there they were still there anyway. She thought about them all day, she saw them all day long, all day long she expected the boys to show up, she heard them wherever she went. It was better when they were really there; that was much easier to take.

She wandered through the park, but couldn't find them. The park was almost deserted this evening. At last she saw a man walking alone, without a dog, without a wife, just someone taking a walk. He looked athletic.

First she followed him for a while; then she went and stood in front of him. She rested her hands on her breasts, pressed her hands against them, pushed her tongue up against her braces, looked the stranger straight in the eye, and said, "Kierkegaard."

The man looked at her. He smiled. "How old are you?" he asked at last.

"Thirteen," she said.

.   .   .

XAVIER LEFT the home of the single mother. Not until he got to the foot of the stairs, to the front door, did he realize that he had forgotten Awromele's custard.

He didn't go back; he ran through the streets on his way to the student hostel on Prinsengracht.

There he took off all his clothes and climbed into bed. He was still shivering. He didn't know where the fever ended and reality began. All he knew was that he felt nothing, that he had succeeded in feeling nothing, that it was so much better not to feel a thing. All meaning was fiction, after all, the product of an overworked imagination.

The Dictatorship of the Majority

NOT FAR FROM THE BEACH, in the center of Tel Aviv, Xavier and Awromele found themselves a little apartment. It was infested with rats and cockroaches, but they were together in the Promised Land.

The authorities had welcomed them with open arms. Xavier had passed himself off as a red-blooded Zionist from old Europe. In fact, it wasn't a matter of passing himself off. He was who he said he was, a Zionist, a man convinced that the Jews should live together in order to be comforted.

Before long, they received their Israeli passports. And, no matter to whom Awromele could not say no—and there were to be many of those, men of all ages, from every country, tourists, soldiers, journalists, Arabs— he always came back to Xavier, like a son to his mother. Sometimes it took a while, but he came back.

One morning in bed, Awromele said: "It doesn't matter, Xavier. We don't feel anything. That's why we'll always be together. Because we don't feel a thing, only death can put an end to our togetherness. That's why we're able to stay together, that's why we love each other. Other people think they feel something. Sometimes, when I can't say no and I go with them, Xavier, I notice that they think that, and I can only despise them for that. That's why I always come back to you, time and time again, because

419

you're the only one who is honest enough, like me, to admit that he doesn't feel a thing."

He took Xavier's hands in his and held on to them. He fetched a pair of nail scissors from the kitchen and began cutting Xavier's fingernails. From little finger to thumb, then the other hand, from thumb to little finger.

"That's right," Xavier said, "that's why we stay together."

"You should take better care of yourself," Awromele said, still holding the nail scissors. "You should think about more than just your language lessons. What good is translating *Mein Kampf* into Yiddish if you neglect your appearance?"

"Awromele," Xavier said, "I can't live without you, either. Funny, isn't it?" He pulled Awromele's shirt up around his shoulders and kissed his nipples. Even though he knew how many others had done so before, and would do so in the years to come, he still had the feeling that he was the very first person to kiss Awromele's nipples, the very first to smell him, the very first, except for his mother, to see him naked.

"Maybe I should go with you sometime when you can't say no," Xavier said, rubbing his hand over his cheek. The wound had healed, but it had left a big scar that Awromele said made Xavier even better-looking. "Maybe that would make it easier. Maybe I should see you when you're with the others. Then I wouldn't have to imagine what you're doing with them—I'd see it, and then it wouldn't be so bad."

"Maybe," Awromele said. "Maybe."

Xavier's nail clippings were lying on a piece of toilet paper. Awromele examined the clippings, picked them up, and put them in his mouth for a moment; he was curious about how they tasted. "What I have to sell," Awromele said, "is my youth, my flesh, the lack of wrinkles, my hair. And there's always something you have to sell, you always have to sell something. Only when you stop selling things does loneliness become something to be ashamed of. But you, you have more to sell than just your youth and your flesh, Xavier. That's why I don't say no. Because I don't want to say no, because you have something to sell that I don't, because someday you'll betray me. That's why."

"But what do I have," Xavier asked, "that you don't? What?"

"Talent," Awromele said.

Xavier laughed; the clippings on the piece of toilet paper fell to the floor. "They didn't think so at the Rietveld Academy; they thought I should open a flower shop."

"Maybe it's not a talent for painting," Awromele said. "I don't know. I know that I can't imagine being anyone else but this, the Jew who can't say no. That's who I am, that's who I should be. But you can be someone else, and you *will* become someone else. You can make other people believe in your transformation. That's talent, and I don't have that. In the end, all I want is a house, just a house, it doesn't matter where; I want to sit with you in a living room and cut your nails. But you'll always want more than that. That's why I don't say no, because it's the only way to make sure you don't lose interest. Only as long as I don't say no, only as long as I sell myself, will you still long for me."

"But, dearest," Xavier said, pulling off Awromele's underpants. "I won't betray you. You don't have to sell yourself to other people, you don't have to go with them. I don't amount to anything."

And then Awromele cooed, and Xavier took him. As he thrust himself into him, he thought about what Awromele had just said. He saw his mother with the knife, standing in her kitchen, talking about rat poison.

"Come on," Awromele said after they had rested for a while. "Let's translate a little *Mein Kampf.* We were always so good at that together."

IN ISRAEL THERE were no longer books by Schiller in their bookcase, but King David had received a place of honor. King David no longer had his picture painted: Xavier had stopped painting. But he still looked at his testicle often, and he talked to him, too. During a crash course at Bar-Ilan University, Xavier worked on his Hebrew. Soon he spoke it even better than Awromele. In order to improve his writing skills, he sent letters to the editors of Israeli newspapers. *Yediot Achronot* printed his first one, dealing with draft exemption for Orthodox Jewish men.

That encouraged him to write more letters. He expressed his views on all kinds of issues, ranging from traffic congestion in downtown Tel Aviv to the peace process to the privatization of state-owned companies. The less he meant it, the better he wrote about it. In one way, the opinion of his teachers at the Rietveld had been borne out: he found work as a photographer. First he worked for a small Russian-language paper, later as a wedding photographer as well. He made a reputation for himself in Tel Aviv and the surroundings.

He began pulling in a lot of assignments, so many that he had to turn some of them down. Word-of-mouth advertising worked very well indeed. Here and there, people whispered about his sexual preferences, but his charm, his bearing, his competitive prices, and his hypnotic brown eyes silenced all backbiting. Before long, he was receiving assignments from high-circulation magazines, glossies, daily papers. People were very pleased with his capabilities as a photographer.

During an assignment dealing with local corruption, he met a councilman from the Likud Party. The councilman, who thought Xavier was a nice fellow, asked him: "Couldn't you do a nice portrait of me? I'm not pleased with ones that have been done so far. You're a sharp kid—I think you know what I mean. A picture should spruce things up a bit, or at least not make things worse than they already are."

Xavier hired a studio and did a fine portrait of the politician.

After the shooting session, the councilman talked to the photographer and became even more impressed by his abilities. The politician considered himself someone with a nose for talent, and even though he had gone bankrupt three times before starting a career in politics, this time his nose for talent didn't fail him.

"How would you like to write a speech for me?" he suggested. "No strings attached, of course."

The speech Xavier wrote made the national papers. From that day on, Xavier began writing speeches more often. Not only for the councilman, but for other politicians as well. He began to see a way in which he might comfort the Jews. The fact that Awromele often did not come home at night still caused him pain. But when he was sitting at the window of their dirty little apartment, writing a speech, with King David on the table beside him, he could forget that pain.

"It's weird," Xavier told Awromele, "but without King David I can't write. He gives me inspiration."

"You shouldn't be so superstitious," Awromele said. In Tel Aviv, he had found a job in a supermarket as well. These days he was a checkout assistant.

THE MOTHER REMAINED lying on the kitchen floor, the night she had mixed rat poison into the cake. She lay there silently, panting occasionally like a woman in the pangs of childbirth. After a few hours, at a little past eleven, she went into the living room and cleaned up the mess. She leaned down and looked at Marc. He was cold, and he had changed color. Reminded of her late husband, she said, "Well, there you go again, out cold."

She cut the rest of the cake into slices and put them on a plate. She took them to the neighbors', but they didn't answer the bell—they were probably already asleep.

Then she went to bed herself. She slept soundly, or at least more soundly than usual. She got up the next morning at eight, put on her bathrobe, and went back to the neighbors' with the cake. She had wrapped the plate in foil to keep it from drying out. It looked good. She had a way with baking.

She rang the bell.

"I made some cake last night," she said. "There's still a little left. I thought, well, maybe you'd enjoy it."

The neighbor, a woman in her late sixties who had never had children and was now living out her twilight years with her husband, peered at the cake, and then at the mother. "My," she said, "isn't that kind of you. How lovely."

"Don't worry about the plate," the mother said. "I'll get it back some other time." She placed the cake in the neighbor lady's speckled hands.

Then the mother went back to her own house. She felt better than she had in ages. She felt satisfied. In the kitchen, she took off all her clothes and examined her body, to see where her lover hadn't taken her yet. There were still so many places left untouched.

Two days later, just as she was sliding an apple pie into the oven, they came for her. She put a few clothes in a suitcase, turned off the oven and the pilot light in the gas heater.

Xavier flew in from Israel for the trial. He waved to the mother a few times from the public gallery. She didn't wave back. She didn't seem to recognize her son.

The judge sentenced her to five years in prison. There were mitigating circumstances: her honorary membership in the Committee of Vigilant Parents, the wounds on her legs, her arms, her groin, and even her breasts.

In the penitentiary, the mother proved a model prisoner. She never complained, she ate well, she was always punctual, and she was polite to the female guards, all of whom she soon knew by name. She learned their birthdays by heart. Whenever a guard's birthday came around, the mother always had a present for her. Usually something she had crocheted herself—a hot pad, a potholder, a table mat, an egg cozy. She spent a lot of time crocheting.

The only thing she didn't do anymore was talk. Not about herself, not about her past. At unexpected moments, though, a smile would suddenly appear on her face. But that was more a nervous tic than an expression of happiness.

She signed up for a course in Italian. Just like You-Know-Who, she had a soft spot for Italians.

.   .   .

AS A POLITICAL SPEECHWRITER, Xavier developed unparalleled finesse, sensitivity, and playfulness. After two years of writing speeches for others, he himself became a Likud candidate for the municipal elections in Tel Aviv.

He possessed the ability to evoke emotions among the electorate. He spoke to the voters with a fire and a faith in the future that no other politician could equal. Xavier Radek had something they lacked. For him, passion was not a matter for irony. That much, at least, had become clear to Xavier: first came power, then came the comforting.

In order to comfort the Jews, he needed power.

"How do you do that?" the campaign manager asked. "Whip up the crowd like that? I thought politics didn't appeal to the emotions anymore."

"Communication is pain," Xavier said. "Don't ever forget that. If it doesn't hurt, there's no communication taking place. Don't make promises. That doesn't help. Everyone does that already. You have to tell them the truth. And truth is nothing but pain. They can only start to believe in it once it has become pain. That's the secret of democracy."

Because of Xavier's ability to draw voters from various segments of the population, the party didn't make a point of his private life.

His opponents tried to use it to their own advantage, but Xavier grew stronger with each attack. The voters didn't want a leader without foibles. They wanted him to be one of them, or at least to be a man they could think of as being one of them.

Xavier knew there was no such thing as meaning. There was only pain without meaning. A politician's job was fleshing out that pain. That was the temporary comfort he could offer his voters. He expressed their frustration, gave voice to their despair; he played upon their fears like an eleven-year-old Russian virtuoso at the keyboard. It was precisely Xavier—who felt nothing, who couldn't feel anything anymore, for feeling was tantamount to falling—it was precisely Xavier who d simulated feeling so convincingly that his speeches were always attended by a few hundred people. Yet he was still nothing more than a candidate for the City Council.

He had made a habit of taking King David wherever he went. Each time, he told the same story. "My parents," he said, "forgot to have me circumcised because they didn't want to know who we were. But I discovered who I was, and I had myself circumcised, when I was almost seventeen. It cost me a testicle. And that testicle is my king. I call him King David." And then, after a short pause: "King David can be your king, too."

"Yes," shouted voters from all walks of life, "make him our king, too!"

And they raised their voices in song. "Long live King David, King David, *hai hai vekayam!*" They lifted Xavier and his jar with the testicle in it onto their shoulders. They danced like that around the gym where the rally was being held. The electorate was waiting for a king.

Xavier was elected to the City Council of Tel Aviv.

But as his power grew, Xavier made enemies.

Not only the members of other parties were his enemies. His greatest enemies were within the ranks of his own party. And in order to combat them, he began assembling dossiers.

Water over the Desert

AFTER EIGHT YEARS in city politics, Xavier announced that he was going into national politics. He didn't want to comfort a municipality, he wanted to comfort a nation, a people.

He appointed Awromele as his campaign manager. Never before had a checkout assistant been given the job of campaign manager. That created a lot of goodwill for Xavier, although in some ultra-Orthodox circles people spoke of nepotism.

Nothing is worse for a politician than to have everyone love him—for then, in fact, no one loves him. If he hungers after power, he must be contentious and controversial.

"Power," Xavier told Awromele, "is the accumulation of missteps made by your opponents. Some of my opponents have not yet made any missteps. For them, we have to arrange a misstep. If they don't make a misstep voluntarily, we have to help them." And he went back to work on his enemies' dossiers.

Occasionally he leaked something out to journalist friends who, in exchange for exclusive stories about his life, were willing to cite Xavier as an anonymous source.

"Look," Xavier said to Awromele in bed one night. "It's just a matter of reading between the lines. Study their speeches, study their draft legislation, study the marks they've made, you'll always find a weak spot somewhere. And then you have to apply deconstruction to that. You deconstruct what they've said, what they've done, what they've proposed, what they've believed in or claimed to believe in, until that weak spot spreads across their entire career like an oil slick. It's like tennis—you have to help your opponent make a mistake, let your opponent beat himself. No one made a greater contribution to the death of communism than Stalin."

Xavier hired six assistants whose work consisted solely of passing along his opponents' weak spots to the media. They were willing to go through fire and water for Xavier. They praised his energy, his charisma, his belief that things couldn't go on like this, that a great of deal of work remained to be done.

Xavier realized that the voter was nothing but meaningless pain, pain to which a leader had to lend meaning. He who accepts that all truth is pain need not shrink from accepting power. He knows power like the back of his hand.

One by one, systematically, and with an unerring sense of timing, Xavier eliminated his enemies, until only one remained.

That was Jossi Dolav. He, too, wanted to be the leader of the Likud Party. Xavier despised Dolav, but that was nothing personal, it was part of his job. Jossi Dolav had started out as a lawyer and, after some idealistic ramblings, had become a professional politician. He had a family and a mustache. Xavier invited him to the bar at the Dan Hotel, close to the beach, where they could talk undisturbed.

"Jossi," Xavier said, after inquiring in detail after his wife and children, "Jossi, you're an intelligent person, a nice person. You're a credit to the party—you would be a credit to any party. That's why I'm pleased that you've chosen our party."

Jossi Dolav smiled. Like so many people, he was fond of compliments, especially when they came from someone like Xavier, who, though younger than he, was very well respected.

Xavier put a few peanuts in his mouth. Then he remembered that he
didn't really like peanuts, and pulled a plastic bag of sunflower seeds out
of his pocket. He cracked the shells deftly and ate the contents with amazing speed. Amid the cracking of shells, he told Jossi Dolav: "Jossi, you want
something that I want. That's bad for you, that's bad for me, and ultimately
it's bad for the party. Withdraw your candidacy and I'll make sure you're
richly rewarded—after the elections, of course, which I will win. An attractive and responsible post as minister in my Cabinet. I leave it up to you.
I'm a generous person, you know that. If you like to travel, I'll make you
minister of foreign affairs. If you prefer to take it easy and you like a nice
massage now and then, I'll make you minister of tourism. Just tell me, you
know how I am, I'm as good as my word."

"I'm not like that," Jossi Dolav said. "I have ideals."

"So do I. That's precisely why I'm talking to you, because I have ideals,
too. That's why I'm warning you. As a friend. As a fellow party member.
Your candidacy is a mistake. You're splitting the party, and ultimately
you'll split yourself. A party that's split can heal again, but a politician,
never. A split politician is a dead politician. Don't kill yourself."

Jossi Dolav shook his head. He put a couple of peanuts in his mouth;
peanut skins were sticking to his lips. "Don't worry about me," he said.

Xavier was eating even more sunflower seeds now, even faster. "Jossi,"
he said, "Jossi, Jossi, it was, what, five years ago when we were still on the
City Council? You remember?"

Jossi Dolav nodded. He looked outside, at the beach, but it was dark,
there wasn't much beach to be seen.

"There was a soccer stadium built back then—-it was your responsibility. I'm sure you remember that, because you've got a memory like an elephant. That's another thing that makes you such a talented politician. It
would be a terrible pity to have such a promising career nipped in the bud,
a terrible pity. Anyway, where were we? Oh yeah, that soccer stadium.
Who did you have build that stadium? I bet you remember that, too. It was
your brother-in-law. That was awfully loyal and insightful of you. Always

prepared to help family and friends in need. Fortunately, that brother-in-law of yours rewarded your insight, to the tune of fifty thousand dollars, if I'm not mistaken."

Xavier pulled out a plastic folder and slid it across the bar to Jossi Dolav. The folder contained photographs and copies of documents. Without looking at it, Jossi said: "Everyone does that. That's the way it works here. That's the way it works everywhere."

"I know," Xavier said, "of course everyone does that. Of course that's the way it works everywhere, and that's the way it works here, too. In itself, there's nothing wrong with it. But you need to ask yourself, Jossi, what is news? Ask yourself that question. Do you think news is something about which you can objectively determine, this is news, and that's no news? No, of course you don't think that. You're not that dumb. News is news when enough people know that it's news. Say, a quarter of the population. My campaign manager and his staff, they make news. That's their job. That's what I pay them for. Of course, you have to let journalists go about their business—that's very important. You always have to let journalists think that they've come up with it themselves. If you take that illusion away from them, they stop being pliable. But listen to me—why am I telling you this? Anyway, we feed the journalists stories the way a rabbit farmer feeds his rabbits. News is a big, unpredictable wave, a tornado, that's what news is. As you undoubtedly recall, your brother-in-law was convicted a few years ago of molesting a girl, a girl who was underage. Stupid of that brother-in-law, to let himself be convicted of something like that. Did he maybe cross somebody? Was he a little too ambitious? Was he traveling in the company of friends who turned out not to be friends at all?"

"What does this have to do with me?" Jossi Dolav snorted. "What does this have to do with anything?" He was starting to lose patience; he was slapping his right hand gently but rhythmically against the back of his chair.

The hotel lobby was almost empty. There weren't any tourists anymore—they had stopped coming because of the terrorists.

"Nothing," Xavier replied, "in fact, nothing. But news establishes connections between A and B, news makes connections, news is the great unknown, news assembles some facts and tears other facts apart. It's our job to inform the voter. You shouldn't forget that. You inform, I inform, that's what we're here for."

"Listen," Jossi said. "I worked for this all my life, for this moment, for this election. I'm not going to let it be taken away by you, by some, some . . ."

"Say it," Xavier said. "Come on, say it, have the courage to say it. Don't stifle it up."

Jossi Dolav put a few more peanuts in his mouth. "I'm not letting you take this away from me. You hear me? That's all I wanted to say, that's all. I'm not letting myself be intimidated—the way you intimidate everyone. I'm not falling for it."

The sunflower seeds were finished. Xavier wiped his hands on a napkin. "If you withdraw your candidacy within forty-eight hours," he said, "in a couple of months you'll be a Cabinet minister. You'll be happy; you'll have power, too. Don't let yourself be misled by the gossip—ministers have power, too, even in a democracy. But if you don't, Jossi, if you don't withdraw, then in a couple of months you'll be a dung heap that everybody, even your friends, will go out of their way to avoid. You'll be a dung heap—and make no mistake about that, being a dung heap is a real drag."

He stood up, shook Jossi Dolav's hand, and said in a friendly, almost conspiratorial tone: "Clothing is the only form of communication that doesn't necessarily have to hurt. Think about buying your suits somewhere else."

JOSSI DOLAV did not withdraw his candidacy for the party's leadership, and within a week there erupted a scandal concerning the funding of the soccer stadium for which Jossi had been responsible.

At first Jossi Dolav dismissed all accusations and said, "It will blow over."

But it didn't blow over. Every day, new details of the scandal appeared in the papers. Before long, it was public knowledge that Jossi's brother-in-law had molested an underage girl, and although of course Jossi couldn't have done much about it, every day he had to answer questions about girls who were underage.

Two weeks later, Jossi withdrew his candidacy. But that decision could not put a stop to reports on the scandal. There was no stopping them. New scandals came to light. It was a cesspool. The public loved it.

Two weeks before the elections, Jossi Dolav put a bullet through his head beneath a tree on the Mount of Olives. Because Judaism forbids suicide, the official explanation was that it had been an accident while Jossi was cleaning his rifle.

The suicide was inconvenient for Xavier, but before the funeral, he gave a speech that moved friend and enemy alike. He spoke of Jossi's qualities, about everything he had done for the country, for the party, for his family. Then the body, wrapped in a prayer shawl, was lowered into the grave. The widow and children cried, and Xavier pulled out his hankie for the cameras as well.

Xavier won the elections with ease. He had almost no competitors left. The competition that was still around stayed quiet, waiting for the storm that called itself Xavier Radek to abate.

Because people still had trouble pronouncing his first name, Xavier now began calling himself Radek for short. And also The Radek, or "ha-Radek" in Hebrew.

HIS ELECTORAL VICTORY was international news. That someone of his sexual inclination could become prime minister of the Jewish state was seen as a sign of hope. The papers wrote: "Perhaps someone like this can make peace with the Palestinians. Perhaps precisely someone like this."

During the victory party, ha-Radek, who had lost his voice from all the

speeches he had given in the months before—a dictator can allow himself to be silent, but a democrat must speak, speak, and go on speaking—
whispered: "This is King David, this is the testicle I lost at sixteen, when
I discovered who I was. At that point, I accepted the consequences of
being who I was. I accepted my people's history. I had myself circumcised,
King David brought me to this country, King David made me win the elections. King David is my king, but he can be your king, too."

He held the jar with the testicle in it above his head, with both hands.

"Yes," ha-Radek's supporters screamed. "Let King David be our king,
too. Let King David lead us through these dark days. Don't let him leave
our side."

Xavier Radek silenced his opponents by publicizing missteps they
had made in the past. But ha-Radek also had houses and highways built,
planted forests and orange groves, let water flow over the desert. Unem-
ployment fell, inflation decreased, the spending deficit shrank. *The Econ-
omist* praised his employment policies and called ha-Radek "the miracle
from Jerusalem."

ABOUT SIX MONTHS LATER, rumors began circulating to the effect
that the Redeemer was a testicle in a jar. At first only on a few obscure
Web sites, but later the leading newspapers and magazines began grant-
ing coverage to King David as well. Orthodox Christians wrote serious
articles about him. Several theologians said, "We may not rule out the possibility that Christ has returned in the form of a testicle." And they supported this thesis with quotations from the Old and New Testaments.

More and more Jews were becoming convinced as well. They saw the
sexual inclinations of ha-Radek as an additional sign that King David was
the Messiah. That a homosexual could become the prime minister of Israel was a miracle. And God's miracles always had a purpose.

Time ran a photo of King David on its cover, with the line "Is This the
Redeemer?" Beaten silly by wars, poverty, diseases, scandals, corruption,

and a sluggish equity market, the world was ripe for a redeemer in a unique guise.

In bed, Awromele asked Xavier, "Were you planning this the whole time, or did you come up with it later on?"

Xavier said nothing. He shivered, the way he had the time he had met the terrorist in Beatrixpark. He held Awromele tight, but he didn't answer his questions. He only kissed him.

Statistics

THE TALL BOY and his friends graduated from secondary school, but they remained friends. Danica was still under their protection. They were loyal. They gave and they took; they knew that taking brought with it responsibilities. He who has taken once must take again. He who has used a person once must continue to use them, otherwise they will get the feeling that they are useless, that you have rejected them, that they no longer have a function. A person without a function is a person lost.

In fact, they had grown tired of Danica. She had developed into a spindly woman. Out of goodness, out of a sense of duty, they continued to make use of her.

Along with their former Greek and Latin teacher, they had formed a reading circle. They talked him into making use of Danica as well. At first he had objected: he had a girlfriend, Danica had been one of his pupils, it would be inappropriate. But finally he realized that such objections were less than sporting. Then the teacher began making use of Danica as well.

"We're doing this to make you happy," the tall boy told Danica, when they met her in the park on their regular evening there. "We could find something better. We do this out of pity. Call it friendship. Is there anything in the world lovelier than true friendship?"

Danica shook her head. She thought about Snoopy, about her brother

Awromele, whom she hadn't seen for years, and about Rochele, whom she'd lost track of as well. She understood that there was only one thing worse than being used by your tormentors: being left behind, unused.

THE BIGGEST PROBLEM still facing ha-Radek as prime minister of the Jewish state was terrorism. All other problems arose from that, no other problems seemed to exist, just as the object of affection is all that exists for one in love. Xavier knew, on the basis of personal experience, that pain knows no progress. Pain can become more intense, or it can decrease in intensity, but the idea of progress is foreign to pain. That certainty safe-guarded him from political missteps.

Via a former head of the Israeli intelligence agency, the Shin Bet, he came into contact with the leader of Hamas. Ha-Radek invited the leader of Hamas to have a bite to eat with him at a discreet location, so that they might get to know each other better. Having a bite to eat with a stranger makes conversation easier—Xavier knew that.

Although the Hamas leader had little sympathy for men who were fond of men, and although he had no truck with Jews in particular, he accepted the invitation. Xavier had sworn to him that the media would never hear about it.

They met at a remote farm in the Negev. With the exception of two interpreters, employees who had both proved their discretion in the past, and Awromele, no one else was present.

The spiritual and political leader of the Hamas movement ate heartily of the roast lamb, after ha-Radek had personally tasted it first. He took two helpings of salad. He was a serious person, but eating soothed him.

After the meal, when the peppermint tea had been served, they sat down together on comfortable cushions beneath a pair of ceiling fans.

"I'm going to level with you," Xavier said. "Both of us have a mission. You have a mission, I have a mission. I want to comfort the Jewish peo-ple, and once we know each other better, I'll explain why. And you want to offer comfort to your people as well. But how can we comfort a people when we have no power?"

The leader of Hamas didn't reply, so Xavier went on. "Even if a family is all you wish to comfort, you still need power. All comforting assumes power. You know that, I know that. Once I dreamed of writing the Great Yiddish Novel, but it turned out that it had already been written. Then I considered becoming a painter, and I painted, every evening, sometimes during the day as well. But now I'm the prime minister. Now I should be able to provide comfort. Yet this is an unusual country. Everyone watches this country, everyone talks about it. This land evokes emotions, just like an exciting book. This is where monotheism was born, this is where the sacred places of almost all the great religions are located, this is where a traffic accident can become international news. Let's not linger too much on history, though, because, to be honest, I don't know very much about it. Politicians shouldn't look back, anyway—they should look forward. But how can you comfort a people when your power is not abiding? How can you make decisions when you have to fear for your power with every decision you make, when you live in fear of falling out of favor? He who has power must keep it. You have power, but your power is threatened as well. Because the people are fickle, and their memory is poor. The people are weak and disoriented by nature. They need leaders to keep them from making missteps. Your power exists because you have an enemy, because you can create for your people the illusion that you are struggling heroically against that enemy. There's nothing wrong with that—every people has its own illusions. But let me put it differently: where would you be without an enemy?"

"Where would *you* be without an enemy?" the aged leader of Hamas asked quietly. His voice wasn't particularly loud; you had to listen carefully to understand him. "All things human," he said, "exist by virtue of having enemies. Without enemies, none of it can exist; it dissolves, vanishes into thin air, becomes more invisible than ashes."

The servants poured them some more peppermint tea.

Awromele was sitting on the other side of the low table. He looked proudly and longingly at Xavier. He would have liked to take him in his arms right then and tell him how much he loved him, but he knew this wasn't the moment for expressions of tenderness.

On the table, beside a candlestick and a plate full of grapes, was King David. Wherever ha-Radek went, he always took King David with him.

The leader of Hamas had already looked at the jar with interest a few times.

"So let's talk about death," Xavier said, putting some grapes in his mouth. "What is death? Scholars say: nothingness. And they are probably right about that. But death does spread fear. That's why death is nothingness only to those who are already dead. For the living, death is always present, like a mother who keeps her eye on you."

The leader of Hamas put a grape in his mouth as well; he liked grapes, he liked all kinds of fruit. He often skipped dinner completely and ate only tropical fruit. He looked at the jar again; he couldn't see it particularly well, but, still, it intrigued him, that testicle. He was old and tired; in the course of his life, he had seen almost everything, but never a testicle in a jar. He had dedicated his entire life to a struggle in which he barely believed anymore, even though he would never admit that, not even to his closest associates, his political heir-apparent, his family. Without that struggle he was nothing, and he didn't want to be nothing. He had been that already, and he had no desire to return to that state. To be dead was one thing, but to be alive and still not add up to anything— never again.

Xavier leaned back. After all these years in the Holy Land, he still hadn't become accustomed to the heat. He closed his eyes tightly, opened them again, and looked at the leader of Hamas. He liked him. The leader had eaten his fill, and Xavier liked people who enjoyed eating.

"I'll speak honestly with you, the same way I speak to my friend here, and to my advisers," Xavier said. He wiped his forehead; the heat was tiring him out. "It's hard for me to take," he said, "the heat. I'm sorry. I was born and raised in Basel. Couldn't Theodor Herzl have picked out a place with a milder climate than this?"

The leader smiled graciously. He knew Basel; he had been there once, years ago, when he was still young. To silence a helper who had turned informant. But he had taken pity on him. He hadn't killed him. He had simply deep-fried his feet. In the end, he always took pity, that's why he wasn't suited for fieldwork. Directing people—that was where his abilities lay, he was better at that. Although he had his doubts about that now as well. "I know the city," he said. "Basel. Lovely town. I was there once. We do business with Switzerland."

"Who doesn't?" Xavier said. "The Swiss banking system brings us all together. Yes, Basel. Have you been there often?"

"Once or twice," the leader said. "But only on business."

Xavier nodded. The leader thought about all the times the Zionists had tried to infiltrate his movement. If you wanted to prevent infiltration, you couldn't show pity, you had to eradicate the informants root and branch, but he had always felt pity for them. He had fried where he should have killed. That was why he had applied himself increasingly to office work, to the logistical preparations for their operations, to finances.

"What I had started to say," Xavier continued, "is that I have no secrets from you. I don't want to have secrets from you. That's the only way for us to get any further. There is a collection of meaningless pain. That collection is also referred to as mankind. But all pain begs for meaning. That is why there is religion, that's why there is art. I used to paint, so I know what I'm talking about. I made dozens, hundreds of portraits of my mother with my testicle in her hand. But back then the world wasn't ready for that yet."

"I'm sorry to hear that," the leader of Hamas said. He had written poems as a young man. He had been just as much a lover of beauty as Xavier was. But now he was tired. Though he longed to work on a poem again, his vision was failing. His eyes were getting worse all the time, and that made it look as though the world was going backwards, getting smaller all the time, withering away, until it became only the things he knew by heart, the bathroom in his house, his office, the path from the bed to the toilet.

"No need to be sorry," Xavier said. "That's how things go. Would you like some more tea?"

The leader shook his head. He'd already had four cups of peppermint tea; more than that would be bad for his stomach.

"Art lends meaning to pain," Xavier said. "You know that. You can call God art as well, it makes no difference to me. All art is God, and God is all art. There is no Godless art. There is only bad art, and art that is far ahead of its day. Like the paintings I made of my mother with testicle, for example. They weren't appreciated at the Rietveld Academy, because the people there were narrow-minded, locked up in something I prefer not to honor with a name."

Xavier had risen to his feet; he shook his fist now and paced back and forth. "I know what I'm talking about," he shouted. "I painted, I lived for art. I know how narrow-minded and prejudiced they were, the anti-Semites of the Rietveld Academy. Those homophobes, those frustrated bu-reaucrats who could do nothing themselves but macramé."

"Take it easy," Awromele said. "Xavier, calm down, now. This gentle-man isn't interested in the Rietveld Academy, this gentleman came here to talk about a truce."

Xavier walked over to Awromele and ran his hand through his hair. As a campaign manager he had been creative, and he was still one of Xavier's best advisers; his loyalty was unswerving. In fact, Awromele was the only person Xavier trusted. Ha-Radek discussed all important decisions with Awromele. Not that he always followed Awromele's advice, but he talked to him about everything. In the shower, in bed, while they were walking their dogs. Xavier had bought two German shepherds—to keep himself company when Awromele couldn't say no again. Then he would let them into the bedroom. They would hop up onto the bed, and Xavier would scratch them behind the ears until he fell asleep. By the time Awromele

got home, the bed would be covered in dog hair, but that was something
Awromele would just have to get used to.

"We should get to know each other a little better," Xavier said, sitting
down again. "That makes things a lot easier. How many children do
you have?"

"Twenty-four," the leader of Hamas said quietly, and he looked at
Awromele again. He saw only a silhouette. That was enough. This
Awromele was interesting, but the prime minister annoyed him. His own
movement was full of young men with more ambition than effectiveness,
and they were lazy, that above all, simply lazy. Spoiled, loudmouthed,
without creativity, without real idealism. Even those who were prepared
to die did so often out of laziness.

"Twenty-four," Xavier said. "That's a fine number. But what I wanted to
say to you is this: politics is an extension of art. Politics is art that doesn't
withdraw to some protected nature reserve. Politics is art that doesn't run
away from responsibility."

Xavier took a big gulp of water. He leaned back on the cushions for a
moment, then sat up straight again. He looked at Awromele. It was for
him that he was sitting in this farmhouse in the desert, it was for him that
he had come to this country. For him. Xavier had no regrets, but sometimes he needed to remind himself of that.

"You send your boys to the supermarket," he said, "to a hotel, a bus, a
roadblock, a pizzeria. They go on their way, full of high spirits. Their parents don't know about it, because when you're young and adventuresome
your parents never know what you're doing. I know how that goes. My
own parents didn't know a thing, nothing. I was swimming in the Rhine
with Zionists when other kids were reading *Donald Duck*. But, okay, they
get themselves something to eat, your boys, or girls, they drink a little
water, and then they explode. Some people call it terrorism, others call
it a legitimate act of resistance. Let's call it kinetic theater. Without art,
there is no meaning."

The leader of Hamas had made up his mind. This man was a clown;

there was no doubt about that now. That's what democracy gave you, clowns. He didn't like the circus, he never had. An uncle of his had taken him to the circus in Beirut once, he had hated it. "Yes, kinetic theater," he said. "You can call it that. If you like. I am not a philologist."

"But effective and committed theater," said Xavier, who had regained a bit of his former enthusiasm. "Because that kinetic theater causes pain and sorrow. It unleashes emotions. It becomes news, which is more than you can say about most theater. How many artists would like to make the news but never do? Not even an *in memoriam*. Do you know what they told me at the Rietveld Academy? They said I should start a flower shop."

Xavier had risen to his feet again.

"Sit down, for God's sake," Awromele said.

The leader of Hamas nodded. The food had been good, but as for the rest, he had the feeling that he had come here for nothing, that he was wasting his time—and he didn't have much time left.

Xavier sat down.

"Okay, I'll remain seated," he said. "I'll remain seated, no problem. I'm an emotional person, I can't help it. That's why people sometimes misunderstand me. There is only one thing that can throw open our joyless wildlife sanctuary. And you've understood that by now. Death. Death is the only thing that can drag art out of the nature reserve where it has made itself ridiculous and superfluous."

The leader of Hamas flicked away a piece of skin from under his eye. He wanted to go home; he'd had enough.

"Your kinetic theater causes joy for some, sorrow for others. Only a few are indifferent to it, and then only because they've never experienced it up close." Xavier saw the leader glance at his watch and said: "Yes, I'll keep this short. You want to comfort your people, I want to comfort mine. That's why we need to perpetuate our power. Power adores the status quo, the way a habitual john adores his favorite girl. Let's help each other out, let's perpetuate each other's power. That's why I invited you here for this meal. Let's keep things a bit under control. That is my proposal. Everything in good time, and all things in moderation. That's the best for all concerned. My proposal is: no more than fifteen deaths a month, and not always in a pizzeria. Go for a little variety. Those people have to make a living, too."

The leader studied his nails. He said nothing.

"I've talked to America about this," Xavier said, "and to the European Union. They know about it, they back my proposal one hundred percent. I understand, you can't always control it, there's a lot of improvisation involved. So let it be twenty one month, but no more than ten the next."

The leader leaned forward. He had a headache. There was a plate of figs on the table; he put one in his mouth, then picked up King David.

"May I?" he asked.

"By all means," Xavier said.

The leader examined the jar from all angles, as well as he could with his bad eyesight. "A fine testicle," he said with his mouth full of fig. "Blue— you don't often see them like that. Is that right, is it blue?"

"He was infected," Xavier said. "That's why he's blue. Yes, you see that very clearly."

"So this is your Redeemer?" the leader asked. And he held the jar up to the light in order to get a better look.

"That's what people say," Xavier said. "Surveys show that fifty-five percent of the population believe that King David is the Redeemer. And who are we to doubt the majority? We mustn't doubt that—that would be undemocratic."

"More and more Christians are also starting to believe that Jesus has come back to earth as Xavier's testicle," Awromele stated proudly. "Almost seventy percent of the Christians in the United States, thirty percent in Italy. In Ireland, it's still less than ten percent, but they're working on that."

The leader of Hamas nodded. "It is truly a fine thing to behold," he said, putting the jar back on the table.

"Fifty," the leader of Hamas said after he had finished his fig. "Fifty a month, and not one less."

Xavier started laughing.

But suddenly he stopped, and his mouth twisted into a grimace.

"Fifty—that's ridiculous," he said. "That's a mockery. That's more than it is now, more than last month. That won't help to perpetuate your power, or mine, either. That won't help anyone. The EU and America agreed to fifteen to twenty a month. I'm telling you this in complete confidence. No, that won't get us anywhere. Have something else to drink, and try one of my chocolate cookies—I had them baked specially for you."

Xavier had to call for them a few times, but finally a servant brought in a big plate of cookies and a fresh pot of tea.

The leader of Hamas ate four cookies, one after another, looked at Awromele, and asked, "And this is your . . . ?"

"Yes, this is my friend," Xavier said, and he looked at Awromele, too. It seemed as though time had left him untouched, as though everything became older and drier and balder except for Awromele. Only the little lines at the corners of his eyes showed that he was no longer twenty-three. "He can't say no, but that's because of his mother. She always told him: Don't say no, the Jews have enough problems as it is. But I like you, and that's not something I say to everyone. I believe we can help each other, and not only each other but also the United States and the EU—no, make that the world, mankind as a whole," Xavier said. "The Palestinian Authority no longer exists; they're a pack of corrupt animals. You are the Authority—unofficially now, but soon it will be official. I'm telling you, as a friend, as someone with your best interests in mind: he who has power must keep it, the rest is just details."

"And how many wounded did you have in mind?" the leader of Hamas asked.

"Wounded?" Xavier asked. "Who's talking about the wounded? What is a wounded person? Someone who couldn't make up his mind, an in-betweener. I'm not interested in the wounded. Wounded people aren't front-page news. You and I should concentrate on front-page news. Leave the regional news on page eight to the executive branch. We're concerned with the dead. That's what we're talking about here."

Xavier took a big gulp of tea. The tea was still hot, and it burned his mouth. After soothing the burn with ice water, he said: "I'll tell you what.

Because we understand each other so well, we'll make it twenty-two—twenty-two deaths a month, and not one more. Twenty-two is my final offer."

The leader laughed. It seemed as though he was only now starting to enjoy this. He said: "You're not taking me seriously. What is twenty-two? What kind of ridiculous number is that? Let's round it off to forty. But only because I enjoyed your lamb so much. Because I appreciate your hospitality, and that of your friend. Your nice friend—what was his name again?"

"Awromele," Xavier said, "Awromele Michalowitz."

"Yes," the leader of Hamas said. "Awromele. My eyes are not so good anymore; perhaps he could come a little closer."

"Awromele," Xavier said, "dearest, would you be so kind as to sit next to our guest?"

Awromele got up and sat down beside the leader of Hamas, who ran his hands over Awromele's face like a blind man. He enjoyed softness. The older he grew, the more he liked softness. In fact, softness was all that remained. The rest disappeared, dissolved. Soft flesh, nothing more, only that, each time anew.

"So your Redeemer lives in a jar," the leader of Hamas whispered. He felt how warm Awromele's face was, he felt the stubble of his beard, the sweat, the lips, the eyebrows.

"Fine," Xavier said as the Hamas leader's hands moved over Awromele's features, "all right, we'll round it off. Twenty-five a month. And then not all of them in Israel, but also the occasional synagogue in Rome, or Istanbul, or Vancouver. Scattering. Wherever art has locked itself up to languish away like a sick dog, it must be dragged from its preserve. The EU and the States know about it, and they say scattering is fine. But everything in moderation. No need for the whole thing to explode. Because then people won't go shopping anymore. Scaring them a little, okay, that's the task of art. Teaching the audience to shiver a little, to wipe the smile off the participant's face, but the rest still have to be able to leave their homes and go shopping. So things can't get out of hand. Are you listening to me?"

The leader of Hamas leaned over and kissed Awromele. First on the cheek and at the base of his neck, then on the mouth. "You don't mind, do you?" he asked between kisses. "That I kiss your friend?"

"No, of course not," Xavier said. "Go right ahead. You are my guest. Besides, he can't say no. And you are an artist, I admit that freely. You are my opponent, but I am not blind to creativity."

Then Xavier fell silent and watched as the leader of Hamas kissed Awromele. He thought: Why can't he say no? What's the real reason why he can't say no? I must ask him, before it's too late.

His hands shaking, the leader of Hamas fumbled at the buttons of Awromele's shirt, but because he was so nearsighted Awromele had to help him.

The leader of Hamas smelled Awromele, the aroma of young life, the odor of youth—yes, that was it, there was nothing but beauty and soft-ness, that's what life boiled down to when you started seeing less and less. And beauty and softness together, that was youth. His hand slid over Awromele's bare stomach. He thought about Basel again for a moment. Long ago, after the operation he had not fully completed, he had visited a strange massage parlor. It had been recommended to him. But this was much better. This was lively, wistful. All true lust was bound together with wistfulness. At the massage parlor, the wistfulness had been eradicated by money. Did beauty have any greater enemy than money?

"How many deaths will that involve, then, on our side?" he whispered.

"We're sticking to a ratio of one to three," Xavier stated. "We've stuck to that for years; it's a ratio we can work with. The United States and the EU have also let me know that they can live with that. Chaos in modera-tion perpetuates power, so that's my offer: twenty-five."

No answer came. The leader of Hamas had buried his face in Awromele's warm torso. He kissed it, he licked off the sweat; it almost made him cry, it was so sweet. There was something about youth that made all politics futile, that made all power pale, that reduced all ambi-tion to a tiring, almost superfluous affair.

"Thirty-five," the leader cried, his hands running over Awromele's trousers and thighs. "I have to take my constituency into account." He felt

Awromele's buttocks. They were hard; he liked that. Not those flabby, gelatinous buttocks—they had to be hard.

"Twenty-eight," Xavier shouted. "Because I'm out of my mind, because I want only the best for you."

"Mmm," the leader said. He murmured something Xavier couldn't understand, and pulled with trembling fingers at Awromele's zipper.

"Twenty-nine," Xavier whispered, "twenty-nine a month."

"Thirty," said the leader, his hand in the underpants now.

There he had the sex organ. He could barely see it, but he felt it growing in his hand. How lovely it was. He was breathing heavily.

"Thirty," Xavier cried. "Thirty, it's a deal. Thirty a month, that's decent, that's respectable. And the States and the EU are behind us all the way. I tell you this in all confidence. They sent their envoys to tell me: don't mess around with us on this one. No experiments. Chaos in moderation is good for all."

"I want to see your ass," the leader of Hamas whispered. And while Awromele was pulling off his gym socks, the leader said: "The interpreters can leave now. Now there's no need for us to understand each other any longer."

"Go away," Xavier told the interpreters. "Go away. Can't you see that our guest no longer needs you?"

Xavier paced the room with a bunch of grapes in his hand. "A flower shop," he mumbled, "I bet they're sorry about that now, and they'll be even sorrier." Occasionally he stopped pacing to look at Awromele and the leader of Hamas. How the leader pushed his way into Awromele and grew wild, almost youthful.

And Xavier wondered where the jealousy was, where the pain remained, the uncontrollable rage, the overpowering sense of loss.

But he understood that what was happening now was perpetuating his power. That made up for everything.

The Unjustly Neglected Principles
of Streicher and Himmler

ALTHOUGH HE HIMSELF would never have admitted it, after years of chaos in moderation, electoral victories, crises, and power that had been increasingly perpetuated, ha-Radek began tiring of politics. He had learned Arabic, he had brought down Cabinets, he had campaigned and been re-elected, he had been maligned but re-elected nonetheless, yet still he missed something. And that missing became increasingly active; it grew like a wound that becomes more inflamed with each passing day.

The number of people who saw King David as the Redeemer no longer increased, but it didn't decrease, either. And those who did believe in the King did so with a rare fire and conviction. Children wrote letters to King David, grown-ups prayed to him, and photos and drawings of King David hung on the walls of living rooms and bedrooms all over the world.

After years of tenderness and tenderness deferred—Awromele still couldn't say no, but he always came back, even if it meant coming back from Cape Town—after all those years, Xavier lay in bed one night and dreamed of his grandfather, in the uniform he had once found so manly.

It was February, and it was snowing in Jerusalem, a rare event. And snow that fell and did not melt right away was rarer still. Xavier awoke. He looked to see whether Awromele was lying beside him. He was. That happened more and more frequently lately; it was almost as though Awromele had finally learned to say no. Xavier got up and went to the window to look at the snow. His official residence in Jerusalem had a little garden that he never used. His two dogs were the only ones who ever walked around in it.

He stared at the snow. He was feared, hated, and, by those who believed in King David, loved as well, yet he still had to admit that when it came to comforting he had made little headway. He could no longer blame it on the need to keep perpetuating his power. Power could never become much more perpetual than his. He was a master in the creation, manipulation, and control of seemingly boundless chaos, but that mastery no long produced happiness or excitement, only a dull sense of reluctance at best. He had already taken every step; his speeches reminded him of speeches he had made years ago, only in a different form. He had seen opponents come and go. He had survived attacks on his life. He was still there. In this world of eternal struggle, ha-Radek was a survivor, there was no denying that. His grandfather would have been proud of him.

Atop a dresser in his bedroom lay the translation of the book by You-Know-Who. He still worked on it in his free time, along with Awromele. The end was in sight, though it had taken them a long time. His free hours were limited.

"Xavier," Awromele called out to him from the big bed. "What are you doing? Why don't you get some sleep?"

Xavier didn't reply. He looked at the snow: he pressed his nose against the windowpane and looked at the mark his nose had made.

It had been a month or two since he had called the mother. Not that she had said anything. She was living in a nursing home these days. The nurse who came on the line brought him up-to-date on the situation that hadn't changed in years. The mother didn't talk to anyone, she remained silent. But she ate well, she was strong. She, too, unlike her father, had proved to be a survivor.

Awromele got out of bed, put on the slippers Xavier had given him two years ago at Hanukkah, and came over to stand beside him. He was wearing light blue pajamas. "What is it?" Awromele asked. "Why are you standing here? It's the middle of the night."

"I'm looking at the snow," Xavier said.

Awromele looked, too, but snow didn't interest him. Then Awromele said: "There's something wrong. I know you. I can tell when there's something wrong." He put his arm around Xavier.

"I've mastered this," Xavier said quietly. "All of this, the politics, this life, I can do it, I know how it works. I've carried out negotiations, I've dragged art out of its preserve, I've raised the body counts and lowered them again. I know it like the back of my hand, this life. But it's not enough." He turned around. "It's nothing, Awromele. This, here, is less than nothing. Art gives meaning to pain. But is this meaning? And is this pain? And if it isn't pain, then what is it? I'm afraid of becoming embittered, and I don't want that. My father was embittered. I don't want to end up like him. That's not why I came here, that's not why I achieved what I've achieved."

"Well, then, what do you want?" Awromele asked. "What do you want? You're trembling."

"It's cold," Xavier said. "I want to astonish people."

Awromele looked at him. The man with whom he had gone to the Venice of the North and then, albeit unwillingly, followed to the Promised Land. The man whose campaign manager he had become, for whom he had come up with slogans the way he had once come up with jokes while stocking shelves, the man with whom he had stayed despite his inability to say no. He tugged on Xavier's ear, tickled his neck, and kissed spots he had kissed before. "You've astonished me," he said. "Me."

"You? You're my friend. You're only one person. That's not enough. One person is nothing."

"Put something on, you'll catch cold." Awromele rubbed Xavier's back and put his hand under Xavier's T-shirt. He felt moles, thicker than the rest of the skin. He knew them the way a person knows a hotel room in which, owing to circumstances beyond his control, he's been living for the last eighteen months.

"Start a flower shop—that's what they said. But is this really so different from a flower shop? I send soldiers to their deaths, children, families. I feel nothing. It's as though I'm arranging flowers and cutting off the dead leaves. I know what to say, what to cover up, I play the game better than the rest, I know the pitfalls. I could go on like this for years, but when I came here I had something else in mind. Is this it, Awromele, is this what happens when you drag art out of its seedy preserve? When I was still painting, thoughts like that never bothered me. I had hope; I was a different person."

Awromele grabbed Xavier by the shoulders, the way you grab hold of a child. "Stop talking about art and preservation all the time. That nice Hamas man can't stand listening to it either, anymore. Just stop thinking about it. It only makes you sad, and other people have no idea what you're talking about."

"They know exactly what I'm talking about," Xavier said, yanking himself free.

But Awromele wasn't about to be put off. Gently, he began kissing Xavier on the neck.

"They know exactly what I'm talking about. They understand me perfectly, the ones who need to understand me. You remember when you told me why you couldn't say no? Because I would betray you, that's what you said. Because I had something you didn't. That's why you had to go with everyone who wanted you, that's why you couldn't say no, because I had talent. Is this talent, Awromele? Look around you—is this talent? Is this what it does to you? Is that what it makes of you?"

"You're blathering," Awromele said, and he caressed Xavier more firmly. The way he used to caress him. "We weren't going to feel anything.

That's why we were able to stay together, that's why we stayed together. Don't feel anything. You promised. There's nothing else you have to do. Feel nothing. That's surviving."

"What do I need to do?" Xavier asked.

"What do you mean? Right now?"

"No, not now. It's nighttime now. What do I need do in order to leave the world behind different from the way I found it? Because, if I don't do that, I haven't comforted anyone, and then we could just as well have stayed in the Venice of the North, with a flower shop, or maybe two."

"Go back to bed. You'll get sick."

Xavier shook his head. "Just take a look," he said. "Look at who we've become."

"Who have we become? I see the same thing I've been seeing for years, what I saw when I first met you, at lunch at my parents' house on the Sabbath. That's all I see." Awromele squeezed the back of Xavier's neck, and Xavier shivered even more, as though he had come down with a fever.

"It stinks in here," Xavier said. "Don't you smell it? What kind of cleanser do they use when they clean this place? Or is it you? Is it your deodorant? The stench is driving me crazy."

Awromele ran his fingers through Xavier's hair. It didn't matter what Xavier said; he was used to his tantrums, with the smashed furniture, the torn clothing, and the vases thrown across the room. "You haven't been getting enough sleep lately," he said. "You've had a hectic program these last few weeks, all those foreign ministers coming to visit. It would drive me crazy, too. You just need to take it a little easier."

"No," Xavier said, "that's nonsense—too hectic, take it a little easier. Listen to you spouting clichés. Nothing but laziness, like something out of the self-help books. The point is not to compete with the mediocre. Competing with the mediocre is only an alternative form of being dead. You have to compete with the ones who have really made a mark on this world, the ones who left it behind different from the way they found it."

"But you'll leave me behind different from when you found me,"

Awromele said. "Can't you see that? Isn't that enough?" He stopped running his fingers through Xavier's hair; he took off his pajamas. "Take me,"
Awromele said. "Then you can feel that I'm here. Take me the way you
used to, right after we met."

"But I don't know if *I'm* here," Xavier said. "I don't know." He looked
at the secret-service man who was walking through the garden. It was still
snowing. What's that man doing there? he thought. Why can't they ever
leave me alone? Why do they have to walk through my garden when I'm
trying to look at the snow? Why are they always there? "You once told me,"
Xavier said, "that loneliness is nothing to be ashamed of. Do you remem
ber that?"

"Yes, of course I remember that," Awromele whispered. "I remember
everything, but let's not talk about that again, not now, not tonight."

"The only thing I see anymore is the shame," Xavier said. "That's the
only thing I see. No matter where I go, wherever I am, whatever bed I lie
in, whoever I'm with, whatever Cabinet minister I talk to, whatever general comes to talk to me, I see the shame, I smell the shame, I taste it, even
when I'm eating. And why is that man walking through my garden? Is that
security? Is that what they call security these days, a little walk around the
garden?"

Awromele was standing in front of Xavier, naked.

"So come up with something new," Awromele said. "Make peace, start
a new war, start painting again, come up with something—but look at me.
Look at me the way you used to look at me."

"But how, but who?" Xavier shook his head; he didn't look at Awromele,
he was looking at the security man in the garden. This was a new one, just
a boy.

"You need a common enemy," Awromele whispered, running his hand
over Xavier's back, down his leg. "If you want to turn your enemies into
allies, you need a common enemy. You know that—you told me that
once."

Awromele was shivering now, too; it was cold in the bedroom when
you weren't under the blankets. "All peace, every alliance, every pact

starts with a common enemy," he whispered, laying his hand on Xavier's crotch.

For the first time, Xavier felt old, truly old. In the light of the flood lamps that had been set up in the garden to protect the prime minister against intruders, he looked at his hands, he saw how old his hands had become. They had changed color.

"But who?" he asked. "What common enemy?"

"How should I know?" Awromele said. "The West, as far as I'm concerned. Look at me. Don't make me wait any longer."

But Xavier kept looking at the secret-service man in the snow. He was standing perfectly still in the garden now, almost like a dummy. As though he had seen something.

"The West," Xavier said. "Okay, the West. As far as I'm concerned."

"Take me now," Awromele said. "Please, take me now. Can't you see how I'm standing here? Really, can't you see that? Take me the way you used to. Before it's too late."

Xavier turned to look at Awromele. He had heard something in his voice that worried him. "Why are you crying?" he asked. "I thought we weren't going to feel anything."

"I'm crying without feeling anything," Awromele said.

"Put on some music."

Awromele put on some music, then Xavier took Awromele.

Afterwards, they lay in each other's arms, exactly the way they used to, and Xavier said: "The West, okay, the West. Where are the dogs, anyway?"

"In their room," Awromele said. "Where they always are."

TO MAKE IT EASIER to find a common enemy, ha-Radek began selling nuclear weapons. First to Turkey, and later a couple of little ones to Armenia, in order not to disturb the balance of power in the region, and because of historical sensitivities.

Then he sold a few to Colombia—he got along very well with the president of Colombia—and to Argentina. It cheered him up; his somberness began melting away. And he became too busy to be somber anymore.

The special envoys from the EU and the United States, who were not pleased with ha-Radek's latest ventures, were thrown out of the country.

And Xavier told the leader of Hamas, who occasionally met Xavier and Awromele for tea at a discreet location, and who always played discreetly with Awromele afterwards: "Who's to blame for our being here? Who got us into this mess? Who created this stupid situation? It wasn't us. I wouldn't have been the one to come here. If I'd known all this beforehand, I would never have come here. We're here because of Europe. Because of the United States. The United Kingdom was here long before we were, and look at the way they left your country behind."

"I'm too ill to be particularly interested in the past," the leader of Hamas said. "Too old."

"You shouldn't think that way," Xavier replied. "You should think about the oppressors, you must never forget the oppressors, even if they have left your country, because you're still living with the mess they left behind."

The leader had his head in Awromele's lap. He always did that when he was visiting ha-Radek. "I'm not sure," he said, "what are you trying to pawn off on me now?"

Whenever the leader came to visit ha-Radek, Xavier tried to pawn something off on him. Sometimes it was only a special tea that helped against rheumatism, sometimes a few weapons, other times a few garden implements.

"I'm not trying to pawn anything off on you," Xavier said. "I'm trying to make something clear to you."

"We've already talked about everything there is to talk about," the leader said. "I'm tired. And your friend is so quiet today."

Xavier got up. He knelt down beside the cushions where Awromele was sitting with the leader's head in his lap. The leader had been smoking the nargileh, and was pleasantly drowsy. Ready to surrender himself to Awromele's still-youthful body.

"I'm trying to explain to you that we have a common enemy."

"*A* common enemy?" said the leader, baring his bad teeth. "Thousands, tens of thousands. Nothing but enemies. Everywhere."

His hand was resting on Awromele's stomach, which had grown a bit plumper—not much, just a little. But the leader of Hamas didn't notice that. These days, the leader mostly smelled things—he didn't taste much anymore, either, but he could still feel, with his hands he felt everything.

"We've been divided and conquered," Xavier whispered. "We're nothing but lightning rods. Without us, the whole region would go up in flames, from Egypt to Syria, from Bahrain to Saudi Arabia, but things don't have to stay that way. Right now we're still pawns. We're messenger boys, don't you see that? But do you know what scares them most? That we'll start working together. My mother said, if fascism hadn't turned against the Israelites, it would still be a vital European movement. We're not doomed to play this bit part forever, we don't have to protect other people's interests until the end of days."

"I'm too old for that," the leader said, licking lightly at Awromele's nipple. "Let's go on doing what we've always done, a few attacks each month, a few reprisals. We can do that—it works out quite well. And it has been working out well for years. My Gaza Strip is full of NGOs, full of sweet, young, enthusiastic Westerners who wouldn't know what to do with themselves if they didn't have us around. When I look out my window, I see them driving around in their jeeps. Their lives would be empty and meaningless without us. Without us they would have no goal—think about them. The first time I visited you, you told me we must take the shapeless pain, the meaningless pain, and provide it with meaning. That's what we're doing. Let's go on doing that."

"But don't you see?" Xavier asked. "Is it really that hard for you to see?"

The leader was planting kisses all over Awromele's stomach. He liked kissing the stomach, pushing his tongue into the navel—that's why he liked to visit Xavier and his friend at this discreet location. There really wasn't much left to talk about anymore. They'd already said everything there was to say.

"So who is this enemy?" the leader asked, after he had done enough kissing for the moment. "He's the enemy," he said, pointing to Awromele, and he laughed. "Come, show me your buttocks, don't make me wait any longer. I'm tired. And old. I want to see them now. I want to feel them."

"The West is our common enemy," Xavier said. "If you're able to see that, then I do indeed have something to offer you. Something you might find particularly interesting. Everything is finite, but we poets, we artists, we have to give form to the finite, to keep it from sinking away in a formless mush."

Xavier had to pee. So he left the leader of Hamas and Awromele alone. They found each other blindly, Awromele and the leader, they knew each other's bodies like old lovers.

That same month, ha-Radek and a group of prominent Israeli scientists and businessmen traveled to Mexico. The president of Mexico was one-third Indian.

"Your ancestors," Xavier told him after the state dinner, "were annihilated by the Spanish. Isn't it about time to do something in return, to restore the imbalance? I have a couple of nuclear weapons for sale. They amount to an extremely good bargain. For you, only for you. Because I think you'll know how to use them. And, if I may be so free, I certainly don't want to meddle in your affairs, but wouldn't it be a good idea to aim a missile with a unconventional warhead at, say, Madrid? They'd find out soon enough. Not even actually to use it, just so they can feel a little bit of what your ancestors must have felt. Just a little bit. You remember what they did to your ancestors? If they failed to bring in their quota of gold, they cut off their arms. The road to the riches of the West is paved with severed arms. In fact, it's sort of like what they did to my ancestors. First comes the labor, then the annihilation. Again, it's up to you, but it's never too late to strike back. You can count on my support. As far as the weapons go, I'll supply them now, you can pay me later. Money should never get in the way of friendship."

"I'll think about it," the president of Mexico said.

But he didn't have to think about it long. In order to perpetuate power, you have to expand it. Standing still meant lagging behind.

THE MORE NUCLEAR weapons ha-Radek sold to various countries, the more rumors began flying concerning a Jewish conspiracy. There were people, and, not the least among them, often people who had published interesting articles about Schopenhauer, who said: "International Judaism must distance itself from the policies of ha-Radek; otherwise it will be impossible for us to distinguish between ha-Radek's politics and international Judaism. We would regret that terribly, but we have no choice."

"Don't let it worry you," Awromele said to Xavier in the bedroom. "Remember what your mother told me? It's love, the hatred of the Jews is love. It's the only love deserving of the name."

But Xavier said: "They don't get it. I am lending meaning to meaningless pain. I have finally started comforting; when it comes to comforting, I have put my shoulder to the wheel at last." Earlier that day, he had delivered nuclear weapons to Bangladesh, under the slogan: "Even one of the poorest countries in the world should be able to join our coalition." Because Bangladesh didn't know how to operate the weapons, ha-Radek had supplied them with technicians as well.

By this time, the European and U.S. ambassadors had left Israel as well. Before they left, they had stated, "We have nothing against the Jewish people, but their leader is a threat to world peace."

A prominent Irish intellectual wrote in *The Guardian* that—in the light of events in recent years, perhaps even of recent decades—Hitler's war against the Jews had to be seen as a pre-emptive war. "All war is abhorrent," he wrote, "as was that of the Nazis. But had they won their pre-emptive war, we would not have to fear for our lives today. And that is something for all peace-loving people to consider."

His public appeal to review afresh the ideas of Streicher and Himmler met with support. Criticism of this renewed interest in a vanquished ideology was also voiced here and there, but mostly by older thinkers and politicians who refused to admit that they had been clinging to unrealistic ideas all those years.

RIGHT-MINDED PEOPLE all over the world agreed: Hitler's war had not been proper, but it had been pre-emptive. And those who viewed him without prejudice had to admit: he'd had his lesser moments, but he was a visionary.

Greetings from Anne Frank

HIS HANDS WERE black with mud, as though he'd been working in the garden, and there was blood on his wrists. His jacket was wrinkled, his shirt torn, he hadn't bathed in two days. He had delivered an ultimatum to the world, then withdrawn to his bunker. There were people who had not understood him, allies who had abandoned him. NATO had its armies on immediate standby, ready to finish the job and lop off the head of the Jewish-Palestinian serpent in the Middle East. But they wanted to give diplomacy one final chance, to prevent unnecessary bloodshed.

Friends had stopped calling him; business contacts with whom he had been on intimate terms for years no longer answered his calls and letters. Yet there were exceptions, people who understood what he was doing, and who supported him.

Even the Jewish people, whom he had hoped to comfort as no other people had ever been comforted before, whom he had served, for whom he had lived, had turned against him, because they were afraid of dying. Fear did not bring out the best in people. Fortunately, there were still a few courageous individuals who said: "This is how King David wanted it. Redemption is now at hand. Those who are willing to heal themselves will now be healed by King David."

Awromele's body, wrapped in a blanket, he dragged behind him.

Awromele had refused to listen to him; he had been unable to say no, he still couldn't. He had gone out into the street.

"They won't hurt me," Awromele had said. "They won't even recognize me. I'll come back, you know that, I always come back. We don't feel anything, that's why I can come back to you, that's why I'm safe with you. And you're safe with me." Then he had kissed Xavier and gone out the door. In his hand he'd had a shopping bag from the supermarket chain he had once worked for.

It had taken the army three hours to free Awromele. They had been forced to wrench his remains by force from the hands of a furious crowd. At the back of the crowd there had been an old, bald man and a woman with gray curls—she was old, too. They had once worked together. They glanced at each other, but they said nothing. In the pocket of her jeans the woman felt the tooth she had carried around with her for years, like a talisman. They saw Awromele's mutilated corpse, then parted ways without a word. And, for the first time in years, the woman smelled the smell she had never forgotten, the smell of dog and desert.

THE FOREIGN PRESS spoke of a revolution. International observers reported that ha-Radek had lost control over his people. That was an exaggeration: the wish was father to the thought. The fear of dying had made some people hysterical, that's all it was, hysteria. Lynching was a distraction. It provided temporary relief; lynching was their aspirin. The crowd had poked out Awromele's eyes, cut off his hands, beaten him with shovels and garden implements, even after he was dead.

When Xavier got to his desk, he stopped. He let go of the blanket. This was how the secret-service men had brought Awromele to him. In an old gray blanket.

"If I were you, I wouldn't look in it," they had said.

He only shook his head. He had not opened the blanket with Awromele in it, which was now lying at his feet. He had made a peeping sound when he breathed, like an asthma sufferer; the ventilation in the bunker didn't work well, or at least not well enough. Then he had said, "Go. I need to think."

The security men had left. Every civil servant who still supported his democratically elected leader was needed out on the street.

Only when they had pulled the door closed behind them did he bend down.

"Awromele," he said, "Awromele." He pulled open the blanket. He tried to wipe the mud and the clotted blood from Awromele's forehead. But it was hopeless, it only made things worse.

He had no idea how long he had been in the bunker. He knew that the ultimatum he had issued would expire within a few hours; he knew that the stale air tickled his throat unpleasantly, that the dust brought on fits of coughing that sometimes lasted for five minutes. But he also knew that he could not give up, not now, now that he had finally started taking the comforting seriously.

The dogs barked; they came running up to him. Xavier petted them. He had named them Saul and Jacob. There wasn't enough water for the dogs; their tongues were hanging from their mouths. Crazed with thirst, they jumped up against him, but he pushed them away. "Go on," he said, "I'll come to you in a minute."

He wanted to be alone with Awromele.

But he had already been alone with Awromele for hours. His sense of time had abandoned him.

That same morning, he had phoned the leaders of Colombia, Turkey, Bangladesh, Mexico, Cambodia, and Kazakhstan, his most faithful allies. Each and every one of them had received unconventional weapons from ha-Radek. His final allies—there weren't many of them, but there were enough. A common enemy, that was all you needed to form an alliance.

The leader of Hamas, he was among them, too. He had assured Xavier that the nuclear weapons given to his movement, which were now aimed at London, would be used at the appointed hour. Ha-Radek had had to do a lot of talking, but he'd finally convinced the leader that they had a common enemy, that they could not go on maintaining the status quo forever, no matter how agreeable that status quo was to some.

He dragged Awromele's body over to a round table with a CD player on it. The music soothed him—Rachmaninoff, Beethoven, Orff. Always the same music, day and night, the same music, so he wouldn't have to hear the buzzing, the buzzing in his ears.

"Dearest," he said, "we're alone now. We're alone at last. It was about time. You don't have to tell me that you couldn't say no. I know that, I know it so well. The way people know that truth is pain. But some of them don't want to know that, some of them can't accept it—that's what's driving them mad. They don't understand that pain is relief. That's why you should have stayed inside, here with me, in the bunker. Look what they've done to you. Now you can't say yes anymore, either."

He opened a cupboard. There were baby clothes in it. Awromele had hoped to adopt a baby, a little Vietnamese girl, a baby no one else wanted. But the crisis got in the way. The ultimatum. The baby had never arrived, because of the international boycott—which hadn't helped, of course. It had at best made a few people extremely rich within a very short period.

He bent down, took Awromele's head in his hands, and pressed it against him. The head that had been beaten with garden utensils so long that you could no longer tell the back from the front. The crowd had tried to set fire to Awromele. The fire had been put out, but the head was charred black.

"I don't feel a thing, Awromele," he said. "Nothing, just like I promised. You don't have to be afraid."

He kissed the head, tasted the blood, the burned skin, the shoes that had stepped on it, he tasted the earth, in the end, that was all he tasted: earth.

"Awromele," he said, "you taught me that loneliness was nothing to be ashamed of. Now I will teach others that as well. It has never been something to be ashamed of. And it never will be anything to be ashamed of."

.   .   .

IN HER BERLIN APARTMENT, Bettina was packing a little suitcase. Everone had been advised to take along warm clothes to the air-raid shelter.

Bettina had been a junkie for ten years. Then she had kicked the habit. She had moved to Berlin and married a Turk. But they had never been able to have children. They had tried everything, absolutely everything, but it didn't work.

She slammed down the lid of her suitcase. "Come on," she said to the Turk. "Let's go, let's get there before the crowd does."

KING DAVID WAS standing beside the CD player. The light in the bunker was unpleasant, too bright in some places, too dim in others.

On the side of a nuclear weapon in the Negev Desert, ha-Radek had had them paint the words "Greetings from Anne Frank." It was pointed at the old West Church in the Venice of the North. On another weapon he'd had painted, "And from Margot, too." That one was aimed at Mer-wedeplein.

Colombia had Spain and Portugal covered; those missiles had the names of various tin and gold mines painted on them. Hamas would see to London and its surroundings. Turkey had the Balkans and Southern Germany, Mexico had the United States, and Cambodia was homing in on France. And ha-Radek himself had two missiles pointed at Switzerland. "Thanks for throwing open the borders," those missiles said.

He glanced at his watch. The top brass had never left his side, the deserters had come from the lower ranks. The fools, the scaredy-cats, the ignoramuses, who finally knew nothing at all about beauty, and therefore nothing about politics, either.

ROCHELE, who had married a puppeteer and had two children, was standing in her apartment in Basel. She refused to go to the shelter. "What good will that do us?" she had told her husband. "We'll only end up eating each other."

She had dressed her daughters in their prettiest outfits, their princess dresses. Then she had made crepes for everyone, and chocolate milk, not from a package but with real cocoa. She was holding the younger girl in her arms.

"Where is everyone?" the child asked.

"Everyone is at home," Rochele said.

"Why?"

"Because this is an important day," Rochele said. "Today the pelican is coming. Do you know what a pelican is? It's a tropical bird. That's why everyone is at home, so they can see the pelican."

"Let's go to the shelter now," the puppeteer said.

She shook her head.

"We're staying here," she replied. "Come on," she told her children. "Finish your chocolate milk."

She sat down on the floor beside her children. There was a game of Copy Cat spread out on the rug.

"Who's going to start?" Rochele asked. Then she looked at her younger daughter, in her party dress.

"Little princess," Rochele said. "Come over here and sit with me. That's what Mama likes."

THE MOTHER HAD locked the door of her room. The nursing home had been evacuated; they had knocked on her door a few times, but in all the panic and commotion they had left her behind.

Although she had only been allowed to eat with plastic cutlery all those years, she had still succeeded in getting her hands on a bread knife, which she'd hidden beneath the sink in the bathroom. Long, long ago, when she had first come to this place.

Now she was crawling around in the bathroom, rooting around amid the old towels and dust, until she found the bread knife at last.

"There you are," she said, sitting on the floor. "My most faithful sweetheart. My lover." She looked at the knife. "You're so handsome," she said. "You're from Italy. You're the prettiest object on this earth. Now I've found you, now I'll never let you go again. Because the knife is warmer than a person."

She didn't undress. She couldn't stand to see herself naked anymore; she couldn't bear to look in the mirror.

Her lover took her with her clothes on, again and again, each time in a different place, at first only in the leg, then in the chest, gently still, and finally in the stomach, hard, with all the strength and love the mother had in her.

DANICA WAS STANDING before her collection of Snoopy things. She couldn't decide what to take with her. Everyone had left the house, but she had stayed with her mother. Someone had to stay with her. Danica had decided that she would be the one to do that. Something that couldn't break, and that wasn't too big, either—that was what she should take to the shelter. But what? There were so many things in her collection that couldn't break and that weren't too big, either.

She had already decided once, and walked away, but she wasn't satisfied with what she'd chosen, and so she came back. Besides, her mother was still in the bathroom, freshening up.

HE HAD CALLED his dogs; he had petted them, scratched them behind the ears, held their muzzles up to his face, tasted the dried slobber around their mouths. "Saul," he had said, "Jacob. You're so thirsty, so terribly thirsty."

Then he shot them. He had fired at least five times: because he wasn't a practiced marksman, a few of the shots had missed. He had cut his index finger on the gun.

Then he knelt down beside Awromele, with the translation of the bestseller by You-Know-Who. The work was almost finished. The notebooks, the notes, the footnotes in a separate folder, the things they weren't sure about, the construction for which they had not been able to find the right words. He had it all with him, held it all in his hands.

"The best way," he whispered, "to say nothing is not to be silent, but to speak, so I'm going to read to you from our book, the book we translated, because we belonged together. We always did, and now more than ever. I can't say the prayer for the dead for you, Awromele. The words won't leave my lips. But I miss you already. I miss you so badly."

He buried his face in the formless mass, all that was left of Awromele's body.

"This is the only prayer I'll say for you," he said. Then he opened the manuscript. He saw Awromele's handwriting, and began reading aloud from the Yiddish translation of the Book of Books. Occasionally he stopped, opened his mouth wide, and howled at the ceiling like a crazed animal.

"*Dos lebn wos a jid firt afn kerper foen andere meloeches oen felker, iz di sibe foen a tipisjer ejgnsjaft, wos hot gebracht Sjopenhoiern tsoem friër dermontn srois-zog, az der jid iz der 'groiser maister foen lign.' Dem jidns lebnsbadingoengen tswingen im tsoe ot dem lign, oen take tsoe a basjtendikn lign, poenkt azoi wi di lebsnbadingoengen foen mentsjn in kalte raionen tswingen zej tsoe trogn wareme malboesjiem.*"*

THEN THE PHONE RANG.

THE TALL BOY, who had become a tall man, had loaded his family, his wife and children, into the jeep. "We're going into the mountains," he'd

---

*"The life that the Jew lives as a parasite on the body of other states and nations is the cause of a typical trait which once prompted Schopenhauer to state, as noted earlier, that the Jew is 'the grandmaster of the lie.' The conditions under which the Jew lives compel him to that lie, and then to an everlasting lie, just as the conditions under which people live in cold climates compel them to wear warm clothes."

said. "We'll be safe there." He had brought along enough food for a month. Cans, cheese, freeze-dried food. Things that couldn't spoil.

He was already sitting at the wheel when he realized that he hadn't told his mistress about it, hadn't said goodbye to her. That wasn't nice. He suddenly longed for her so badly. He wanted to see her one last time, even if only for a moment, even if it was only for five minutes.

"I'll be right back," he said. "I forgot something."

He left the door of the jeep open and began walking hurriedly towards his mistress's house.

"Don't take too long," his wife shouted after him. "Don't leave us waiting here too long."

"IT'S TIME," said the voice on the phone, which he, for a fraction of a second, didn't quite recognize.

He tilted his head to hold the receiver against his shoulder, and picked up King David. In the white light, the testicle looked bluer than ever.

"Yes," he said.

The conversation didn't take long. It didn't have to take long.

He hung up. "Redeemer," he whispered to King David. "Redeemer."

He carried the King over to Awromele's body, and knelt down with the King beside the translated manuscript by You-Know-Who.

"Listen," he said, "here it is. 'A person can easily change languages, that is, he can use another language; but in his new language he will continue to express his old thoughts, his character will not be changed. The clearest demonstration of this can be seen in the Jew, who can speak thousands of languages yet always remains the same Jew.' "

A few minutes to go. He closed the book. The notebooks, the sheets covered in footnotes, he put away.

"I'm going to tell you a fairy tale, Awromele," he said. "A bedtime story." He held one of his beloved's hands, half charred, a hand attached to the arm only by a single strand of flesh.

"My grandfather," he said, "worked in a place they called 'the anus of the world.' And as you know, Awromele, the good comes from the anus. Do you hear me? Just tell me if you can't hear me. This is your good ear, isn't it? It's nothing to be ashamed of. But the anus is everywhere. Wherever you go, it's there. Whatever direction you start walking, whatever street you turn into, everywhere you go, you run into the anus of the world. It's always there, everywhere, you can smell it, you can feel it, you can see it. But it's nothing to be ashamed of, Awromele. Just like loneliness is nothing to be ashamed of. And you don't have to be afraid. Suffering is the emergency exit of beauty, and we took that emergency exit. We have to learn to speak the language of the future. The language you taught me, Awromele."

Like a dog, he licked the black, clotted blood from Awromele's face. "Is this it?" he asked. "Is this the meaning of pain?"

DANICA RAN DOWN the deserted street with her Snoopy pajamas in a plastic bag. Her mother was still in the bathroom. She was putting on her wig.

"WHY AREN'T WE in the shelter?" Rochele's elder daughter asked.

"Because we're fine right here," Rochele said. "Come on, I'll make some more chocolate milk for the two of you."

"When's the pelican coming?" the younger girl asked. She was too tired; she'd been whining for a while.

"In just a little bit," Rochele said. "When you see him, I want you to shout, Pelican, look at me. You have to stamp your feet on the floor and shout, Pelican, look at me."

Then Rochele's two daughters stamped their feet and shouted, "Pelican, look at me!"

HE WAS LYING on Awromele's body, on what was left of Awromele. The corpses of his dogs were lying a few yards away.

It stank inside the bunker. It stank of old blood, rotting flesh. Almost nothing was working anymore, not even the ventilation. He remembered the teeth of the Armenian who had watched over the synagogue in Basel: he remembered the lunch he'd eaten at Awromele's house; he remembered happiness. It broke him.

"Awromele," he whispered, holding his friend's head, a head that was gradually coming loose from the body. Nothing was attached anymore. Awromele had been brought to him as a collection of loose parts. A collection of flesh and bones, wrapped in an old blanket.

"Do you hear the music, Beethoven, Awromele? Everything else has fallen silent, no pleas, no complaints, no declarations of love in which no one believes anymore. Only he speaks. Can you hear it?"

He got up. He was holding the head loosely in his arms; it had no color anymore, it was pure black, from the back, from the front, from the side. He carried it to the table, and sat down beside King David.

He held the head in his lap, rocked it back and forth like a baby that needs to go to sleep. That's how much he loved this head, even now that it was only a head, without a front or a back, without eyes or ears, a head like a soccer ball.

He had Awromele's head on his knees, held it with both hands. He hummed for a few moments. Then he stopped and said: "I came to comfort. But the only comfort you people have is destruction."

He held up the head, pressed it against him, planted hundreds of little kisses on the burned crust. "Awromele," he said. "Are you listening? Our only comfort is destruction."

"THERE'S THE PELICAN," Rochele said. She was standing at the window with her younger daughter on her arm. The little girl's mouth was brown from the chocolate milk.

"There's the pelican. You can see him now."

The publisher would like to thank the heirs of A. Hitler for their kind permission to include here excerpts from *Mijn kamp,* published in Amsterdam in 1938, Yiddish translation by Willy Brill.